THE PLEASURE PRINCIPLE

As David's arrogance dawned on Natalie, he had already bent down and swept her into his arms. Caught off guard, she writhed in protest as he buried his mouth against hers, but it took only a moment before she melted against his deliciously hard chest. His mouth, his body, it was all good. but she had to stop this . . . this madness.

She pulled free of his embrace, dizzy with desire. But when she saw the self-satisfied smile on his face, she slapped him again before she stepped back. But he kept coming toward her. The evening was getting out of her control.

BOOK YOUR PLACE ON OUR WEBSITE AND MAKE THE ARABESQUE ROMANCE CONNECTION!

We've created a customized website just for our very special Arabesque readers, where you can get the inside scoop on everything that's going on with Arabesque romance novels.

When you come online, you'll have the exciting opportunity to:

- View covers of upcoming books

- Learn about our future publishing schedule (listed by publication month and author)

- Find out when your favorite authors will be visiting a city near you

- Search for and order backlist books

- Check out author bios and background information

- Send e-mail to your favorite authors

- Join us in weekly chats with authors, readers and other guests

- Get writing guidelines

- AND MUCH MORE!

Visit our website at
http://www.arabesquebooks.com

THE
Pleasure
PRINCIPLE

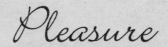

SHIRLEY HARRISON

ARABESQUE

★ BET
BOOKS

BET Publications, LLC
http://www.bet.com
http://www.arabesquebooks.com

ARABESQUE BOOKS are published by

BET Publications, LLC
c/o BET BOOKS
One BET Plaza
1900 W Place NE
Washington, DC 20018-1211

All Kensington Titles, Imprints, and Distributed Lines are available at special quantity discounts for bulk purchases for sales promotions, premiums, fund-raising, and educational or institutional use. Special book excerpts or customized printings can also be created to fit specific needs. For details, write or phone the office of the Kensington special sales manager: Kensington Publishing Corp., 850 Third Avenue, New York, NY 10022, attn: Special Sales Department, Phone: 1-800-221-2647.

First Printing: May 2004
10 9 8 7 6 5 4 3 2 1

Printed in the United States of America

before his fingers made a sensuous journey along her neck and down her arm before finally dropping to her waist.

"We were about to make love ten minutes ago," he emphasized in a whisper. "What we both want and waited for hasn't changed because of what just happened."

Natalie's short-cropped hair bounced wildly as she shook her head. "This was a mistake." She sighed, and pushed out of his grasp.

Now what the hell is that supposed to mean? David dropped his arms, frowning as he watched her move away from him across the room. Impatient, he followed her. It was obvious that she blamed him for the evening's bad turn of events—but to what degree?

When he moved closer to her, she turned her back. Perplexed by her mood, he slid his hand beneath the dark, curly hair that reached his shoulders, remembering how earlier, Natalie's willing fingers had liberally tousled his mane. He massaged the tightness in his neck as he began to think that his patience was lost on Natalie and her unreasonable attitude.

"All right, you want to let me in on what's ticked you off, or will you keep walking away with that damn passive-aggressive attitude?"

Natalie spun around to face him, her eyes sparking with unmistakable defiance. "Don't start with me, David—not tonight." She turned away again and stepped into her skirt, twisting it into place along her body.

"At least you're still talking to me," David said evenly. His eyes followed her firm curves being pressed into the softly woven skirt. He was keenly aware that her anger had done nothing to dampen his arousal. "So, I'll try again." He crossed his arms in front of his chest. "I thought you understood when I explained earlier about—"

". . . How your ex-girlfriend used her key to walk in on us in bed?" Natalie let out a hollow laugh. "Save your breath. There's not that much understanding in the world."

He dropped his arms. "You think I planned something

like this?" When she didn't respond, he turned away in frustration. "Sheree knew it was over a long time ago. I made that crystal clear. I can't help that she kept my key and decided to surprise me. Who could have guessed she'd use it tonight of all nights?"

David heard more than saw something coming his way as he turned, and then swiftly ducked in time to avoid the cell phone Natalie threw with amazing accuracy.

"Hey, what the—" he shouted, lifting his head cautiously. The phone caromed off the wall behind him before falling harmlessly to the floor.

"Will you stop going on and on about you and Sheree?" she shouted back. "Don't you get it? The problem is with us."

Puzzled, David drew in a deep breath. "What are you talking about?"

"Your old girlfriend showing up was bad enough. But, it doesn't change anything, though it did stop us from . . ." Natalie continued looking sideward at David. ". . . From making a mistake."

"That's bull," he argued and moved toward her. "You want me as much as I want you." He stepped closer. "And, I can prove it."

"There's more to consider, David." She abruptly spun from him to walk away. "I . . . I can't do it."

"Whoa . . . wait just a minute." David caught her arm and pulled her back to face him. "You can't make love to me?" His scowl softened. "Baby, after the way we fought to keep our hands off each other these last weeks, I didn't think that was a problem."

Natalie frowned before she snatched away her arm. "Not that, David. This," she started, waving her arm in a wide gesture, "this whole relationship thing. I don't know that it'll work."

"Sure, we have some differences to deal with. But we talked about them, and we still ended up here tonight—body and soul," he reasoned. When she didn't respond, he moved over to the wall. Leaning against it, he studied her demeanor—calm and deliberate.

"What's really going on here, Natalie? You're a smart woman, and you always talk straight, but right now you're not making much sense. In fact, you sound like you have a case of cold feet and you're using Sheree's appearance as an excuse to run."

"I am not." Natalie pivoted around to confront him with her hand on her hip. "I don't have to run and I don't need an excuse to call off tonight. But why shouldn't I leave? Aren't you the one with the unfinished business?"

"You think I'd play you against another woman?" His eyes clung to hers for a sign of trust, but to his surprise, she showed no reaction. "Can't you see how much I . . ." David said, raising his guard, ". . . how much I respect what we have?"

Natalie sighed wearily. "And what's that—our friendship, a mutual love for your sister who's my best friend? That's all we have, David. And we'll lose that if we keep doing this."

David pushed off the wall. "I'm talking about something bigger between me and you, damn it. Why shouldn't we try for that?"

"Because we'll end up hurting each other and then lose everything."

"That won't happen—we won't let it."

"That's not guaranteed."

"Nothing is." His eyes narrowed suspiciously as he reached out a finger and tilted her chin up. "You don't want us to work out, do you?"

"I didn't say that."

The insincere denial angered an already frustrated David. "Now you're lying," he accused her.

Natalie slapped his hand away and stepped back.

"We had—no, have—the beginnings of something that could work, and you know it." David's stare didn't waver. "But, why are you giving up on us so easily? Unless . . ." He slowly started toward her. " . . . Unless it's because you realize your feelings go deeper than you expected . . . that you love me."

Her eyes squinted into an icy glint before his steady gaze. "Spoken like a true man," she barked, before she strutted away and slipped her feet into her shoes. "Just because I question the sanity in what we're doing, you think I'm confused; and that, of course, must mean I'm in love," she mocked.

David continued as though she hadn't spoken. "Now, that little revelation of love sure as hell would screw up your control of things, wouldn't it? In fact, I bet it scares you to death. That's it, huh? You're running because deep down inside you're a coward."

"Where are my clothes?" she now shouted, and snatched up David's shirt from the bedcovers. "You're not bullying me into an argument, because I'm leaving."

"Why are you afraid, Natalie? I'm willing to stay put and work things out." When he heard her snort in derision, he blurted out, "You're a woman—isn't your holy grail supposed to be a committed man?"

Furious, Natalie yanked David's shirt onto her arm. "You think that nice little sexist comment will make me stay?"

David's eyes had strayed from her face and dropped to her jutting breasts covered only by the thin slip, which left little to his imagination as she strained to swing her other arm through his shirt.

"Maybe what I *need* is a man who wants the contents as much as the packaging," she said in a bitter tone.

"And then, again," David retorted, taking the bait as he raised his gaze slowly from her breasts to meet her sparking eyes, "maybe you're scared that you've *found* him."

Having only managed to fumble a couple of buttons closed, Natalie abandoned the effort. She quickly stomped away from David in stiff dignity to grab up her purse. *Oh, hell*, David thought, and took off after her.

"You see?" she yelled. "This is what I have to deal with.

You always know best, forcing decisions on me," Natalie huffed as she made her way through the bedroom and to the front door. "God, I can't breathe when you're like this. You . . . you take up all the air."

"And your answer to everything is sarcasm or over-the-top drama," David responded, only a step behind her. "Say what you mean."

"You want it straight? All right," she offered, and turned the front door lock. "I'm not right for you. You need someone more pliable to complement that huge male ego of yours."

David flinched, and his hardened tone turned nasty. "If you feel that strongly about my needs, why didn't you say so? We could have jumped into bed right from the start and satisfied my huge male ego."

"And if I remember correctly," Natalie remarked sweetly from over her shoulder, "that was my original suggestion." She turned the doorknob.

David reached around and stayed her hand. "Have you even heard a word I've said? Why do things have to be your way or no way?"

But she stood with her back ramrod straight, intractable to his words.

"Damn, Natalie . . ." He leaned into her and rested his head atop hers, breathing in her essence as though it were the elixir of life. "We agreed to slow things down and take our time because we had a lot to lose, but if you leave this way, it means you don't want to try anymore."

Natalie turned the knob once again.

This time, David didn't stop her, but neither could he stop the ultimatum that tumbled from his lips. "If you leave now, we're through."

"You're right. We're now officially over."

As Natalie cleared the door, she turned, her dark brows arched in disdain. "When you come across the rest of my clothes, you can mail them to me." She closed the door with a resounding thump.

David stared at the door a full minute, the finality of the slam echoing in his head as he debated in anger on whether to go after her.

He pushed his hand into his pocket and pulled out the key he had confiscated from Sheree a scant thirty minutes ago, though not soon enough to avoid tonight's catastrophe. And what had come over Natalie tonight? She was a provocative woman, and even dangerously irreverent on occasion, but David didn't think he had ever seen her so removed from her usual pleasure-seeking ways.

He frowned at the thought. No matter the circumstance that passed her way, Natalie had a knack for squeezing some measure of satisfaction from it; she referred to it as her pleasure principle—pleasure equaled power and control—and by indulging that whim, Natalie had experienced just about everything. David shook his head in confusion. Damn if Natalie wasn't pretty much a borderline narcissist on a good day; so why should he give a damn that she walked out tonight?

It was then that he admitted to himself the very thing he had accused Natalie of denying. Inexplicably, and with no warning, she had gotten under his skin, and he wasn't even sure when it had happened. But, he couldn't admit it to Natalie, a woman who equated a committed relationship with a loss of independence. To share his feelings would only serve to push her further into denial about hers.

David was in a sticky predicament. He let out an expletive and, with exploded force, threw the key across the room.

It wasn't true what David had suggested—she was not in love. She couldn't be. How could she have let it happen? Natalie let out the deep breath that she had been holding. *So, why did you let it happen?* The scolding mantra and repeated denials swept through Natalie's head as she sat behind the steering wheel of her car still parked in the shadowy space outside David's condo. And what of David? Did he make a lucky guess or had she become that transparent?

Natalie had lived her share of relationships in her almost thirty years, but she had always controlled their depth and breadth—until now. How could she have allowed David to slip under her guard and make her break her cardinal rule to never become emotionally involved with a lover? Natalie slapped the steering wheel in frustration.

Technically, he wasn't even her lover.

Natalie had been so sure she could handle a . . . a fling with her best friend's brother. It was supposed to have been pure pleasure—flirty, carefree, and, break-out-in-a-sweat sexy.

It hadn't played out like the others, though. From the beginning, the emotional pull for David had spiraled away from her, possibly because she had nurtured a secret crush since high school. It was only when Sheree had barged in on them tonight that she realized how serious she had become, because, for the first time that she could remember, Natalie was jealous of another woman.

She peered into the rearview mirror and noticed a misshapen, dusky rosy bruise—about the size of a quarter—on her neck. It was a passion mark.

She frowned as she fingered the tender spot, and remembered how a relative had explained the danger of passion marks years before. *It's a seductive brand that seals ownership,* she had been warned as a teenager. *It tells others you are a possession for another's pleasure.* The warning had stayed with Natalie, and while she had done her own share of branding, she never allowed a boyfriend to mark her with possession—until tonight.

Unnerved by her slipup, Natalie wiped hard at the evidence. Earlier, she had yearned for nothing less than David's complete possession. His heady scent, of aftershave and sandalwood, was embedded in his shirt she was wearing, and gently reminded her of how much she had wanted him tonight.

Betrayed by her emotions, Natalie rubbed harder at the

soft mark until her skin began to sting. But instead of erasing recent memories, her actions invoked the past. Snapshots of her childhood stalled in her mind's eye: her compliant, stay-at-home mother, a workaholic father, and she, a curious child clamoring for their affection.

It wouldn't happen to her . . . love, marriage, babies, and the whole brokenhearted scene.

With fortitude revived, she straightened up in the car seat. She would not become trapped by useless emotions and live under a man's will, forced to beg for affection and money while stifling her true self with unexpected responsibility. She had wanted desperately to have sex with David tonight, but the price she'd have to pay, loss of control over her own life, wasn't worth it.

Natalie started the car and forced a smile to set her resolve. She wasn't afraid of life and planned to live it to its fullest, but on her own terms. And after one last glance in the mirror at her neck and the still evident mark and all it embodied, Natalie drove from the parking lot and away from the trap of love.

Chapter 1

A Year Later

After five straight hours without a break, the windowless office on the fifteenth floor at Innervision Industries had finally begun to close in on Natalie Goodman.

She raised her head from the sea of figures she studied on the computer screen and, rubbing her tired eyes, turned around to her desk and reached for another spreadsheet from the looming hefty stack. With the new sheet in hand, she settled once again into the soft leather chair behind her heavy antique desk, but this time her gaze roamed lazily about the room.

Though it lacked a window view, the well-appointed office located on her client's Atlanta premises had been a surprising boon. She looked up into the recessed ceiling lighting that superbly enhanced the desk lamp's radiant arc and enjoyed the warm glow.

Shortly after Natalie's arriving at Innervision, her appreciation for the room's impressive detail—from the dentil molding along the high ceiling to the wainscoted walls—had grown considerably. While conducting audit reviews for clients that could last for months, Natalie was usually shown to an office only a notch above a closet, which could easily double as a supply cabinet and was just as dour. She had noticed one oddity with this prize space, though: the desk, as well as a few other pieces of furniture, was bolted in place.

Natalie smiled at the peculiarity. Granted, nailing furniture to the floor was one way to cut down on employee pilfering, but this company needed to do better than that. From what she'd seen so far, the technology giant's profits were disappearing, yet their forecasts projected solid gains. Natalie hadn't figured out why the discrepancy, but in time she would—she always did.

Her gaze skipped across her file-strewn desk. The disarray represented the mental challenge she enjoyed. But, rather than giving her peace of mind today, it reminded her of another challenge; only that one was less predictable and had an extraordinary physique to match his inflexible scowl.

Natalie blinked away the unsettling vision of David Spenser and, in a habit borne of frustration, tapped her pencil eraser against the desk. The closer the day neared for David to return, the harder it was to maintain her focus. To say her feelings were mixed about David's return would be an enormous understatement.

Uncomfortably warmed by his memory, Natalie suffered the sweet heat that streaked through her. Damn. He was in her head, and her treasonous body knew it. She tapped the pencil faster. *Come on. Focus.*

The phone rang, blessedly interrupting her thoughts. Natalie scooped it from the cradle and gave her name.

"Hi, it's me," a crisp, pleasant voice replied.

Natalie immediately recognized the voice as that of her best friend, Davina Spenser Hardy. "What's up?" Natalie asked, putting down the spreadsheet.

"Just a reminder about dinner tonight."

"As usual, you have impeccable timing."

"Well, we both know that's a lie." Davina's light chuckle echoed through the phone. "I've been setting up my temporary studio in the house."

"Hey, that's great. I'll have to see it," Natalie said. Davina's artist career had taken off in the last two years and she was beginning to book shows now that the baby had been born.

"What about your day? Are things still bad around there?"

"I'm beginning to have second thoughts about this project," Natalie said as she stretched. "Maybe I shouldn't have agreed so quickly to take it on."

"Hey," Davina chided. "You're one of Lang & Myers's best accountants. That's the reason they offered it up."

Natalie leaned back in her chair, humored—and at the same time buoyed—by her friend's words. "Yeah, you're right," she crowed. "I am good at what I do."

"You're a virtual bloodhound when it comes to cracking numbers," Davina teased. "And you don't give up easily. But, everyone deserves a break from work, and seeing as you're little Jake's godmother—"

"Oh, I haven't forgotten about spending tomorrow with you two," Natalie cut in quickly. "I'm keeping my promise."

"Good."

Jacob James Hardy, called little Jake since his birth two months before, was Davina and Justin's first child. Although Natalie was surprised at having been asked to be the godmother, she was moved by Davina's confidence in her. However, since she had no idea of what constituted child-rearing, and whether her own wild side might interfere, Natalie's doubts about her suitability for such a lofty position continued to linger.

"Where is the lump of sugar, anyway?"

"He's with his daddy meeting more relatives that keep dropping by."

Natalie heard the pride in Davina's voice at having acquired such a large family through marriage. After all, before the baby's birth and since her father's death last year, Davina's only known blood relative had been her brother, David.

"You know, that kid's gonna be spoiled rotten."

"That's where you come in." Davina's voice was firm. "You're the balance he'll need."

"Me . . . balanced?" Natalie laughed. "I've been called a lot of things, but never that."

"Trust me. I know you better than you know yourself."

Natalie couldn't deny the claim. They'd been inseparable since middle school, going their own ways only during their college years. And when they met up again shortly afterward, it was as if they'd never parted.

Since Davina's marriage to Justin, they'd made adjustments, though. Now, with the baby's arrival, they were reduced to weekly get-togethers, which they worked hard to honor. Natalie disliked the self-pity sway her thoughts were taking, and sat up in the big chair.

"Okay, I'll admit you know me," she said. "But then you'd know I don't have a clue about raising children."

Davina laughed. "I can't wait until you're married and have your first baby. You'd be surprised at how much of it comes naturally."

Natalie groaned. "Please, you know where I stand on your state of grace, and I won't be joining you in it any time soon."

"Look at the way Justin and I adapted to marriage and a baby," Davina reasoned.

"You and Justin are a rare pair."

"I always thought the same about you and David."

A short, loping silence passed between the women.

"David and I are fine with our breakup." Natalie pulled her fingers through her hair, glad that her friend couldn't witness her discomfort. "But it's understandable that you miss your brother."

"And you?"

To her dismay, the unexpected question caused Natalie's voice to break. "I . . . I . . . What are you talking about?"

"Well, for starters, you never bring up his name; and the last two times he came home, you managed to be either unavailable or tied up with work. You haven't even seen him since he left for D.C. last year."

Irritated at the conversation's turn, Natalie frowned. "This sounds like an interrogation."

"No, it's not. I only want to know if you're okay with seeing David this weekend after so long."

Davina's surprising bluntness drew a nervous chuckle from Natalie. "It hasn't been *that* long. And it's not like we were engaged. We dated; we broke up. End of story."

"Okay, okay," her friend conceded. "But, my brother and my best friend—it has a nice ring. You know, legally, you'd be my sister."

"Didn't you get three of them when you married Justin?"

"Which reminds me—Alli is joining us tonight."

Alli Hardy, in her early twenties, was the youngest of Davina's three sisters-in-law and managed to hang out with Natalie and Davina whenever she could.

"What's she up to now?" Natalie asked, knowing she spent her days as a management assistant at Hardy Enterprises, her family's company.

"Don't say I didn't warn you, but she wants you to meet some guy she knows."

Natalie cringed; but before she could respond, she heard a light rap against her partly opened office door.

The dark head that appeared from around the other side was a familiar one. It belonged to Carter Johnson from security operations. She straightened up in her chair and gestured for him to come in. With his tough demeanor, Carter resembled just what you would expect a security expert to look like. Only his version dressed in cosmopolitan business suits and maintained a spit-polish shine on his wing tips.

With her head averted and voice lowered, she spoke to Davina. "I have a visitor. Carter."

"Not that tall, silent dude who handles security you spoke about?" Davina giggled. "Sounds promising."

Natalie rolled her eyes. Everybody was a matchmaker. "Lose the thought before I pick you and Alli up later, all right?" She replaced the phone and looked across the room to Carter, who had still ventured no farther than the door's threshold.

"Did I interrupt?" The polite words were brusquely spoken.

"Not at all," Natalie answered as she pulled her suit jacket from the back of her chair and slipped it on.

Earlier that week, Carter had asked her out, and she suspected he'd only dropped in now for the answer. Seemingly determined, he had asked her out on several occasions since she'd been here, even though she had been just as consistent in turning him down.

"What brings you down from the executive quarters?" she asked.

"Blakely. He'll see you this afternoon."

In her surprise, a frown knitted at Natalie's brows. "Don't tell me—he's finally deigned to give me some of his precious time when I asked for an appointment two whole days ago?"

"Try harder to work *with* him," Carter suggested. "You won't gain much testing his tolerance for your authority on this case."

"Don't be too sure," Natalie grunted unkindly.

"Didn't your mother teach you that sugar will trap more flies than vinegar?"

Natalie's frown deepened. Carter worked under the auspices of Gilbert Blakely, Innervision's curmudgeon of a CFO—chief financial officer—so his favorable comments were expected.

"My business professor taught me that traps aren't necessary when you have your knowledge and facts in place."

Carter bit at his lip as it slowly curved into a smile. "All right. It's your case, your call."

"How did I merit the personally delivered message, anyway?" she asked.

Carter's brows lifted in another bow to humor. He leaned against the doorjamb and crossed his arms, his big, dark hands a stark contrast to the neat white cuffs they rubbed against.

"That was my call."

Natalie stood from her chair while she gave Carter a strained once-over. His features, a series of strong angles and shadows, were wrapped around a mysterious aloofness that made him the subject of office curiosity, some of which had reached Natalie's ear. Like her, he was also new around here, though he had arrived at least six months prior to Natalie.

She slowly walked around to the front of her desk. He was as tall as David, though not nearly as muscular, and probably close in age, say early thirties. It wasn't that she was immune to Carter's brand of sexuality; it was just that she was indifferent. Now, it seemed, only David's particular handsomeness could heat her blood anymore. She drew in a pleasurable breath, and sighed.

As she eased back against the desk ledge, she focused in on Carter's curious stare, and realized she'd done it again— zoned off as she compared David to yet another man. Recovering quickly, she smoothed out her skirt before she returned his gaze.

"How can you work with someone as bad-tempered and obstinate as Blakely?"

"I take my own advice," Carter replied. "But from what I see, you handle him pretty well."

Natalie's brows rose a fraction. "Weren't you offering me advice a minute ago?"

"It was merely a suggestion," he clarified. "Given your driven personality, I'm not surprised that you draw conflict."

"For your sake, I'll take that as a compliment."

"I only meant that it's expected that you have to deal with"—the small smile crept up again even as he lowered his voice for emphasis—"misguided men."

"I admit I'm no shrinking violet," she said with a shrug of her shoulders. "And the right word for what I have to deal with is misogynists. They come with my profession, though."

She folded her arms across her chest. "So, how does a security staffer get paired with the likes of Gil Blakely?"

"It's no mystery. I'm an adviser for his security needs," he explained.

Natalie grinned as she twisted around to reach into a stack of papers on her desk. "I forgot about all of those secrets floating around on accounting spreadsheets these days."

"More than you think," Carter replied.

After a quick rummage, she found the document request she had prepared and then sent to Blakely.

As she turned back to face Carter, she was amused to observe that her crossed legs had distracted him. In fact, his gaze was still traveling along their nylon-encased length. Natalie wasn't vain, but she wasn't blind, either, and over the years had become well aware of her effect on the opposite sex. Men—when it came to parts of a woman, they were drunk happy. It was the sum that scared them to death.

"I can meet Blakely before I leave at four," she said, and watched as Carter's dark eyes quickly rose up to meet her unabashed smile. "Will you see him before then?"

He nodded curtly. "Sure. I can tell him."

"Thanks." Natalie's attention returned briefly to the memo in her hand before she noticed that Carter had not left. She looked up.

"Is there something else?" she asked expectantly.

"No," he said, and straightened from the door. "That's it." The pause before his answer had been slight.

Carter dropped his arms and, with a silent nod in her direction, disappeared through the doorway.

Puzzled by his actions, Natalie shook her head before she glanced at her watch. Four o'clock would be here before she knew it.

In a couple of days, David would be here, too.

Once again, she was immersed in a pool of sweet dread. A myriad of questions that centered on him floated unanswered in her consciousness. Did she really want the answers? She inhaled a deep breath to clear her head, but for just another moment she enjoyed her body's shiver as it played willing accomplice to her memories.

She pushed off the edge of the desk and stretched her stiff muscles.

"Okay," she mused out loud, "back to the business at hand." *Before I prepare to face off with Blakely.*

Knowing she had only to assert herself to invoke the bad-tempered Blakely's disfavor, she grinned with mischief and without the slightest guilt. In the end, he would have no choice but to bow to her requests, and that fact alone would make him furious.

She returned to her chair, the impish grin still gracing her face.

Pressing the cell phone to his ear with one hand, David Spenser reached across the crowded bar counter with the other. He nodded to the busy bartender and then grabbed up the two bottles of beer that had been set out, his attention divided by the phone.

"Vinny, it's me again." He used his sister's childhood nickname as he let out a deep sigh, impatient at being connected to her voice mail for a third time in as many hours.

"I arranged a flight out this evening instead of the weekend," he continued, and recited the flight number and arrival time while he worked his way through the noisy happy-hour crowd to return to his sidewalk table.

"Right now, I'm out with a few friends from the office before I leave for the airport, but I'll call when I get into Atlanta. Later." David closed the phone and dropped it into the starched pocket of his white dress shirt. With the cuffs turned back, his tie loosened, and sans the suit jacket left on his chair outside, he presented a striking portrait of a sophisticated young professional cruising his way through the popular Georgetown bar.

As he slowly edged his way toward the door, David ignored most of the primal glances he drew from the women he passed.

In fairness to his disinterest, he was used to the attention;

but for some time now, it had ceased being the novelty it had been years ago. Natalie—he'd bet on it—was responsible for the change. He smoothed his hand across his head, a habit he'd recently developed after having cut his longtime shoulder-length hair in favor of a shorter, conservative style. He was curious about Natalie's reaction to the haircut, but in the same moment thought, why the hell should he care?

David easily returned a statuesque brunette's smile with his own cheeky one, and thought his situation ironic. He had picked up an irritating habit of comparing every woman he came across to Natalie. And damn if she didn't still come out as the one he preferred.

The one he preferred. An uncomfortable reality rode him about his return to Atlanta and the guarantee that he'd see Natalie this time around. In fact, he hadn't been able to shake the feelings for the last few days; it was like a head rush—he had thought little of anything else, day and night, and used any excuse to succumb to a memory that involved her. Was she seeing someone else? Of course she was. She'd moved on; of that, David was sure, and he needed to do the same.

A scowl had slowly formed and deepened by the time he exited the bar doors. He stepped outside into the warm, spring sunshine to rejoin his friends for what could be their last drinks together in D.C.—that is, if he decided to remain in Atlanta this time around.

"Is she here yet?"

Gilbert Blakely barked the words at the middle-aged blond woman who sat behind the computer in his reception area.

"If you're referring to Miss Goodman, the answer is no," she replied evenly. "Mr. Johnson said she'd be here at four o'clock." She turned from her work to give her boss a patronizing look before she resumed her typing. "You'll just have to be patient for another thirty minutes."

Blakely let out a brisk grunt and huffed through the area

that abutted his office suite. His irritation, prompted by this upcoming meeting with his personal thorn in the side, was not helped by the receptionist's composure.

"Women," he mumbled and threw open his own office door before he pushed it shut behind him.

Anxious fingers brushed back brown hair mixed with thatches of salt-and-pepper gray from his receding hairline. He looked across the spacious suite to assure himself that he was alone, and made a determined path to his desk.

"That damned Goodman girl is becoming my personal nightmare," he mumbled out loud. "She knows it and she damn well likes it, too." Blakely sighed as he came around his desk and easily pressed his fit, sixty-year-old body into his oversized executive chair.

He unlocked and then opened his side drawer before he slid back a wooden panel to reveal three attached video screens, each one boasting a width of no more than five inches. Below the screens lay a series of manual controls, along with an RCA plug for a listening device.

Blakely pushed down on the front of the drawer, and the screens tilted for optimum viewing. He picked up a sleek, silver cylinder with a dark head—it could easily have been mistaken for a common highlighter marker—from the top of his leather desk blotter. Rearing back in his chair, he pointed the cylinder at the screens.

"All right, little miss, let's see what you're up to now."

With a light press to the cylinder's head, all three screens sprang to life in crisp black and white. Blakely leaned forward to peer at the focusing images.

Each screen offered a different angle for viewing the well-appointed office located ten floors below.

And every aspect of an unaware Natalie's movements, from packing her briefcase to straightening her skirt, played out in real time on the screens for Blakely's benefit.

Chapter 2

At exactly one minute before four o'clock, Natalie strolled through the empty reception area on the twenty-fifth floor and made her way to Blakely's door. With her knuckles poised for a knock, his voice boomed out to her from the other side.

"Come on in."

Did the man have a spy in the hall? Opening the door, she pulled a luggage caddy behind her as she crossed the threshold into his large office. The wall-sized window looked out onto an uneven skyline of gray concrete that morphed into green, rolling woods set as far as the eye could see to the west.

Blakely had already come from around his desk to greet Natalie, his eyes shrewdly observant of her entrance as they gazed out from his ruddy face.

He thrust out his hand. "I see you're punctual. A good habit."

While he pumped her hand stiffly, Natalie detected a pale aura of smoke and, possibly, the sweet stench of scotch encircling his expensive suit. She disengaged from the handshake. Blakely returned to his desk, but Natalie stayed put near a plush sofa, and waited for him to choreograph their next moves.

They shared a mutual dislike of each other, and the impression had only grown stronger from that very first meeting when Blakely all but dismissed her in front of her accounting superiors at Lang & Myers, and then patently ignored her input in the ensuing discussion. His look of surprise when he learned she would lead the audit review had been priceless.

"You're calling it a day already?" His eyes darted from Natalie to her briefcase after a time.

"Shortly," she replied, and stepped toward his desk. "Mr. Johnson said you wanted to see me."

"Ahh . . . Carter. Go on," he said, and gestured to the chairs around the room as he sat down behind the desk. "Sit down."

Natalie chose a tufted, straight-back chair near his desk as opposed to the heavily cushioned sofa behind her. She watched Blakely pick up her letter from his desk and emit a series of grunts while he studied the enumerated list.

"I wanted to meet with you as well," Natalie began quietly. "I thought you might have a few questions . . . about the issues I raised."

"You're damned right about that," he charged in instantly.

Natalie almost jumped as his voice boomed over her, though she quickly settled in for the bout to come.

"What is this about?" he continued, and narrowed his eyes at her before waving the document in dismissal. "I don't see the need to pull this much paper. It'll take someone on staff the better part of a few days to collect all this." He looked at the list again. "And your questions for the accounting managers—why are they necessary?"

Natalie took in a deep breath and prepared to lock horns with Blakely. "If you give me full computer access, there won't be a need to pull paper; and I could have gone directly to the managers for answers by now, but you told me I'd have to run all requests through you."

"To avoid a useless waste of employee time."

"Actually, Mr. Blakely, it would have been much quicker—"

"We're in the middle of a quarterly report," he interrupted. "Now, getting back to my question, Ms. Goodman, what does all this have to do with you not signing off on a review we're paying your firm good money to certify?"

"Granted, some of my requests might not be clear initially. But together they'll help me form the basis of reasoning for some of the accounting entries."

This time, Blakely drew in a loud breath, obviously unhappy with Natalie's response. "You're upsetting my operation, putting off your decision. Time is money, young lady. Did you know that every review prior to this one has been handled in just half the time you've taken?"

Natalie knew that fact only too well. It had been mentioned more than once, and by her own managers, too. She sat forward in her chair and in one long breath told Blakely the same thing she had told them. "Maybe if they'd been more thorough then, you wouldn't be losing profits along with shareholder confidence now, Mr. Blakely."

She sat back and stared off with the older man. "Remember, Innervision is hemorrhaging profits, and I've been charged with finding out why."

Natalie pressed stiffly against her chair as they both sat through a controlled silence that was thick with attitude. She spoke first, and tried to delete the sarcasm from her voice.

"I'll tell you what I can do, sir. I'll be out of the office part of next week on personal business, so I can give you more time to gather the remaining data."

Blakely was still not appeased, and boldly grunted his continued disfavor as he looked up from the paper he now shuttled to the side of his desk, his eyes straying once again to the caddy tied down with her briefcase and work papers.

"Why do you cart your work back and forth like some homeless employee?" he asked. "Don't we provide ample storage space in that office you're using?"

Natalie blocked the distinct urge to kick the man and serenely followed his gaze to the overstuffed caddy. "I prefer to store my work papers at Lang & Myers. That way, it keeps conflicts of interest issues to a minimum. It protects you, too, until my final report is prepared for you and the CEO, Mr. Monroe, as well as the board."

"Of which, I'm also a member," he reminded her.

"I'm aware of the fact."

With a snort, Blakely pushed back in his big chair and began to roll an oversized silver highlighter through his fingers while Natalie tried not to roll her eyes in contempt.

"You can tell me, then, about your preliminary findings."

"No, I'd rather not say right now." No progress was being made, and Natalie stood up from her chair to end the session. "Mr. Blakely, things will go smoother if you'd just let me do my job. Mr. Monroe promised full—"

"Cooperation," Blakely recited with a bit of sarcasm. "I know; I was there."

"Then I trust you'll provide me with computer and employee access, as well as the documents from that list."

Slightly uncomfortable in the shadow of his stare, coupled with the silence that followed, Natalie turned from the desk and started for the door. "If you have any questions before I return, you can always talk with my operations manager, John Callaway." She slid her purse strap onto her shoulder. "Hopefully, sir, you'll have everything I need when I return."

Natalie didn't expect that the obstinate Blakely would oblige her with a nod of agreement, and he didn't. Under his watchful eye, she left through his door, closing it solidly behind her. Once she was out of his sight, she exhaled a noisy breath as she pulled the caddy past the receptionist that now tended the area. When the blond woman offered an understanding smile, Natalie smiled in return.

Though she was petite in a powerful profession, Natalie was not easily intimidated; but Blakely was one man she wouldn't miss once this audit was over. They had only exchanged words on a handful of occasions. Even so, there was something disturbing about him, even sinister.

She entered the empty hallway and moved toward the express elevators that were privy only to the executive level.

It took a while for the elevator to arrive on the seemingly

deserted twenty-fifth-floor suite. The empty, low-lit corridor was almost ghostly in its silence with only the shadows of oversized frames from abstract paintings for company.

When the elevator doors finally opened, she stepped in and hurriedly dragged the luggage caddy behind her. Unfortunately, a wheel jammed in a groove between the floor and elevator carriage. Shoving the caddy to dislodge it was a mistake, because when she did, it overturned, and her briefcase and folders slipped from beneath their cords and spilled out onto the floor and into the elevator.

"Damn," Natalie muttered, and stooped to block the closing doors. She quickly stretched her arms to gather her things.

"I'll help with that."

Natalie literally jumped at the deep voice coming from above her—nearly losing her balance, in fact—and craned her neck to look up into the dark visage that now loomed above hers.

"Carter," she exclaimed in relief and pressed her hand to her chest. "You scared me to death."

"I'm surprised you scare at all," Carter replied. "Give me a hand with this," he said to someone behind him.

When Natalie stood, she saw that a younger man with thick dark hair accompanied Carter. She didn't know his name but she recognized his face only as an employee she'd seen on occasion.

Before she could manage a reply, the men had edged her aside and proceeded to grab up her files.

"Thank you, but I could have managed." Natalie made the tactful protest amid her cringe when she saw them haul her papers up from the floor in typical male helter-skelter fashion.

With a defeated sigh, she watched Carter strong-arm the wheel from the floor groove. Once the caddy had been freed, she followed her belongings and the men into the elevator.

"What floor are you parked on, Natalie?" the younger man asked, his free hand poised before the button panel.

"Ah, level two. Do I know you?" she asked with a squint.

"Sean Miller in accounting." Sean tried shaking her hand before he realized his arms were full.

"Oh, let me take those," Natalie said, reaching for her files.

"No," he protested, and bent over the carrier. "I'll just re-stack them for you."

"So, how do you know my name?" she asked.

"I've seen you around—you're with our outside account-ing firm." He looked up from his handiwork, his face bright from the exertion, and grinned. "And I asked Carter."

Surprised, Natalie pivoted from Sean to Carter, who stood quietly against the elevator wall with his arms loaded. She arched an inquiring brow at his stone expression.

"Sean is helping me with a project." He shrugged his shoulders. "He asked, and I obliged."

Natalie opened her mouth to remark, but the elevator had already come to a smooth stop and the doors slid open. Sean quickly stepped out into the cement corridor. She followed and Carter brought up the rear.

Natalie reached for her briefcase, still held by Carter. "I appreciate you and your friend's help, but I'm a big girl and I don't need an escort all the way to my car."

"Actually, you're not that big." He passed her bags to Sean, who proceeded to strap them down with her other files, and turned back to Natalie. "We had a security breach in garage parking last week, so you can never be too care-ful."

"Well, why didn't you just say that? Though, something tells me you and Sean aren't giving personal escorts to every-one in the building." She fished her keys from her purse as Sean wheeled over her luggage caddy.

"True." Carter took up steps alongside Natalie as she walked to her car. "Just wanted to make sure you were safe, that's all. Mr. Blakely will be happy to know it, too."

The unexpected reference raised Natalie's hackles, and

she looked over at Carter. "I'm no fool. Blakely wouldn't care if I was kidnapped. As a matter of fact, he'd welcome it."

Carter eased into a smile. "I think I spoke too soon earlier. There is something big about you after all—your mouth." He darted her a teasing look. "I'd bet that it gets you into trouble on a regular basis."

At the same time his humor doused her anger, another thought—a totally unexpected one—occurred to her. She could avoid the weekly matchmaking by her friends that waited for her tonight if she already had a date lined up for the weekend. Carter. She gave him a sidelong glance. What the hell? At least he wasn't altogether unknown.

"Carter . . ." Natalie stopped and turned to face him, her voice low. "I'm curious. Why do you keep asking me out? I think if someone told me no, even once, I'd say to hell with him and move on."

He folded his arms, the same lineless expression claiming his face. "I don't have a problem with no. I figure you have your reasons, and it's fine with me. I just try again."

Natalie considered his take on rejection for only a few seconds, and then gave up. It didn't make a bit of sense. "Well, you may think I'm sending mixed messages, but if your offer is still good to go out this weekend and try that new Eastern restaurant, I accept."

"You do?" Carter shifted his weight, as though he was considering her change of mind. "All right. How about Saturday, eight o'clock?"

She nodded. "But, this is a friendly dinner, okay? We can, I don't know, exchange tips on working with Blakely, or something like that."

Carter allowed a small grin to soften his face. "Or something like that."

Natalie's car was parked only a few yards away and she said as much. "I believe I can handle it from here."

"I'll see you Saturday, then."

As Carter started back for the elevator where Sean waited, Natalie remembered he didn't have her address.

"Carter," she called out. "You don't know where I live."

"I work security, remember?"

She grinned and then laughed at the implication. "Please don't make me regret this," she warned.

But when she turned and made the remaining few steps to her car, she frowned with second thoughts, the regrets arriving a tad late. David always did warn her about being impetuous.

David.

Natalie sucked in an audible breath as she unlocked her trunk. *Two more days.* As she settled her bags inside, she could hear the elevator arrive for the men and then leave.

Now, alone in the parking deck, and assailed by her doubts about accepting a spur-of-the-moment date, something else occurred to her. Carter and Sean had appeared from nowhere as she left Blakely's office. In light of Carter's cryptic comment about Blakely's concern for her, how far-fetched was it that Blakely might have sent Carter to follow her, but for what reason? Carter didn't seem the type to play anybody's lackey, especially for a bully like Blakely. But, could she be sure? He did work for the man.

The unsettling possibility that once again she had let impulsiveness get the better of her caused her to glance over her shoulders before she slammed down the trunk and then quickly slipped into the relative safety of her car and locked the doors.

Chapter 3

"I'm not interested in your boy-toy pick of the week," Natalie said between bites of salad, and looked across the restaurant booth she shared with Alli and Davina. It always came to this when she took a pass on one of Alli's "perfect" matches.

About five years their junior, Natalie saw much of her younger self in Alli; it was the very reason Natalie now plied her with a spirited grin. "If this one is so great, you go out with him."

When she was met by silence, Natalie asked her friends, "What's with you two, anyway, playing like middle-aged matchmakers? You think I'm missing the commitment boat when I don't go on one of your arranged dates?"

"Well, look at you," Alli said. "You're short-tempered—"

"And preoccupied," Davina added with a nod.

"Or maybe we should just say more than usual." Alli glanced to Davina for confirmation. "Telltale signs, don't you think, of a woman who needs some real T.L.C., and in a hurry?"

"She needs love, Alli," Davina said. "And you can't hurry that."

Natalie laughed at her friends. "That's the last thing I need."

"Why not?" Alli asked. "It does feel good . . . at least for a while."

"Because love complicates everything, especially sex," Natalie explained. "And I prefer mine without the love issues."

Davina let out a loud sigh. "I hate it when you talk like that."

"Oh . . . so that's where you're headed again," Natalie said, sagely nodding her head. "Listen, the love train is plumb out of fuel. And being older and wiser now, a one-night stand isn't all bad." She grinned at her friend's rolling eyes. "It can have its benefits."

"Mmm . . . she may be right about that," Alli replied slyly. "A little impromptu brown-skin magic between the sheets, preferably satin, can help anything."

Davina shook her head. "Now you've got Alli sounding as crazy as you."

"I don't know," Alli said. "It doesn't sound all crazy."

"You're right, you don't know," Natalie quipped right back. "You haven't dated regularly since you dumped poor, clueless Chazz. You need to get some more life experience." Her gaze now flitted to Davina.

Davina laughed as she waved off her friend's stare. "This discussion is between you and Alli, so don't drag me into it." Her brow raised a fraction. "But, it doesn't change the fact that you have been a little tense and edgy lately, and not just about work."

"Okay, so on occasion I don't want to go out; but I can go home and take a long, leisurely shower." She smiled before she winked at Alli. "Pretty soon, the tension is washed away and I'm just fine again, thank you."

"Oh, my God." Alli chuckled out loud at the confession. "Just don't name the shower massage. That's when we'll know you've gone over the edge."

Davina grinned even as she solemnly shook her head at her friends. "You ought to stop it, Natalie. And, Alli"—she nudged her sister-in-law next to her in the booth—"don't encourage her bad behavior."

"I still want her to go out this weekend," Alli said.

Natalie lathered creamy butter on another honeyed roll. "I am doing just fine with my life. Anyway, what's so hot about this particular guy, Alli, that I *have* to go out with him this weekend?"

"Because when David gets here, he needs to see you with a life," she blurted.

The knife hovered in midair as Natalie frowned at Alli. "What?"

Alli set off a loud jangle from her ubiquitous African bracelets as she quickly smoothed a tendril of short hair behind her ear. "I can't believe I said that."

"Somehow, you did," Davina added with a sigh.

"So, that's what everyone thinks? That I'm this sad sack since David left?" Natalie set the knife down and pushed her salad plate back.

"Well, at least you're one good-looking, well-dressed sad sack," Alli explained.

"Drop it, Alli," Davina warned.

"All I meant is David should know what he's missed out on."

"I'm supposed to take advice from the woman who flirted with him outrageously when they first met?" Natalie reminded her.

"Eww . . . I would never do that again." Alli waved off any concern. "Anyway, that was before I knew he would practically become my brother."

"We like setting you up to see if we can make love happen. All you have to do is go out with one of our picks once in a while," Davina suggested, smiling to lighten the mood. "Even Alli does that for me. I mean, we're not talking long-term commitment."

"No, we're talking worse. A blind date can be an eternity, and I won't do it. If I want a date, I'll get my own." Natalie looked at her friends' skeptical expressions as she gently pulled apart the buttered roll, pleased with herself that she'd had the foresight to plan ahead.

"Anyway, I already have a date Saturday night," she announced.

Alli and Davina exchanged surprised looks before they turned back and spoke simultaneously. "Who?"

Natalie slowly trained her eyes on Davina, who prepared to sip from her tea. "Carter Johnson," she said, and smiled as her friend sputtered her drink.

Alli's eyes turned shrewd. "That tall dude from your client's office?"

"I thought you'd turned him down," Davina said, wiping her mouth with a napkin. "What changed your mind?"

Natalie shrugged. "I suggested that new restaurant, the Casbah in Buckhead, so I figured dinner at a place I've wanted to go to wouldn't be all bad."

"I . . . I don't know what to say." Davina looked squint-eyed at Natalie. "Who'd have thought you'd be so easy to get out?"

"I think it's great, girl." Alli flagged her thumb up in approval. "If nothing else, you'll get a good meal out of it. But, ooh, what I'd give for David to see you there, having fun with another man."

"Don't even think about it," Natalie warned. Alli had a knack for rooting up trouble and Natalie didn't need any well-intentioned interference to add to her already unsorted emotions about David's return.

"Actually," she continued, "I hope I didn't accept too quickly." She then recounted to the women how Carter and the young intern had appeared out of nowhere as she left Blakely's office and then proceeded to hustle her and her bags to the parking garage. "The truth is, I only know him from a few conversations in the building."

"He is security personnel," Alli assured Natalie. "Don't they get checked out pretty thoroughly to weed out the odd-balls?"

Davina casually leaned back against the booth. "The only thing odd is that you *let them* hijack you to your car."

"Well, later on, a crazy thought did occur that maybe they'd followed me, courtesy of Mr. Blakely's orders."

"Are you serious?" Alli asked, frowning. "Even if this Blakely guy does bite like you say, what are the odds that the old coot bothered to cook up a conspiracy against you?"

"I know, I know, it's a wacky idea," Natalie said between chews of bread. "I've racked my brain for a valid reason, and I can't come up with one, other than our mutual dislike of each other."

"Alli's right," Davina charged in. "What's the point of getting worked up over nothing, unless you're trying to find an excuse to cancel this date?"

Natalie smiled and eyed another plump roll. "Okay, my voices of reason have spoken." She stretched her fingers toward the bread basket and spoke jokingly. "Just don't rule out kidnapping if I fail to show up at one of little Jake's christening parties."

"Hey—" Davina shook her head good-naturedly, and her unruly head of curly hair, a trait she shared with her brother, danced along her shoulders. "No jokes about kidnapping and conspiracy stuff. We don't want a repeat of that summer drama, do we?"

Natalie's brows furrowed at the none too distant memories that had left an indelible mark on their young lives. "You're right," she agreed solemnly, and sank her teeth into the honeyed roll.

Two summers ago . . . it had been filled with surprises and unexpected danger when she and Davina had turned sleuth to uncover the mystery behind the identity and lost paintings of Davina's artist father.

In fact, it was during those perilous events that Davina and Justin had met and fallen in love. Natalie had considered her friend's engagement a much-deserved and picture-perfect conclusion to that dangerous time. It had also heralded Natalie and David's simmering attraction.

Unfortunately—or fortunately, as the case might be—the two couples' endings hadn't played out in the same way. She and David were afflicted by the identical latent tendency to undermine relationships, specifically their own, she thought sourly. And while she remembered—as though it were yesterday—how they had lobbed angry words at one another their last night together, she could no longer recall them.

"Earth to Natalie . . ."

She looked up into Alli's concerned gaze, and instantly sobered from the reminiscence. "I was thinking that Davina's right—the last thing we need is more intrigue, real or imagined." She settled her salad plate back in front of her.

"Why don't we just forget what I said, and I'll forgive you both for trying to match me up again, okay?"

"A truce," Alli teased, "at least until we find out how the date with Carter went."

Davina smiled at Natalie and leaned into the table. "It's forgotten. But tomorrow, we're going to spend the day doing absolutely nothing, just like we planned."

"Oh, why didn't you tell me? I want to come," Alli complained at their side.

"You have to work," Davina explained, but continued on, turning to Natalie. "I'm figuring the baby should be more than enough to keep you clear of conspiracy traps *and* occupy your mind, you think?" Davina asked.

That remained to be seen. With a smile of acquiescence to her friend, Natalie sipped from her tea before she absently reached for the last roll.

"No. It shouldn't look like an inside job at all." Blakely spoke tersely into the phone as he flicked his wrist and looked at his watch. "I want things done cleanly. No trails back to anyone on our side of the fence," he emphasized.

"Just get the papers to me before the night's over. Am I clear?"

When he heard the affirmative response he wanted, he clicked off the cell phone. And, it wasn't a moment too soon, because his wife's footsteps could be heard in the hallway outside their bedroom door.

"Gil, honey," she called out. "We're going to be late for dinner. What's taking you so long?"

"I'm coming, I'm coming." As Blakely grabbed up his jacket and headed for the door, he swallowed the peptic acid that rose in his throat and wondered if he'd feel any better about this whole damned thing come tomorrow. He'd better, he decided with a grimace . . . or else.

Natalie pushed her dinner plate away before she shrugged from her suit jacket and draped it across her lap. "If I eat another thing, I'll burst," she complained, and leaned back against the padded booth.

"Well, thank goodness there's nothing left on your plate . . . or ours . . . to eat," Alli observed dryly as the waiter cleared away their dishes.

"Interesting how you've found your appetite," Davina said, "just as I've lost mine."

"You've got jitters over all those plans for the christening," Natalie replied. "You were like this for the wedding, too."

"That explains me. What about you?"

"What do you mean?" Natalie cocked a suspicious brow while she raised her water glass to her lips.

"You're eating like you're doing it for two." Davina similarly hiked her brow at Natalie. "Nothing's been going on long-term between you and Carter that you haven't shared, is there?"

This time, Davina laughed while Natalie choked. "Okay, so it's not that."

"Are you aware that you sucked down a whole basket of bread?" Alli pointed out. "Did you even taste it?"

Natalie's look turned to horror. "I ate that many?" She inhaled deeply and, cupping her breasts in the sleeveless silk sweater, looked down to check her waist. "I bought that skinny dress just for the christening. Now I probably won't even fit in it."

Davina shook her head. "I'm worried about you, girl."

"Why? Because I'm vain."

"Who wouldn't be if a new dress won't fit?" Alli countered. She slid from her seat at the booth and stood up. "Ladies, I'm off to the powder room. Be right back."

As Alli stepped away, Davina slanted her dark brows at her friend and sighed. "Why do you complain about your weight? You've had the same hourglass curves since junior high. And you know I've been jealous of them ever since."

"No need, anymore." Natalie leaned back in her seat. "I happen to know Justin thinks you're as sexy as they come."

With a widening grin, Davina crossed her arms on the table's edge. "I've heard David say the same about you."

The heat rose from Natalie's neck and encased her like a glove. "Let's not talk about your brother, okay?"

"Oh, suddenly he's *my brother*," Davina mocked. "And why not? He mentions you."

Natalie's attention was immediate, though she remained detached under her friend's watchful gaze. She drew her finger lazily across the condensation that accumulated on her glass. "Okay, Davina, I'll bite. What does he say?"

"Actually, the same thing as you—that he doesn't want to talk about you. Funny, though, how both of you are interested in what each other has to say."

Natalie wrinkled her nose at the trickery and, kicking off her shoes, expertly swung her legs up and onto the long booth seat. "We've both moved on."

"The more I think about it, the more I don't think so." Davina peered at Natalie. "You're also curiously thin-skinned about David. Does it bother you that he's coming home?"

Natalie jerked her eyes at her friend, and then quickly looked away, unable to respond except with a chuckle and a negative shake of her head.

"Maybe the fire's not out between you two after all."

Natalie reached over and tugged Davina's hand. "Leave it alone." With a sigh, she released her friend's hand. "David and I weren't suited from the beginning, and you know it."

"Been there, done that. It started out the same way with me and Justin, and look at what happened."

"Nothing happens, Davina, unless the couple wants it to." Natalie could feel her frustration rise. "Wishing won't make it so."

"But, don't you see?" Davina pressed on. "You have to face your unresolved feelings."

"And what makes you think they aren't?"

"I've been thinking. For someone who believes in squeezing as much pleasure from life as they can, you've not been your usual carefree self since you heard David was coming back. Have you even been on a date since Jake was born?"

"I've gone out."

"Okay, two times."

"I'm dating Saturday night."

"Suspiciously right before David returns, I might add. And is it really a *date* date?"

"If it'll make you happy, why don't I just sleep with him right off the bat? That'll prove it's a date and that I'm over David, right?"

Davina looked stricken. "You'd better not." When Natalie grinned, she joined in and spoke in a low tone. "Okay, you've made your point."

"I'm a big girl, and I know all about choices, which I make alone."

Nodding her head, Davina smiled. "Somebody else is involved in that choice, too. There's a lot to be said about the powerful effects of what Alli called brown-skin magic between satin sheets."

The conjured image was acute and Natalie swallowed hard, not in the least humored by her friend's joke.

"Seriously, Natalie, I don't think it's too late to talk—"

"I see now that David and I should have just sat you down and explained everything at the time."

"What I'm saying is that it's never too late to work out your differences," Davina persisted, not in the least put off by her friend's sarcasm. "And, I have a strong hunch David wants the same thing."

That would be the worst that could happen. Exasperated, Natalie ran her fingers through her feathered tufts of hair. All she wanted to do was make it through the next two weeks while David was in town. After that, he'd be gone again, and she could return to life without him in it.

She leaned back against the booth, closed her eyes, and allowed David to fill her mind's eye. She'd be forced, soon enough, to deal with the man in the flesh. A tired sigh escaped Natalie's throat as she realized Davina was still talking, not yet giving up her arguments on the sense of reconciliation.

Natalie tried holding on to her smile to make light of a subject that still had the ability to squeeze her heart. Instead, the smile faded as she shifted on her seat and averted her face from her friend's gaze. She loved Davina above all else, but when she had a mission, it was hard to turn around her pit bull attitude.

"I'll treat for dessert if you promise to change subjects," Natalie offered.

Anxious tugs to Natalie's arm were accompanied by Davina's giddy whisper. "Oh, my goodness. Look at who Alli's bringing over."

The words set off alarms as Natalie's eyes abruptly flew open. She straightened up in the booth, her dread real that Alli's latest "perfect" blind date had actually shown up at their dinner.

I'm going to kill the little minx. She turned her head and followed Davina's gaze across the room.

Two men, tall with steady strides, had moved beyond the lighted entrance and now made their way through the dimly lit aisles to meet up with Alli, turning heads of curious diners as they moved. One, dressed in a dark suit, took the lead and bent to hug Alli. It was Justin. Natalie's wide eyes quickly cut to the other man who was only a step behind and was dressed more casually in a knit sweater and slacks. The sweater hugged a beautiful physique.

Recognition jerked her body forward. David.

Natalie's heart lurched, her silent shock palpable as the private vision she'd produced only moments before now actually took shape.

It was then that David looked up from behind Justin and claimed her stare from across the room. Warmth suffused Natalie's face, and a real fear—that she was far from being over David—began to set in.

Chapter 4

Natalie's breath lodged in her throat for the seconds it took her eyes to sweep over David's face. He was as handsome as she'd remembered, maybe even more so, with his deep-set eyes and firm lips set against cognac-brown skin . . . except that his usually long hair—

"Look, Natalie," Davina exclaimed. "He's cut his hair."

David had always resembled a charming rogue to Natalie with his hair worn long and, for business, usually tied back neatly at his nape, but it was now short against his head. The thought of what else had changed ran swiftly across her mind.

She reclaimed his silent gaze, but only for a moment before their prickly past rose up and crept into their eyes. Instantly, they both looked away.

Natalie jerked her head around to Davina, an accusation of the worst kind poised on her lips. But her friend saw it coming and spoke first, her excited eyes darting between Natalie and the approaching men.

"Natalie, I know what you're thinking, but I swear I had no idea he was coming tonight. I wouldn't keep this from you."

"I know." She took a deep breath to brace herself in the time remaining before David and the others joined them.

"What about Alli? Do you think she set this up?"

"If she did," Natalie said evenly, and with a good deal of malice, "I will personally make her regret not sharing it." She looked up just as the group reached the table, and before she could steady her heart, it lurched again, topsy-turvy, in her chest.

"David!" Davina was sliding from the booth like lightning, and soon became enfolded in her brother's wide embrace. "It's so good to see you." She stepped back and lightly brushed his head, speaking at a fast clip. "You cut off your beautiful hair. Why didn't you tell me you had changed plans? Was this a surprise Justin and Alli cooked up?"

Natalie watched the others wordlessly from her seat, waiting for her inevitable moment with David. She did catch Alli's eye and took some satisfaction in the fact that the younger woman's grin made a rapid fade as blame was being assigned.

Justin stepped around the others and slipped his hands against Davina's waist. "I had nothing to do with it. I'm just the chauffeur," he said, and kissed her cheek.

"I'm innocent, too," Alli explained with a look to Davina and Natalie. "I just happened to see them walk through the door on my way back to the table."

David's smile had become as wide as his baritone was deep. "Why don't we sit down? And if you'll give me a moment, I think I can explain everything."

When Davina slipped back onto the booth seat, Alli pushed her brother in his wife's direction. "You sit over there."

David turned to acknowledge Natalie from her seat in the corner. It was a moment he savored up close. She was the same sensual, exotic flower that defied description and she had never looked lovelier—or more vulnerable, under the circumstances. He'd have to tread carefully.

"Natalie . . . it's good seeing you."

"You too, David. Welcome home."

Her noncommittal voice was pleasant, yet aloof, something that immediately disturbed him. He wondered if she was boiling over inside, like him. David got his answer as he saw her fidget against the seat. She was just as uneasy with this first public meeting as he.

"Now wait just a minute," Alli announced in mock shock. "Is that any way for old friends to greet each other?"

"Of course not," Davina said.

"True," Justin added with a wide grin from her side.

"For goodness' sake, man," Alli continued as she nudged David to Natalie's side of the booth. "Hug her like you're really glad to see her."

He didn't miss the eye contact between Davina and Natalie before her large beautiful eyes returned to him. He leaned over and drew Natalie into a gentle one-arm hug amidst the group's vocal approvals. But no touch was gentle when it evoked memories of spent passion a scant year ago.

David released her and, turning his head slightly, took in her signature fragrance. Giving in to temptation, he kissed her cheek. When he pulled away, their eyes caught and held in an intimate connection they both understood. So much for time and distance healing things.

"We can have the waiter bring another chair," Justin offered.

"That's not necessary," Alli said. "David can sit on our side of the booth. Natalie, can you slide over?"

"Sure," Natalie grunted and edged closer toward the wall.

The abrupt request was a surprise, and David, aware of Alli's meddling, thought Natalie would choke on the words she didn't say. He smiled and slid into the space Natalie vacated, with Alli following him into the booth to take up the outside seat.

It was a snug but comfortable fit for three people, and as David inched over to allow more space for Alli, it was hard for him to ignore Natalie's delicate femininity only a hairbreadth away. It was just as rough on Natalie when David's well-muscled thigh settled easily against her soft one. Of course, both reacted to the intimate contact with a jolt.

Natalie's lips twitched into a smile as she turned slightly toward him, ostensibly to alleviate their constant touching. "Weren't you going to tell us how you ended up arriving two days early?"

"My schedule cleared at the last minute," he said, turning to the others. "And I managed to get an earlier flight, but I wasn't trying to surprise anyone."

Alli's brows rose. "So, why didn't you let us know?"

David casually leaned back in the booth and stretched his arms out across the back of the seats. "Oh, I tried calling Vinny on her cell, but she didn't answer."

Davina frowned. "I was home with the baby all day until Natalie picked me up this evening. I wonder why my cell phone . . ." Her voice tapered off as realization set in. The others chuckled when she rummaged in her purse for the turned-off phone.

"You do have to turn it on for it to work," Justin pointed out.

Alli turned to David. "That still doesn't explain how you ended up here with Justin."

"I heard one of his voice mails at the house," Justin explained. "And I figured Davina had no idea about the new plans, so I met him at baggage claim and brought him straight over here where I knew I'd find the three of you." He looked at David and, with a grin, added, "I thought he looked a little hungry."

"We can get a waiter for your order," Davina suggested.

"No, no," David demurred, and gave Justin a wicked glare. "I ate before I left D.C." He ignored the friendly gibe thrown by his rascal of a brother-in-law, a man who had gone from being a sworn enemy once upon a time to a respected brother figure.

"It's pretty good seeing everybody, though," David said.

"If you miss us so much, are you back to stay?" Alli asked.

"You do have a new nephew," Davina added.

"Yeah . . . I've thought about it," he said, his reply purposely enigmatic as he felt Natalie's eyes upon him.

"Okay, first things first: what's with the hair?" Alli asked. "Or, should I say lack of it?"

"What about it?" David joked, and ran a hand across his head. "You don't like it?"

"Personally, I'd be fine if you were bald, my handsome brother; but then again, I'm only one opinion. What do y'all think?"

Davina took on a pensive air before she let loose with a chuckle. "He's definitely edgy, and less raffish, but it does make him look older."

"I like to think *wiser*," David corrected with a grin.

"It's about time," Justin chimed in.

David turned to Natalie, and could feel her stiffen at his attention. "Come on," he coaxed. "Don't hold back your opinion on my account."

"No chance of that," she replied amidst the quiet laughter from the others. "I've always been straight with you."

As more laughter circled them, David hesitated, measuring her in that moment. "That's what I'm afraid of."

"Not to worry," she said.

David's eyes followed her lips as they parted in a curved, stiff smile.

"Because I like it."

"Good,"Alli announced. "We've decided we can live with the new you."

As the conversation continued to flow around them, David's arm slipped from the top of the booth, either through inadvertence or by design, to Natalie's shoulders.

Like water on a hot skillet, David pulled his arm away, where it then collided into Natalie's side and breast. As he recoiled from yet another electric jolt, David's glance met Natalie's in joined frustration, and they both squirmed as he returned his arm to rest across the back of the seat.

"David?"

"What?" he asked thickly, and looked around to his sister.

"She asked twice if you're staying in the poolhouse this time," Alli said, giggling at his confusion. "Pay attention."

Casually amused, he smiled at Alli. "As tempting as the offer is for maid service and daily hot meals, I'm staying at my house this time." David had become a familiar figure at the Hardy family's large estate, but he preferred the privacy of his own condo, even if his sister had occasionally used it as her art studio during his absence.

"Have you had time to have the condo cleaned?" Natalie asked Davina. "Canvases were everywhere the last time I was there."

David jerked his head around to Natalie, remembering quite well the last time she'd been there—with him. From the twist of her brows, so did she.

"What I meant," Natalie explained, and darted her gaze to David, "is the last time I was there with Davina, just before the baby came, she still had work piled against the walls."

"I've set up a studio at home until I find a new one, but we haven't done much moving since Jake was born," Davina explained.

"So, just stay at the house. Mom wants you there, too," Justin added. "In fact, the whole family is so preoccupied with the christening next week, your chances of spending time with Davina and the baby are better if you're settled in at the house." He shrugged. "Hell, at the end of some days, I have to get in line to kiss my own wife and son."

"That is so untrue," Davina said, laughing as she leaned in and gave him a kiss.

Alli rolled her eyes heavenward. "Can you two please stop?"

David watched the affection between his sister and Justin and smiled, pleased that she had found a deserved happiness in her husband's large family.

"I'll figure a way to manage on my own," he said. "But, don't worry. I'll be around for my nephew."

"About all that's necessary now is babysitting and diaper changing," Alli quipped.

"This is probably as good a time as any," Davina said, and exchanged a glance with Justin before she straightened in her seat. "We want the best for our baby, and that means surrounding him with a well-rounded group of people who have his best interests in hand."

"What are you talking about?" Alli said.

"Yeah," Natalie chimed in. "I'm not being dumped as a godmother, am I?"

Godmother? David drew a deep breath and looked across the table at his sister. *What is she up to?*

Davina and Justin quickly spoke together. "No, Natalie, nothing like that."

"Vinny, when you called me about the christening—" David began.

"Just tell them, Davina," Justin interrupted. "Go on."

"Tell us what?" Alli asked.

"We asked Natalie to be Jake's godmother right after he was born," Davina said, smiling at her friend. "And she agreed."

"And even though David is a relative, Davina wanted him to be an extra-special part of Jake's life in a way that transcends their blood relation," Justin said.

Davina's grin began to grow. "So we asked David, too, and he agreed."

David felt Natalie's body tense next to his, and she turned wide eyes in his direction that proceeded to impale him.

"You mean, you're little Jake's . . . godfather?"

"I guess she wanted to surprise us," David replied without inflection.

"This is just flat-out wonderful," Alli said, clasping her hands. "What a great idea."

"Yes, it was inspired, if I may say so myself," Davina agreed in a self-satisfied voice, and darted her gaze from David to Natalie. "Can it get any better? My brother and my best friend are godparents to our first baby."

And while Natalie slumped back in her seat with a rather hesitant smile pursing her lips, David nodded as he considered the repercussions the announcement would have on his life in the days to come. God save him from meddling women.

"We only found three of the files you wanted," the man whispered into the cell phone as he sat on a desk in a small wall office. "But they're dated weeks ago."

"Keep looking for more recent ones," the voice replied from the other end. "Don't take any originals from the files. Copy and then replace everything just as you found it. After you finish, get out of there without being noticed. Is that clear?"

"Yeah, yeah." The leader of the two-man team sighed absently, and picked up a silver-framed picture from the desk. "We are professionals, you know. It's not like we haven't done this before. Shorty is copying the papers now." The couple in the framed picture—a small, attractive woman posed with a tall man—were in formal attire in a garden, as though at a wedding.

"Well, just don't get caught this time. Call me back when you've cleared the building, and I'll meet you." The voice on the other end abruptly signaled off the phone.

The two burglars had entered the building with the cleaning personnel and then separated, steadily making their way to the upper floors. The cleaning staff wouldn't be happy to learn they'd be held accountable for the unplanned larceny of office electronics.

"What did he say?" The man called Shorty was intently snapping digital shots of pages spread out over a worktable from nearby stacked folders.

"Nothing new," the leader replied, and set the silver frame precariously near the desk's edge before he dropped the cell phone into the painter's pocket of the cleaning uniform.

"Just keep working while I try to find another file with a recent date on it."

"You know, I don't like him." Shorty rose up from his stooped posture, his complexion ruddy from a combination of exertion, liquor, and heredity. "Don't like him at all. He acts kind of uppity, if you ask me."

The leader had started to browse through more cabinet drawers, and now turned to his partner. "Look, I know what you're gonna say, but just shut your trap, and get back to work, all right? As long as his money's green, that's what's important, right?"

Shorty grumbled, and began snapping again. "Yeah, that's what we're here for—the green."

Although some of the moments had been difficult, Natalie had managed to keep her composure while crowded in next to David. And despite his denial of hunger, another appetizer had been ordered with a round of cold drinks as the five friends discussed a variety of topics, including the upcoming plans for the christening. Before Natalie realized the time, another hour had breezed by.

"Davina, weren't you supposed to call that photographer Alli found about the christening?" she asked.

Alli looked at her watch. "You know, he's at his studio now; and didn't you want Justin to talk with him, too?"

Davina tugged at Justin's arm. "This is perfect, you showing up. Alli, you can introduce us to him tonight. That is, of course, if David and Natalie don't mind."

Natalie reflected David's confusion as she asked her friend, "Don't mind what?"

"Each other's company."

"Why wouldn't they?" Alli asked with a sly grin. "They're the godparents, not to mention friends, too."

"Hey, if it's about riding along with you tonight, don't worry. I'm tired and don't need to go. All I want to do is crash in my own bed," David said, and swung a smug gaze at Natalie.

"Oh, I feel the same. You know the kind of day I had. Just go on and take care of your business. I can go on home." Natalie had spoken slowly as she watched Davina. "But what does that have to do with anything?"

"Everything," Davina said, "because you won't mind this little favor. You see, it would really help if you could drop David off at his condo for us."

"Of course," she managed to reply in an even tone. And as David's leg pressed into hers like a hot brand, she swallowed hard before she turned and smiled sweetly at him. "We don't mind at all, do we?"

Chapter 5

Had it been up to Natalie, she would have continued to seethe quietly—and preferably alone—in her car for the entire trip to David's house. However, knowing David, he wouldn't let the silence last too much longer; never mind the fact that he was responsible for another screwed-up evening.

Consumed by frustration over the night's misguided direction, she took the upcoming turn without applying the brakes.

"You handle this car like you're on a German autobahn," David observed dryly as he held on for the tight turn.

Natalie darted a frown in his direction. "If you didn't want to ride with me, you should have spoken up."

"And spoil that insane notion in Davina's head that we make this perfect couple?" He let out a hollow chuckle and shook his head in confusion. "And by the way, she means that in more ways than just as godparents. Where did they get that idea, anyway?"

"Don't ask me. I keep telling them we're not a couple. So, I'm as surprised as you are."

"I noticed," he said, and returned his gaze straight ahead. "That was a pretty sad attempt of theirs back there to cover up this little arrangement."

Despite being irritated by David's proximity, she wanted to smile. "They mean well, so what can we do?" When she felt David's gaze, she frowned instead. "Your sister is in this really happy place right now, and she wants everybody there with her; she's misguided, but I love her, anyway."

Natalie turned to find David still watching her. "What now?" she asked. "You've forgotten how I look?"

"I forgot how different you and my sister are, yet you both have this interesting loyalty for each other, despite . . ." He paused for the right word.

"Despite each other's faults?" she finished with a snort. "You never could grasp that concept."

"But I can respect it." He looked away. "We still have to deal with everybody's good intentions, though."

"They're *my* best friends and you're related to them. What's the point in having them committed?" She exhaled deeply. "We'll just have to see this through for the time being, that's all."

"You're actually going to see something *through*?" David emphasized in amusement, and shook his head in mock surprise. "This I've got to see."

Natalie swerved into the next curve without the benefit of the brakes, satisfied when David was, once again, pitched to the side.

"All right, all right, that was uncalled for, so you can back off." The apology was accompanied by a deep sigh before he gave his attention to the dark city outside his window.

Natalie now itched for an argument, the one thing guaranteed to keep her focus from the electricity they seemed to create when they were together. She wondered if he felt it, too, and tried to restrain the dangerous train of thought.

With her heart beating rapidly, Natalie pressed her lips into a straight line to avoid a slip of the tongue. The restraint lasted for about another mile before she stole a glance at David's strong profile only a moment before his dark eyes trained on her. Heaving a sigh, she decided to let the chip tumble from her shoulder.

"You had to know showing up like you did tonight wasn't going to be easy."

"True, " David agreed. "But I didn't know what to expect, either." He turned so he could watch her as she drove. "You dumped me, remember?"

Provoked, she flashed her eyes at him. "I remember that was your choice because you don't respect my right to an opinion."

"What? Is that what you told Davina?"

"No."

"Does she know about . . . you know, how we broke off?"

"Why would I tell her details of that sordid story?"

"Sordid? What was sordid about it?"

"Well, your girlfriend did show up. Oops, my error," she added huffily. "Your ex-girlfriend."

"Since when did you make yourself into the injured party?" David dropped his arm from the seat and stared ahead. "You're obviously over the whole thing, so I can't see why you're acting as if you're upset that I'm here."

Natalie was ready to pick up the chip that lay between them and hit him over the head. "I can see you're still arrogant as hell about the whole situation, and as usual making it all about you."

"And you're still trying to control everything in your universe." He glanced at her. "You've managed to move on, though. I hear you're dating."

"And I heard you weren't exactly sitting at home on Saturday nights in D.C. pining over little old me."

David crossed his arms and chuckled. "So, you got updates from Alli, too, huh?"

Natalie gave in to a smile and decided she and Alli would talk later on. Finally feeling more relaxed, she stifled a yawn with the back of her hand and changed the subject.

"You took me by surprise tonight, that's all, and I don't like surprises." She punctuated the last words with another yawn.

"Yeah, I know." He turned to her again, and rested easily

against the car seat. "You're also dead tired. You've let out a half dozen yawns since we left the restaurant. And when you're sleepy, you're—"

"An evil woman." She politely finished their private joke, and glanced in his direction before she joined him in another smile. As she'd hoped, it worked to release more tension between them. "I am a little tired from the long hours I've put in on a project at the office."

"So, how is your firm these days?" David asked. "I hear you're on their fast track."

"If the fast track is working my butt off, then that's where I am," she said, and told him about her promotion with Lang & Myers since he'd left town.

"I don't know if the corporate ladder is what I want to climb anymore," David said.

Natalie raised a brow at him. "You're thinking about breaking out on your own?"

"I didn't say that, but as time passes, it looks better and better, even though I'd be buying into even more hard work." He touched her shoulder in a gesture of familiarity. "Surely you've had the same thoughts. As smart as you are, you'd be a fool not to have considered it."

Her look quickly became a glare. "So now I'm a fool for not embracing your ideas?"

David groaned out loud. "Wrong word."

"Look at you. You went off to D.C. to fortify your position with your law firm."

"I know, but you have to widen your horizons before you can decide where you want to be." David looked at her uncertainly. "All I said was you should consider the option, seeing as what's happening in corporate America."

"I agree there's not a lot of moral commitment to the employee base, and it's all over the news about how the boardrooms lack integrity."

"And as a result," David argued, "there's no morale. It's kill or be killed by top management's poor decisions."

"I don't know if that's the rule. My experience is that

Lang & Myers is very much employee friendly. I even happen to have a pretty good working relationship with my manager." She yawned again.

"No one's corporate-proof, Natalie. Not even a smart woman like you."

"It's my decision, though. I'm grown, so don't tell me what to do and expect me to hop to your word alone," she spouted proudly, enjoying their spirited exchange. She didn't realize how much she had missed that.

"If you say so," David said with a grin. "But you might want to know that you're missing the expressway turnoff to my place."

"Damn." Natalie saw her chance to make a last-second exit deteriorate when another car blocked her lane change. Annoyed, she slapped the steering wheel. "Damn, damn."

"And you say I have no patience," David said, chuckling at her frustration. "Anyway, it's obvious that you're tired."

"I know," Natalie groaned. "Why did you have to buy a condo in the sticks with only one way in?"

"At the time, you thought it was a great investment."

Natalie squirmed. Damn him for reminding her.

"Tell you what," David said. "Since it's quicker to go straight to your house rather than circle around to go back to mine, why don't I drive your car home tonight? Tomorrow morning, I'll pick you up and we can both go to the Hardys' and I can get my car." He touched her shoulder again. "That way, we can avoid your going to sleep at the wheel."

For a moment, Natalie's emotions enjoyed a spike over the fact that she'd definitely see him again in the morning, but she struggled to hide her bewildering reactions to the man.

"The idea does sound tempting," she said, and darted her eyes at him, though his were already focused on her. She would keep it simple. No explanations or reasoning on the why or why not. "All right, and thanks."

"My pleasure, Natalie." His eyes remained steady. "Always, my pleasure."

The smooth, whiskey richness of his voice rolled over her in the dark car. And then, when he smiled, its whiteness accentuated in a passing car's lights, Natalie felt herself melt under his gaze.

It was so easy to remember their last time together, before it all turned bad. She wondered if his thoughts were trapped in the same time and place as where hers had lodged. Silken sheets and cloud-puff pillows, rock-hard limbs, and . . . and . . . She shook her head to clear it of the unbidden vision, lest she miss her own exit coming up soon.

Natalie pulled into the driveway of the town house she had purchased shortly after Davina had become engaged. The two-story, four-sided brick building consisted of two units encircled within a stone courtyard that was cordoned off by a black, wrought-iron fence.

A single length of stone fencing, around which grew shrubs and flowers just beginning their spring flourish, separated her yard from her neighbor's. Security lights blazed high above their heads and emphasized the well-kept cluster of town houses laid out on the softly rolling landscape.

David had always been impressed with Natalie's good taste and business sense. But, that had never been their problem, he lamented as he opened his car door. When it came to work and finances, she was a woman who played by the rules, but didn't necessarily live by them. Life, Natalie believed, was meant to be lived to its fullest.

"Pop the trunk," David said, climbing from the car. "I'll take your bags inside."

Natalie acted on the request and tiredly swung her legs, one at a time, from her car. "I think I can sleep for a whole day," she said. "In fact, don't rush here too early tomorrow. Noon should be soon enough for me."

"I promise I'll call before I pick you up," he said, humor in his voice, and walked to the rear of the car where he lifted the trunk door.

Natalie came around the other side to join him, her jacket and purse slung over her shoulder as the overhead lights caressed her stunning figure. David studied her soft features a moment before he quickly returned his attention to the open trunk and its contents.

"It'll take some getting used to your hair being as short as mine," Natalie said and, impudently, reached up to touch a sweep of hair near his temple. "All in all, I think D.C. treated you well," she added.

David caught her hand in a reflexive action as she moved it away. "I can say the same about you. Independence fits you and you wear it to a tee."

At that moment, a thread of understanding attached them. If they were careful, they could still be friends. He squeezed her hand before he let it drop.

"How do you carry this much stuff around every day?" he teased, referring to the corrugated box of files along with the luggage carrier strapped down with two more bags.

"Believe it or not, I usually have more," she explained. "I made an earlier stop by my office and left some things there before I picked up Davina and Alli."

He shook his head in humored disbelief before he reached in and grabbed a hold on the carrier and lifted it from the trunk. As he turned to set it on the ground, he realized Natalie had walked away.

David's eyes were drawn to her every confident move down the paved walk to the front door—from the shapely legs that disappeared under the skirt, the firm backside that swayed seductively with each sure step, to the slender, straight back that supported ample breasts he had yet to experience. She was some put-together package, and the familiar tightening that encased his groin confirmed the fact.

When she disappeared through the front door without a backward glance, David chastised his train of thought. Here he was acting like a rutting stag when sex was probably the furthest thing from her mind right now. *Move on. She already has.*

With a sigh, he lowered the carrier to the asphalt and reached into the trunk for the box.

Some of the papers in the box must have taken a spill during Natalie's wild drive, since a number of the white sheets of paper lay scattered in the trunk. He gathered up the loose papers to return them to the box.

One sheet instantly caught his attention. Unlike the other business-looking documents, this one was handwritten and contained only a few words in large, dark block letters.

David picked up the sheet and gave the words a cursory glance, his intention being not to invade her privacy. But then, he read them again, and this time a harsh frown covered his face:

BE CAREFUL.

Chapter 6

Leaving the door ajar, Natalie moved through the tiled foyer and switched on the lights. It helped to be at home amid familiar comforts when David's appearance tonight so easily rattled her nerves.

She dropped her jacket and purse on the bowfront table sitting at the foot of the curved staircase, which led to the second floor and her bedroom. As had become her habit when arriving home tired, she put off climbing the stairs and, instead, shook off each of her pumps where she stood.

Natalie closed her eyes and leisurely stretched away a mixture of anxiety and exhaustion. She savored the powerful sexual vibrato launching through her body that David had ignited; yet at the same time, she was determined not to reveal it. And, since she did not intend to imagine herself in love, she'd just have to force herself to settle down until David left town. She could do it.

"Natalie, what's this?"

Full of resolve, as well as curiosity, she returned to the living room where David was setting the box on the floor next to her luggage carrier.

"What are you talking about?" she asked.

When he turned to her and thrust his hand out, a sheet of white paper hung benignly from his fingers.

"This."

She took the paper and read the large, handwritten words printed in a block style. Confused, she brought her gaze up to David's stern one. "Be careful?" She inspected the paper more closely. "What makes you think this is mine?"

"It was in the trunk with your files."

"My trunk?" she repeated in disbelief.

"You haven't gotten yourself into any trouble, have you?"

"Well, thank you for that inspired bit of confidence," she replied, tartly. But his gaze remained steady.

Natalie sighed as she walked past him to sit on the plush, cream-colored sofa, giving her attention to the words on the paper. "It's somebody's gag—probably set up by Davina or Alli—about you," she said, and looked up at David. "You saw how they acted tonight, giving us space, leaving us alone."

When David's look turned blank, she rolled her eyes impatiently and explained. "Do I have to draw you pictures? You know . . . be careful of what I decide about you and me . . . that sort of thing." She arched a slim brow before offering him a shrewd smile. "What can I say? They're our friends."

"So there is a you and me?" he asked with a straight face.

Natalie's brows turned sharp as she deadpanned a reply. "They're playing a joke, okay, and I can take it. Lighten up, will you?"

"Why would two women who know you as well as they do resort to a bad joke when you tell everyone we're only . . ." He shrugged his wide shoulders. "Old friends?"

Natalie swallowed hard in the face of his lawyer's logic, and while tucking her legs beneath her on the sofa, she drew on a bit of her own analytical common sense. "All right, so it wasn't them. Stop acting like there's something sinister about the whole thing."

"I didn't say that, but it deserves more thought than you're giving it."

"That's because I haven't the faintest idea what I need to

be careful about," she concluded, and flipped the sheet of paper over. Out of sight, out of mind.

Natalie watched as David walked away and stuffed his hands into his pockets. He was a big man—tall, with an athletic frame—and it was hard to forget how his size had always made her feel: safe, comforted, even sexually powerful. An erotic shiver of want ran along her body. Natalie blinked and turned her head from the yearning thoughts that could spread heat through her with the ease of a silken feather.

All evening, her body had willingly swelled with strong emotions she had tried to ignore for months. This painful resurgence, without a doubt, was due to the simple fact that she and David shared an intense physical awareness of each other. That meant they shouldn't be near each other—not now, not ever—because no matter what the barriers had been in making a go of their relationship, physical attraction had not been the problem.

And, damn if it still wasn't.

She would keep her distance and she'd be fine. And before she knew it, he'd be gone. Again. Like a thief in the night. But, not with her heart. Not this time. The disjointed thoughts bounced in her head and she squirmed on her seat.

"Natalie?"

She looked up and found David standing over her, his hands on his hips.

"What?" she snapped, irritated by the seductive musings, and straightened up on the sofa.

"You were thinking about something?"

She pulled her fingers through her hair. "Only that the note has a simple explanation for its owner. And, that wouldn't be me, an average CPA."

"CPA, yes." He grinned down at her. "Average, never."

"Still, I wonder how it got in my trunk. No one has access to my car or keys."

"I will tonight." He took careful steps toward the window before he turned to her again. "Did you let someone else use your car recently? A boyfriend—"

Natalie shot him a withering glance that quickly staunched his words.

"Okay," he said, his hand raised. "So, no one uses your car. The note could have been mixed into your files at the office."

She stifled another stubborn yawn. "You of all people know about client confidentiality. I don't leave files out for people to rummage through."

"Maybe someone found a way."

David's words clicked into Natalie's brain, and in a momentary flash the occasion of the accidental spill of files in the elevator filled her head. *He* had helped her pick them up; *he* had carried them down to the garage.

"Carter?" She mumbled the name in recollection.

"Who?" David asked.

Natalie looked up and realized she had spoken out loud. "Oh . . . it's nothing," she quickly added, and filed the disturbing thought away for later.

"What's that supposed to mean?"

"This note doesn't have to be aimed at me," she continued. "Suppose there was a flyer about something else nearby and I picked it up with my things and put it in my trunk?" She watched as David dropped down onto the chair opposite her.

"So, did you recently pick up a flyer?"

"Not that I can remember."

He shook his head, as though to clear it of her cockeyed logic. "Okay, let's drop it." He lifted a brow in concern. "Just . . . be careful."

They both grinned at his words before they relaxed against their chairs. Soon, as though to magnify their attraction, an awkward quiet ensued.

David sat forward, his arms resting on his thighs. "The last time I was here, you had just moved in and the place was pretty much empty." He looked around the room. "You've done a nice job of making it yours."

"Thank you. I don't plan on being here forever, but it suits me fine right now."

And while he took in the raised ceiling, the spacious living room, and the balcony that overlooked the foyer, Natalie experienced an unexpected burst of pride at his continued tacit approval.

David turned to her, his smile wide and white, and close to a dare. "So, are you going to show me around?"

She unfolded her legs to rise from the sofa, but David was already standing and without effort, pulled Natalie to her feet. Her emotions, made fragile simply by his proximity, warred with the sensibility of what she was about to do. She should tell him, urge him, to leave, but . . .

"If you're not too tired," he added, towering over her.

"Sure," Natalie said, with no hint of regret. She drew in a deep breath that included the tantalizing smell of his cologne. "We, ah, can start with the patio."

She stepped in front of him to lead the way, confident that this small fix for her emotional habit would assuage David's growing power over her senses. Or at least temporarily.

The office documents, photographed digitally earlier that evening, had been transferred back to paper form and handed over to their new owner within a few hours' time.

The tall burglar leaned patiently against the black limo that squatted like a fat cat in the dark alley. He watched as the new owner, sitting in the shadowy backseat, used a penlight to peruse the stack of printed pages. Finally the man gave the signal that all was fine, clicked off the bright beam, and thrust a small wrapped package through the window opening.

The green.

As if on cue, Shorty separated from the adjacent brick wall and swept up the wrapped, compact package. Dropping the handles of the large canvas bag he dragged behind him, he tore open the paper and counted the small stack of bills.

"There were no personal, handwritten notes?" the man asked from the backseat. "They must be stored someplace else."

"We took what was there," the leader responded. He could see that the man was flipping through the papers again, and he straightened up from the car. Uneasy that the man was unhappy with the night's work, he offered a plan to salvage this job.

"If you like, we can follow the woman to get what you need; we can make it look like a mugging, steal—"

"No." The directive issued through the window was final.

"It's all here," Shorty blurted into the quiet night, and passed the stacked bills to his partner before he reclaimed the handles of his bag.

"What's in that thing?" the man in the limo asked.

"Uh, just a few odds and ends," Shorty explained, darting his eyes to the swollen canvas bag on the ground. He raised his eyes to his partner for help.

"I told you not to remove anything," the man in the limo growled before he twisted around in his seat. "You were to leave everything exactly as you found it."

"Aw, it's just a few things that were sitting around the place that'll bring in a few bucks. They'll blame it on the cleaning people," Shorty reasoned.

"And maybe they won't if the property is traced back to you," the man threw back.

"Damn, Shorty," the leader complained in a low voice as he stomped the ground. "Can't you do anything right? Why'd you have to drag the damn thing over here, anyway?"

"Open the door," the man ordered. "Set the bag in the car."

"What?" both burglars queried in unison.

"Take this little something extra for your trouble," the man said and pushed another envelope, though thinner, through the small window opening. "Now, set the bag on the seat," he commanded again.

With a nod of agreement from his tall partner, Shorty

opened the middle limo door and shoved the heavy bag onto the seat inside. At the same time, the leader grabbed the proffered money hanging from the window and performed the honor of counting the second set of bills.

"If you need us again," he said, stepping away from the car as Shorty closed the middle door, "you know how to get in touch."

But, the cracked window was already summarily closing on his words and, without preamble, the limo came alive with lights as it shot forward and exited the dark alley.

"You know, I still don't like him," Shorty said, standing in the middle of the alleyway, shaking his head. "I don't like him at all."

"Shut up, will you?" his partner complained. "And let's get out of here."

As soon as the limo cleared the corner and merged into the late night traffic, new orders were given to the driver from the backseat.

"Circle back to that office building they just left. When you get there, I want this bag placed near the loading dock so it'll be found quickly by security."

"Yes, sir," the driver, responded, and turned the limo at the next light.

They had come full circle through the two-story town house—an uncluttered environment that bespoke Natalie's style—clean lines and bold colors highlighted by eclectic, antique pieces she had handpicked—saving the downstairs study for last.

David followed Natalie into the study that had become her office, and came upon a wall of bookcases that dominated the room. He stopped at the first shelves of books that flanked the large window and smiled when he recognized a particular grouping as Natalie's diverse erotica collection. As he remembered, her titles ran the gamut, from the classic to the irreverent. He touched a bound volume by Henry Miller, and another by Anais Nin, which had been a gift from him in honor of some occasion.   He smiled at the memory of less strained times between them.

"Have you added any new ones to your collection?"

Natalie joined him at the shelf and with a devilish smile, pointed out a thick volume titled, simply, *The Limerick*.

"I found it at a secondhand store." Her smile grew wider. "It has to be the funniest collection of limericks I've ever seen."

"Hmm . . . looks innocent enough from the outside," David said as he pulled the volume from the shelf, and flicked it open near the center. His eyes immediately lit upon one of many five-line ditties that would make a sailor blush, and he let out a deep laugh before his gaze sought out Natalie's.

"You think Vinny will allow her son to visit his god-mother with this kind of stuff in the house?"

"Why not?" she questioned, crossing her arms. "She's the one who pointed the book out to me. Anyway, Davina's an artist, and erotica is just another art form," she argued. "And like any good art, it's supposed to arouse the senses."

"Well, I agree it arouses, all right," he said in mock sincerity. "Listen to this one: 'This prudish young teacher from Prussia—' "

"Give me that book," she said, snatching it good-naturedly from his hand.

David laughed as he watched her replace the volume and strut away, all passion and sass in everything she did. He liked seeing her this way, unfettered and unguarded. Unfortunately, in Natalie's mind, that also meant unattached. He raised his eyes to the object of his thoughts as she adjusted the blinds at the window.

On the outside, David was the picture of control; but on the inside, the entire evening was eating him alive. Ever since he'd caught his first glimpse of her earlier, he realized how much he missed her, and the evening became a constant reminder of what they had let get away.

Right now, his anger over why they had ended, an ill will

he had nurtured these last months, well, it seemed to have dissipated. He now wanted some answers—and only Natalie could provide them.

"Don't do that."

Natalie's words made David realize he had been staring at her as she stood at the window.

He frowned and took the few steps to join her. "Don't do what? Stare at you and stir up the past? Does it make you uncomfortable?"

She frowned and took a step back. "We were doing so well tonight. So, why are you doing this?"

"Maybe I figure a year is a bit long for us to be mad at each other."

With an angry set to her mouth, she straightened her shoulders and made to rush past him toward the living room. "Speak for yourself."

"Oh?" David quickly clutched onto her arm and drew her back. "Is that all you have to say about it after so much time? That you're still mad?"

She tried pulling away. "Well, excuse me if I don't want to go back—"

"That night, you accused me of not having any patience. Believe it or not, I've actually been working on the skill; but damn, Natalie, if you don't manage to try it at every turn."

She stopped and, angling her head, stared up at him in comic surprise. "You remembered that?"

He nodded his head. "I think about that night a lot."

She allowed herself to draw on his clean, masculine scent. "Yeah. Me too," she admitted.

A thick silence accompanied the two as they slowly left the study for the living room.

"So, did you miss me?" David asked. He watched as her eyes grew wide in search of an answer. Would she admit what he wanted to hear?

"Isn't it a little arrogant for you to be asking that kind of question?"

"Come on, it's a simple one. Just answer it."

She stopped and looked up at him. "Yes. I still miss my friend, the one I can get mad at, and laugh and share things—anything—with."

David devoured the perfectly oval face that was turned to his, the soft feathered hair that lay against her head, the large eyes and soft lips in the flawless brown skin. He pressed his hands into his pockets. "Good. I missed you, too."

"So, is he back?" she asked, and continued their stroll into the living room.

"Well, that depends on you."

She quirked her brow at his words.

"How much of the past are you willing to own up to?"

"David . . ." She entered the living room through an open arch with David following. "I don't want to do that."

"What was it we argued about that night, anyway?" he asked, pressing on. "Do you remember?"

"Does it matter? We know the end result."

"Yeah, a year lost."

"That we can't go back and fix."

"Can't we?" David asked. "Look at us . . . we're still standing after all that. We can do whatever we want."

They had reached the front door.

"For our friends' sake, then, let's start by fixing the friendship," Natalie suggested.

"All right. We'll *start* there."

"David, don't make this impossible for me by bringing up the past."

"In that case, we won't know what could have been."

"And maybe that's for the best."

Disappointment claimed David and he pressed his hands deeper into his pockets. Natalie had confirmed that the past was still a chasm between them, a lover's leap that, with a false step, could lead to the death and oblivion of his slim hope. He turned to Natalie just as she did the same to him, intent on speaking one last thing on his mind.

"Why did you—"

"Why didn't you—" she blurted.

They had spoken in the same moment. And just as abruptly, they stopped.

David swallowed hard and, pulling his hands from his pockets, asked the question that had haunted him for some time. "Why did you leave me that night, without ever looking back?"

"Why didn't you stop me?"

He sighed heavily, his voice filled with resignation. "Because it was what you wanted."

Chapter 7

Natalie looked into David's face and blinked, shocked by the simple truth in his words. On the path to meet his dark eyes, she was, instead, drawn by a sensual pull to his mouth.

She broke off the troubling possession and stepped backward, which landed her clumsily against the door.

David moved toward her, a knowing smile on his face at her sudden awkwardness.

"Like it or not," he said, "at some point we'll have to clear the air between us, and that means going back."

He bent down and, after a slight pause, brushed a gentle kiss across her forehead. Taking a couple of steps back, he turned and headed down the driveway for her car.

Natalie exhaled a long held breath, her sleepiness momentarily stayed as she ran a hand across her mouth, her gaze moving with David. It would not be easy having this potently attractive man around her.

She abruptly moved behind the front door and then closed it solidly. Given the direction of her thoughts, Natalie's plans to go directly upstairs to bed were well intended; but when she reached the foyer table, it was the unexpected, strident ring of the phone sitting there that stopped her. She picked it up before the second ring sounded.

"Hello?"

"Natalie, it's me. You didn't call me back today."

When she heard her mother's voice, the absent thought that she should have relied on the caller ID before she picked up floated through her head. She had enough to deal with already.

"Mama, I said I would." The sound of her own harsh words made her instantly contrite. "It's just that I . . . I got tied up with some things this evening, that's all."

"You always say that when you don't return my calls."

Natalie pursed her lips at the chastisement and slowly counted to three. "I'm sorry, but it's late and I'm just getting home."

"I didn't want you to forget about your little sister's birthday party next month. Do you think you can make it home to be with us?"

Natalie barely knew her stepsister, but she supposed that wasn't the child's fault. "Sienna will be, what, seven? She couldn't care less if I was there, and Miami is not my home anymore."

"It's still your family's home, and I want you girls to know each other better. Your sister Marilyn is coming all the way from Washington state and she's staying the whole week."

And you'll keep on reminding me of it, too. Marilyn, Natalie's oldest sister, had made a clean break from the family problems right after high school, ending up far away from the rest of the Goodmans. Both girls had been long gone by the time their divorced mother remarried and surprised everyone with Sienna.

"I may not be able to leave town, Mama. I'll have to wait and see how things look at work next month." Natalie paced the foyer, impatient to get off the phone.

"I know your job up there is high-powered, but it wouldn't hurt you to take a break now and again so you can meet somebody nice like your sister and Davina did."

Natalie blew out an exasperated held breath. "I've got to go."

"At least think about coming for a few days, okay?"

"Sure," she said, running her hand through her hair. "I'll talk with you later, Mama."

She replaced the phone stiffly on its cradle and moved past the table to the staircase. It occurred to her that in a perfect world, she had just blown an opportunity to talk with her mother about her mixed feelings for David. Wasn't that what a girl did with her mother—talk about fears and expectations? She grasped the wooden banister and lightly treaded onto the first step, thinking that she should call her mother back. Now.

Hers was not a perfect world, though. Natalie's parents were divorced, she was estranged from her father and avoided her mother, and damn if her oldest sister didn't constantly bring up the unresolved feelings Natalie still carried around about their youngest sibling.

By the time Natalie reached the third step, the idea of making the connection with her mother had all but faded. Once again, the link that could save the chain of understanding between them remained broken.

When Natalie reached the top of the stairs, her momentary lapse into a perfect world had been completely forgotten.

"David," Justin called out as he crossed the cavernous kitchen at his home. "Mrs. Taylor told us you were down here."

"You're back from the photographer," David observed and, straightening in the tall bar chair he occupied at the granite breakfast counter, set down the remainder of his sandwich. "How did it go?"

"Smoothly. They didn't need me, but I figured you knew that."

"Yeah . . . it was a little obvious." David grinned. "Where's Vinny?"

"Upstairs, nursing Jake. She'll be down a little later," he said and, loosening his tie, settled onto one of the chairs next to David. "I see Mrs. Taylor insisted on feeding you," he commented dryly of the family cook and housekeeper. "I'm surprised she didn't set out a three-course meal."

David smiled. "Don't think she didn't try."

"So, what happened with you? I thought Natalie was taking you home."

"I decided I wanted to see my nephew tonight, that's all. I've been upstairs in the nursery with him and Mrs. Hardy."

He reached for his bottle of water and held it up in a toast. "To your son and my nephew-slash-godson. Justin, that's one fine, healthy kid we've got on our hands."

"I know," Justin said, and with a proud smile stretched across his face, he reached over the counter and grabbed up another bottle. Raising it high, he tilted his head in acknowledgement.

David pushed his plate away and leaned onto the counter. "I hope you haven't changed my little sister too much since I've been gone."

"If anything, she's changed me," Justin responded and, with that, cocked a concerned brow David's way. "You look worried. I thought we'd gotten past your doubts about our marriage—"

"Oh, we have," David assured him. "It's just that for a long time she and I only had each other, and I was the one who watched out for her welfare. Now I get the feeling she's reversing our roles. She worries too much."

"She just wants to see you settled down and happy, like her. That's all."

David looked up. "So, she has mentioned something to you?"

Justin nodded. "I think she's a little guilty about deserting you to marry into a brand-new family." He smiled. "And like a woman, she wants what she has for you, and Natalie, too."

"Good God," David said, frowning. "She's playing matchmaker for Natalie?"

"She figures if you two won't fit together, you will with somebody else."

"Yeah—that would make sense to her." He let out a deep and uneasy sigh at the prospect of his sister setting Natalie up with another man.

Justin's eyes darted toward the doorway before he slanted his brow at his brother-in-law. "So, what did you do with our little godmother?"

David made a playful snort at the title. "She was dead tired," he said, and explained their revised arrangement. "I'll pick her up in the morning and we'll both come back here for my car," he added.

"Good—I'm just glad you're not any the worse for wear after being blindsided tonight." He leaned back in his chair and suppressed a laugh. "You had to see her at some point, right? So it was a good thing that you jumped on in and got it over with."

"I jumped in?" Shaking his head, David chuckled. "Spoken like the true sadist I know you can be."

"It was that rough, huh?"

"In more ways than you know," David muttered before he drank from the bottle.

"Whatever happened, anyway? One day you two were together; the next, you were surprising us all by taking a temporary work assignment in D.C."

"It's complicated, and I can't explain what I'm still trying to figure out for myself." David stretched his legs out before he looked over at his friend. "Did you know tonight was the first time we'd spoken since I left last year?"

"Damn." Justin gave him a skeptical look. "You did a good job of hiding it. What were you thinking, letting me drop you in on her at the restaurant like that?"

"Because you were right. It had to happen, and when it did was as good a time as any."

"So, what's the bottom line? Everything's fine, and you go your separate ways?"

"We sort of talked and, yeah, we're still friends." David took another swig from the water bottle before he realized that Justin was staring at him. "What? You don't think we can pull that off?"

"I don't know—I saw something else tonight, too. In fact, I thought both of you looked pretty uncomfortable squeezed in there with each other, checking each other out, like you were ready to explode."

"We were friends before; we can go back."

"At best, you were oil and water." Justin chuckled. "It's a tricky business, getting back to that comfort level after you've been lovers and more, especially if you didn't have any say in the change to start with."

David set the bottle down hard on the countertop. "We weren't lovers."

Justin's brows rose. "I see."

"Probably not. Natalie is pretty open-minded and more comfortable than most when it comes to sexuality, but she's a lot more complicated than you realize at first glance."

"Well," Justin said with a short grunt, "all of this explains some of what I saw going on tonight."

David drummed his fingers on the counter. "Yeah, we started out keeping things slow on purpose, so we wouldn't screw up what we had; of course, things went sour anyway, and here I am—"

"—calling the woman you've got a hell of an itch for just your friend." Justin shook his head. "Hell, yes, that'll drive you crazy all day."

David watched as Justin heaved a deep sigh, rose from his chair, and then circled around to the other side of the counter.

"The first thing you've got to figure out is what kind of itch you're dealing with. If it's short-term . . ." Justin smiled easily. "Well, I think you know how to scratch that. But, what about long-term, the kind that won't go away? Now, that one's more serious."

David knew exactly where Justin was headed and uncertainty claimed his thoughts. "I'll admit that the woman drives me crazy. Most of the time, I don't think she gives a damn about what I do or where the hell I do it."

"Yeah, you've both got it bad."

David glared at the insinuation as he watched Justin reach under the counter and pull out a familiar-shaped whiskey bottle followed by two glasses.

"Since you're here, and it's late, you might as well stay the night. I've got something stronger for your mood if you do."

David waved off the offer. "Nah, I need to keep a clear head."

"To figure out women?"

Frowning, David said, "You're right." He reached for one of the glasses.

Chapter 8

The phone rang out for the third time before Natalie's hand snaked across the bed, grabbed it from its cradle, and wedged it between her ear and the pillow.

"This had better be good," she slurred sleepily into the receiver.

"Wake up." Davina's voice sailed gaily through the phone. "I've been waiting all morning to call you."

"What time is it?" Natalie complained, and valiantly tried to hold one eyelid open long enough to focus on the small clock near the phone.

"It's late, already past eight."

Natalie pressed deeper into the sheets. "Shouldn't you be pleasing your man or something at this time of morning?"

"Been there, done that, and he's left for the office," she said in good humor. "Come on, tell me how things went last night."

Natalie yawned at her friend's expected comment and, giving up on a quick return to sleep, rolled onto her back. "Actually, I thought you were David calling. He drove my car back to his house last night."

"So, you had a great night after all," Davina blurted happily.

"Aside from being manipulated by my best friend, it was fine."

Davina laughed at Natalie's candor. "Well, I'm just happy you're not bailing on being godmother because of David."

"More than anything, David and I are friends," Natalie said, though the words sounded strange on her tongue. "And, yeah, it was a surprise, but what you want is what counts."

"Uh-huh . . . that's sort of the way David put it with Justin last night."

Natalie's eyes flitted open. "You saw David later on last night?"

"After he left your house, he came here."

She turned over on her side. "He was supposed to go home. Is everything all right?"

"Not to worry," Davina said with a chuckle. "He came by to see Jake. When I joined them, though, he and Justin were already closed up in the library talking over drinks, so I left them there. I understand David didn't look none the worse for wear."

"Maybe not then," Natalie said, yawning. "But I'll personally change that if he drove my car after a night of drinks with Justin."

"Oh, he wouldn't; Justin would never have let him leave, anyway. In fact, I don't know that he has even left for home this morning. I can run downstairs and check if you want me to."

"No, no," Natalie said. "He stayed put, and it's too early for him to be up while on vacation."

"Sounds like you've learned him well. You know, I've got this friendly little bet going with Justin," Davina announced in high spirits. "Suddenly, I'm feeling pretty good about my chances."

"As long as it doesn't involve me."

"Want to hear the details?"

Natalie sat up on the bed and pushed back her tousled hair. "I know the kind of bets you and Justin make, and I don't want to be part of anybody else's sex games."

"Okay, then, I won't tell you. And stop being so crabby. This particular wager doesn't involve you . . . directly."

"That means it's David." With a sigh, Natalie dropped back onto the pillow. "You'd better hope he doesn't find out."

"I know my brother well. He'd help Justin if only to teach me a lesson. Anyway, even if Justin loses, I make sure he wins," she said, chuckling devilishly. "Why do you think he goes along with my bets?"

Natalie let out a groan. "You're killing me."

"So, what time is David picking you up?" Davina asked. "Oh, and plan to stay for dinner tonight. Everyone will be there for you and David."

"He won't get here until much later this morning—" She stopped when the singular beep from the phone indicated another call. Twisting the handset around to read the numbers, Natalie was sure it was David this time.

Her employer's name and number lit up on the screen.

Puzzled, she sat up in the bed. "Davina, let me get back with you. I've got to take this call."

"Is it David?"

"Bye, Davina." She quickly flashed the other line. "Hello?"

"Natalie, it's John from the office."

His voice gave nothing away, yet it was oddly disconcerting to her. John Callaway had been Natalie's boss almost since she'd joined the firm, and she couldn't remember him ever having called her at home.

"This is a surprise. Is something up?" she asked.

"Can you come down to the office this morning? There's been a burglary in the building."

Natalie frowned. "Are you serious?"

"As serious as this triplicate incident report I have to file before the day is out. I'm calling everybody in to check for missing property."

"Everybody?" Resigned to the fact that she had to get up, she pressed her fingers against her eyes. "That should make you pretty popular today."

"If I don't, the insurers will make it an issue when something goes missing later. I know you planned to be off today, but all I can say is, sorry."

"No more than I am," she muttered hastily.

"You're pretty organized, so you shouldn't have to spend much time with a form."

Natalie grunted in consent. "I'll be in as soon as I can."

"That's all I ask. By the way," he began, "how did things go between you and Blakely yesterday? Did he come around to your way of thinking?"

"Why don't I fill you in when I get to the office?" she suggested.

"That'll work," he agreed.

After exchanging good-byes, Natalie dropped the phone back onto its cradle. She pushed her craving for sleep aside and hopped off the bed. Tugging her tank top over her head, she walked toward the bathroom; only then did she remember yet another bump in this rocky morning.

David still had her car. "Damn," she muttered out loud.

With his eyes closed in light sleep, and a smile playing on his mind, David savored the touch of Natalie's fingers sweeping along his neck and her body weight pressing seductively against his chest and groin while he lay sprawled on his back, only to have the pleasingly erotic dream interrupted by a knock and then a distant voice.

"David, are you in there?"

It was his sister's voice. "Come on in," he called out, and swung his legs to the floor. David sat up in the bed and immediately recognized his surroundings, a fact that surprised him since he'd imbibed more than a few drinks last night.

Davina stepped into the room located in the guest wing of the Hardy mansion and, leaning against the elegant wallpaper, flicked the wall switch.

"Good morning," she said. "How are you feeling after last night?"

David rubbed his eyes against the soft overhead light. "I'm good." When she didn't readily respond, he squinted at her. "Something wrong?"

"Natalie is trying to reach you," she said.

"Oh?" he asked, his attention alerted on Davina, who now broke into a smile.

"My, my . . . it's sort of nice to see all of that concern pop out of you like that," she teased.

David sighed. "She made it pretty clear she didn't want to be bothered this morning, so what's going on?"

"She got a call from her office. Something happened last night and she has to go in and fill out an incident report."

"Which means she needs her car." He stood up and headed for his luggage stacked in the corner just as Davina moved away from the wall to join him.

"I'm glad to hear you and Natalie had a pretty successful reunion last night. You think you might try to get together with her again?"

"Just cut to the chase, why don't you?" David's grin widened as he looked over his shoulder at his sister. "You're reading way too much into that fantasy of yours."

"Well, it's my fantasy." She walked around so she could face him. "Justin says leave it alone and be happy that you and Natalie are still friends."

"I say trust your husband's advice."

"There was a time I never thought I'd hear that sentiment from you."

David laughed. "Times change, and so do people." He pulled his leather toiletry bag from the suitcase.

"At least you can make sure Natalie spends the day over here like she promised. You know she'll end up going to that office, start working on something, lose track of time, and then end up staying there all day."

"Like you do when you start to paint," he pointed out.

Davina grinned. "Just get her back over here as soon as you can."

He started for the bathroom at the other end of the guest suite, leaving an inquiring Davina in the middle of the room.

"The only way I can do that is to follow her around this morning." When he didn't hear a response, he turned to look back at her.

"Will you do it?" she asked.

It was hard to gaze at his sister these days and not see her uncanny resemblance to their long-deceased mother. So, how could he refuse her, even though he knew he was playing into her matchmaking fantasy?

"Sure, why not?" He winked at her and walked away.

"David?"

He turned to her voice and bumped into her open arms. He spread his own wide and held her close to him. "What's this for?" he asked with a laugh.

"Nothing," she said. "I'm just glad you're here now with me and Jake."

David grinned as he rocked his little sister in his arms. "Me too, Vinny."

Natalie opened her door to David's impressive form standing there in casual slacks and a light jacket on the bright spring morning. Even with dark shades disguising his gray stare, she could feel it on her, bringing unaccustomed warmth to her neck.

"That was fast," she said, and stepped back so he could enter the house.

"Davina said the problem at your office was important," he said as he followed her inside.

"I don't think it'll amount to much." Natalie closed the door behind him and walked toward the table at the staircase. "Employees just have to account for property on an incident report. The building was burglarized."

"I guess that's as good an excuse as any to take your day."

"I work for a CPA firm, remember? We can be pretty anal about reports."

Natalie turned from the table and almost collided into David only a few feet away where he lounged against the wall. He had removed the sunglasses, but she could still detect a restless energy in his intense stare that brought back their conversation from last night. They had to clear the air at some point, he had warned her then.

His gaze slipped from her face and moved over what she wore.

Natalie followed his eyes and looked down on her black wrapped linen skirt and heeled sandals. She pushed back a sleeve on the white, cowl-necked sweater tucked in at her waist before she looked up at David.

"Is something wrong with what I'm wearing?"

His brow rose a fraction before he once again met her gaze. "Davina was worried that you might cancel plans to come over since you got that call, but I don't believe you're planning on staying at the office."

The close contact with David was both disturbing and exciting, and Natalie took a step backward.

"I intend to drop you off at Davina's for your car. That way, you won't be stuck with me for who knows how long."

David stepped forward. "I have a better arrangement. Let's go straight to your office so you can take care of business first. That way, there won't be hell to pay with Davina for getting there late."

He reached around Natalie and picked up her purse and jacket from the foyer table. "I'll just ride along with you and make sure we both end up at the right place."

He had spoken with a firm finality that gave Natalie no room or reason to challenge his decision. She leaned her head back and gazed up into gray eyes that narrowed in a critical squint, and then tried to figure this mood.

"All right," she said. "We'll work with your plan."

As they left the foyer for the front door, David handed

Natalie her things. The tension between them could be as taut as a bowstring when silence surrounded them, and she impetuously searched for some subject that would lessen her strain.

"Are you ready?" David asked, pulling his sunglasses from his pocket.

"You've got the sunglasses out early. Could that mean you have a hangover after all?" she teased.

"Some of us know how to drink," he retorted, referring to the well-documented fact that Natalie was not a drinker of any repute.

She snorted at his comment. "At least you were smart enough not to try and drive home last night."

"Oh, I'm no fool, but I also remembered I was in your car."

Natalie's face burned that Davina had shared her sentiments with him.

"Come on." David grinned down at her as he opened the door. "Let's get going before we use up all of our goodwill right here. There's a lot of day still ahead of us."

With a perfunctory hand lightly at her back, he escorted her through the front door and to the car.

Chapter 9

Natalie slowly pushed open the door to her office and peeked inside. She hadn't known what to expect, but it looked nothing like the ransacking spectacles she saw in movies. In fact, it looked much like it did when she had left yesterday.

"So far, so good," she said to David, who stood behind her. "It shouldn't take me too long to check things out."

They entered the small but neatly appointed office where Natalie immediately began to visually account for her office computer and other electronics. Having noted the usual items marked for theft, she pulled open the top drawer of a wide filing cabinet.

"You don't lock them?" David asked from across the room.

Natalie threw a glance from over her shoulder to where he comfortably lounged against the door frame. Their twenty-minute ride to the office had been filled with cautious small talk. It said a lot that neither of them wanted to break their brokered peace.

"I don't have to since our main office entrance is off the building's master lock system."

"Not anymore," he responded, and moved farther into the room.

Smiling, Natalie said, "You may be right about that." She turned back to her perfunctory review of items stored in the top drawer, and fingered through computer disks, tablets, and an assortment of other small items. Satisfied that nothing was missing, she closed the drawer.

"Do these burglaries happen often?" David asked.

"I can't remember there ever being one in this office," she said. "We require coded entries to get into our suites and the computer room, so no one, except for employees, can come in here after hours. Even the cleaning crews perform their jobs during the workday. I've always felt pretty secure around here."

David had now wandered over to her desk. "All it takes is one event for companies to realize they're vulnerable." He glanced her way. "The same goes for people."

He had deliberately alluded to her and himself. Warily, she turned from the cabinet in time to see the remnants of a smile on his handsome face. When her look threatened to become a stare, she hastily turned away.

"I suspect your legal clients have more interesting issues than the ones we get in this office."

"Not necessarily," he said. "It depends on what you want. Trash for one company can be highly classified information in the hands of another." David rounded the desk and trampled across something that lay on the carpeted floor.

"What's this?" he asked.

Curious, Natalie watched as he stooped and picked up a silver-framed photograph. A shudder of humiliation flowed through her body when David's expression revealed recognition. They'd taken the picture together at Davina and Justin's wedding. Natalie had placed it on her office desk as a strong— and private—reminder of her volatile emotions where David was concerned.

He turned to Natalie, a spark of humor gracing his eyes. "A good-looking couple."

She hid the embarrassment and walked grandly toward

David. Snatching the framed photo from his hand, she boldly set it back down on its regular spot on her desk.

"I must have knocked it over," she suggested, moving back to the filing cabinet.

"Maybe your burglar upset it," David replied, lifting up the picture again to inspect it.

"I doubt that, seeing as everything else looks to be in place. Since I'm here, I can grab up a couple of files to take with me, and then we can leave."

"Vinny warned me about that," David said, breaking into a leisurely smile.

"What did she say this time?"

"That you'd manage to squeeze in some work and forget the time."

Familiar with her own filing system, she slid a finger along brown, legal-sized accordion files that lined the back section of the drawer. "The work will come later this weekend," she replied absently.

When she didn't see the file she wanted, she repeated her search. "I'm working a particularly messy audit right now, and time is my enemy," she said to David, who had joined her at the cabinet.

"Yeah . . . Davina told me your latest project is kicking your butt."

Natalie's eyes finally lit upon the file she wanted, and she reached for it. "Hmm . . . that's odd."

"What?" David asked.

"The file I was looking for. It shouldn't be here." She pulled it out and set it on top of the cabinet. Her eyes and fingers systematically perused the folders again. "Here's another one."

"You misfiled?"

"I don't know. I take client notes home all the time, but not their source documents. I'm pretty sensitive about them getting lost," she explained, replacing the brown folder. "So, I won't commingle the files, but these were."

David laughed. "Are you serious with this filing?"

She rolled her eyes at him. "Yes, I am."

He propped an arm against the cabinet. "Well, you did say you've been busier than usual."

"Yeah, I know." Natalie stooped to open a second cabinet drawer, and after a minute of thumbing across tabs, she sighed as she rose up next to David. "As far as I can tell, those were in order."

David grunted. "Interesting."

"What do you find so interesting on your day off?" A deep voice spoke from the doorway.

Natalie looked up to see her immediate manager entering the office. John was both a champion and friend to Natalie and she, in turn, liked the liberal and reformed hippie who still managed to claim a thick head of graying brown hair in his middle years. She smiled as she greeted him.

"Hi, John, I planned on stopping in to see you next." As a partner, John with his mentoring had been instrumental in the other partners allowing Natalie to flex her abilities into areas that may have precluded an aggressive female. In exchange for his support, she tried to make sure he'd never regret his stance.

"I heard you were here, so I brought an insurance questionnaire by for your signature." Even though he spoke to Natalie, his eyes had circled to David in a silent query.

"Oh, I'd like you to meet a good friend of mine." She turned to David and introduced the two men, who shook hands.

"You heard about our burglary?" John asked.

David smiled. "Natalie mentioned it before we arrived." He turned to her now. "I'll just wait out in the reception area until you're finished in here." Turning, he nodded to John. "It was nice meeting you."

"Same here," John offered and watched as David cleared the door. "So, is everything accounted for in here?"

Natalie drew a deep breath. "Yeah, I believe so, except that I'm losing my touch when it comes to filing." She reached for the file on top of the cabinet and walked back to her desk.

"What are you talking about?" John asked as he followed her.

"I came across a few things that were, I guess you could say, misfiled."

"So?" His softly planed face presented an eager grin. "Okay, I can see where misfiling something would be unusual for you, to say the least."

Natalie smiled, too, and sat in one of the chairs across from her desk. "So I'm a bit on the obsessive-compulsive side."

"Do you remember which files were out of place?"

She nodded. "That's why I checked the rest." She looked up at John. "They were all Innervision files."

"No kidding?"

She nodded again, and added a shrug. "Coincidence, I imagine."

"Maybe not," John suggested, claiming the remaining chair in front of the desk. "Remember, you've been working on Innervision almost exclusively for weeks, so you're always in those files. Are they pretty current?"

"No. I'm still collecting data from their accounting department."

John grunted as he rested his chin against tented fingers.

Natalie grew curious at his silence. "Tell me, are you worried that this burglary might compromise the audit if word gets out?"

"No," he said, and forced a small smile. "The burglary last night was pure larceny, that's all." He looked at her. "I just don't want your results held up any more than they need to be, and you know lost or compromised records would only prolong the process when Blakely is already on you to hurry it up."

"I agree." Natalie sighed and slowly turned the file in her hands.

"Now it's my turn to ask you, are you worried over something?"

"Don't mind me." Natalie immediately thought better of

mentioning any of her concerns and waved her hand in dismissal. "So, is anything missing from the office?"

"So far, everything we've found came from the workstations."

"That's the common area."

He nodded. "Which is why security decided to question the cleaning staff."

Natalie wasn't surprised at security's quick conclusion—it reminded her, oddly, of Carter and Blakely.

"You wanted to know how the meeting went with Mr. Blakely?" she asked.

He grimaced in good humor. "Just the finer points."

"Let's see," she said, and counted on her fingers. "He wasn't happy with my records and computer access request, felt I was totally unreasonable for wanting to speak with managers, and he wants things wrapped up last week." She leaned back in the chair and looked at John. "I'm surprised he didn't call you to complain after I left his office."

John released a telling sigh. "He did. In fact, he instructed his accounting staff to release some of the computer disks you wanted to review. They're waiting for you at Innervision."

"Really?" Natalie grinned. "I'm impressed by his speed." But the grin faded when John didn't smile. "Okay, what else did he say?"

"Tell me, Natalie. Are you sure you need to keep digging into already plowed ground?"

The analogy made her lose her humor. "John, I trust my instincts, and something's there. The payroll is way out of balance, and there are a lot of strange transfers between capital accounts that just don't make sense when there's no documentation to explain the entries."

"I saw the company's projections for next quarter, and to be honest with you, they look good . . . just as good as the last two quarters," John said.

"The devil is in the details. You taught me that." She shook her head, exhibiting her own uncertainty. "You've been where

I am, and you know how you get that gut feeling that something isn't adding up—"

"Yeah, I know what you're talking about." John grasped the chair arms and pushed himself forward. "But it makes business sense, in this particular instance, to cut yourself free of this case. Time is not on our side."

"Why? Because their annual meeting is coming up and they want to look good?"

"No, Natalie. Because they're our client, and we serve them."

John had made his point clear; however, out of habit, Natalie continued her stubborn push. "Is that what you want me to do? Pull out and just certify this thing as is?"

"I didn't say that. It's still your call."

"Then, what are you saying?"

He tapped his fingers against the chair, as if in deep thought. "Make sure any move you make is necessary; but whatever you do, you've got to do it swiftly . . . and carefully."

Then and there, Natalie knew. John was being pressured to move her along. Who else besides Blakely was doing the pushing? Even worse, she wondered how long John would hold up to the pressure and allow her free rein. Their gazes froze in a subtle understanding before Natalie spoke firmly.

"I appreciate whatever support you can offer."

John rose from the chair and then pointed to the insurance form on the desk. "Sign this thing so you can get out of here. Your friend is probably anxious to leave, too."

Natalie relaxed at the change of subject and signed her name. "He's a lawyer, so he's used to business dragging on."

"A lawyer, huh? Local firm?"

"Bennett, Parker & Richardson."

He nodded as though he appreciated David's affiliation with the reputable, long-standing law firm. "I believe we've done work for them before."

She handed the signed form to John before she got up to gather her things.

Joining Natalie at the door, John patted her shoulder in a friendly good-bye.

"Go on," he said. "Enjoy your day. That's an order."

Natalie smiled at his departing figure. "I will," she called out. The smile quickly faded, though, as her last tumultuous twenty-four hours rolled over in her head.

When she joined David in the reception area, he put aside the magazine he held and stood up. Tilting his brow, he looked at her thoughtfully.

"Something's bothering you. Come on," he said, holding the door open. "Let's get you out of here."

"Do you mind if we make one more stop before we meet Davina?" Natalie asked. "I have to pick up some items at my client's building."

As they walked side by side to the car, David glanced over at her. "I think I have detected one change in you. I don't think you've ever frowned this much."

Natalie darted a smile at him, surprisingly comforted by the simple fact that he accompanied her. It felt good to embrace their past . . . if only for a moment.

"I'm trying to figure out some things, that's all."

"Like what? Maybe I can help."

"Mmm . . . I don't think so, even though it would be nice to have a sounding board." She looked over at David. "I miss Davina for that, you know, but she's got her hands full right now with a new baby and husband and her own art career gearing up again."

"Yeah . . . Vinny's pretty happy with her life right now, and she deserves it."

Natalie gritted her teeth, hating to sound pitiful. So, she intentionally added a little cheer to her voice. "Don't mind me. It's all this work I have that's talking, that's all."

Tilting his head, David looked down at her, uncertainty in his eyes. "Does this have something to do with your client, Innervision?"

"David . . ." she warned.

"The name's no secret. It's in the public record that your

firm is their outside accountant, and their name was written on the boxes I took into your house last night."

"All right, counselor." She turned his way. "Can we talk hypothetically?"

"No details, names, or facts."

She grunted at the game. "What do you think about coincidence?"

"It depends. Some say there's no such thing, and I'm inclined to agree most of the time. Where are your keys?"

She produced them.

He took them. "Why don't I drive to your office and on the way, I'll be your sounding board for whatever's bothering you?"

Natalie smiled, warming to his take-charge manner. "Okay, it's a deal."

Natalie and David stepped off the elevator and onto the empty fifteenth-floor elevator lobby at Innervision's downtown office building.

"My office is farther down the hall," Natalie said, drawing him in that direction.

David looked around at the contemporary décor. "I heard something about the company a while back."

"Good or bad?"

"Can't recall. What does this Blakely guy have against you, anyway? I'd think he'd be careful about having a complaint filed against him."

"I don't think he cares. What he does care about is whether the company stock is trading high."

David grunted. "He sounds like a head case."

"Shhh . . . someone's coming," Natalie warned when she saw a figure turn into the other end of the long corridor and head in their direction.

"If he's that much of a pain, I guarantee everyone already knows." David's voice was low and full of amusement. "They won't hear anything that hasn't already been said."

Natalie's attention had shifted from David to the figure, and as it drew closer, her eyes widened with recognition. There was no mistaking the ramrod-straight, dark-suited form headed for them. It was Carter. She looked away quickly, not wanting to draw his gaze.

Unaccountably anxious over the fact that David was about to meet her Saturday night date, she felt a shadow of annoyance rolling over her.

Chapter 10

With Carter less than twenty feet away, Natalie had neither the time nor the patience to be irritated by a dilemma of her own making; so she made the best of the bad situation. She met it head-on by boldly catching Carter's eye and holding the contact as they came abreast in the hallway.

"This is a surprise, running into you down here," she said.

Carter had slowed to a stop. "What are you doing here?" He swung his head in David's general direction before he returned his attention to Natalie. "I thought you were off today."

"I am, but my meeting with Blakely got results after all, and I'm picking up some work he left for me."

A smile began to creep into his stony features. "So, your patience was rewarded."

"I wouldn't quite call it a reward."

Carter's eyes had meandered back to David at about the same time David's hand shifted possessively near Natalie's back. Turning to David, Natalie casually managed the introductions as she measured the scrutiny in his eyes.

"I'd like you to meet a coworker of mine, Carter Johnson."

"Carter . . . Johnson." David's expression darkened with an unreadable emotion before he extended his hand with a polite nod.

"And, Carter, this is an old family friend, David Spenser."

"Nice meeting you," Carter replied.

Sizing each other up, they exchanged a firm handshake.

"I was just on my way to my office," she said, watching Carter and David eye each other curiously.

"In that case," Carter said, "I'll see you later." Stepping away, he moved past them down the hallway.

David let out a grunt. "I don't like him," he declared as they rounded the corner.

"You only just met him," Natalie said. "Anyway, he works security for Blakely."

"All the more reason for this 'old family friend's' concern," he said, emphasizing the introduction. "And didn't I hear his name somewhere before?"

Natalie ignored him. "The office I use is not too much farther." She led him through an open threshold with the title ACCOUNTING printed in bold letters on the wall.

"Hey, Natalie, what are you doing here?"

Surprised by the voice, she turned and saw Sean, the junior accountant who'd helped her on the elevator yesterday. She smiled at the weird luck in running into Carter first, and now Sean.

"I thought you were off today," he said.

"And I don't remember sharing that," she teased. "Actually, I am, but I came by to pick up some things." Once again, she could tell David's curiosity was piqued as she introduced the men. Intentionally needling him, she introduced him as she had to Carter.

With that done, she started for her office again. But, Sean tagged along.

"You haven't had any more nasty spills, have you?" he teased.

"No, not today," Natalie said, groaning at the expected revelation to follow.

"A spill? What happened?" David asked.

"Oh, I just knocked over my luggage caddy yesterday,"

she quickly explained before Sean could open his mouth. "That's all."

Sean laughed as they entered the accounting offices. "She'd still be stacking all of that stuff back up if it wasn't for me and Carter."

Turning to Natalie, David frowned. "I keep hearing his name."

Sean looked puzzled. "What name?"

Ignoring both men, Natalie returned the smiles and greetings from other employees they passed in the open work area. "Sean, I'll have to see you later."

"Sure thing," he called out as Natalie continued on her way. "It's good seeing you."

Natalie looked over her shoulder and saw that he no longer trailed them. In fact, he was already picking up a phone in one of the glass cubicles along the wall.

"You'd think we're all old friends or something around here," she said. "I only learned Sean's name yesterday."

David grinned. "You're like a Pied Piper to the male population."

Darting a look over to him, she raised a brow at the comment. "Is that supposed to be a dig or a compliment?"

He studied her thoughtfully for a moment before he pressed his hands into his pockets. "Sometimes I don't think you realize how much of an impression you make. Don't sell yourself short."

She turned to face him fully. "And what's that supposed to mean?"

David gently turned her back toward the hallway. "Where's your sense of humor today? It was a compliment," he whispered near her ear.

As they continued their walk, she was acutely conscious of David at her side. She had to admit she'd enjoyed his company this morning, but would that enjoyment last? Before she considered an answer, they had reached her office door. She opened it and David followed her inside.

"When you said your office here is hard to describe, I see what you mean," he said. "This is nice, except there's no window."

Natalie walked over to the desk, inserted a key in the gold keyhole, and opened the long drawer.

David looked up at the ceiling as he circled the room. "You think this room used to be something besides an office?"

"Maybe," Natalie said, immediately spying the memo Blakely had left for her. "But how do you explain the furniture bolted to the floor?"

"Damn, you're right," David exclaimed with a chuckle while he nudged the desk with his leg. "I wonder, what that is about?"

"Nothing leaves the room but the chair." She spoke absently as she quickly perused the memo, noting the part that listed the produced documents. Blakely was only allowing her to review payroll spreadsheet disks for now. Other expense categories were *currently* unavailable. Natalie scratched her head. What did that mean?

"You've got that look on your face again," David said as he came to a stop in front of her. "Did you find what you wanted?"

"Yes." She looked up at him. "But everything is being held by a senior accounting manager." She looked at the sheet again. "A Myra Grayson."

David reached over and playfully nudged her lips into a smile. "Hey, I thought we agreed in the car that you were going to forget this place for a few days and not let Blakely or these other problems get to you?"

She smiled for his benefit, and then closed and locked the desk drawer before she glanced at her watch. "Look at the time."

"I've kept an eye on it. We can get back to the house in plenty of time for lunch."

Natalie looked apologetic. "After I go back to the accounting department."

David grinned and shook his head as he walked to the door. "Come on."

They closed the door and then split up, with David headed for the elevator to wait for Natalie, who went back through to accounting.

When she came upon a door with the name M. L. GRAYSON stenciled in gold on the wall next to it, she knocked.

"Are you looking for me?"

The voice came from behind Natalie, and she turned. A small woman who appeared to be in her early forties, with pale skin and keen features, was walking across the room toward her.

"Myra Grayson?"

Myra nodded as she spoke matter-of-factly. "And you're the auditor."

"Yes, Natalie Goodman. I believe you're holding some things for me?" In a word, the woman was best described as mousy. Her fine, brown hair, parted on the side, lay limply against the white starched collar that accompanied her brown business suit. Sensible pumps moved her quietly across the carpeted floor.

"I only learned of your request this morning and I didn't expect to see you until next week." Her words seemed apologetic as she moved past Natalie and opened the door. "Please, come in."

Natalie followed her into the office and immediately wrinkled her nose at the clutter. Stacks of papers, in some form, occupied every bit of surface space, even the chairs.

"Sorry about the mess," Myra said from behind her desk. "We're preparing reports for the big stockholders' meeting, and you know how crazy things can get."

"I can imagine," Natalie replied, thinking that the poor woman looked completely dumped on. "Listen, if you haven't had the chance to pull the documents, I can come back."

"Oh, I have them." The woman lifted a sturdy manila envelope from her desk and held it out to Natalie.

"That's great," she said, taking the package. "I'll just call if I have further questions."

"Ah, I believe you're to direct questions through Mr. Blakely."

"But weren't the reports compiled by your teams?"

Myra looked suitably embarrassed by that observation. "I'm sorry, but I was told to give you the disks, that's all."

Realizing it would be useless to query the woman, Natalie nodded her understanding. "Thank you," she said, and turned to leave the crowded office.

After Natalie left, Myra stared at the empty doorway, a sharp knife turning like a spit in her stomach. She thought this must be what it felt like to be handed a death sentence—while the outcome was inevitable, each day's delay was its own bit of death.

Resignedly, she picked up the phone.

Gil Blakely reared back in the chair behind his desk, and chewed on the end of a pencil. He needed a smoke, but he couldn't even bum one off his staff—no one smoked any damn more because of the no-good liberal do-gooders—and his wife would raise holy hell if she found him with one.

He clicked the head of the silver remote control, and the television screens went dark at the same time his private line rang. He picked it up.

"I've been looking for you," he stormed, knowing instinctively who the caller would be. "Where've you been?"

"I was off-site most of the morning," the caller answered unhurriedly, "and just returned."

"I got a call that she was downstairs to pick up the disks."

"I heard your message."

"She was in her office, but I couldn't catch much of the conversation on the audio feed, and she didn't stay long." He shifted on his chair. "She had a man with her. I don't know if that should be a concern or not."

"I can check it out."

He grunted his acceptance of the plan. "You do that. I'll firm up things on this end."

"If that's all—"

"By the way, that was good work last night for such short notice." He paused for a reply, but when none came, he continued. "I don't say that often, because I think you'd know if your work was below par."

"I believe I would."

"You're damned right about that," Blakely said and chewed on the pencil. "You're damned right."

The morning had been like old times for Natalie and David. On the ride to Davina's house, they joked about being godparents, scrutinized their careers, and very carefully sidestepped the subject of their own unpredictable relationship. And so far, they had kept their word to put aside their differences for the sake of the christening and their friendship.

The Hardy estate soon rose into view, and Natalie remembered Davina's vivid description of her initial visit to what would later become her home. She had likened that first look to a glimpse into an enchanted castle that came complete with turretlike windows at each wing. Davina had been right—the place was breathtakingly beautiful.

Natalie darted a glance over at David as he drove through the tall iron gates surrounding the estate's entrance and then brought the car to a stop in the courtyard drive.

"We're here." His unnecessary announcement broke their silence.

"I see," Natalie muttered similarly, and pulled on the door latch to get out.

When they met each other at the front of the car, David dropped the keys into Natalie's open hand. He pulled his sunglasses from his eyes and, for the span of a moment, studied her with a curious intensity that caused her to lower her own gaze.

"I remember now where I heard that name before."

Natalie jerked her head back up, blinking against the noon sun's bright glare. "What name?" she asked.

"Carter," David said with quiet emphasis. "The dude back at your office."

"Oh, him," Natalie replied, tucking her keys into her purse.

David nodded. "The first time was when we were talking about that note last night. You said his name, like you remembered something about him."

"I . . . I did?" she stammered. The elevator encounter immediately flashed before her eyes and she looked up again. "You must be wrong," she said with a straight face. "I mean, how could he be connected to that? I barely know the man."

"Really?" Mockery hung in the soft breeze.

She set her chin in a stubborn line. "We agreed to drop the subject of the note."

"Yeah . . . we said a lot of things last night." He gave her a sidelong glance as they slowly crossed the gravel-covered drive that led to the front walk.

"Your problem is you don't like Carter; you've already admitted it."

"He works for a man who has no respect for you. That alone should be reason enough to stay clear of him."

Natalie stopped to face David, strangely on edge over his references to Carter. "And what makes you think I don't?"

"I keep hearing his name connected with yours."

"That's not true, but what about it, anyway?" she asked. "You're in town all of a day and you're already dictating what I should do."

"All I did was offer some advice."

"I didn't ask for it."

"Still, it wouldn't hurt you to show some caution for a change, that's all."

"I am not yours to worry about."

". . . Anymore is what you mean."

"That was your call," Natalie huffed. "Remember?"

Clenching her teeth, she drew a full breath and haughtily turned to step away. However, her shoe's delicate heel skidded out from under her, and she felt herself begin to tumble off balance. In an undignified panic, she gasped.

"Oh—"

Chapter 11

"Oh—" Natalie squealed again.

David was right there, though, and quickly halted her fall. Before she knew it, she was lifted up and into his arms, and he continued on across the drive.

Finding herself suddenly pressed against David's hard chest brought on an unwelcome surge of excitement. With the tantalizing smell of his aftershave washing over her like a disturbing storm, she knew she should not be so close. She twisted to look up at him.

"David," she asked, enjoying the rocking motion of his arms as he walked with her, "what are you doing?"

"I think I just saved your butt from falling," he said, tightening his grip as he stepped, surefooted, across the ground.

"You know what I mean," she demanded, no longer amused, and squirmed against his arms. "Put me down."

He glanced at the slipperlike pointed-toe shoes that hung precariously on her feet. "You can't walk on the ground in those lethal-looking things. You'll kill yourself."

"We're on the sidewalk now." She grated the words out through her teeth.

"I'd be careful about being so ungrateful if I were you."

He darted his eyes toward the upper part of the house. "We're being watched."

Looping her arm around David's neck for support, Natalie turned to follow his gaze at the house. She could make out Davina standing at a second-story window waving at them.

Natalie quickly looked away and turned into David's warm breath against her cheek. "Well, this is just peachy," she said, her eyes darting across his face. "How do we explain you carrying me all the way up the walk?"

He grunted. "It's easier than explaining why Jake's godmother is wearing a cast at the christening."

She sighed. "You've got a point."

"By the way, what I said earlier—it came out wrong."

Natalie pulled back and eyed him with a skeptical nod.

"I wasn't trying to tell you what to do," he explained. "In fact, you've done all right—taking care of yourself while I was away."

She challenged him with a frosty gaze. "Is that your idea of an apology?" However, the ice was instantly charmed into a thaw when she saw his smile and mischievously arched dark brow.

Natalie averted her eyes. "If so, it's lousy, you know."

By now, they were near the front door and David loosened his hold just enough so that Natalie's feet touched the ground.

"No matter how badly you want one, I'm not giving you an argument," he said, still preventing her from leaving his arms.

The smile in David's eyes contained a sensuous flame and Natalie was, once again, unsure of her own emotions. She pushed out of his arms and, stepping back, smoothed out her skirt just as the front door opened.

"Natalie . . . David."

It was Davina with the shawl-covered baby against her shoulder.

"Hey," Natalie called back, and quickly composed her

features before she rushed up to the door. Dressed in capri pants and sandals, she thought her friend was the picture of a confident mother aware of her family's love. She drew Davina and the sleeping baby into a hug.

"See," she said, "I told you I'd be here, and it's not even noon."

"Barely," Davina said drolly as she pulled back and received a similar hug and kiss from her brother. "That's why I put David on your tail."

"She's delivered," he said, and turning to Natalie, added, "And in one piece."

Davina gestured toward the door with her head. "Come on in. Mrs. Taylor is setting lunch out on the patio."

"I'll be in shortly," David said, and turned toward the path that ran alongside the house. "I'm going around back for a sec."

Natalie could only watch with an odd twinge of disappointment that he'd sauntered off, carrying his tall, athletic body like a graceful cat.

"So, what was that about?" Davina asked, her Cheshire Cat grin about to split her face.

"You know your brother," she said, her stare never waning as David moved farther away. When he disappeared around the curve of the house, she turned to her friend and spoke matter-of-factly. "What do you want to bet he's checking on that car? I swear, I can't believe he left it here the whole time."

Davina let out a laugh. "You know that's not what I'm talking about. Why were you being carried—"

"I know exactly what you're talking about," Natalie quickly cut in. "I almost fell, that's all. It was nothing." She lied easily about the nothing part—it took no trouble imagining his hard chest pressed against her . . . his smell—and shifted her attention to little Jake, cooing sweetly as she watched him.

"Liar," Davina said evenly, and winked when Natalie shot her a twisted scowl. "You know you liked it."

Natalie grinned as she peeked under the shawl. "Lucky for me this little fellow is now in my life. Her finger gingerly stroked the soft downy hair on his creamy scalp. "He's much more my speed." She let her pinky become grasped in his tiny hand when he stretched in sleep. "Oh, Davina, he's so beautiful and . . . and precious."

"Here," Davina said, shifting Jake around. "You can hold him."

Natalie's eyes stretched wide as a mild panic claimed her. "No, I don't—"

"You're a godmother. You've got to get used to this." Davina was already efficiently transferring the child onto Natalie's chest.

With the baby nestling against her body, Natalie stiffened, gripped with fear that she might drop the squirming child. She could also hear Davina's chuckles behind her.

"Stop laughing," she gritted out. "I'm new at this." Remembering David's comment about her shoes, she quickly stepped out of them.

"Girl, what are you doing?" Davina picked up the discarded shoes.

Natalie had started to bounce the fidgeting baby back to sleep. "Until I get the hang of this, I'm thinking safety first."

Davina's laugh echoed through the clear spring air. "I can't wait until you get the chance to change a diaper or two." She pointed Natalie and little Jake toward the door. "Let's go inside. We've got some talking to catch up on. Maybe we'll even talk about that fall."

Natalie could see the determination set into Davina's features, and gave in to whatever would come next. "Oh, well. I did promise to be yours all day. Lead the way."

After looking in on his car, David stepped outside of the attached garage and pulled down on the metal door until it rolled with a heavy groan to the ground. He then methodically latched it at the base of the center brick column. The simple details helped to keep his mind occupied and off Natalie—and everything about her.

It didn't work, though. He wanted to know about this Carter dude. To make matters worse, Natalie didn't seem to be in any hurry to explain *her* relationship with the man, which only managed to intrigue David more.

"David?"

He turned at the shout, knowing it belonged to Elizabeth Hardy, his sister's mother-in-law. A wide grin spread over his face as he quickly strode across the back drive and onto the manicured lawn to greet the small dynamo of a woman who, in the short time David had known her, had unselfishly attempted to fill a void that had been left by the death, years ago, of his mother.

Mrs. Hardy had been settled on her knees in front of a garden bed of colorful flowers. Now, holding her wide-brimmed hat with one hand, she stood and let David sweep her into a bear hug.

"Oh, goodness," she said, laughing, craning her neck up to take him in. "You're looking as handsome as ever, even with your hair cut off. It's good having you home again."

"It feels good being here."

"Well, if that's the case, you should move on back," she said, her eyes twinkling with amusement. "Come on." She motioned to the park bench nearby. "Sit and talk with me for a minute before we have lunch. It's been a while since we've done this."

David claimed the seat, enjoying the crisp breeze and the slightly pungent odor of mosquito spray mixed with the floral fragrance cast off by the garden. Mrs. Hardy had returned to kneel before her flowers. It did feel good being back home in the South.

"Vinny probably told you I was here last night," he said.

"Yes, she did." She cut her eyes over to him. "But, I also heard it was spent mostly in the library." Her gentle voice held a hint of censure.

"You know I wouldn't normally come over here without seeing you," he explained awkwardly. "But, last night . . . well, it got a little complicated, and I ended up hanging out with Justin."

"Where's Natalie? I thought she'd be here today, too."

"She's inside, with Vinny. We just got here."

Mrs. Hardy looked up. "So, is she last night's complication?"

Her directness caught David off guard. "You, ah, probably know we're not seeing each other anymore."

"Indeed, I do. I also know you two were the picture of happiness at Justin and Davina's wedding." She shoved the trowel into the soil. "Do you know what happened?"

He shifted on the bench as the picture on Natalie's desk loomed in his mind. They had been happy, or so they thought. "Sometimes things just don't work out the way you want."

He heard a loud snort, and realized Mrs. Hardy was staring at him with her hands on her hips.

"David, I'm almost sixty years old. You don't think I know that sometimes things don't work out?" She grinned as she peeled off the work gloves. "Now, you want to try that again?"

He wasn't sure whether it was the earnestness in her soft brown eyes or her blunt assessment. Whatever it was, it led him to speak the truth. "I wanted more than she was willing to give."

"Should it matter—how much she gave?"

David frowned. "Sure. You want to feel as though the other person is willing to meet you at some point in the relationship."

Mrs. Hardy joined David on the bench. "I've had the privilege of knowing you and Davina only a short time, but I understand the serious family issues you've worked through."

"Yeah," he said with a wry smile. "We had to throw off a lot of baggage."

"So, have you considered that maybe Natalie has baggage to be worked through, too?"

"Natalie?" David didn't think for a moment that she had the kind of problems he and Vinny had faced. Their mother had died in a car accident when they were kids; and their father, a talented artist before his wife died, had eked out a meager living and drowned his misery in alcohol after her death, finally succumbing to its complications only last year. Natalie's family, on the other hand, had been intact, and was nothing like his.

Mrs. Hardy touched David's shoulder and broke into his reverie. "You say you want more than Natalie is willing to give. What if that's all she's able to give right now? Would it make you see things any differently?"

Uncertainty crept into David's expression at her words. Did he give up too soon on Natalie? Maybe he should try again, and in time, things might change.

Standing up, Mrs. Hardy stretched her back and then tossed her gloves to the ground where they joined the trowel. "You know, Mr. Yamata, our gardener, hates when I dig out here," she said, surveying the bulbs she had planted.

David stood with her and eyed the flower bed. "So, why do you do it?"

"Because after so many years, he expects it of me," she explained with a grin. "Let's go back up to the house. Mrs. Taylor should have lunch set out by now—she knew you'd be here, so she planned some of your favorites."

David threw his head back and laughed. "Aw, you're spoiling me, but I love it." Linking her arm through his, he escorted her back up to the house.

"Are you happy, Natalie?"

The odd question caught Natalie off guard in the brightly decorated nursery. She looked over at Davina where she sat in a wide rocker, her feet tucked and crossed beneath her, and a pillow cushion enfolded in her arms.

"Sure," she answered. "But it's all relative, you know."

Natalie reached down and tucked the crocheted shawl around Jake's middle as he lay sleeping in his baby crib. "Am I as happy as you?" She grinned and turned from the crib. "No one is as happy as you, girl."

"You wouldn't say that if you could see yourself around Jake. You love babies."

"Before now, only from afar—that is until I got this chance with Jake, thanks to you and Justin." With one last glance at the baby, she walked over to the love seat near the window and dropped onto it. "I still feel like I should know more, being the godmother and all."

"Be yourself," Davina said, smiling gently. "That's all Justin and I want from you and David."

Natalie's heart did a little tumble at his name. "Just be myself. Well, that's a sad cry from what David wants." It had happened so quickly. She had voiced her thoughts—and verbatim at that—out loud. She looked around to Davina and groaned, "Tell me I didn't say that."

"You did." Davina grinned. "When I saw you all up in his arms on the walk . . ."

Natalie leaned back on the sofa and crossed her legs. "Oh, I know exactly what you thought, but it's not happening." In a flash, a cushion landed in Natalie's face. She let out a yelp just as Davina's laugh filled the room.

"I can dream, can't I?"

Natalie pushed the cushion aside. "Dream, yes, because everyone won't have your Cinderella ending." She stood and threw the cushion back at a ducking, giggling Davina. "And everyone doesn't want it, either."

"There's nothing wrong with wanting my loved ones to settle down like me." She drew in a deep sigh. "The problem is you're still holding on to your crazy idea that relates husbands and commitment to a poison pill."

"Yeah—who'd ask for it willingly?"

Davina turned and stared in reproach. "If it's possible, I think you've gotten worse."

Natalie paced across the soft Berber carpet in her bare feet as she talked. "Don't you agree that women are entitled to—even deserve—pleasure?"

"Of course."

"Well, the majority don't get it once they're married. Why? Because they give up control, their power. I don't plan on being one of those unlucky souls."

"Oh, God." Davina rolled her eyes upward. "Not that pleasure principle stuff again."

"What's wrong with it?" Natalie's voice rose as she warmed to her subject. "Men have always known that sex and pleasure is about power." She made a looping fist in the air. "Whoever enjoys it holds the brass ring. I simply intend to keep my power."

"By going for pleasure without commitment? You know that's empty. Even worse, you're describing an adolescent male."

"It's control over your own life," Natalie popped back.

"Snap out of it, girl."

"In fact, marriage is all about power, with man as the ultimate captor and the woman, his captive. I mean, think about it. How often does the woman ask a man to marry her and get to be the conqueror?"

"But, what about love? That evens the playing field."

"Humph . . . Love is a form of insanity."

Davina threw up her hands in exasperation. "How can the woman who encouraged me to open my heart to Justin close her own to the same possibilities?"

"I urged you to go for the power, after you had that horrible debacle with Lawrence Parker down in Miami." Natalie stopped pacing to eye her friend. "Seems like you totally ignored me. You're so besotted that you'd forgive Justin anything, and he knows it."

"But he loves me too, so we're insane together." She giggled. "Natalie, that's the fun part."

"Yeah," she conceded as her voice turned serious. "You two may very well defy the odds."

"There is one thing I've learned. Love may not be smooth, but it's worth the effort." Davina looked at her friend. "And you know what? When you let yourself fall in love, you'll know I'm right."

"Now you snap out of it," Natalie warned and picked up her pace around the room. "I don't want to do the love thing and get married. I want a life that lets me live out my own dreams my way." She stopped in front of Jake's crib in the corner, drawn once again to the tiny form there.

"Those things aren't mutually exclusive with a special person."

Natalie looked back over her shoulder and deadpanned, "You mean you're not my special person anymore?"

"I'm serious, Natalie."

"So am I. With a little judicious application of the principle, even a one-night stand can be managed beneficially."

Davina let out a loud, resigned snort. "Fine. Be pigheaded," she said and crossed her arms in a huff. "You'd never admit it, but you sound like you're running from something. Don't forget, I know what happened to your parents' marriage."

A stab of guilt pierced Natalie. "Don't—"

"I'm not bringing it up, but you know as well as I that it scared you. Admit it, especially to yourself."

"Scared . . . me?" She snorted in derision. "It opened my eyes; and before I'd submit myself to a lifetime of pain and suffering like my mother, I'd work free of charge for Gil Blakely."

"Ahem."

Natalie and Davina looked up and saw David in the doorway, his arm stretched out as he leaned against the doorjamb. He was watching them.

"Oh," Natalie said. Her eyes had widened in surprise. "We didn't see you there."

"I know." His face didn't reveal his mood as his eyes sought Natalie's. "Mrs. Hardy asked me to tell you lunch is ready, out on the patio." David pushed away from the door and, with a quirk of his brow, left them.

* * *

Gil Blakely had been in an expansive mood all day, and this evening, as he sat across from Merlin Ford, Innervision's director of general accounting, he allowed a grin to gather on his face. Although he still wasn't in possession of all the information he wanted, he believed he had enough to predict the next steps of the nosy auditor certifying the books.

"You talked with the senior managers?" he asked the somber director. "Did you explain the plan to hit our profit targets for this quarter?"

"Well, sir . . ." Merlin squeezed his nose, and then cleared his throat, an obvious delay for whatever he had to say. "The problem is their concern that you promised they wouldn't have to make any more questionable adjustments between accounts."

He shifted in his chair before he continued. "When they first agreed to make those transfers in the accounts, that was three quarters ago, and it was a onetime thing. And, as you know, they've had to make adjustments every quarter since then."

With each of Merlin's words, Blakely was quickly losing his buzz. He leaned forward.

"I've been through this with you before. This is all for the good of the company."

"It's the continuing issue that, frankly, concerns all of us, sir."

"We simply ran into a little problem. So we had to make a few shifts of expenses here and there to increase our bottom line. But, it was for the sake of the stock value." He waved his hand. "It's a temporary fix, that's all. When we announce our new acquisition and merger coming up next year, these little problems with runaway expenses will take care of themselves."

Merlin's rotund shape pushed back against his chair, as if to give him ample breathing room, and he let out a sigh. "I think we all know this is no longer temporary. It's not good accounting, either—not in the short run, and surely not on a continuous basis."

He continued to speak worriedly, his voice almost a whine. "Sir, we've backdated invoices, made up journal entries." He ran his hand across his face, covered with a pale sheen of fear. "And with the rumors about the reviewer taking a more in-depth look at the figures making up the financial reports, my managers are balking at preparing another bad one right under her nose."

"There won't be a problem with Miss Goodman."

The director's voice lowered to a whisper. "Sir, we're talking about almost a . . . a half billion dollars in false entries and questionable transfers this last year alone."

"There won't be a problem," Blakely repeated.

"My people want to know what they're supposed to do when Miss Goodman asks them directly for backup to explain the entries, and it's only a matter of time before she does."

"She won't ask. Everything she wants—documents, interviews, access—comes through me, so I'll know about it first, and can prepare. Now, I want you to get your people back with the program." He slammed his fist on the desk for emphasis. "I don't care what you have to do. Promise them your job, if you have to. But, damn it, they agreed to do this before, and now is not the time to abandon the ship, not in the middle of this storm and just before a stockholders' meeting."

He abruptly stood and dropped a set of papers on Merlin's desk. "These are some of the notes she made over the last weeks. I already gave you the list of documents she wants and what I decided to let her take a look at."

Merlin looked at the copied sheets, and spoke as his eyes scanned the lines. "Where did these—" He stopped in midsentence, as though rethinking his question. "I'll . . . I'll call you this weekend after I look over this."

"That's more like it." Blakely slapped the portly director

on the back. "I can't tell you how much the company appre-
ciates your discretion, not to mention that of your managers,
over this, ah, little matter."

"You met them once in your office, sir. Myra—"

He didn't care. "When I get your call, tell me what they
make of all this, and in what direction that auditor is going
so we"—he smiled at Merlin, a man he'd hired and given
two promotions in the last three years—"can cut her down at
the knees."

Merlin didn't return the smile, but carefully laid aside the
papers and looked up at his superior.

"I, ah, hope you're talking figuratively this time, sir."

"Of course," Blakely said, his smile widening to display a
broad set of teeth. "For now."

Chapter 12

Dinner at the Hardys' was always a family affair, and though it was their Sunday gathering that had become the not-to-miss event, this one, on a Friday night, was turning out to be just as special due, in part, to David's arrival and the presence of both godparents.

All afternoon and into the evening, though, Mrs. Hardy had hinted at something else; and surprise, along with vibrant conversation, crackled in the air.

The huge table in the dining room could easily seat thirty, but it had been modified to accommodate only the twelve adults present tonight. And with each course, the mood grew lighter. Stuffed with Mrs. Taylor's delicious meal, everyone seemed to be winding down as they settled in with dessert.

Natalie loved the energy in the room, and was continually amazed at the closeness the Hardys held for each other. Davina and David were lucky to have acquired a family like this one after having lost their own to tragedy. She smiled to herself, thinking the Hardys were definitely not the Goodmans.

She slid her spoon into the deceptively simple creamy baked Alaska and looked across the table at David. He was talking with Michael Hennessey, a well-known professional football player and Carolyn Hardy's fiancé, and seemed oblivious of Natalie's stare. Her gaze spread along the table, past Carolyn, to Alli, and then to the oldest Hardy sister, Stephanie Rogers. Stephanie was seated across from her husband, William.

On the other end sat Mrs. Hardy. She was next to the ever-attentive and longtime family friend, Douglas Bradley, who was also a widower. Mrs. Hardy caught Natalie's eye and smiled before she resumed talking with Eugenia Graham, the late Mr. Hardy's sister.

While closing her eyes a moment to enjoy the delicious blend of meringue and ice cream in her mouth, Natalie's attention was drawn back to David. This time, his eyes were on her. Cocking his brow, he offered only an enigmatic smile before he returned to his conversation with Michael.

Since David's unexpected appearance in the nursery, Natalie had not been able to grab a moment alone with him, and now she couldn't figure his mood. It bothered her that he might have heard something deeply personal in those moments he'd stood at the door. She didn't like talking about her family to anyone—not even Davina. Clearly, though, it shouldn't matter since she and David were no longer involved. Hadn't they agreed to that fact?

"Do you think he heard our entire conversation?" Natalie asked in a whisper to Davina seated next to her.

"If you're still carping about this afternoon, stop it. He didn't hear anything he probably didn't already know, anyway."

"Easy for you to say," she snorted, and ate another spoon of dessert.

"Natalie . . ." The voice came from the other end of the table. "What about you? Are you anxious about being a godmother for the first time?"

She swung her head in that direction and saw Eugenia Graham's gray head leaning forward to look down the table.

"Oh, just a little," Natalie replied with respectful humor. "I've never been asked to play a special role in anyone's life.

So, as long as Justin and Davina don't come to their senses before next week, I'm game."

Amid good-natured aahs and smiles, Mrs. Hardy said, "Oh, you're going to make a wonderful godmother, Natalie. And, David"—she turned her attention on him—"you're going to be good for each other. Personally, I don't think little Jake could be in finer sets of hands."

"And since we're here tonight partly to honor the godparents, I'd like to make a toast." Justin raised his wineglass, and the others at the table followed suit. "Davina and I couldn't agree more on two people we respect and value with our friendship and love." He turned to Natalie and David and offered a nod. "Thank you for accepting the challenge to show our firstborn how to live life."

As glasses tinkled against one another around the table, everyone drank to their success; Davina squeezed her arm in support. Natalie had been moved by the encouraging words, but they all only enhanced her feeling of inadequacy. What did she know about children? She barely handled her own life. What did David think? Amid the talking and laughing that had ensued, Natalie sipped her wine and took a moment to peer over the edge of her glass at David. He saluted her with a private nod and smile.

Out of the corner of her eye, Natalie saw Mrs. Taylor come in and hand Mr. Bradley a flat, though large, rectangular box.

She turned to Davina. "What else is going on?"

"I don't know," Davina replied, looking down the table.

"I believe this is the surprise Mom mentioned," Justin offered with a grin, and taking his wife's hand in his own, he rubbed it. "We'll see in a moment."

Mrs. Hardy stood up and tapped her water glass with a spoon. "I need everyone's attention again." She set the glass down and beamed a broad smile.

"There's a tradition in the Hardy family that started over six decades ago." Mrs. Graham, along with Mr. Bradley, now stood and fiddled with opening up the box at the table alongside Mrs. Hardy. "Justin, Carolyn, and Alli became aware of the tradition when Stephanie and William's two children were christened. So, I'd like to explain the tradition to the godparents, a new member of the Hardy clan, Davina . . ." Her eyes now sought out Michael. "And, of course, to a future member, Michael."

Everyone smiled at a grinning Michael and Carolyn while Mrs. Hardy stepped back and helped take the lid off the box. And then, attention returned to that end of the table.

Inside the box, packed in clouds of pink, blue, and yellow tissue paper, was a christening gown, a white cotton and lace frock complete with the slip. Mrs. Hardy held it aloft on its small hanger.

Amidst the oohs and aahs, everyone stood from their chairs, and then moved forward for a closer look.

"It's absolutely beautiful," Davina remarked.

"Justin's father, Jacob, was the first to wear it back in the thirties," Mrs. Hardy explained.

"And I was the next to wear it," Mrs. Graham added, stepping up. "Mama told us it was a gift when Jacob was born, and she could tell it wasn't your everyday child's dress gown; oh, no. It was expensive." She laughed. "In those days, money was hard-earned and even harder to come by; but with it being so beautiful and precious, Mama decided to use it for all of her children's christening ceremonies."

"A funny thing happened after that, though." Mrs. Hardy's eyes washed over the group that had now crowded around her as she told her story. "When her children grew up, she passed the gown on to their children. And now that all of my children, their many cousins, and their cousin's babies have worn it, it truly has become a Hardy family christening gown tradition."

"I don't know how many more babies it'll take before this gown retires." Mrs. Graham touched a corner near the hem. "It has a few interesting spots on it; but then again, it has been worn at least thirty times by active Hardy babies."

The group laughed at the comment as Mrs. Graham continued. "Each child's name gets etched on this scroll kept with the gown, and it'll be little Jake's turn next week."

"Davina, you want to take over the gown, now?" Mrs. Hardy held it out to her.

As she moved forward to accept the tradition with Justin next to her, Natalie felt a lump in her throat. She sidled to the back of the group, surprised at her reaction to things she had vowed never to embrace.

"Sort of gets to you, huh?"

Natalie looked up and realized she had backed right into David. He gave her a smile that sent her pulses racing.

"Go ahead," he teased. "Admit it makes you want to chuck those ideas of yours about matrimony and babies."

His infectious grin set the tone and Natalie playfully sent a punch at his shoulder. "You rat," she said, the heat stealing her face. "You did hear us this afternoon."

He grinned and pushed his hands into his pockets. "Didn't hear a thing I hadn't already figured out."

Natalie rolled her eyes and stepped away from the dinner group that had begun to mill around the dining room in small talk.

"One thing I didn't know until a few minutes ago is that"— he gave her a pointed look—"you're scared about being a godmother."

"Don't you think I should be? I'm not your average, overeager caregiver, you know."

"You'll be all right." He leaned against the wall near the buffet and watched as Natalie poured out a glass of iced water.

Natalie was aware of his attention. The intensity of his stare was arousing, to say the least, and her body tingled with excitement. She fumbled with the glass.

"I've sort of warmed to the idea that at least I won't have the job alone," he said. "Just like Mrs. Hardy said, we can rely on each other, right?"

"I suspect there'll be other godparents running around

here pretty soon." She motioned to Davina and Justin, standing cozily together in the room. "How much you want to bet Jake won't be an only child for long?"

David grinned. "Yeah, I agree. Marriage has been great for Vinny. I couldn't have planned it better."

"I admit, they do make that *institution* seem"—Natalie groaned the word—"inviting."

David stretched his arm out to the buffet, brushing against Natalie as he leaned close to her ear. "You shouldn't be so down on marriage. It's what you make it. In fact, you were one of the big matchmakers for those two, and I see how taken you are with Jake; so why be squeamish?"

Natalie gave her back to David, but could feel him step closer. "I'm not squeamish; I just view it differently than most women my age, I guess. Let's leave it at that."

In a quick thought, she whirled back around to face David, and found herself almost flush against him, but she didn't move away. "Anyway, life is about squeezing out the pleasure."

With humor in his eyes, David said, "Hey, I can understand that. Nothing like it."

Natalie's wide grin turned into a chuckle. "Like now. It's been a good day."

David nodded. "Yeah, it has. I've missed my friend, but I think I found her again."

"With all that we don't agree on, I guess we forgot the really simple stuff that we can agree with."

"Today's good feeling doesn't have to end." He leaned into her a little, his voice lowering for her ears. "We could find a way to spend some time together. The day's not over yet."

"Is that what you were thinking about when I caught you staring at me at the table?"

"You have no shame, woman," he mocked with a smile. "And let's be clear; you were staring at me." Light smoldered in his gray gaze. "If we can't have tonight, we could have dinner tomorrow night."

Natalie froze at his words and the room momentarily tilted on its axis. Instinctively, she knew the pleasant day of lunch and dinner had come to a dangerous end, and all because of that thoughtless moment in a parking deck.

"I . . . uh, I can't have dinner tomorrow," she said in a rush, and set her water glass on the buffet. "We could do it Sunday?"

He straightened and looked down at her. "I thought you said you were pretty much free through next week because of the christening." He laughed. "So what is it? You've got another date lined up or something?"

Natalie swallowed hard, wincing at the facetious words. "Well, actually, yes, sort of."

David's smile slowly faded in acknowledgement, but his stoic silence that followed only managed to incense an already guilt-ridden Natalie.

"Well, that's that." He lifted his wineglass and tossed down the last swallow.

"What? You weren't even supposed to be back in Atlanta until tomorrow."

Confused, David frowned at her logic as he set the glass on the buffet. "What's that supposed to mean?"

"You're acting like you expected me to pine away and stay home until your miraculous return."

"No." He spoke insolently. "I never expected you to give up a thing for me, and it seems you didn't."

"And you did? You didn't even have the decency to tell me you were leaving town last year."

"You made it clear you didn't want to have anything to do with me." He glared at her. "Is that what this is all about? I figured, why bother telling you? You didn't give a damn then, and you don't give one now. It's obvious, since you're right back in the saddle, getting your pleasure where you want it."

"Humph! And you expect me to think you didn't while you were in D.C.?" she retorted right back.

It dawned on Natalie, as it did on David, that the room had become silent and they were the awful center of growing attention. When they turned and faced the others, Natalie smothered a groan.

"Let's get out of here," she whispered, and stepped back toward the door as David took the lead.

"Ah, excuse us for a moment," he said, and backed up the few steps to the double French doors, Natalie sidling along with him. "We just need a little air."

"There's plenty of air in here," Alli observed suspiciously as he took hold of the doorknobs.

"Alli . . ." The warning came in duplicate from her sisters.

David drew the doors closed in front of him and then turned around to Natalie. Out of sight of the others, they stood apart and glared into each other's eyes, like prizefighters sizing up their opponents.

"I might as well ask," David said. "Who is he? How long have you been dating?"

Natalie planted her fists on her hips. "You don't get to ask me that. It's none of your business."

"According to you, nothing ever is." He strode away from her, calling out over his shoulder, "You know what—why the hell do I bother with you?"

She quickly caught up with him as he turned the corner in the hall, pushing his elbow to turn him around. "You have some nerve, David, walking off, acting all indignant, when you're the one repeating the same things that caused us trouble before."

"Oh, it's my fault?" he asked. "You're the one who can't see any good for the bad."

"I call it as I see it," she argued, her eyes flashing. "At least I'm not being impatient and judgmental—jumping to the wrong conclusions all the time like you. You're just angry because things aren't going the way you want them."

"I'm not angry. I'm disappointed because I thought this would turn out to be a good day." David turned on his heels. "I'm out of here. There's no talking with you."

"David, don't you dare leave me here with these people by myself."

"Watch me."

Natalie watched him walk off from her for the second time that day. When he reached the doors that opened onto the back patio, and kept walking, she let out the breath she held.

"Damn you, David Spenser."

"He'll be okay."

Natalie whirled around at Mrs. Hardy's voice, and was immediately contrite at having uttered the curse in her presence. "Oh, I'm sorry. I didn't know you were there."

She raised her brows as she put her arm around Natalie's shoulder. "Don't worry about me. I know enough about men to understand how they can make you say things you don't mean. And as for David, he's probably taking that hot car of his out for a spin. It'll do him good, but he'll be back."

"You probably think we're a sad duo for little Jake." Natalie shrugged her shoulders miserably. "But, David makes me so mad."

She smiled. "You and Alli are two of a kind—fonts of emotions. One moment you're moved to sentimentality, and the next you're angry. But that's okay, because it'll be a different one in the next moment."

"David hates that about me."

She turned Natalie around and they walked back down the hall. "No, I believe that's what he loves."

Natalie wasn't sure if she'd heard the older woman correctly, and darted a glance at her, only to see her brow quirked in amusement.

"Come," Mrs. Hardy said. "Davina has gone upstairs to get Jake so we can all spoil him in the salon. He'll at least need his godmother to act as interference."

Natalie smiled and, reluctantly, allowed herself to be led back with the family even as her last thoughts damned David once again. *He'd better get back soon.*

Almost two hours later, David hadn't returned and Natalie made her excuses to Davina and left.

The drive home was filled with scenario after scenario of how she could have explained how the date with Carter came about. In each situation, though, she always ended up arguing with David for some unreasonable comment he made.

She hit the steering wheel in frustration. There was just no winning with him, even in her thoughts.

Natalie turned into the entrance of her community and made her way to her town house. As she came upon her driveway, the car lights briefly illuminated something at her front door steps. It looked like a package.

Rather than drive her car into the garage, she stopped at its entrance and got out. Walking up the drive, she recognized a bouquet of flowers sitting on her doorstep—a mixture of fragrances uniting in the crisp evening air.

"David," Natalie said, and her heart took flight. "Aw, he's apologizing."

She dropped her purse and, stooping to scoop the vase into her arms, took a deep whiff of the flowers. "Ahh . . ."

Her mood was buoyant as she read the attached card out loud.

"Looking forward to tomorrow night at eight. Carter."

And just as suddenly, all pleasure left her. She pushed the card into the bouquet.

Natalie chided herself. She'd have to make the best out of this situation. She was going out with Carter, and she would have a good time. After all, she needed a night out, regardless of the reason, David's attitude be damned.

Still, if this was the right thing to do, why did she feel so bad? She hugged the flowers to her chest, and leaning back against the front door, closed her eyes as she drew on the fragrance again.

Chapter 13

Natalie turned around in the bedroom and critiqued her image in the cheval glass, all the while dancing to the churning urban beat offered from the radio.

Davina had come over earlier with the baby and, for tonight's date with Carter, had suggested this two-piece outfit with the shirred, fitted top and skirt that rode low on Natalie's hips. Sexy wasn't exactly what Natalie had been aiming for on this particular evening, but the red color had done an excellent job of lifting her mood. She popped her fingers to the sweet downbeat that floated through the air.

The reflection aimed back at her was ready to have a good time. What the hell, Natalie figured, and walked into her closet for a pair of shoes. She would have fun tonight, and she wouldn't waste it wondering about David and what he thought.

It took less than a minute to choose a striking pair of four-inch leather heels that left a good deal of foot exposed. She smiled, already feeling better about the evening ahead.

Ding-dong!

The doorbell rang with an almost gleeful gusto. Natalie looked at the bedside clock. It was eight o'clock, straight up. She had to give points to the man—he was punctual.

She slipped into the shoes and grabbed up her purse. As she turned off the radio and flicked the light switch on her way out of the bedroom, the phone rang.

"It never fails," Natalie muttered, but didn't miss a step as she went down the stairs. She reached for the phone on the foyer table while eyeing the caller ID screen. It was her mother. Instinctively, she stayed her hand from answering the ring. Mercifully, that was the last one before all went silent.

Ding-dong!

She let out a held breath. When she returned home tonight, she'd call her mother. *I will.* Definitely, tonight, she told herself, and buried her feelings of guilt and selfishness in the promise before opening the door to Carter.

Natalie didn't expect anything less than the nattily dressed man she saw at the office, and he didn't disappoint her, either.

"Hi, you're right on time," she said, smiling. She could tell that he wasn't disappointed, either. He cast an approving glance over her that was emphasized by a significant lift of his brows.

"As usual, Natalie, you're looking lovely." His eyes flowed downward. "And tall."

"Thank you." She pulled the door shut behind her. "I'm ready if you are."

"Fine with me." They walked toward his car sitting at the end of her drive. "Did you get the flowers?" he asked.

"Yes. Thank you. The florist had to leave them because I wasn't at home."

"I know." They had reached the car and he opened her door. "I brought the flowers over and left them."

Surprised, Natalie looked up as she ducked her head to get into the car, but Carter's face was cast in shadow before he pushed the door closed.

As he walked around the car to get in, Natalie couldn't shake the fact that he'd found her house and then come over without her knowledge. Damn David again for planting the notion that Carter couldn't be trusted. Was he right?

Carter slid behind the wheel. "Ready?"

"Sure." She turned to look at him. "Let's go."

Natalie and Carter arrived at the Casbah in Buckhead, and were immediately transported into another century.

Carter slowed his walk as he took in his surroundings. "All I can say is, wow."

"Me too."

The Mediterranean restaurant's décor was a hedonist's paradise, an experience in the meeting of sumptuous moods. With the feel and resemblance of a lavish, opulent Moroccan tent settled in the desert, long, sheer curtains hung along the back walls and windows, where they softly billowed on a light breeze that blew in from air circulating through tall door openings.

Tapestries of all sizes and all manners of ornamentation covered the walls, and thick, multipatterned rugs caressed every inch of the floors. The entire place was ablaze with bold color.

"Ooh . . . I love this," Natalie said, her eyes bright with curiosity and interest as they were shown to a large table near the middle of the room.

The low-slung tables occupying the room were in different sizes, some against the walls and others shaped to form a semicircle around a large space in the center of the restaurant. The tables were covered with red linen and surrounded by a host of colorfully decorated pillows, long, overstuffed stools, and legless chairs draped in purple cloth.

The seating was meant for relaxation since it didn't appear that any diner was ever more than a foot above the floor. Some couples near the wall had reclined on the padded sofa benches while they ate with their fingers from large trays of salad and fruit. It was early yet, and the restaurant was maybe at half occupancy, but Natalie could see a steady flow of customers appear from her seat location.

The musicians' area was across the room next to one of the large openings with flowing curtains. The Eastern rhythms—using drums, tambourines, and wind instruments—provided a steady, lilting beat that caused even the most unlikely of patrons to tap their feet and sway like the wind.

"Off with your shoes," the waiter urged them in a heavy accent, and gestured toward other guests who had done away with theirs.

Laughing, they complied, and Carter sat in the sloping chair with his legs stretched out to the side of the table. "I swear," he said, grinning from ear to ear. "This takes some getting used to. I feel like I'm in a beach chair."

While Carter ordered drinks, Natalie wiggled her toes into the plush rug. "Ooh . . . I can get into this."

"Yeah," he agreed. "I think this place fits you to a tee."

"So, what do you think?" she asked.

"Well, it's different." He leaned back as he planted his gaze on Natalie.

"I knew you'd hate it."

"If so, then why did you suggest it? Do you always try to alienate your dates?"

"We're not using that word, remember? To me, the important thing is that you are willing to try something different."

"Okay, I passed your test. Now, tell me about this place I'm willing to try."

"Well, it's wildly popular. I don't know why you haven't heard about it. They serve great couscous dishes, and the entertainment is first-rate."

"Couscous?" He raised his brows. "Entertainment?"

She laughed and rubbed her hands together. "Get your tips ready because they have belly dancers."

"Well, then, that should help the interesting food digest easily."

"You'll love it," Natalie said, and shifted so she could look at him. "So, tell me. You're not from this area, are you?"

"I've only been here since I joined Innervision just under a year ago." His brows knitted as he regarded her. "Did it bother you much that I came to your house yesterday?"

She carefully felt out his query. "Maybe. I don't like unexpected visitors, especially from a man I hardly know. Besides, a call would have been much more appropriate."

"I never figured you for appropriate. Quite the opposite," he said, humor in his voice. "But, I understand. You're in control, and don't rock your boat." When she smiled in response, he nodded. "I see."

The waiter arrived and set their drinks down before he explained the five-course meal procedure and began to take their order.

Natalie helped with Carter's choices, finally agreeing on a lentil soup for starters. Carter wasn't too game for the more exotic dishes, but accepted the Cornish hen appetizer. The waiter suggested a variety of Moroccan salads from which both of them could sample, and then he excused himself.

A scant moment later, Natalie was sipping from her drink when she looked up, almost choking from the view ahead. Coming through the door was Davina, followed by Justin and Alli. And David.

Her attention immediately perked up, and she straightened as best she could in the chair, craning her neck to catch their procession through the door. How on earth could this be? Hadn't she just lived this very same scenario two nights ago? Her growing frown's intensity alerted Carter.

"Something wrong?" He followed her gaze across the room.

"Ahh . . . that remains to be seen," she replied, her mind a crazy mixture of excitement and dread, and took another sip of her drink. Her eyes continued to squint at the small group standing at the entrance.

* * *

"Are we in the right place?" David asked, holding the door open for Alli.

"I think I've already asked that," Justin said, and turned to Davina. "So, what's up with this restaurant?"

"Stop it, both of you," she said. "I told you about it."

The two men looked around with obvious skepticism written on their faces, and then transmitted their disgust to each other in one look.

"I don't remember you telling me this much," Justin said.

"Yeah, otherwise I don't think I'd be here," David added.

"I wanted to try it out." Davina looked back at Alli, who was busy scanning the room. "So did Alli. Right?"

"Ah, yeah, right," Alli said, looking around.

David's mood was not good and he pushed a hand into his pocket and looked around, too. Justin was glancing at his watch, and the women were acting weirder than usual. He heard a tiny squeal from Alli and turned. Something interesting must have caught her eye as she scooted near Davina where the maître d' checked for their reservation. To his relief, though, shortly thereafter, they were led into the dining room.

Moving deeper into the restaurant, David thought it resembled something out of *The Arabian Nights*.

They followed the host to a table that was set up near the musicians, and just as they became interested in their chairs' design, David looked up and found Natalie in his line of sight, directly across the room. Incredulous, he froze for a moment before he announced the discovery to the others.

"Will you look at what we have here?" he said, his eyes still trained on hers in the low-lit room. "Natalie's here. With her date." *Carter from her office.*

"You're right," Davina said.

"Yep. That's her, all right," Alli agreed.

"Davina—" Justin started.

"I'll be right back," David said, and strode away, his gaze unwavering as it pinpointed his destination.

"David, don't you dare do anything that gets us thrown out, you hear?" His sister's words hit him in the back as he moved across the room.

"What does she see in that pompous jackass?" David asked the rhetorical question under his breath as he came upon them. Carter was sitting just a little too close to Natalie, he decided, and she didn't seem in the least ruffled or surprised that David had appeared.

"Carter?" David planted his feet in front of the table and looked down at the two. "I'm David Spenser," he said with a bland smile. "We meet again. I tell you, as often as I've heard your name and bumped into you in the last forty-eight hours, *we* ought to be dating." He let out a sour chuckle.

Carter bounded to his feet to shake David's hand, recognition in his eyes. "I remember meeting you at the office yesterday. Nice seeing you again, too." They both looked down at his shoeless feet.

"And what brings you to this particular restaurant, *Mr. Spenser?*" Natalie looked up from her chair, a leisurely smile curling her lips.

"And hello to you, too, *Ms. Goodman.* I tell you, it's a small world."

"Too small, if you ask me," she said.

"This little outing was cooked up by my sister." He turned and motioned to the group still standing at the table near the musicians before he looked back at Carter. "I'm sure if she'd known that our good friend Natalie was going to be here, she would've booked a table together."

Carter turned around and looked at Natalie, who was fervently shaking her head at him. He turned back to David. "We, ah, still have seats free at our table." He looked over at the group. "How many? Four of you? Come on over and join us."

Natalie struggled to rise up by herself from the floor. "I'm sure they don't want to do that." She stood in front of Carter and reared back to glare into David's face. "Do you, David?"

"Actually, I think it's a great idea," he said, looking over Natalie's head to Carter. "Thanks for the offer, man." He raised his hand and signaled to Justin and the others to come over. At about that same moment, a great sigh escaped Natalie.

"We've already ordered our meal," she complained.

"Just the appetizers," Carter said. "Natalie knows a lot about this restaurant; she was a big help with the menu."

"Is that right?" David asked, turning his attention on Natalie. "I'm glad you mentioned it."

When she gave him a daggered stare, he ground out his own derisive smile.

"In fact," David said, "I think I'll sit right next to her. I'm going to need as much help as she can give."

Chapter 14

"So . . . you're the Carter we keep hearing Natalie talk about," Alli said, an eager smile dazzling on her face.

Lifting her head, Natalie was incredulous at the cheeky comment, quite aware by now that Alli's game was to make David jealous.

Alli had done a pretty good job of it, seemingly infatuated herself with Carter; and he, too, hadn't seemed to mind that Alli, seated on his other side, had monopolized his attention and the table conversation since the group had first sat down twenty minutes ago. Now, she was lapsing into another discussion.

Natalie looked across the big, circular table and eyeballed Davina until she was forced to look up. In a helpless gesture, Davina hunched her shoulders in defeat that things had gotten out of hand. She then busied herself by tearing off a crust of bread from one of the huge, dimpled loaves that had been set out on the table, avoiding Natalie's eyes.

Meanwhile, in his chair next to Natalie, a muscle flicked at David's angular jaw as his eyes narrowed on her.

Natalie raised her voice above the growing din of the fast-filling restaurant. "You joined us just to glare at me?"

"It's hard not to," he said, his voice low as his eyes took in all they could about her. "You're looking . . . nice."

"After the week I've had in the office, I deserve to let loose a little tonight," she replied. "And I thought Carter might prefer if I ditched the black suit and pumps."

He grunted his displeasure at the name, pushing aside the soup he'd sampled earlier. "Tell me, whose idea was it to come to this place—yours, or your, ah"—he nodded toward Carter, who was busy with Alli—"date's?"

"No one asked you to follow us."

He let out a deep masculine laugh that was quickly lost in the music and chatter. "You think I'd pay to come eat on the floor with my shoes off, and on purpose?"

Natalie leaned into him. "No, you wouldn't—that would take a person looking for a new and different experience."

As David measured her with a cool, appraising look, Natalie was aware of his pleasant scent, a light manliness that floated into her head. It was almost intoxicating, and she didn't want to move away.

"Congratulations."

"Huh?" she asked.

"On rounding up somebody new and something different," he said.

Natalie jerked her head back, unhappy that he'd twisted her words. "You don't like the restaurant, then leave."

"Uh-uh. Not a chance," he said with a wide grin.

Natalie looked across at Justin, her eyes pleading for help.

"Don't look at me," he said with an equal grin. "I'm just an innocent victim in all this, listening to the music and sampling the food."

Carter turned from his conversation with Alli and leaned toward Natalie. "Everything all right?" he asked as the waiter set two more large, ornate platters in the middle of the table, after having whisked away the remnants of their last course.

"Just fine." She spat the words out before she turned and

leaned in close to him. "You shouldn't have invited them over," she whispered gruffly.

"What was I supposed to say to your friends?" he answered softly. "They seem pretty nice—for the most part, anyway." He nodded toward David. "Is something going on between you two? He seemed okay the other afternoon."

David now turned and leaned toward them, innocence glowing in his eyes. "Something wrong?"

Natalie rolled her eyes at him, but he dared to stare right back with benign curiosity. She turned back to her food and ignored both men.

So what if David was irritated that she was out with Carter and enjoyed this little turnabout? Why should she care enough to let it get to her? Admittedly, a part of her was glad that he still showed an interest; yet she felt compelled to let him know, despite her own rising passion when he was around, that he didn't own her, and that he couldn't dictate what she could do.

She heaved a sigh. Was that screwed-up thinking, or what?

She watched him talking easily with Justin, effortlessly hiding the displeasure he'd shown her.

If the truth be known, she wanted nothing more than to be here with David—alone, maybe on a plush sofa seat like the one Justin and Davina lounged on, but in his arms, with his mouth . . .

Alli's sharp laughter, mixed with the jangle of her jewelry, cracked through the heavy layer of sounds in the restaurant.

"It's hard to believe it took this long for you two to go out," she was saying to Carter. "But, of course, maybe you were dating someone else. And God knows, Natalie sure wasn't—"

Natalie's eyes drew into a frown at the same time David's leg collided with hers beneath the low table.

"—sitting around at home," she added.

"What are you, Alli, the *Enquirer*?" Natalie snapped matter-of-factly.

Justin laughed as he looked across the table. "Nothing like sharing good food—"

"What's this?" David declared as he leaned over to inspect the exotically detailed platter he found in front of him.

"—and good times with friends," Justin finished.

"It looks good," Alli said. "But how do we dish it out without a serving fork?"

"With your fingers." Natalie looked up, realizing that she and Carter had spoken at the same time.

She raised a brow at him, but continued. "Like this," she explained, and reached into one platter filled with colorful salad greens, roasted vegetables—too numerous to identify—and filled three fingers before she turned to one of several dipping sauces nearby, and touched the food to one. "That's it. Go ahead and try it."

As she brought the ultimate concoction to her mouth, she realized she was still the center of attention. Straightening up, she chewed on the sweet and nutty mixture in her mouth and looked at her fellow diners.

"What?" she asked. "Go on, what are you waiting for?"

Davina reached over and tentatively imitated Natalie's motions, followed by Justin, and then the others.

"Mmm . . . it's not bad," Davina announced between chews.

"Of course not," Natalie challenged. "Isn't that why you're here, to try new things?" She selected a morsel from the second platter.

"I thought that was *your* driving force." David whispered the comment as he followed her example and next sampled the toasted hens buried in couscous and green pods. "Do you always act out your pleasure principle?"

Natalie paused a moment. So, he did hear a little more at the door yesterday than he'd let on, which accounted for his poor manners last night and again tonight. He probably thought Carter was going to become the one-night stand she'd mentioned. It'd serve him right to get all aggravated over that prospect, she decided with a smile.

"You should try my principle," she said, and licked her lips from the chicken she chewed. "You'd be surprised at how freeing it can be."

She reached for her large linen napkin, but it slipped from the table and dropped to the small space between them. David reached for it at the same time as Natalie, but in doing so, trapped her hand beneath his under the tablecloth.

"I've got it," she whispered.

"No, you don't get it at all."

She looked into his eyes, only inches from her own. "Well, then tell me."

His hand closed tightly over hers. "Don't act like you're blind or a fool, because you're neither." He held her stare as she snatched at her hand, but the movement only dragged both of their hands into her lap.

Natalie squirmed at the intimate connection inches from the juncture of her thighs.

"You want to push me away? Go ahead, push all you want," he whispered at her ear. "But we know we have some unfinished business."

"And your point is?"

"I don't intend to let you just walk away this time, because you don't want me to."

It wasn't what Natalie expected to hear from the angry David of last night. He slowly released her hand, but his own slid back across the curve of her thigh, as though to mark it in memory. He then quietly placed the napkin on the table before he turned to the platters of food and resumed conversation with the others.

Natalie swallowed hard, and darted a glance down at her scorched hand and thigh. She didn't like this hellish place that she'd been cornered into. And it was all because she and David didn't fit into any of her neat categories she used for relationships.

He wasn't a former lover in the true sense, yet she could recall, with red-hot accuracy, simple intimacies they'd shared that could even now heat her blood. He was a friend, yet she wanted to break her own principle and sleep with him so badly that she could feel the tingle and taste the sensation.

Natalie was in this weird midpoint where she needed protection from her own traitorous thoughts, and she'd never get it under David's scrutiny tonight. She looked across the table at Davina, and saw her friend smile—lost in something her husband was saying against her ear.

"Whew." Natalie's senses were becoming hyperactive. Her nipples ached, her thighs throbbed clear to her center core, and a glowing shiver of heat steadily emanated from inside. Something had to give soon with David or she could spontaneously combust on the spot.

The evening progressed, and David didn't stop with his looks and dares that, at every opportunity, proved his earlier point. As the sultry music played, and the food materialized nonstop, Natalie's thoughts grew bolder and bolder when she looked at David. His gaze continued to wrap around Natalie like a scorching blanket, and settled as a tingling in the pit of her stomach, only to start all over again.

Over an hour had passed since the group had joined as one. The music was now gradually changing tempo, and the waiter was quickly clearing away dishes. The group had settled into a familiarity that included Carter, though to Natalie, David's cynicism occasionally stuck out like a sore thumb.

"Natalie mentioned that you work security for your company," David said.

Carter nodded. "But I'm sure she didn't say anything too flattering. She doesn't hold the work in too high a regard," he added.

"Maybe it's the company you keep," she said, smiling.

"I understand you're a lawyer in a well-known firm," Carter said to David.

Natalie looked up at his comment, unable to remember sharing that with him, and wondered if David thought she'd been discussing him.

David, though, was shifting in his chair. "Do you like the security field?"

"It has its advantages," Carter replied.

"I'll bet it does. . . ." David left his meaning hanging.

Justin quickly spoke up. "I have a friend in the security business; he's a local private eye," he said. "He does quite a bit of work with the firms around town."

Carter raised his brows. "Oh . . . I might know of him. What's his name?"

Before Justin could answer, the restaurant lights blinked and the noise level dropped appreciably as the rhythms played by the musicians took a deeper, more primal beat and the flowing curtains near the large doorways dramatically lifted.

"The entertainment's about to start," Natalie said.

"What entertainment?" David asked, looking around.

"You didn't hear? There are belly dancers," Justin said, leaning back to enjoy the show. "Carter told me about it during one of your discussions with Natalie."

David grinned and eased back in his own chair. "Now I see why you didn't up and leave a long time ago."

In fact, it appeared no one had left the now packed restaurant. Even the staff had lined the walls to watch the show. The sultry music had the full tables of diners swaying to the beat, and the small group's table was no exception. Suddenly, a series of tambourine and drum rhythms announced the dancers—four shapely women in a single file, already bobbing their hips to the heated beat—as they came through the side entrances.

The saucy, henna-painted women were dressed in gold, silver, black, and teal-caped harem attire, and under a spotlight, pranced through the tables to enter the center area.

The lead dancer, a black-haired beauty named Anya, explained the art of belly dancing—the dance of love, as they called it—and how the body is used to interpret the music's mood. In an eye-opening display, they then showed the techniques that made the art so sensual.

Intrigued by it all, Natalie looked around and saw that all of the men had ridiculous glassy-eyed smiles on their faces. Pleasure was about the power—and the dancers controlled the room right now.

The dancers immediately went to work. The garments were made to accentuate their every body movement, from twisting hands and nimble feet to jutting breasts barely covered and hips undulating with fierce abandon.

Natalie thought it was enough to make the women glassy-eyed, too.

To further emphasize their abilities, the dancers balanced candles, swords, even daggers and water gourds in their hands and on their heads. Numerous veils were attached to their headpieces, and came off in a coquettish seduction aimed at the audience.

All wore their hair long, and flowing down their backs, and they showed wide, seductive smiles that were indicative of the pleasure they were getting in presenting their craft.

Instinctively, Natalie turned to David, but saw that his eyes, like the others at the table, were glued to the dancing women. To their credit, though, the agile beauties had mesmerized the entire room of men and women.

Dance after dance was outstanding, but one, with an exceptional acrobatic movement, stood out. The teal-veiled lead dancer, Anya, tore away her veil; suddenly, her swaying hands and limbs floated wide apart as her fluid, butterfly-like bend backward kept getting lower and lower, and the music tempo became faster and faster, until her hair dragged along the carpet and her head nearly touched the floor. She then sensuously contorted her body in ways that kept the steam level high amid the chorus of cheers in the room before she began to rise up again.

The audience loved it, and showed their appreciation in rousing ovations and applause. The dancers were clearly an attraction for the restaurant—this was an opportunity to witness the premiere moves of some of the country's best belly dancers.

Diners were already holding bills aloft to tuck into the waist of the harem outfits, and the dancers walked among the tables to collect the tips.

"Did you see that?" David asked, reaching for his wallet. "I swear she touched the floor."

"The way all of you were gawking at them, you ought to tip very well," Natalie said.

"Oh, yeah," Justin said, pulling bills from his wallet. "Anya should be tipped for that back bend alone."

Davina grimaced. "It looked like it hurt."

"Yeah, that was pretty freaky," Carter agreed with a chuckle.

"I didn't know everybody would react this way," Alli said. "It almost makes a woman want to take belly dancing lessons."

"Almost," Natalie and Davina said in unison, before they laughed.

While the men tucked the bills into the dancers' waists when they came to the table, Davina said, "Jeez, it must take years of practice to get your body to go in two directions at once."

"I don't think it's that hard to roll your stomach and shake your butt at the same time," Natalie said. "All you have to do is a takeoff on the *bootylicious* bounce. Hey, I even saw Oprah do it on her show."

"Easy for you to say," Alli said while the others erupted in laughter.

"I'm telling you," Natalie said, caught up in everyone's lighthearted mood. "It's just mind over matter and, of course, knowing how to move, that's all."

Caught up in the moment, she began to undulate in time to the hypnotizing percussion beat being played by the musicians.

"Come, then." The nimble, dark-haired dancer who had managed the difficult back bend appeared from nowhere and took up one of Natalie's hands. "For audience participation—you'll be great." She looked to the men. "Tell her, guys."

"No, no," Natalie said, pulling her hand back. "I was just kidding."

"Ah, I think you want to perform the dance of love," the dancer insisted, and looked at David seated next to her. "Maybe for the one you love, huh? Come on."

"Go on, Natalie."

"Do it."

The support came from all around the table, with David being the notable exception.

He had turned silent and his earlier smile had vanished as he now watched her with a critical squint. Though he didn't say it, his face spoke disapproval for this and, in Natalie's mind, practically every other action of hers. And because she did sense his displeasure, she went for the brass ring.

"Okay," she said, and started to get up. "I'm game."

And with a parting smile to David's growing frown, she allowed herself to be helped from her chair by the dancers.

Chapter 15

David gritted his teeth as he studied Natalie making her way from the table, every beautiful curve of her body swaying in exaggerated defiance of the silent challenge he'd inadvertently offered. When she joined the belly dancers in the center of the floor, and was introduced as tonight's guest dancer, applause filled the room.

"Leave it to Natalie to spike up the action," Alli said.

"Actually, Natalie is the action," Carter said with a chuckle.

"You're right," Davina agreed and looked at her brother. "You can't sit back when she's around; she's quite fearless."

David met his sister's probing eyes, but gave up no clues to his own inner turmoil. He leaned back in the chair, intent on enjoying Natalie's impulsive show. If she wanted to prove something, which was usually the case with Natalie, then let her. Seeking her out on the floor, he let his eyes roam her figure at his leisure.

She was the shortest of the group; but to David, she was also the sexiest—her hourglass figure put emphasis on an already bare waist David was sure he could span with his hands. He drew a deep breath while he watched the dancers drape a netted, golden sash embedded with bells around her hips.

The sash hugged her firm butt and accentuated her sleek thighs, all the while touting an exotic chime with each move. Finally, a matching diaphanous veil was fitted across her face, leaving only her eyes exposed to express emotion. She was a siren, dressed in red and gold, ready to cause havoc; and when David raised his gaze to her eyes, he could have sworn they smiled back at him. A challenge?

Scowling, David shifted on the chair as the lead dancer, Anya, stepped behind Natalie. As she stood there, Anya placed her hands against Natalie's hips and, in a rocking motion, demonstrated how to move, thrust, and roll the belly in time to the music. The musicians then picked up the cadence with a lilting, infectious beat that accommodated each hesitant hip swing.

"Look at that," Alli exclaimed with a laugh. "She's actually doing it."

David could see that and more, and moved restlessly in the chair. Suddenly, he realized why he hadn't been happy about Natalie being up there. He was jealous that she was sharing her sensual side. He didn't want to share her with others, and especially Carter and a room of strangers.

Initially, Natalie's movements were cautious; but as the music soared and the audience got into the act, she became more at ease with the technique, and she grew bolder.

With each audacious thump of Natalie's hips, David's thoughts turned primal and lusty as he unconsciously answered her with a thrust of his own, his blood rising at the thought of the exquisite delight she presented. She was a feast for the eyes and a promise of release to the body. . . .

"David . . ."

He felt a kick come from under the table and looked across at Justin and his sister, who had leaned toward him.

"Close your mouth," she said, teasing him as she giggled. "You're drooling."

David ignored her humor as he let out the breath he'd been holding, quickly returning his attention to Natalie's sinuous dance. If she continued on this way, it was going to take some amount of control on his part to get through the rest of the evening with his dignity still intact.

Pulling her shoulders together in a come-hither move, Natalie swayed forward, her eyes on David for a moment, and her hips shimmying to the music's vibrato and the dancers' encouragement. Turning, she began to lean backward, similar to the approach one took for a limbo stick, her face lost in the gossamer veil. The lush move was sensuous in its simplicity, and caused most in the room to applaud to the beat, as they'd done before. They were beginning to come to their feet.

Natalie tried Anya's deep back bend, not with so much of the earlier dancer's acrobatic worth, but with a waving, bouncing motion that propelled her far enough down to amaze the crowd. With her final seductive dip, amid the percussion's insistent throb, the crowd responded with cheers at her effort.

Swallowing deeply, David felt a familiar, pleasurable tightening in his groin, and shifted once again in the chair while Natalie regained her footing and snatched away the veil. And as the music reduced its tempo and volume, the crowd, including staff from the back, gave her loud applause. Pressed by the group of dancers to take a bow, Natalie took a deep breath, as well.

"Wasn't that great?" Anya called out to everyone, and motioned for Natalie to step forward and take another bow for the appreciative audience.

David reluctantly stood with the others to give Natalie her due. He could see in her eyes, bright with excitement, that she loved this . . . this control. She would go so far as to call it power. It was a sobering moment to David, too. He wouldn't deny that Natalie was well settled in his blood, and he was going to have her as his—with or without the commitment she avoided. He would simply have to convince her to be of the same mind.

Natalie beamed with the blood rush of accomplishment, and looked across to her table of friends who had stood to clap eagerly with the crowd. Instinctively, she searched out David's face and found that his eyes were exactly where she wanted them: on her.

She hoped that he was as uncomfortably warmed by her performance as she'd been all evening by his bold reminders of their past that her body couldn't forget.

Wearing a wide grin, she reached out to receive the gift Anya presented for the performance: the gold-threaded sash and matching veil. She stroked the butter-soft material, suddenly intrigued by the idea of what this must feel like against naked skin.

"I think I should start the apologies about now," Natalie said as she twisted on the car seat to face Carter.

He darted a glance her way as he drove her home. "For what? We had a great dinner, and the entertainment . . . well, the entertainment was unbelievable. I mean, the belly dancers, and you—" He stopped to glance her way again. "Where did you say you learned that limbo move?"

"Stop it," she said, laughing. "Don't make it out to be more than what it was."

"Your friend, David, was the only one who didn't have much to say afterward. What gives with you two?"

I wish I knew. Natalie took a deep breath before dropping her head against the seat. "We're trying to navigate some rather sharky waters right now." She turned to him. "Does that make it any clearer?"

He smiled. "As mud."

"Good. Now, about that apology on account of my friends." She looked straight ahead and let out a desperate sigh. "I figure I owe you one."

He chuckled out loud. "I told you that's not necessary, but is it really that unpleasant, being in debt to me?"

"Except for the fact that you take up with the likes of Blakely, you're not that bad." She turned his way. "Alli sure seems to think so."

He smiled. "Taking your friends as a whole, I didn't have a problem with them. They seem okay."

Surprised by his forgiving attitude, she turned sideways on the car seat. "Still, David's behavior was borderline, and—"

"All right, then." He looked over at her. "How about I decide when and how to cash in?"

She frowned. "Am I about to regret something here?"

He turned the car into her subdivision. "If you're worried about me becoming a stalker, don't, even though I did come over last night without your permission."

"Don't take it personally. I only agreed to let you meet me at my house because I figure we work together, and I do know a bit about you."

"You won't get any argument out of me when it comes to your safety." Carter pulled up in front of her house and stopped the car. "I'm the first to say that it always pays to be careful."

"Be careful, huh?" She looked up at him, remembering their time at the elevator, and then the note. "Why did you say it like that?"

He turned to her. "That it pays to be careful? I guess because there are a lot of crazy things going on in the world."

Even though his face looked blank, Natalie bit at her lip and, on impulse, asked him if he wanted to come inside for a bit.

Carter pulled the key from the ignition. "All right."

Once inside the foyer, she led him to the living room where she dropped her things on one of the couches and offered him a seat on the other.

As he took the seat, he looked around the room. "Nice place."

With her arms crossed, she remained standing. "Thanks." And then, without hesitation, she got to the point. "I found a note in my car when I got home the other evening. Did you slip it into my bags on the elevator the other evening at the office?"

Carter, already sitting back on the sofa, slid forward to the edge. "Whoa, you're going real fast here . . . a note? What are you talking about?"

"The note that found its way into my bags sometime between when I left Innervision and arrived home. Did you leave it for me to find?"

"I haven't the vaguest idea of what you're talking about."

Natalie sighed, and relaxed her stance. "There was a note with the words 'be careful' in large print left with my things." She turned to Carter. "I found it when I took my bags from my trunk Thursday night."

"And you think I left it there?" he asked flatly.

"I'm figuring you had the opportunity when you helped me at the elevator, remember? You wouldn't let me carry my own things to my car. And a minute ago, you reminded me that I should be careful, which is exactly what the cheesy little note said." It hadn't all tied together for Natalie, but she needed to start somewhere.

Carter's perplexed look slowly turned into a smile. "You're making a Grand Canyon jump. What I said in the car was just a—"

"One thing I've noticed about you tonight is that you don't 'just' say anything." She watched as Carter's brows rose from the reprimand, and he leaned back on the sofa again. Natalie, with her lips pursed, sat on the other one.

"You told David you knew he was a lawyer with a local firm," she accused. "I never told you that."

"Well, I may have heard it from Alli, or someone else at the table," he countered.

"Did you?"

He drew a deep breath as he braided his fingers. "Actually, I don't recall—"

"And the food we were served tonight . . ." Her eyes turned into twin squints. "I think you're more familiar with Mediterranean food than you let on, aren't you? I mean, I boned up on it beforehand." She waved her hand in the air. "But that's the kind of thing I'd do."

Carter laughed as he shook his head at her comments.

"I'll bet you even let me think I twisted your arm into going there."

"Or, maybe I just read up on the place, too."

"I saw you dive into that salad after your comment. You were handling that stuff too well for a first-timer." She peered at him curiously from her chair. "Someone once told me there's no such thing as coincidence. And you know what? I think there's a lot more to you than you're letting on, Mr. Carter Johnson."

"Okay, I did check out David."

"Why?"

"Curious about the other man, I guess, and because I can." He stood up from the sofa. "And yes, I've been to the Casbah, but it wasn't part of some devious plot." He smiled with open hands. "I wanted to make a good impression tonight. That's all."

"Now I'm beginning to wonder if there isn't more to your tenacity in getting me to go out from the start."

"And you'd be selling yourself short," he said with a glance. "Don't ever doubt that you're very good with detail." He grinned. "It's no wonder you're an accountant."

Natalie grunted off the compliment as she stood, too. "So you didn't leave a cryptic note for me to find?"

"Obviously, someone's playing a joke on you with that."

She scratched her head in thought. "Yeah, maybe. I had all but forgotten about that note until tonight." Slowly, she started to pace the room. "It's not a funny joke, though, when I don't get the punch line."

"So, who do you know that would do that? One of your friends? David?"

"No, they would have admitted to it by now." She stopped and looked at Carter. "Sean was with us at the elevator. Do you think he did it?"

Carter shook his head. "For what reason? I thought he barely knew you. I'd say look to your friends. That's your best source." He glanced at his watch.

"It's getting late," Natalie said.

Running his hand across his head, Carter nodded. "I'd better go. It was a nice, and interesting, evening; but I hope my, uh, confession didn't hurt things between us."

Natalie smiled as they walked to the door. "No, but I appreciate your honesty."

"So, we're still speaking friends?" he asked.

She smiled. "We're still speaking friends."

They stepped through the door and were immediately bathed in the bright light that illuminated the small porch.

"You and your friends were talking about all your plans between now and your godchild's christening." He stopped in front of Natalie. "Are you coming into Innervision next week?"

"Unfortunately, I'm doomed to have a face-off with Blakely in the near future, but I've managed to put it off until Wednesday."

"Well, I'll see you then." He took a step forward and bent toward Natalie, but she tilted her head ever so slightly and his lips made a soft landing against her temple.

They both smiled at the mishap. "I was only going for the forehead," he said.

"And I was just making sure," she teased.

With a final grin, he left her on the porch and walked back to his car. "Don't forget you owe me," he called out.

Natalie waved and walked back into the house. Locking the door, she thought over Carter's answers, which he'd given quickly and fully, and with little subterfuge. So, why was there something niggling at the back of her mind?

She needed to get some exercise in before bed, but she wanted to take a quick peek at Innervision's list of auditors. Kicking her shoes off at the base of the stairs, she moved toward her study where David had taken her files.

On top of the desk, beneath a crystal paperweight, sat the note. It was in that moment that it dawned on Natalie what had seemed odd. Not once had Carter shown any curiosity in looking at the note she had so earnestly accused him of leaving.

* * *

Ding-dong!

When Natalie turned her ear toward the doorbell, her rhythm was thrown off and she missed the jump, causing her feet to become entangled in the thick exercise rope.

"Oh, hell," she panted, aggravated at the interruption, and bent over. With hands pressed to knees, she caught her breath from the strenuous exercise. Turning, she took a quick glance at the clock in the bookcase. It had been thirty minutes since Carter left, so it wasn't him at the door. Or was it?

She straightened up and, dropping the rope where she stood, left the study for the front door, her padded sports slippers silent as she walked through the foyer.

Ding-dong! Ding-dong!

Annoyed by the caller's insistence, she pulled at the towel draped around her neck and blotted the moisture on her face, her neck, and then the front of her sports bra.

She looked through the peephole, and her eyes widened even as her heart pounded in double time. It was David, his square jaw visibly tensed.

A sweet shock of energy sluiced through her center, and Natalie gave no thought to the consequence of allowing him in. She simply wiped her sweaty palms against her fleece pants and turned the locks to open the door.

Chapter 16

"What are you doing here?" she asked, looking up at him.

It was as though David kissed Natalie with his eyes—their intense chemistry's reaction sent a delicious shudder through her heated body. He seemed to be able to take her all in at one glance; but then again, so did she.

He still wore the casual suit from dinner, which set off his athletic body well. A shaft of light from the porch struck his short, curling hair in such a way that it gleamed like black rain.

"Can we talk?" he asked in a husky whisper.

Natalie could feel herself being drawn into his spell and took a deep breath. "I can't imagine why I'd want to do that."

"Okay, then I'll talk."

"Your actions tonight already said volumes. In fact, I'm surprised you don't suspect I have someone here now."

Vetoing her earlier decision, she started to close the door, but David stopped her.

"I probably deserved that," he said, his deep voice apologetic. "But, Natalie, please . . ."

She sighed as her heart thumped wildly.

". . . Give me the chance to say a few things."

Relenting, Natalie released the door, and allowed him to

come in, but left him there while she walked back to the study.

David's appreciative eye followed the hypnotic sway of her hips. She was about attitude tonight, and he had a lot of ground to cover.

"You're exercising this time of night?" he asked, closing the door. "You'll never get to sleep."

"Apparently you haven't taken notice of my appetite." She looked over her shoulder at him. "Unlike Davina, I have to exercise," she said, turning into the study.

David joined her there, but succumbed to his wayward thoughts once again when she bent over to move the jumping rope and weights.

It didn't matter what Natalie chose to wear—it was impossible to hide the fact that she had exceptional curves beneath. Even now, with the baggy gym pants, her bare midriff and flat stomach gave preview to the flare of curvaceous hips farther down.

"Well, what are you waiting for? You can speak your mind whenever you're ready," she said, turning to him.

No, I can't. David's eyes strayed upward and stopped at round, full breasts safely encased in the brightly colored sports top, which did nothing to ease the ache he'd carried all evening. His gaze traveled across delicate facial bones carved around a full mouth, and short tufts of black curls held back with a sports band—and flawless, chocolate skin. *Focus,* he reminded himself.

"First, it wasn't my idea to eat at that restaurant. I was as surprised as you were."

"I suspect Davina will have to fess up to that."

When she strolled the few paces to her desk, David's gaze pursued her. Office files were spread across the desktop as though she'd been working. He walked over and joined her.

"When I saw who you were with," he continued, "well, I'll admit that it pissed me off."

"So, you took advantage of Carter's goodwill just so you could make my evening miserable."

"I was out of line, true, but you weren't entirely innocent tonight, either." Deliberately casual, he walked forward until he stopped in front of her, and then pushed his hands deep into his pockets. "I didn't like the idea that you chose to be with someone besides me."

Natalie leaned back and looked David fully in the face. "We were doing so well together at the Hardys', and I tried to tell you that tonight wasn't a *date* date, and that you and I could—"

"I know, I know. Davina and Mrs. Hardy have already raked me over the coals," David tried to explain. "It's one thing to know you're dating when I don't see it. Up close, it's a killer."

"And that justifies your impatience, arrogance, and—"

"What about you and that dance?" he asked, frowning at her dead-on analysis. "You shook and shimmied in front of the whole room. Don't tell me that wasn't to get back at me."

"So, you figure we're even?"

David could only smile, and when she joined him, it broke the ice. "I honestly didn't come here to make things worse. In fact, I'm going to show restraint and not even ask if you kissed Carter good night."

"Why should you care? You'd be asking as a friend, anyway."

David wouldn't answer, but instead drew her curious stare. It was time for them to cut the friendship pretense and get to the chase.

When Natalie frowned, it was as though she'd read David's mind. "I need a drink of water." She moved around him and left the study for the kitchen.

David followed her to where she stood facing the counter. "What's wrong with me not wanting anyone kissing you but me?"

"Because friends don't indulge in meaningful kissing." She stood on her toes and reached into the cabinet for a glass when she felt David brush against her from behind, easily reaching over her. He retrieved the glass and then set it on the counter.

"I decided tonight, right about the time you put on that gold veil," he said quietly against her back, "that this friend deal didn't work for me. No friend should have the thoughts I had tonight about another friend."

Natalie slowly turned around to face David, and found herself flush between him and the counter.

She held her breath. "How do you suppose we change from being friends?"

Leaning in, David gripped the counter on either side of Natalie, effectively trapping her to him.

"By doing this. . . ."

He bent his head and brushed a gentle kiss across her temple and cheek.

". . . And then, this." His last words were smothered against her lips when he captured them.

Natalie's heartbeat skyrocketed as she allowed the pleasure to unfurl. The first touch of his lips was a delicious, persuasive sensation she didn't want to end; as his hungry mouth covered hers again and again, she rose up on tiptoe and parted her lips to take in each erotic kiss. But, she wanted . . . needed more.

In the midst of a storm of initial emotions, Natalie was achingly aware that only their mouths touched.

Instinctively, David and Natalie reached for each other at the same time. She wound her arms inside David's jacket and around his back, stroking his smoothly rippled muscles with abandon. His hands had already begun to caress her sensitive lower back, exploring its hollows and sides in time with the movement of their mouths.

Pressing against him, Natalie couldn't get close enough, and she let out a groan when she felt his erection, hard as stone, waiting for her. Natalie knew, without a doubt, they were quickly coming upon the point of no return.

David stroked the upper curves of her hips before his hands

found their way into her loose waistband, slipping under the sports thong's thin strap, to explore and then cup her twin cheeks.

Thinking she would explode from her heated blood, Natalie encircled his neck with her arms as she gave herself over to the forceful domination of his lips and thrusting tongue.

Suddenly, finding herself being lifted in David's hands, she wrapped her legs around his hips and then pressed intimately against his strong erection, rocking in a timeless rhythm of their own making.

Holding on to her last corner of sanity, she turned her head and buried her face in his neck, taking in his husky scent and breathing a kiss there.

"David, what are we doing?" she managed to whisper. His breathing was uneven against her cheek, and she knew he was deeply affected, too.

"Killing the damn friendship."

He set her down gently on the counter, his hands moving to curve around her waist as he captured her mouth again.

"I want to make love to you . . . tonight . . . now."

Love. Natalie's eyes opened. Other men had said that to her, but with David it meant something different. She didn't have the will to say no, so she feebly tried to dodge his probing kisses.

"You want more." He leaned into her, whispering in her hair. "I saw it in your eyes that first night I was back, and you know we'll be good together." He kissed her again. "I can't understand why you won't let our bodies join and make music."

A warm glow flowed through Natalie in knowing that he wanted her, but the news gave her no peace or satisfaction.

Reluctantly, they finally separated a few inches; and then, taking a deep, unsteady breath, Natalie pulled back to look at him from her perch on the counter.

"Why did you come here tonight and open all of this up again?" She stroked his dark brow and then trailed her fingers down his face as she talked. "It didn't work for us before, David, so all we had to do was accept that it was finished."

"But, does it feel finished for you?" He traced his fingertip across her lips, still moist from his mouth. "Or do you have wild thoughts and vivid dreams about what could have been?"

Awareness caused Natalie's eyes to flutter closed for a moment. She couldn't answer him, because he was right.

"It's hard for me to look at you and forget how we were that last night together or even a few minutes ago." His finger dropped to sear a path between her breasts to her navel. "That kind of memory in a man's head can drive him crazy, Natalie, especially if he knows his woman feels the same way."

His woman. Natalie swallowed as a delicious warmth rose like a tide inside her. "Right now, sex is this uncharted game for us, but suppose our fun turns out to be something much more serious like . . . maybe love?" She tilted her head. "Then what?"

"Then I guess we'll have to run out and get married and prove your ideas about relationships wrong."

"That's if both of us end up feeling the same way." She gazed deeply into his eyes. "What if only one of us feels love? We'll end up hurt, angry, and . . . and think of all our friends we share. It would all be screwed up forever."

He smiled as he stroked her arm. "So, you're afraid I'll fall in love with you, and then you'll have to break my heart because you're not into that 'happily ever after' stuff?"

"Yeah, sort of."

"Or, you could be thinking you'll end up falling in love with me, and then I'll break your heart." David's expression sobered. "The way your father broke your mother's heart."

Natalie frowned. "What are you talking about? Did Davina tell you—"

David caught her hands up in his and, leaning into her, held them between their bodies.

"She didn't tell me anything. It doesn't take a rocket scientist to figure out that your issues with commitment are probably rooted in your past." He sighed. "But it seems to be my curse that I want to make love with a woman whom I can love, but that woman only wants sex with a man she can't love."

"Okay, so I sound a little crazy when you put it like that. All the more reason to stay clear of me." She let out a tentative smile. "Out of sight, out of mind, you know."

"I tried that in D.C., remember?" David asked, cocking his brow at her. "And it didn't work—for you, either, it seems." He kissed the soft cleavage that formed above her sports bra.

Natalie closed her eyes for a moment and stroked his hair. "We have to consider the consequences of having sex."

He raised his head. "Making love," he corrected. "And not as friends, we won't." David's arms straddled her again on the counter. "From this point on, as long as you know where I'm coming from, I can wait for you to figure out whatever it is that's going on in that head of yours. But not as a friend."

Natalie swallowed hard, not happy over the decision she had to make.

"Tell me, Natalie, why does everything get your pleasure treatment, except this one important thing—our mutual pleasure?"

She looked down at her hands. "My principle only serves to remind me to do what makes me happy." She turned her gaze back up to him. "Becoming lovers can turn into misery."

"Don't expect me to apologize for trying to change your mind . . . and I will. Remember, though, patience is not one of my virtues."

He kissed her, deeply and thoroughly. It was surprisingly gentle . . . and brief.

Stepping back, David winked. "Just a little something for both of us to think on, that's all."

He squeezed her hands, turned on his heel, and strode from the kitchen, leaving Natalie sitting on the counter, curling her toes in anguish.

* * *

Gil Blakely finally received the awaited call at home from Merlin Ford late Saturday night. He made an apology to his wife before he retreated to another room in the mansion that offered more privacy.

"All right," he said, adjusting comfortably in an oversized lounger. "What do you have for me?"

"Let's see, Mr. Blakely—" The rattle of paper could be heard. "I reviewed those notes you gave me, and from what I can see, she has lots of questions, but most are geared toward imbalances she detects in some of the capital accounts as well as payroll."

"Well, damn it," Blakely cursed. "I gave her access to most of the payroll spreadsheets."

There was an expectant pause on the other end of the phone before Merlin fumbled out a response.

"It should be okay if she doesn't pry too closely into individual entries. She could move on to something else on her list. But if that happens, we're right back to the original problem—producing documentation."

"We'll delay her, until after the stockholders' meeting."

"There's just so much dancing that can be done before we have to admit there's nothing to produce."

"I want things quiet for that meeting."

"Sir, we've been capitalizing expenses by the millions, loans have been reported as income, and half of the payroll is nonexistent staff—"

Blakely moved the phone away from his ear and glared at it before he replaced it.

"Now, you listen to me. If I hear you whine like that again, I'll personally come into that office of yours and snatch your tongue out through your nose." He caught his breath before he continued. "Stop making excuses, and tell me things can happen. Is that clear?"

"Yes, sir," Merlin replied stiffly.

"Good. Be in my office bright and early Monday morning."

He rang off bluntly with the cowed Merlin and immediately dialed another number. It was answered within the second ring by a deep voice.

"Good, you're in," Blakely said. "When's that auditor, Ms. Goodman, supposed to return here?"

"Wednesday."

"Are you sure?"

"I am."

"Schedule a meeting with the others. I want to know every move she makes from here on out."

There was a deadening silence before the voice on the other end asked, "Why the urgency? What's changed?"

"She's got the accountants running scared, and I don't know if I can trust them to keep it together awhile longer."

"I see."

"If she's got a plan we haven't anticipated, then I want to know it, too. You understand?"

"Perfectly."

"Good. Good. She's ambitious, so she'll ultimately take the advice of her firm at some point." He pinched his nose beneath his reading glasses and sighed. "If not, we might just have to let her meet up with old George Webster."

"Webster, sir?"

Blakely let out a snort and quickly scribbled notes on a pad in his lap. "Before your time," he muttered absently. "Now, where was I?" he continued, and prepared to read a list of to-dos into the phone that needed immediate handling.

Chapter 17

Carter looked at his watch as he strode through the Woodruff Arts Center's main lobby. At midmorning on a Monday, the immense downtown artistic center was just beginning to hum with patrons lining up at the box office for tickets to any number of local events, including Alliance Theatre productions, and the latest exhibit openings at the High Museum of Art.

Stopping for a moment, Carter took in the panoramic view around him, turning slightly, until his eyes found their subject. There, on one of the center's signature red contemporary leather couches, sat his appointment, Conrad Preston, local PI.

Based on the description the black investigator had provided over the phone—bald, salt-and-pepper beard, and with the demeanor of a former policeman—Carter was sure it could be none other. He headed toward him.

It hadn't taken long to find the private eye Justin Hardy never got the chance to name the other night at the table. It turned out that Preston's services were quite sought after; and with his connections, he would have access to lots of information. And it was information that Carter needed right now.

He joined the older man who was now standing, and was instantly intrigued by the piercing, hazel gaze that met his straight on. They extended their hands in a greeting.

"Conrad Preston?" Carter asked, shaking his hand.

The investigator bobbed his great mahogany head. "And you must be Carter Johnson," he replied. "Please, call me Connie. Everybody does."

"Then, Connie it is. We can walk across the street to a café." He looked down at the sofa, waving his hand toward it. "Or, we can sit right here, if you'd like."

"Here is fine with me," Connie said. "I'm comfortable wherever my clients are." He was a big man, but he fluidly settled his bulk back on the sofa before he produced a folder.

"This is for you," he said, handing Carter the folder. "It contains information about my agency, our rates, and the standard agreement."

Carter opened the folder and took a brief glimpse before he closed it and set it down beside him. "I'll take your word; but like I said on the phone, your name came up in a discussion with a local businessman, and that was good enough for me."

Lifting his heavy brows, Connie smiled. "Do you mind my asking who, so I can thank them for the referral?"

"I'd rather not say right now. In fact, I'd like to keep this entire meeting, including what I need, between us."

Connie gave a sage nod. "That's standard procedure, so let's get on it. What kind of information are you looking for?"

Carter reached into his pocket, pulled out a sheet of paper, and handed it to Connie. Leaning back, he rested his ankle on his knee, and stretched his arm across the back of the couch. "I want you to find out what happened to this man and where he is now."

Connie looked at the paper and then raised his head to look over at Carter. "George Webster?"

He nodded. "I'll tell you what little I know to get you started, but your window to get this for me is pretty small."

Connie leaned back against the sofa and, similarly, rested his leg over his knee as he pulled a small pad and pen from his shirt pocket. "Well, we don't need to waste any time, so let's get started."

Carter smiled, deciding that Connie would fit his bill perfectly.

Natalie had testily avoided the subject of David for the rest of the weekend—which Davina readily picked up on and complied with—and used the time to work on Innervision files at home. By Monday, however, there was just so much sitting in front of a computer she could take, and on such a beautiful day, before her brain rebelled. She decided she needed a break, even if it meant running into David. With that possibility covered, she pulled a sweater over her jeans and T-shirt, and then took the long road to her friend's house.

Once there, while Davina took a break and puttered around in her new artist's digs—temporarily set up in one of the extra rooms at the huge estate—Natalie took the opportunity to playfully get to know her godchild. She still wasn't quite sure if it was disappointment or relief she felt when she learned David was not around.

She sat on the floor in the sunny solarium near a wide bay window with her back against the wall. Curled in a blanket on his back, and resting against her raised knees, was little Jake.

Basking there with the baby in the simple warmth by the large windows and the endless plants, Natalie felt relaxed and, well, exhilarated, and attributed the almost joyful sensation to the talk she and David had shared. She had dreaded the very idea of discussing what had come between them that night long ago, but now she realized it had helped her define her emotions, even though they were, as yet, unresolved.

He wanted her as desperately as she wanted him. The only thing standing in her way was fear that, in the long run, she would end up the loser—just like her mother. Natalie let out a sigh, remembering she'd forgotten to return her mother's unanswered phone call this weekend. Damn.

In an attempt to erase the problems from her head, she kissed Jake's tiny hands, and inhaled his clean, innocent smell of baby oil and powder. In justification of what she lightly labeled forgetfulness, Natalie figured her mother had only wanted to know about her decision to return for Sienna's birthday party next month. A call later on would suffice, she decided; or, she could call Marilyn, her older sister, and find out what, if anything, was going on.

Totally engrossed in the baby's miniature features, Natalie didn't hear the soft footsteps behind her.

"I hear you've been spoiling him rotten, rocking him to sleep in your arms whenever you get the chance."

Natalie jerked her head around and saw Mrs. Hardy coming across the room, followed closely by David, who carried a small gift bag. An automatic smile of recognition registered on Natalie's face before Jake's wide yawn and fidget quickly recaptured her attention.

She cheerfully greeted them as she rebalanced the baby on her legs. "Can you believe a few days ago I was afraid I'd drop him? Now I'm beginning to love it."

"Did you ever help with your youngest sister? Sienna, isn't it?" Mrs. Hardy asked, taking a seat on the window bench.

A dark bolt of guilt struck Natalie again, and hit her fully in the chest. The Hardys had met her mother and little sister at Davina's wedding.

"I was on an internship in college when she was born," Natalie explained lightly. "So, I didn't get a chance to be around her much when she was Jake's age." She looked up. "She has a birthday next month."

"Oh, she is such a beauty, and so precocious when I saw her last. You have to let us know when they come up to visit you."

David came and stood near her. "I'd forgotten about your new sister, Natalie."

Natalie changed the subject. "Have you ever noticed how peaceful it is just holding babies? Besides, you can't do anything else when you're doing this, can you?"

"You're learning the secret," Mrs. Hardy said, and crossed her arms. "I used that excuse with all four of my babies."

Natalie smiled, and when she looked up, caught David's curious eye.

"You do look pretty comfortable sitting there, sort of like a Madonna," he offered as he joined Mrs. Hardy on the window seat.

Suddenly, Natalie's smile dissolved and she looked down at the sleeping baby. "Mrs. Hardy, you just told me I shouldn't be sitting around holding him all the time, and here I am saying how much fun it is." She darted a sheepish smile at the older woman. "I'm already turning out to be a poor excuse for a godmother."

"Oh, no," Mrs. Hardy said, laughing. "I was teasing about that, but I did mention to the reverend that you and David might want to talk to him about what to expect as godparents. That way, it won't be an uneasy role for you."

Natalie was embarrassed and looked at David with accusing eyes. Had he mentioned her misgivings?

"Don't be angry with him," Mrs. Hardy said. "He and Davina have been nothing but supportive, but Reverend King comes across your kind of doubt all the time, and he has a prepared session he offers to godparents, at their request, before the ceremony."

"I just learned about it, too," David said to Natalie. "He'll also tell us what will happen in the ceremony and what we'll have to say, that sort of thing."

"I talked with the church secretary on Sunday. And, if you'd like, the reverend can see you and David this evening, together or separately."

Natalie smiled at the gesture. "Thank you," she said, before turning her eyes to David. "Will you go?"

He smiled back at her, and nodded his head. "Sure. You want to do it together?"

She nodded her agreement just as the baby let out a great yelp and squirmed against the blanket. Natalie, instantly attentive, was conscious of Mrs. Hardy standing next to her, and tried quieting him. In the span of a few seconds, Jake was letting out loud bawls as his little face turned red from the effort.

"I think he's hungry or needs a diaper change," Mrs. Hardy said, bending over to inspect him, yet she didn't take him from Natalie's ministering arms.

"Or both," David suggested.

"Davina asked me to check and see if he's ready for his feeding, and he probably is. Do you want me to take him upstairs?"

Relieved by the offer, Natalie lifted up the baby so Mrs. Hardy could take him. She then quietly watched as the more experienced woman cooed him quiet in a matter of seconds.

"We'll be back later," she whispered to David and Natalie, and hummed a little song in the air as she left them.

"Did you see how she did that?" Natalie asked, watching them leave the room. "I'm still scared to be left alone with him when he does that red-faced thing." She felt a warm nuzzle near her ear, and turned toward it, only to find David stretched on the floor beside her.

"So, you've got a beautiful and precocious sister, huh?" He smiled as he dropped back to recline on his arms. "I'm thinking it runs in your family."

Natalie found herself becoming warm with a blush, and hated that David would notice. She turned her face away, but stretched her legs out alongside him, taking in the warmth coming from the sun-drenched windows.

"So, why haven't I seen you since Saturday night?"

"I did some work on those files I picked up from my office," she admitted, and closed her eyes.

"I see. So, it wouldn't have anything to do with avoiding me, huh?"

She opened her eyes and saw David's head poised above

her. "No, and excuse me, your huge ego is blocking my sun," she said, smiling. "It had nothing to do with you at all."

"I called you yesterday," he said, not moving.

"I know. I was there."

"And you wouldn't answer? I wanted to come over."

She darted a smile his way before she closed her eyes again. "What was the point of having a frustrating evening?"

"You're admitting it would've tested your control, huh? Well, I must be making some progress." He reached into the small gift bag he'd brought in with him. "I wanted to hand-deliver a little package."

Natalie opened her eyes and saw that David was dangling a tiny pair of electric-blue lace bikini underwear in the air by one of their delicate elastic straps. She immediately recognized them as the ones she'd left somewhere in his bedroom that night long ago when they'd come so close to having sex.

She laughed as she snatched them from his fingers. "Give them to me."

"My cleaning lady found them—your shirt, too—and then laundered them with the rest of my things. Your shirt's still in the bag. They've been folded and neatly nestled with my boxer-briefs—and quite happily, I might add—all this time," he said, smiling. "If I'm not mistaken, I believe your last instructions to me were to mail them."

Natalie snorted at his memory. "Does your cleaning lady accept this as a regular part of her duties, doing laundry for your women?"

"She made an exception in your case. It seems that when I told her they were yours, she said she liked you. You have what she calls spunk."

Natalie's eyes stretched with humor. "You didn't say all that to the poor lady, did you?"

"I figured the chance would come around when I could return them." He inched closer to her on the floor. "And what do you know? Here we are again, with a poolhouse sitting empty and available."

She rolled over to rest on her side and faced him. "We're not just picking up where we left off. We still have to think this through all the way, so"—she whispered close to David's face—"don't even think sex, yet."

"Not even if I know you're thinking it?"

"I'm going home alone tonight."

David quickly dipped his head and kissed her, gently pulling her bottom lip with his mouth. Natalie fought the urge to return the kiss, but only for a moment. She reached for him, though David's hand had already looped around her and was firmly pressed against her butt, heating her to the core.

"We can always do other . . . things," he said, his voice trailing off in an erotic suggestion.

She grinned against his hungry mouth. "Now you sound like Clinton."

"I don't mind that. You want to play Lewinsky?"

She poked him in the ribs and scooted back, but he, in turn, began to tickle her. Doubled over, their one-upmanship play turned into a laughing slapstick of tickles, pokes, and dodges until Natalie collapsed backward into David's arm in defeat, kicking her legs and squealing, "Stop, stop."

"So, are we having fun yet?"

Alli's voice broke through their noisy romp on the floor, and they turned in her direction. Natalie, rolling over onto David's lap, grabbed up the lacy underwear from the floor. She balled them into her hand before she looked up, a devilish smile on her face as she shrewdly surveyed Alli.

"Well, well, well, if it isn't Benedict Arnold's younger, darker cousin," Natalie accused, brushing back her hair. She had yet to squeeze in a private word with Alli since the restaurant debacle.

"Say what you want, but the other night went pretty well," Alli retorted with a matter-of-fact smile. "Okay, so Davina won her bet, but I'm figuring David has to be a hell of a lot better than a long, leisurely shower."

David's brows had ruffled with confusion when he looked at Natalie.

"What is she talking about?" he asked, just as Natalie lobbed a shoe toward the door at their laughing friend.

It was early evening and, after spending the entire afternoon with her friends, Natalie walked to her car in the Hardys' drive. It had been a while since she'd spent consecutive weekdays doing something other than L & M's work.

The plan was to stop by the church on her way home for the counseling session with the minister, and David would meet her there. Lost in the evening's plans, she was taken by surprise when Alli came charging from behind to take up the pace with her down the garden walk.

"Girl . . ." Natalie's hand fell to her heart. "You just about scared me to death."

"So, you really are okay with that little intervention Davina planned at the restaurant? It was all her idea, you know. All I did was keep Carter occupied so you and David could talk."

Natalie grinned at the younger woman. "Are you trying to ease your conscience?"

Alli's shoulders sloped in relief. "Well, I just didn't want you hiding in the garden, ambushing me when I least expect it."

Natalie laughed out loud. "You think I'd do that to you?"

"Don't get me wrong, I would, too." Alli glanced at her. "But see, it all worked out the way it should. You and David are back at it again, and Carter means nothing to you, right?"

Natalie stopped and turned to Alli. "Listen, you have to remember that Carter is simply someone I work with. I don't know him—I don't know him at all." They turned and slowly resumed their walk to the car.

Alli let out a sigh. "Sounds like you don't trust him, either."

"That's not quite right," Natalie replied. "Carter works for my client, Innervision, and I don't trust anyone at Innervision these days."

Chapter 18

It was almost ten minutes past their appointment time. Natalie sat in the straight-backed chair in the minister's study and listened to the soft, almost baroque music that played in the background.

She had already observed his numerous plaques and civic awards that were set about the room. Next, she took in the several diplomas framed in glass behind his desk, and felt a degree of guilt at taking up precious time with her simple issue.

The minister had people to save and sick church members to visit. So, why was she even here? An even better question, though, centered on David's whereabouts. He was now almost fifteen minutes late. Where was he?

"Natalie?"

She jumped at the deep voice, twisting her neck to see Reverend King come through the door and prop it open behind him.

"David hasn't arrived. I asked Sister Lawson upstairs to show him in when he does." He reached up to a shelf behind him, which housed the stereo, and turned the music off.

The sound of silence in the oak-paneled room was deafening to Natalie. Close up, she could tell the minister was not as old as she had first thought him to be. Admittedly, she didn't adopt a home church when she first came to Atlanta; but, like Davina and David, she considered this one as her own—when she attended, that is. Suddenly, her attendance record shamed her. Did they check that sort of thing when you talked with the minister? She was going to rot in—

"Natalie?"

It was Reverend King's voice. He was talking to her. She looked up from her reverie. "Yes, sir?" When she saw his indulgent smile, Natalie felt as though he'd read her embarrassing thoughts.

"I was saying we could use this time to discuss some of your personal misgivings until David arrives." He cocked a curious dark brow her way as he stood behind his desk. "Is that all right with you?"

Natalie let out a breath. "I don't mind."

He sat down in his tall-backed leather chair. "First, congratulations on being asked to be the godmother to little Jacob Hardy. Second, I find it always helps for young godparents to understand that they play a very special role apart from just promoting Christian faith for the child."

"Oh?" He had captured Natalie's attention. "What is that role?"

"To show the child, as he grows older, how to live a full, balanced life."

A smile began to form on Natalie's face. Maybe this had been a good idea after all, she thought.

"In fact, Mrs. Hardy tells me you excel in that aspect."

She relaxed against the chair. "I try to be happy in the things I do."

"Then, you have a great attitude, and should have no problem as Jake gets older and needs someone to talk to besides what he'll describe as his out-of-touch parents."

Natalie shared a laugh with the minister before she tried to explain her confusion.

"How can you be happy in your life and decisions, yet at the same time balance all that with being a role model for an impressionable child?"

"That depends on your definition of *happy*."

The way he said it, Natalie thought he made the word sound frivolous. She sat up in the chair and gave her definition. "Feeling pleased about decisions I make that affect me."

"But, is that really happiness . . . or just a form of vanity?"

The knit of Natalie's brows tightened as she considered what he said.

Reverend King let out a broad smile and leaned against his desk, commanding Natalie's attention. "What makes you doubt your ability to be happy and at the same time live up to moral ideals? Unless"—he raised his finger as he answered his question—"you've limited happiness to simply being one kind of expression: pleasure expressed through physical contentment."

"Well, isn't that what it is, what we're taught?" she countered. "When you're happy, you feel good, right?"

He touched his chest. "Happiness, pleasure, whatever you want to call it, starts from within," he said, "and comes from a rainbow of colors and emotions that boil down to that happiness or pleasure." He relaxed back in his chair. "The pain of childbirth can be excruciating, but the proud mother will tell you she's never been happier. Ask any couple in a relationship. Love is the happiest state of all, yet it's filled with moments of pain and hurt and regret."

Reverend King's words were sobering, and Natalie couldn't respond as her own emotional rainbow flashed by her.

"Okay, what if you're right, and I need to rethink my ideas of what happiness and pleasure are? Then what?"

"You might want to consider finding the source of that false view. And that usually lies somewhere in your childhood."

"Oh."

He smiled. "Yes, that can be daunting. But talk with your parents. Now, that's a quintessential role model that usually leads to false ideas."

"How so?"

"Well, in an effort to serve up the right model for their kids, parents will make sacrifices that can appear as misery and discontent in a child's eyes. Yet, the parents don't see it that way at all. On the contrary, the sacrifice is part of a greater happiness. What clears this up? Communication." He sat up. "It's not uncommon at all to take on the wrong model for happiness from your parents."

Natalie's stare became blank as her mind's eye blinked to a vivid display of domino-effect doors falling over and into each other.

Meanwhile, upstairs, Reverend King's secretary was holding the phone to her ear, and speaking with a church member at the same time she greeted David.

"They're waiting for you," Sister Lawson said, and pointed to the stairs on her left. "His study is the first door downstairs. I can take you down in just a moment."

"Thank you." David strode to the stairwell and, cognizant of his tardiness, decided not to wait. He gave a quick glance to the secretary still on the phone before he quietly loped down the open staircase.

The hallway was empty of other church members at this hour. David heard voices he supposed belonged to Natalie and Reverend King, magnified by the evening silence, and becoming clearer when he stepped from the stairs.

"You aren't forever marked by your parents' mistakes unless that's a choice," the minister was saying. "You have a lot to give, regardless of the current state of your family."

"But, I did it. I'm the one who ripped the family apart."

"You were a child and in no way responsible for their decisions."

Frowning at what he'd heard, David pulled up his momentum near the open door in order to avoid an awkward appearance in the middle of a sincere confession. Quickly turning about, he began to retrace his steps, but not fast enough to avoid hearing more.

"You should talk to your parents about your guilt."

"They're out of my life, and I plan to keep it that way," Natalie was saying.

Just as David caught sight of the stairs, he heard the secretary's light, careful steps upon them.

"Oh, there you are," she said to David. "I hope you didn't get lost down here. I can take you in there, now."

"Great," David said. He fell into step with her as she chattered on during their short walk to the open study door, where she knocked, and then stood aside.

David looked through at Natalie, who raised her head and smiled when she saw him. He returned the smile, though it didn't touch his eyes as he remembered Mrs. Hardy's words that Natalie might have baggage to work through—and it seemed she might have some things to work through after all.

The session was over within the hour, and as David escorted Natalie from the church to the parking lot, he asked her about it.

"Feel better?"

When she simply nodded, David looked at her hard. "You're in pretty deep thought to be feeling better about it."

Natalie darted a smile at him before she spoke. "It wasn't what I expected, I guess, and he said a lot of interesting things, below-the-surface things."

"After tonight, I'm making a vow to get to Sunday service a little more often than once a month."

Natalie giggled. "I said the same thing, too. At least I know that if I'm not in church twenty-four/seven, I won't be responsible for stunting Jake's spiritual growth."

"I'm with you on that one."

"Were you as surprised as I was to learn that Reverend King used to be a practicing psychologist?"

David nodded sagely. "I think that's why his counseling sessions are so popular." When she started to pull on her sweater against the cool night air, he helped her. "You're going home now?"

"I'm afraid so. I plan on trying out a little computer creeping on my own tonight."

"Computer creeping, huh? I didn't know you could get around a hard drive that well."

"I can't, but since Blakely keeps blocking the full access I want, I'm trying some tricks of my own. That way, I can confront him with specifics that he can't ignore. And then, he'll have to give me what I want."

He looked over at her before they started to walk again. "Maybe I can help. I learned a little about hacking through one of my corporate cases involving product espionage."

"Thanks for the offer and all, but no, thanks. And, while the company might be nice, I don't need the distraction," she said, glancing at him. "That is, if I'm going to get any work done."

David smiled, pleased that she considered him a distraction. "I probably won't see you tomorrow."

"Oh? Where will you be?"

"A day trip into the mountains with Justin, Michael, and Mr. Bradley. If it's late, we might stay at the cabin overnight."

"The Hardys are great for you and Davina."

"Yeah, they're pretty hard to beat." He looked over at Natalie walking beside him and tried to see through the patina she presented to the outside. "You never talk about your family back in Florida. Why?"

"No reason." She looked up at him. "Nothing to talk about, I guess."

"You know how I feel about family—hell, we didn't have much of a unit, for one thing. It took a while, but I finally got it that family is just an accident of birth, and sometimes you get less than what you *think* you deserve."

"I can agree with that," she said.

"It's no one's fault; it's just life. So, what you do is create your own. It's what Davina and I did before she met Justin, and we're still doing it."

"You're lucky that it turned into something good," Natalie said. She folded her arms against the chill before she turned to David. "Can I ask you something?" When he nodded, she asked, "Are you happy?"

He grinned. "What kind of question is that?"

"It's something I discussed with Reverend King tonight." She looked up at him. "Well, are you?"

"Yeah, when I think about it, I am pretty happy."

"Even though we haven't figured out our situation, and you're at a crossroads with your career?" she challenged.

He nodded. "I think it's because of what I don't know yet—the unpredictable things." He looked at her puzzled expression. "I think they give my life texture, and a reason to get up in the morning."

They walked the remaining distance to the car in silence. When they reached Natalie's Acura, it looked rather pedestrian when parked alongside David's spotless, low-slung sports car. The car had been a singular extravagant purchase after his artist father's sizeable art estate had been valued and then divided.

"As much as you love that expensive little thing, why didn't you take it with you to Washington?" Natalie asked as she unlocked her own.

"Oh, you mean despite the fact that the firm made a car available to me while I was there?" David teased.

Natalie grinned as she watched him follow her around to her car. When she opened the door, he leaned in close and whispered against her ear.

"You were with me when I picked it out, remember? It reminds me of us, but in better days." He straightened up. "I also knew that if I left it here, I'd come back, and I'd see you."

With one hand, he pushed her car door, and it was closed again. His other hand encircled her waist, making contact with soft, bare skin in the process, and he turned her around to face him.

"Since I can't go home with you . . . a good night kiss will work."

Natalie held on to his arms as he tilted her face up to his and gave her a deep, long kiss in the shadows of the church's great oak.

Her lips, at first taste, were cool, though pliable to David's demanding ones; but soon, Natalie was comfortably nestled between her car and David's strong body. They quickly became victims of heat generated by a kiss that signaled a private longing between two adults who knew there was more to come. The inevitable was bound to happen.

It was as if they realized at the same moment that they should stop, and they broke apart.

David raised his head and smiled. "Yeah, I would say I'm very happy right about now."

Natalie wore her own self-satisfied grin and playfully pushed him off her before she climbed into her car. "I've got to get out of here if I don't want to be up all night."

"Don't work too hard," David warned, and closed her door.

Natalie smiled and, backing out, drove from the parking lot under David's watchful—and more insightful—eye.

Chapter 19

Natalie wasn't keen on the idea that she would have to butt heads with Blakely so early in the day, and on her first day back. It was an inevitable action, though, when she'd entered her office earlier that morning and didn't find the remaining documents waiting for her as she'd requested.

To make matters worse, Natalie still didn't have access to a senior manager with whom she could discuss the problematic accounting entries that were growing in number.

As she now entered the foyer of Gil Blakely's office, his secretary waved her on through.

"He's waiting for you," she said with a commiserating smile.

"Thank you."

No sooner had Natalie knocked on the closed door than she heard his gruff response ring out from the other side.

"Come on in, it's open."

Natalie stepped through and remembered the spacious executive office just as it had been during her last visit. She crossed the room and stopped just short of him seated behind the enormous desk.

"Have a seat," Blakely said from his big chair.

Natalie thought she detected a faint, antiseptic odor hanging in the air—as though it camouflaged a more noxious one, like cigar smoke.

"No, thank you. I won't be staying that long."

"Suit yourself." His eyes drew her into his sight as he steepled his fingers. "So, what can I do for you?"

"I received part of the documentation I requested, but I'd like to know when you'll release the rest."

"Sit down," he said gently.

"I'm not—"

"Sit down."

Surprised by the harsh demand spewing out, Natalie complied, and took the nearby chair immediately in front of his desk.

"Now, let's get some things straight. It doesn't matter how badly you want your list of items—you get nothing until I decide it's necessary."

"What do you consider necessary, sir?"

"That's what you'll have to come up with. I'll know it when I see it, though."

"I've learned that you approved dipping into another division's reserve account to pay operating costs. You even went so far as to rename the set-aside account, making it that much harder to identify and locate. That's tantamount to concealment, sir."

Blakely grinned. "Is that what this witch-hunt of yours is all about? As far as I'm concerned, that reserve account was unnecessary, and we were well within our rights to use that hundred million somewhere else. I like to call it aggressive accounting, and it was approved and signed off by *your firm* in the past."

Natalie got up and placed a sheet of paper on the desk in front of him.

"What's this?" he asked, picking up his reading glasses from the desk.

"I looked at the accounts on the disk you made available and I made a list of questionable variances. The payroll spreadsheets, for instance, fluctuate wildly by as much as a

quarter of a million dollars. Now, if you take that one vari-
ance, along with some of these other entries here"—she
pointed them out for him—"we're now up to millions of dollars in unexplained expenses that aren't showing up on the
balance sheets." She looked at him. "So, where are they?"

He studied the sheet for a moment before he looked up at
her, his expression remaining unchanged. Reaching up, he
removed his reading glasses, effectively dismissing her concerns. "Have you spoken to John?" Before she could answer,
he continued. "Some of your questions here are simply legal
accounting procedures already approved by your people."

It infuriated Natalie that he would try and implicate her
firm just for asking about the entries. She was sure that he
was telling a bald-faced lie to buy more time. No one would
approve disguising such explicit operating expenses in a
public financial statement.

"Is that all you're going to say, sir?"

He leaned back in his chair as he folded the glasses. "Like
I said, speak with John. I've already asked the audit committee to put off this review until after the quarter, or at least
after the stockholders' meeting. It's become time-consuming
in view of our other obligations, and they're taking it under
advisement."

Bells went off in Natalie's head. "You didn't inform me? I
have a right to rebut." Natalie drew a deep breath. "This is
my project and the team and I have spent months—"

"Much longer than was necessary." He stood up from behind his desk so quickly that Natalie was taken aback.

"Do you know who I am? I am a respected board member, an upstanding CFO in this country, and I authorize checks
to pay your firm millions each year for services rendered."
He pressed his hand deep into his pocket as he gestured with
the glasses. "Do you think you're going to just waltz in here
and derail my operation because something doesn't look
right to your young eyes?"

He now set the glasses on the desk and leaned forward.

"Now, when you have some hard evidence that things are not what they appear, then I'll look into it." He came from around his desk and stood back on his heels. "Beyond that, take me before the audit committee if you dare."

When Blakely let out a breath, Natalie thought it was like that of a fire-breathing dragon.

"And if you go that route," he went on, "you'd better be ready to defend your own firm, as well."

Blakely watched Natalie put a stranglehold on her anger and abruptly turn to leave. Rather than slam the door, though, she made a dignified and quiet exit without so much as a swish from her hosiery.

He nodded his head in dark humor. "Got to give it to her—she's got good control," he mumbled. "But get in my damn business if you dare, little girl," he warned the empty door. "It'll be the last time."

The phone rang and he turned to look at the dial to see who had gotten through on his private line. It was Merlin Ford. He picked it up as he moved around the desk.

"Blakely here. What can I do for you?" He paced near the window.

"Well, sir. There's a bit of trouble you might want to hear about."

He stopped his pacing. "Speak up, then. What is it?"

"It's Myra Grayson and Bill Daniels, the accounting manager who's been helping her work on the, ah, quarterly reports. They want to resign."

"What?" his voice boomed into the phone.

"And they want it to be effective"—he cleared his throat—"ah, immediately, sir."

Blakely pinched the bridge of his nose as he resumed his pace across the office. Preparing to count to ten, he got no further than two.

"Where are they now?"

"They're—they're in my office, sir."

"Keep them in there. I want to talk to both of them. Now."

* * *

Natalie took another swig from the Coke can and found that her temper had moderated somewhat. After leaving Blakely, she had needed a break from her closed-in space and had found herself at the soft drink machine in the lobby.

"The nerve of the arrogant bastard," she declared, as she now walked into her office. No sooner had she dropped into her chair and let out a sigh than her phone rang.

She grabbed it up and spoke her name into the receiver.

"It's John."

"Hi, John. What can I do for you?" The moment she uttered the words, she knew. Blakely. He'd put in a call to her boss.

"I wanted to know how things were going."

Natalie leaned back in the chair and, picking up a pencil, allowed her cooling temper to settle even more. "Are you asking for my side of the story?"

She twirled the pencil between her nimble fingers during an almost imperceptible pause. Almost.

"You know how it goes. He's an important client, and I expect him to call when things aren't proceeding on his expected path."

"He won't budge on my requests, saying that I can either wait until after the big meeting next week and the end of the quarter, or I can go ahead and sign off on the audit and be done with my 'witch-hunt' as he calls it."

Natalie sat up in the chair, anxious for a willing ear. "John, he's hiding something. The more I dig, the more odd and confusing entries—"

He cut her off. "I'm going to be over there, anyway, so why don't we talk over a cup of coffee during your afternoon break?"

She swallowed her disappointment at not being able to share what she knew right now. "Sure. That'll work. I'll see you then."

She hung up and, crossing her arms, leaned back in the

chair, curiously uneasy with John's bland reaction to her enthusiasm.

"We understand exactly how you must feel, being asked quarter after quarter to help out the company's financial condition, making transfers that you're not completely comfortable about . . ." Blakely went on and on, laying it on heavy and hard for the two senior managers who sat across from him on the comfortable couch located in Merlin's office. When Blakely wanted—no, needed—his way, it was what he did best.

"But what you're doing is for the good of us all, I promise you. We are getting this spending under control." He slapped his hands together for emphasis. "And this is the last time we're going to come to you for this type of help; but we can't do it this time without you, ah, Myra . . ." Blakely looked across the space at the small, pale woman he believed he had met once before and who answered to a name that fit her perfectly.

"And you, too, ah, Bill." He turned an intent, fatherly gaze onto the baby-faced accountant who, incredibly, managed to display the same nondescript qualities as did Myra.

"Tell me, what is it that you need to be assured of so we can get you to stay with the Innervision family?"

Myra had sat quietly on the sofa, her hands folded politely in her lap, during the entire session she'd listened to her superiors. Blakely cocked his brow at her now.

"Ms. Grayson? Surely you have concerns if you're considering resigning."

"I do." The quick interjection came from Bill, and the others looked at him now.

"Go ahead," Blakely urged.

"Sir, I'm scared that I'll be held responsible for making changes and backdating invoices as I was told to do, if the SEC does an investigation," he said, looking from Blakely to Ford and back again.

"That won't happen," Blakely promised, and darted his own glance to Ford. "First of all, what you've done is not illegal. As CFO, I'm given leeway to make adjustments within reason and as I see fit. . . ."

Blakely was in his element of persuasion and pressed it on the unsuspecting managers with a lion's prowess over prey. As he talked, Bill asked more questions, but Myra remained stoic in her silence. Even so, Blakely could see the waver in her brow, and after a little while, he knew it was time to end the talk.

"Just remember, and I assure you of this, I take full responsibility if any questions come up."

They all stood from their chairs.

"Well, I do feel a lot better after talking with you today," Bill offered. He gave a nervous smile to the others. "I guess it would be pretty hard to match my salary outside if I ended up quitting without notice."

"Good thinking," Blakely said, and extended his hand to Bill's, shaking it. "I like common sense in my employees. Thanks for sticking with us." He turned to Myra, and squeezed her small, lukewarm hand. "A lot of employees are counting on you. Don't let me and Innervision down."

When she ventured a nod, a small smile appeared on her strained face; but she quickly looked away, almost as if she was embarrassed, and followed Bill through the door.

Blakely looked at Ford before he called out behind them, "You won't regret your decision, either."

The afternoon break crowd in the cafeteria had been sparse, and Natalie had no trouble finding a private table for two near a window with John. He had listened to her comments, and even commiserated at times, but he seemed steadfast in concluding that she had to end the audit review, and soon.

Frustrated, Natalie now watched as he sipped the last of his coffee.

"And, that's just it, John? Ignore all of these unaccounted-for numbers showing up all over the balance sheets that no one"—she looked John in the eyes and lowered her voice—"no one wants to talk about?"

She leaned over the table, toward him. "I checked the last review, and I see some of these same odd figures there, too. Whatever is going on has been going on for at least three quarters."

"You're talking about a full-fledged investigation, Natalie." He set the cup down, seemingly unconcerned with her worries. "I'm trying to get you to close this down in less than ten days, and you're talking about something now that could last ten months."

"Mr. Blakely won't even allow me full computer access so I can review live journal entries."

He smiled. "Can you blame him? He's the CFO. You're accusing him of all kinds of malfeasance."

"But if I could use their computers to look up just the computerized entries, I can follow an entry to its original purchase order or invoice and see the justification they used."

"Natalie—"

"That way, I wouldn't have to pull his precious accounting managers off their projects."

"Think about it," John reasoned. "You're also accusing us of the same thing if you make this into an issue with the audit committee."

"I don't intend to drag Lang & Myers into anything."

"What if you have no choice?"

Natalie sat back on her chair. So, Blakely had made John aware of his threats. She was sure dejection played out on her face, but she didn't know what to say to him anymore—not after he made it clear that whatever she said would more than likely fall on deaf ears. The answer to her question, how long it would take for John to bow to pressure to speed her along, had been answered.

* * *

"She still down there?"

Gil Blakely had burst through the door of his office, his brusque question meant for either of the men who already occupied the room.

"She's just searching the computers again." The voice rose up helpfully from a stooped figure near an elegant cherry-wood cabinet built into the wall.

Blakely's fingers plied through his sparse, brown hair as he blazed a trail to his desk. The day was slowly collapsing into ruin.

"Did you find anything else out?"

The question was directed to the tall man in the well-cut business suit, who was turned away as he hung up the phone at Blakely's desk.

"She's taking another close look at the payroll," was his response. "In fact, she was able to access a good amount of the detail she discussed with you this morning from the main-frame computer this weekend." He turned and faced Blakely as he thrust his hand into his pocket. It was Carter.

"Well, damn, Carter. What's she doing in the computer without access?" He came around the desk.

"Getting for herself what you won't give to her willingly," Carter replied. "I put a report of what she looked at on your desk."

"It would've been nice to have had this when she came in here this morning. Don't we have systems in place to avoid that sort of thing?" He let out a stiff expletive as he looked over the document. "That damn girl is getting on my nerves." Blakely sighed as he dropped into his chair.

"She has low-level clearance, but there are ways to ma-nipulate that level by requesting information attached to a higher clearance level."

Letting out a louder sigh, Blakely continued to read the report.

"By the way, that was John Callaway on the phone just then."

Blakely looked up. "What did he want?"

"He wanted you to know he was handling matters on his end."

Blakely picked up the silver cylinder from his desk before he opened the side drawer to expose the video screens.

He pressed the cylinder head and heard the familiar hum that meant the closed-circuit system had powered on.

"She can't make anything of what she was able to access." He looked up at Carter. "Can she?" At the men's silence, Blakely shook his head, seemingly incredulous at her spunk to try anything against him.

"She's an accountant but she's got an analyst's intuition," Carter said.

The stooped body from the cabinet had now stood and came over to join the other men. It was Sean from accounting.

"A thinker," Sean said. "She makes these separate, detailed work papers with all kinds of notes and comments stuck in the margins."

Carter cocked an eye in Sean's direction. "And how would you know that if she doesn't leave them here?"

He grinned. "I caught a look at them in the elevator the other night while you were doing the intro thing with her." He took a seat in front of Blakely's desk. "I already checked out her office downstairs while she was out, and it was clean. Nothing there. Nada."

Sean passed an odd-shaped, pewter key for the cherry cabinet to Blakely. "Everything's organized again, sir."

Blakely hefted the key in his hand as he looked at the young man. "You sure you haven't used your special skills to make another key like this, have you?"

Sean smiled. "Oh, no, sir. I'd never bite the hand that took me from my life of crime on the street and dressed me up to become a junior accountant."

"Yeah, you're one of my better urban relief projects. And as long as you work on my projects, you'll be just fine." He set the key in his side drawer.

Carter shook his head, and walked toward the window.

"Is it guaranteed the Goodman woman won't find anything she can use?" Blakely asked Carter.

Carter exchanged a glance with Sean, giving the nod to the younger man.

"She won't be able to track any discernible pattern," Sean quickly explained. "Everything's pretty much layered and renamed."

Blakely fumbled with the remote control. "I have no intention of taking orders from Lang & Myers's equal-opportunity experiment, and not about an operation that I've built up," he grumbled. "She ought to be home doing something she's probably good at—like making babies—and not here hassling me."

Belatedly, he realized what he said wasn't exactly politically correct, and he looked over at Carter's tall, imposing figure where he now stood near the desk, his dark face masking whatever internal emotions he experienced.

Blakely depended on Carter's expertise in security and electronics, as well as his silence and trust. So, he did what he had to do to preserve their long-standing semblance of respect. He apologized.

Shaking his head in a sign of regret, Blakely sat up in his chair. "Sorry about that, Carter, but you know what I was getting at." He let out a dismissive chuckle as he pushed back from his desk and motioned to the screens.

The camera on screen one was positioned just over Natalie's left shoulder and could zoom in on the material at her desk. She was standing alongside the desk.

"Hell, look at her," Blakely continued, his eyes shrewdly following Natalie's movements. "See what I mean—she's pretty enough, but you can't deny that body of hers is made for babies." He snorted. "Of course, I know you see that, seeing as how you didn't object to the idea of getting her to go out with you."

His attention had moved to screen two, with its camera positioned at the door. It gave a wide, front view of the desk.

"Career women." He shook his head in disdain. "She ought to be married and at home."

Finally, he shifted his attention to the third screen, covered by a camera positioned in the ceiling with a view of the entire room. It captured Natalie as she moved from the desk to the chair in front of it.

Carter had watched in studied silence from his same spot with his arms neatly folded. Now he made a move forward and looked at Blakely.

"What will you do if she does stumble onto something?" he asked.

Blakely glanced over at Carter before his attention was drawn back to the woman on the tiny screen as she kicked off her shoes and raised her legs to rest in the other chair.

"Let's just hope it doesn't come to that," he said with a frown. "In fact, she should pray that she's not as smart as she thinks she is."

Natalie thought her small office looked pretty much akin to Myra's from the way papers covered just about every surface. She had hit upon a plan to borrow previous-year files from the audit library to compare with figures from the current one. It was all an attempt to measure how out of line the numbers had become.

She stretched like a lazy cat and knew it was late even without a window from which to gauge the remaining sunlight. Glancing at her watch, she wasn't surprised. It was already past six. Quickly packing the bags she would take with her, she prepared to leave the office.

As she traveled to the elevator and then down to the parking deck, it occurred to her that she hadn't talked with David. She wondered how his mountain trip had turned out. Since she hadn't heard from him, maybe it meant he would surprise her with a call tonight.

She smiled at her concern. Maybe it wouldn't be so bad

to see him—even invite him over. Maybe they could grab a bite together, she thought as she unlocked her trunk.

Natalie released the bungee cords on the carrier and then lifted her briefcase into the trunk. The Acura's trunk, though roomy, carried extra shoes and that sort of thing for business emergencies, so Natalie reached in to push aside some of the items.

While doing so, she came across a sheet of paper lying innocuously beneath a pair of shoes—paper she immediately suspected belonged in one of her client's files.

"Oh, no," she muttered out loud. "Don't tell me I've lost some of my notes."

She snatched up the paper to confirm what she suspected, but was frozen where she stood when she saw big, bold words in black stare up at her:

WATCH YOUR BACK.

Chapter 20

Natalie looked up when she heard the light rap on her office door at Lang & Myers.

"Yes?" she called out, already rising from her chair when she saw Belinda, the records clerk, peek her head through.

The perky clerk was all smiles. "Hi, Natalie . . . I brought you a visitor from out front."

She had already skirted around her desk and reached the door before Belinda could move aside to make way for the visitor.

"David," Natalie said. An elated smile whisked across her face as she spied him towering behind Belinda. She caught up David's arm and pulled him into her office as she said to the clerk, "Thank you," and then managed to close her door on the woman without appearing rude.

"Why didn't you call me back last night?" She rested against the closed door and gave him an accusing look. It had been two days since she'd seen him, and good Lord, she actually missed him.

"So you missed me, huh?" David grinned as he moved toward her.

"Oh, please. It's just that Davina said Justin was returning last night, so I left a message for you to call me, thinking that you were at home." She regarded him now with a speculative gaze. "And, you didn't. That's all."

David stepped close, almost touching her, before he stopped. "We stayed an extra day, but we didn't make it back until this morning." He touched her hair, running his finger along a silky curl. "When I heard your message, I decided to come here instead of call, and for the same reason you wanted me here."

His silky baritone was an addiction and Natalie suppressed the sexual energy bubbling inside that begged for freedom. She closed her eyes and allowed him to lean into her; but just as the heady sensation of his lips against her neck began to curl her toes, and breathing in his smell was not enough, she broke away and ducked under his arm.

Natalie moved back to her desk across the room and safety. She shouldn't be indulging in pleasure. There was something more important to discuss right now.

"That's not why I wanted to see you so fast," she said, and reached into her desk drawer and pulled out a business-size mailer. She then extracted two sheets of paper. "It's this, David."

He was already crossing the room, his attention riveted to the paper in her hand.

"I found another note in my car trunk last night."

He looked at the paper. The one on top had the words *WATCH YOUR BACK* printed on it. He looked at the second sheet of paper, which carried the first warning, *BE CAREFUL*.

Natalie watched his reaction and expression grow serious. "I already compared them. They look like the same block writing, even the same kind of markers. Cheap ones, though. Look at how smudged the tips of the letters are."

"Yeah, you're right. The ends are split from wear." He moved about the room in a slow pace as he studied the paper. "Tell me again how you found it."

"I left the office around six-thirty and went to the parking garage, and when I opened my trunk to store my things, there it was." She let out a nervous laugh. "I guess I can lose that flyer in the garage theory, huh?"

He looked at the notes again before he looked over at Natalie. "Together, these sound like warnings."

"They do, don't they?" She sat down behind her desk. "When I found it, I tried to slough it off, like we did the first one. . . . Anyway, I called Davina, but she was busy with the baby, and when I called you your cell phone wouldn't even ring, so I left a message at your house."

"I'm sorry I didn't get your message last night. It's hard getting a signal in the mountains." He came around her desk and sat on the edge, crossing his arms in thought. "Does anyone know about this besides the two of us?"

Natalie realized she had told Carter about the first one the night they'd gone out. Something told her this revelation wouldn't sit well with David.

"I did mention the first one to Carter the night we were at the restaurant."

He dropped his arms and, looking down at her, frowned. "You told him? Why?"

"Well . . ." Natalie silently groaned as she looked up at him from her chair and told him the full details of the elevator run-in. "I asked him, point-blank, if he had left the note or knew about it, and he denied any involvement."

David shook his head at what she'd done. "Of course he would."

"I believed that he didn't leave it, but what concerned me was whether something else was going on." She sat up in the chair. "For instance, when I told him, right there in my apartment, about the note, he never even asked to see it, as if, maybe"—she looked at David—"he knew what it meant." Her brows knitted with confusion. "Does that make sense?"

"You always suspected something about him from the beginning, when you mentioned his name that first night."

"Well, he was the only person, besides, Sean . . ." At David's blank look, she explained, "The young guy you met at the office." When he nodded understanding, she continued with her original thought. "They were the only two who had gotten close enough to plant something in my car."

"And you agreed to go out with a man who could do something like that?"

Natalie stood from her chair, brushing against David as she rose to his sitting height. "I didn't know it at the time, and these notes are from someone who's attempting to warn me—"

"Or threaten you." David took Natalie's hand and pulled her toward him, settling her in front of him and between his knees. "The man is not being up front about something if he's resorted to putting notes in your damn trunk every few days. And what about Sean, the other name you mentioned? What do you know about him?"

Natalie shifted her shoulders. "Even less than I know about Carter. He's a junior accountant, a trainee position, I think."

"Yet he works with a top man in the security division?"

Natalie sucked in her breath, and not having an answer, remained silent.

David, still seated on the desk, leveled his eyes at Natalie. "How do you feel about this? Are you scared?" He tilted his head at her. "I think this is something you should bring to your boss's attention, alert security about Carter—"

"He is security."

"In that case, we should show these to the police." He started to stand.

"David, wait." She pushed him back to the desk and then stayed his arms from rising up and around her. "I've been thinking this through on my own, and all night long. That's why my message said to call me at this office. There are things going at Innervision's offices that are business related, and I don't believe the police can deal with them . . . or at least not at this time."

David frowned at the serious words. "Can you talk about it?"

"Only in the most oblique way, and I don't even want to do that in the offices. It's almost lunch. Can you spare some more time and maybe walk with me in the park?"

David dropped his hands to her waist and pulled her to him. "Sure, I can do that." He drew a deep breath that magnified the concentration lines along his brows. "I don't want you in any danger, Natalie."

Grinning, she saluted smartly. "Aye, aye, sir." Intensely aware of his hands still at her waist, she turned slightly and, leaning toward her chair, grabbed up her suit jacket. "Let's go."

With a gentle squeeze to her waist, he stood and joined her as they left through the office. As they neared the front suites that provided luxury offices for the senior partners, John Callaway crossed their paths on the way to the exit.

"Natalie, off to lunch?"

She nodded respectfully, though she was still a little miffed that he seemed to be changing sides on her over the review. "I'll be back in the office a little later if you need to see me."

His eyes had shifted to David, where they remained. "No, no, we're fine. David, ah, Spenser, isn't it?"

"Yes," David said, opening the door. "Good memory."

"Enjoy lunch," John said.

Natalie smiled and left through the door with David.

The few blocks' walk through the skyscraper downtown buildings had been brisk and reviving due to the breezy mid-morning that would easily turn hot by midafternoon.

They had passed the time as Natalie recounted for David the seemingly unconnected events of the past days, and how possibly they could all fit together. She didn't know how yet, but something told her they were related.

"It starts with an innocuous little note that doesn't make sense in the scheme of my life. Next thing you know, my office is burglarized, and I'm the only anal staff member who recognizes a few files, Innervision's files, mind you, out of order.

"So, I get a second note left in my car, and it's a lot more in-your-face—I guess because, what, I'm not being careful like the first one warned?" She looked at David and saw that he was still listening intently.

"And then, lo and behold, I return to L & M's office this morning, and I discover that the personal radios and TVs and coffeemakers and such that were stolen in the burglary have all been recovered in a nice burlap bag sitting right on our building property." She sighed. "Go figure."

"You're right," David said. "Too much to be a coincidence."

They had reached the park entrance. David passed a hot dog to Natalie from the street vendor, and then he took one for himself. They crossed the street into the park and strolled along the redbrick sidewalks of the city's popular Centennial Park, built and named during the city's host duties to the 1996 Summer Olympics.

"So, what makes you believe they're connected to you and your work at Innervision?"

"My career was pretty ordinary until I embarked on this need to extend a particular audit review. Suddenly, my previous prowess on the balance sheet is being called into question. And it's all Blakely. He has been fighting me tooth and nail on everything. I can't give you details, but he doesn't want to explain anything and it's getting both personal and ugly."

David stopped a moment and looked at her. "Do you want to take that kind of abuse?"

"I can take care of myself, and I won't give him the satisfaction of running over me."

They had worked their way around the park's front periphery and now sat on one of the cement benches facing the spectacular spouting fountains in the park's center to finish their drinks.

"So you think someone is warning you to back off whatever it is you're uncovering?"

"Unfortunately, I don't know what that is, yet."

"Someone must think you know more than you do."

"In their own way, maybe they're trying to help," she said.

"Or like I said, they want to scare you into backing off. You know the legal ramifications of signing off on a review you don't believe in. With that said, I don't blame you for standing your ground."

Natalie's concentration dropped as she looked past David's shoulder and spied, across the street, the unmistakable figure of Carter. And he was talking to a man they had all come to know very well, a friend of Justin's, Connie Preston, the private eye.

"David . . ." Natalie's voice had dropped to a whisper. "Look across the street, near the construction."

Spurred by her anxiety, he jerked his body around to follow her gaze.

"Do you see them?" she whispered.

"I wonder what he's doing talking with Connie."

"Remember Justin mentioning something about a friend of his in the security business, too, at the restaurant?"

"Vaguely, but then the belly dancers came out and, well, you know the rest of that story." He looked back at Natalie, whose stare hadn't retreated from the men.

"They do have a common interest," she said, and now looked at David. "They're in the security business."

"Spying, too. Justin had Connie do a pretty good job of it on me and Davina before he knew us."

"You're right. Connie specializes in investigations. But, why would Carter meet him in the park if it's Innervision business?"

David turned back to Natalie and saw the worry evident on her face. "Whatever he's doing, I want you to stay away from him until we know more about these notes. Someone's getting into your car. . . . Maybe I could pick you up from work—"

"David, you're sounding like a mother hen. I'm not afraid of being harmed physically."

"A threat is a threat—at least promise me you'll have a security guard walk you to your car. "

"Okay, but it's only a warning that something else is going on."

"If you won't bring this to your boss's attention, and you feel threatened in any way by Innervision—"

"Nothing will happen." She turned to him, and placed a hand over his. "David, I'm sure it's all related to this audit, and that's all I can say." She tilted her head. "You know that."

He grabbed up her hand. "You're stubborn as hell. If there's anything I can do, you let me know, okay?"

"I will."

"Come on, John gave us sort of a peculiar look when we left, so you think he's checking the clock?" He laughed. "He probably thinks we're having a little afternoon delight. I sure hate to disappoint the man."

Natalie laughed. "We haven't been gone an hour."

"Hey—you work magic with the time you're given."

Grinning, they walked back toward the office. Though Natalie did throw another cautious look over her shoulder at the distant figures, and thought she saw Connie hand something to Carter.

"Is this what you have for me?" Carter opened the folder Connie had handed to him and, removing his sunglasses, glanced over the three pages that contained stacked paragraphs of information. A few paragraphs had snapshots attached, all of which were male, Caucasian, and between the ages of twenty-five and forty-five.

"Preliminary findings, that's all." Connie shifted his stance and folded his arms against his broad chest.

Today, with short sleeves and his signature notepad in his pocket, Connie had dispensed with the suit and tie he donned for a new client's introduction. This was their third meeting, and in as many different places.

"After narrowing down the findings based on your basic description of George Webster's occupation and skills, I came up with these candidates."

While Connie had talked, Carter had already begun to peruse the thumbnail sketches of the thirty or so possibilities on the pages.

He had only gotten as far as the middle of the second page when he stopped reading.

"This one," Carter said. "This could be the George Webster I want."

Connie stepped closer to peer at the selection. "We didn't have a picture available, but you're sure? There's another page to look over."

Carter smiled and settled the sunglasses back on his face. "All I need to know is in that paragraph. He has a business degree and he's a former Innervision employee." He pushed the file back at Connie.

"Find a picture," he said. "And then see if you can track his whereabouts."

When the phone rang that night, Natalie pushed away from the desk in her study and, out of habit, read the caller ID. It was David. Again.

He had called her earlier, after she had arrived home from work. It was just to make sure she hadn't received another note and that she was okay. She actually liked the idea of someone checking on her, making sure she was safe, and wanting to know how her day had gone.

She picked up the receiver. "Hi, David."

"At least you're answering my calls tonight. How's it going?"

Natalie curled up her feet in the chair. "I feel like taking a shower and hitting the sack, but I'm in the middle of ideas, so I've got to slop along until I have something concrete to take to my boss."

"You know, when lovers talk on the phone, they're supposed to say things like, 'What are you wearing?' or, 'When I see you again, here's what I'm going to do to you'—"

She interrupted his suggestive talk with a laugh. "We're not lovers, and you're not coming over tonight, but if it'll make you feel better, I'm wearing sweats."

"Well, you can't blame a man for trying."

Natalie smiled, enjoying the banter.

"I noticed something," David said.

"And that is?"

"We've disagreed a lot today, but we didn't argue or get carried away, did we? Not one time. We handled it like we cared about each other's way of thinking."

Natalie dropped back on the sofa and allowed her smile to flow through her. "I did notice that. But, I didn't want to say anything, you know, and mess up the Karma going on. After all, it's only been a day."

"Are you ready for the christening weekend coming up," he asked.

"Yeah, a lot's going on. We have that dinner at the Hardys' tomorrow night, and the christening on Sunday and the all-day dinner and party afterward."

"And then—"

"And then by this time next week you'll be preparing to head back to Washington." Natalie sat up, her joy dissolving at her words. The momentary silence on the other end didn't help her, either.

"It's hard to believe two weeks can speed by so fast."

"I, um, have to go," she said, speaking quickly. "I've got to get back to this paperwork."

"So, I'll see you tomorrow night at the Hardys'?"

"Sure." She let out a hollow chuckle. "After all, I am a godmother these days. Save me a seat."

They exchanged good nights and Natalie hung up the phone.

It had happened, and she hadn't even noticed how involved she'd become. She didn't want David to leave . . . not for a while, not ever. Damn, but she was in love.

Chapter 21

Access denied. Please see your LAN administrator.

"Damn." Natalie pushed away from the computer's flashing screen and crossed her arms in disgust.

Although this was the first denial she'd received for the afternoon, the warning had already flashed dozens of times that morning. Innervision's computers seemed ready for every amateur attempt she had tried in order to get into the details for an oddly named account with an equally unusually large figure applied to it.

Natalie stared at the entry on the spreadsheet she was trying to break into. Two hundred million entered as *prepaid subsidy*. It had no invoices attached to it, nor a history to explain its existence, yet it had been tucked away in the capital accounts. Who signed off on the sizeable capital expenditure?

Natalie had been up late. She was tired, and now flexed her neck. Each new discovery she came across managed to put her on edge, but she knew she had to press on to figure out the source for this most recent entry she'd unearthed last night.

If she could only open the file, she could then cross-check

and see what kinds of capital costs were associated with it to justify the large fees. But, she kept coming up empty.

After a few more futile attempts, Natalie gave up trying to open it. She decided to take a much-needed break and get a shot of caffeine from the cafeteria.

With a windowless view surrounding her most of the day, Natalie capitalized on this opportunity to sit near a window as she sipped on her drink. Her thoughts, though, had already returned to the problems that awaited her in that office.

"This is some surprise, catching you in here. You seldom leave your office."

Natalie sat up at Carter's voice, and immediately became guarded, the fact that she knew so little about him rising up like a wall. "Hi," she greeted him. "Do you want to join me?"

"Yes, thanks." He slid his suited form onto the chair across from her and clasped his hands together on top of the table. "I'd planned to look you up before the day was over."

"Oh, really?" Natalie asked. "Why?"

"That debt you figured you owed me—are you ready to pay up?"

Natalie squinted at him. "Maybe I should ask, what's the cost?"

Carter crossed his arms on the table. "It's not that bad. In fact, you might even like the bill."

She smiled. "All right, I'm game. What do you want from me?"

"Go with me to Innervision's stockholders' party next week."

"You mean that gala that Blakely keeps saying I'm going to ruin for his stockholders if I don't sign off on the review?" she asked with a raised brow.

Carter nodded. "It's a glorified dinner party for the bigwigs. You know, all of those senior managers you've been wanting to interview will be there, too."

Natalie had already considered that possibility. She also knew that David would have a fit when he found out she accepted; but how could she not go when she'd have all of those brains in one room to pick? Once again, her appearance would aggravate the hell out of Blakely.

"You're serious?" she asked. "Does Blakely know you're asking me to come to his shindig?"

He shifted on the chair, as if it were a minor issue. "It's a big party. I doubt if he'll even know you're there. In the end, though, it's your call." He lifted his brow. "You can think about it over the weekend. An answer on Monday is soon enough."

"Okay. I'm figuring this is a formal affair?"

"Right." His grin turned into a white smile. "Though I'm sure you can be appropriately audacious, regardless of the dress or occasion."

Natalie's smile reached her eyes against her better judgment. She didn't want to like Carter, and on a number of levels. So, she didn't want to give him the idea that she was interested in him beyond the office, and she surely didn't trust his motivations, what with all that had happened, and she wasn't totally convinced he had nothing to do with the second note.

"And when should I plan my audacity?"

"Next Tuesday night. It'll be in the main atrium downstairs." He rose from his seat. "Think about it, and I'll check with you later."

Natalie nodded and then watched him walk off and exit through the doors. She now stood, too. Dropping her cup in the trash receptacle, she headed for the door, preparing herself to go back and tackle the growing stack of accounting entries that seemed to have materialized from nowhere.

If she didn't have something more concrete by the beginning of next week, she would have to bow to the pressure and sign off on the review. Maybe this was what the previous reviewers had been faced with—mounds of questions with no clear answers.

As Natalie neared the exit, her glance took in the room and she saw Myra seated by herself near a window. Almost against her will and without a second thought, Natalie turned in the woman's direction. *Blakely will be mad as hell,* she told herself. But then again, what was wrong with having a friendly break with another employee?

She came alongside the woman's table. "Myra, what an opportunity, running into you like this."

Myra's sad eyes flew up and took in Natalie, and it was as though they'd been caught in deadly headlights. She snatched up her change purse sitting on the table, and prepared to scramble from the booth seat.

"I was just leaving," she said.

"No. Stay for just a moment, please." Natalie's hand touched the woman's shoulder even as she blocked an easy egress. She felt Myra's sigh of concurrence as her shoulder dropped.

"Okay." Myra sidled back into the booth as Natalie crossed over and sat opposite her.

"How are you and that report doing?" Natalie asked, her tone friendly.

"Coming along, keeping me and the other managers busy," Myra replied, her smile hesitant as she raised her eyes to Natalie's. "You know Mr. Blakely doesn't want me talking to you."

"I know, but there's really no logical reason why we can't. Do you think his demand is working simply because he knows you won't go against him?" Natalie pulled a napkin from the holder and wiped her hands, ostensibly to give Myra a moment to respond.

"I have to take orders from my boss, Mr. Ford, and he takes them from Mr. Blakely. There's a hierarchy here, and we respect it, Ms. Goodman." She picked up her cup. "You don't work here, but it's how we've survived this long." She drank deeply.

"Everybody knows your Mr. Blakely is a bully, but at what cost do you survive, Myra?" Natalie lowered her voice. "I know you don't like him; I don't think anyone around here does. So, defy him for once and help me with a question or two."

The woman's eyes darted around the room, as though she expected to be watched. "I've got to go." She made to leave again.

"Wait, wait." Natalie's hand snaked across the table and caught Myra's arm. "I can be a bit blunt at times. I'm sorry, and I don't mean to insult you, but I'm trying to find out something about an odd account I found. It's called prepaid subsidy and it was buried in the capital accounts."

Natalie saw a flicker of recognition in Myra's brows. "Do you know what that is?" she pressed. "When I try to get into it, I keep running into firewalls."

Myra drew a deep breath. "You're looking for names." She dropped her head and looked at her cup, her voice dropping to a whisper. "Start with a list of subcontractors."

Natalie stared at the small woman a moment, trying to figure out what she was talking about. "Subcontractors in the capital accounts?"

"I've got to go. . . ." She was sliding across the booth.

Natalie reached for her arm. "You say I should—"

Myra shook Natalie's hand away and grabbed up her cup. "I've . . . I've said too much as it is."

"But—" Natalie watched as the woman launched herself from the seat and almost ran for the exit.

As she slumped back, all Natalie could do was shake her head and consider the unexpected suggestion given her by Myra.

Natalie had returned to her office, anxious to try out Myra's suggestion. The woman had looked pretty bad, she thought, as though she'd lost her best friend. Settled once again in front of the computer, Natalie entered the proper codes, and finally got to the point where she had constantly hit the proverbial firewall. She entered the new subsearch request, as Myra had suggested.

"Subcontractors." She muttered the word as she typed it in, and then hit the send key.

Within seconds, a separate window was superimposed on the screen and a new account with that name expanded onto the screen.

"Whoa . . ." Natalie scrolled down through, surely, a hundred entries. Interestingly enough, all of the subcontractors appeared to be individuals, and some with quite exotic-sounding names. She chose one of them and requested a separate breakdown of that contractor's payments because, unlike the others, she saw it listed at regular intervals, and in different name forms.

Randy Synn. *He has an odd name,* she thought, and requested all forms of the name for payment history over the last four quarters.

"All right, Mr. Synn, let's see what Innervision has been paying you." Natalie waited a few seconds before the request completed. She peered at the screen. Fifteen entries blinked out at her.

The contractor's name showed up three different ways, and was being paid almost cyclically. Every quarter showed a group of payments made.

After a search, Natalie could locate no explanation of the work performed, and no corresponding work orders for the journal entries. There was no way to scrutinize the transaction by going back to the original journal entry to see how it was justified. Natalie shook her head. What was going on?

She sat back and rubbed her eyes, and looked again at the figures on the screen. She also thought about the other accounting entries she'd combed through. And it all began to make some kind of strange sense to Natalie.

If she was right, Innervision was aggressively renaming their operating costs—millions of dollars' worth of current expenses, like salaries, contractual work, benefits, and such, that would reduce their bottom line and worth to Wall Street—and tucking them away into capital accounts, where the expenses could be legally deducted over a much longer period.

But the figures Natalie had amassed so far were for only a few accounts, and one quarter. Making a quick estimated calculation for other accounts, and over four quarters, she came up with a staggering figure that had extraordinary implications, both internally and publicly.

Natalie let out a deep breath, looking over her shoulder as a shudder of what this could mean overtook her. And what of all the previous reviews? Did this implicate her company, the outside accounting firm? John Callaway was the partner assigned to Innervision. Was he aware of the fraud?

Rising from her chair, Natalie paced the room, her heart pounding with a combination of fear and elation that she'd been on the right track all along. However, David had warned her about jumping to conclusions, so she had to think this through.

All right, she thought, they had to have support for these figures as well as all of the other anomalies she had found. Surely there was a way for them to reconstruct these expenses. But as she considered their demeanor and the stonewalling she'd faced in the past week, she suspected this was what Blakely wanted kept from her.

Another thought occurred to her, and Natalie stopped her anxious pace. The notes. Was this why she was warned to be careful and watch her back? And by whom?

It was beginning to come clear, and Natalie knew what she had to do. She had to keep silent or she would tip her hand, the numbers would be fixed, and she would be labeled a troublemaker. She also had to continue looking for more.

Natalie turned in the room, suddenly desolate that she couldn't share these details with anyone just yet. Not John, and certainly not Davina or David. David would demand that she stop investigating on her own and bring in the authorities. Natalie couldn't do that right now, because it was all mostly circumstantial discoveries. She'd do what she had to do.

Walking briskly to her desk, she sat at the computer and

then slipped a CD-RW disk into the burner port to download the open files. She had to protect herself.

Natalie was sure she was the last to arrive at the Hardys' for dinner that night. She hadn't planned it that way, but after having left the office late, and then returning home to take a shower and change clothes, she was just happy that she hadn't arrived in the middle of dinner being served.

Alli met her at the front door, her bracelets sounding a musical chorus along her bare arm. The two women greeted each other with a friendly hug before Alli stood back and smiled.

"Well, aren't you dressed to kill tonight?" She referred to the black pleated miniskirt and silk waist shirt Natalie wore under her jacket. Heels and hose finished her outfit.

"Careful . . . I've had one hell of a day," Natalie warned, a twinkle in her eye.

"Maybe we can fix that."

Natalie heard David's deep voice as he came up behind Alli, and her heart gave off a delicious thump.

"I can only hope so," she answered. He was exceptionally handsome tonight, wearing a dark suit, and rather than a tie, he chose a pale knit sweater that hugged his sculptured chest. She was aware, as she stepped into the brightly lit foyer, that Alli had quietly left them.

She turned to David, only to see that his gaze was otherwise occupied as it boldly raked over her. She was by no means blind to his attraction, and after the disquieting day she'd had, his eager affection was welcome.

"Has everyone gone in for dinner?" she asked.

"No." He moved toward her. "Some of us are just hanging out in the salon right now, messing around until it's ready. We have time."

"Good. After the day I've had, I really rushed to get here." He stepped closer, and dropped his hands to her shoulders. "How did things go at the office today? Anything you want to tell me about?"

Natalie wanted to share, but she couldn't. "I can't say anything, you know that."

David nodded. "As long as you think it's safe—"

"And it is," she assured him.

"Then, I'll try not to worry."

He leaned down to kiss her; Natalie parted her lips and raised herself to meet him.

Peals of laughter, followed by conversation, could be heard coming from the adjacent room, and it kept them from indulging the kiss awhile longer.

Dragging his mouth from hers, David gazed into her eyes. "I think we're making progress."

It was hard for Natalie to think clearly with him so close, but she agreed. They were building toward something, and it now seemed inevitable.

He drew her with him toward the salon. "Come on."

They entered the elegantly appointed room and worked their way to the group of sofas where Justin and Davina, Carolyn and Michael, and Alli were laughing.

"We could hear you at the door," Natalie said after she greeted the group. "What's so funny?"

"We were talking about the christening Sunday and the baby names that Davina and Justin played around with before they decided on the final one," Alli explained.

"I swear, there are a lot of peculiar names out there," Carolyn offered.

"And thank goodness they didn't use any of them," Alli added.

"Actually," David said, joining Natalie on the couch, "I wanted one of those really long African names my friends had back in elementary school. The longer, the better, I thought."

"Yeah, but when it came time to spell and pronounce it," Michael said, laughing, "you realized you were better off with that short, simple name."

"How simple was Hennessey?" Carolyn said of Michael's last name, and the group chuckled at the irony.

"You have to give parents the benefit of the doubt if they're trying to be inventive," Davina suggested. "I have one of those unusual names, but I would never have agreed to stick my baby with one of those clunkers."

"No, you just wanted to make him a Junior," Justin said with a grimace.

"I love your name," she said, leaning in to her husband. "And that will be the name of our next son," she added.

"We all could have had worse," Natalie said from her seat. "You should be glad you didn't get stuck with a name like Randy Synn," Natalie said, before she received a host of chuckles.

"Are you serious?" Alli asked.

Natalie nodded as she remembered the name from the accounts. "It's real."

"First of all, what adult would willingly claim it as theirs?" Davina offered.

"It could work if you're a porn star," Carolyn suggested merrily as she looked at Michael.

Michael's broad smile deepened into laughter. "She was a stripper," he announced, meeting her gaze.

Their comments were a surprise, and Natalie joined the others who turned to the couple.

"You know someone by that name?" Natalie asked.

Michael nodded as he tucked his arm through Carolyn's. "I think it's her stage name." He looked at Carolyn for confirmation, but she shook her head.

"You tell them the story," she said with a grin.

"Well, this all seems coincidental, but when Carolyn and I first met, there was this dancer we knew who went by that name."

It was Carolyn's turn to nod as she laughed. "Just cut to the chase. The woman was a stripper at the Sheik's Harem at the time."

While the friends had another round of laughs, Natalie's

brain absorbed the information and was now running with it. "That's the so-called gentleman's club in midtown, right?"

"If it's still there," David said.

"It's still there," Michael said. "But surely your Randy Synn isn't the same Randi we're talking about. You're talking about a man, right? We're talking about a woman."

Natalie drew a sigh as she hunched her shoulders. "Actually, I don't know." She turned to David. "It's an odd name I came across while I was doing some work today, and I just figured it was a vendor's."

"Oh, yeah, she's vending all right," Carolyn said, and the group joined her in a laugh.

Natalie's brows raised as her thoughts tunneled deep. "In that case, the name I found must belong to someone else."

While another subject quickly rose up in the group, an idea had already begun to form in Natalie's head. She smiled as she turned to David seated beside her, only to find him slowly shaking his head as he curiously regarded her.

It didn't deter Natalie's thoughtful smile. What if the two people were one and the same?

"No way . . . no way, and that's my final answer." David crossed his arms in defiance of the ridiculous proposition. Natalie had cornered him in the library after dinner with the preposterous plan. And it was just like her not to think through an idea before acting on it.

Natalie rested a hand on her hip. "Fine. If you won't take me to the Sheik's Harem, then I'll just have to find someone who will." She spun around and headed for the door, the short skirt revealing slender legs and thighs.

Damn that woman, David thought, and sped after her. Grabbing her by the arm, he hauled her back around to face him.

"Why do you want to do this, anyway? It's dangerous, not to mention reckless." Still faced with her resolute stare, he sought out other reasons. "We're not detectives, Natalie.

And . . . And you shouldn't be in that kind of place, anyway."

"Good grief, David. You don't think I know about lap dances?"

"It's one thing knowing what it is. It's another to watch it performed."

She let out a sigh. "All I want to do is go there, talk with some of the women, and see if there really is a Randi Synn working there." She lowered her voice. "Can you imagine what this could mean if there's an exotic dancer on the payroll?"

"You don't know what you're doing."

"Like I said, if you won't go with me, I'll get Alli to go." At that moment, Alli came into the library.

"Sure, I'll go." She looked at Natalie. "Go where?"

"And we'll ask Carter to escort us," Natalie said, her voice a dare.

"We will?" Alli asked, smiling and totally in the dark.

David wanted to strangle Natalie's beautiful neck right about now. If he didn't take her to the club, he knew she'd find another way. And he damn sure didn't want it to be Carter.

"All right," he said. "I'll take you."

"Me too?" Alli asked.

"No," David said as he looked into Natalie's smiling face. "Tomorrow night at eight, Natalie and I are going on a date."

Chapter 22

David maneuvered his sleek sports car into a secluded parking space at the Sheik's Harem.

After he had picked up Natalie at her house, they had gone out to eat, a contentious meal wherein he'd tried to talk her out of this foolish idea. She had prevailed, however, with the simple argument that it wouldn't hurt to know if such a woman existed at the club, and if that particular woman had ties to Blakely.

She also reiterated the threat that she could always find someone else to escort her there, though she preferred that it be David. So much for his negotiation skills, he thought.

Turning off the ignition, David looked across the dimly lit car at Natalie seated next to him.

"All right, you're here," he said.

Natalie had straightened up to look around the parking lot. She took in the garishly bright and colorful lights that adorned the roof's perimeter, the faux columns that towered in front of the double-door entrance, and the security men in dark suits who patrolled the entrance.

"So, what's your plan?"

"I'm thinking I'll keep it simple," she said, still observing the scenes outside the window. "I'll go inside, and ask around about a Randi Synn working here."

David shook his head. "I don't think it'll be quite that easy."

"Let me finish," she argued. "I'll inquire discreetly, and if she's actually here, I'll ask her about Blakely and Innervision." Natalie smiled. "If she says no, I can gauge her reaction to see if she's lying."

A helpless chuckle escaped David, and he shook his head again.

"It'll work, David," Natalie protested. "I'm keeping it simple."

"First, there's a no-fraternizing policy at these clubs, and it's well posted, too. You don't get one-on-one time with these girls unless there's a fee involved, negotiated before service is rendered, and then only if she's available or wants to be available."

Natalie tilted her head. "Well, I'll just have to buy Miss Synn's time."

"In the club or privately?"

"Okay, I'll bite." She sighed. "What's the difference?"

David laughed. "How much cash did you bring?" At Natalie's grimace, he once again shook his head. "Admit it; you haven't planned this at all, and you're flying by the seat of your pants."

"Well, do you have a better idea?"

"Me? This is your show, not mine," he said. "You can't go into a strip joint, especially an upscale one like this, and start asking questions like some rank amateur detective."

He watched Natalie study one of the guards, possibly a bouncer, as he walked with two women toward the building's side door.

"Are you listening?" David cautioned. "These clubs have all kinds of activities going on, and a lot of it's illegal, back-room stuff, like gambling and prostitution. You don't want to get caught snooping and asking questions, because the least that will happen is you'll get thrown out by some aggressive security. The worst could be a whole different matter."

He realized she hadn't heard a word he'd said. Instead, her attention was still drawn to the security guard who now appeared to be opening the building's side door and letting the women with him pass through before he closed it and began to walk back to the front.

"David, what's he doing?"

"Looks like maybe a shift change or time for a nightly show. I suspect he's escorting the women through a private rear door as they arrive for work." He turned to Natalie, his brows rising suspiciously as she sat up and began taking off the jacket she'd worn over her shirt and skirt. "Why?"

"Because that's how I'm going to get in. Through the back." She tossed her jacket onto the tiny backseat, and began to unbuckle the leather belt from her Lycra skirt. "I'll follow the women in, say I'm a new dancer, hang out in their dressing room, and find Randi Synn for myself."

"You're insane," David said, his eyes studying her as he wondered what she'd do next. "They'll know you don't work here."

"I'll improvise. You saw those other women, right? I'll just have to blend in with them." Natalie quickly began to undo some of the buttons on her sleeveless shirt. At about halfway down, when she had exposed a lacy black bra, she turned her back to David. "Help me out. Reach under, please, and unhook my bra."

David twisted around in his seat and looked at her, deciding this surely must be hell. When he hesitated, trying to decide if this was absolutely crazy or what, Natalie looked over her shoulder impatiently.

"David, come on. Unhook me."

"I can't believe I'm going along with this harebrained stunt of yours." Scowling, he gingerly reached under her now loose shirt—her supple skin's warmth was like an aphrodisiac— and caught the bra's tabs in his fingers. With only a minor fumble, he managed to unhook it, though his hand lingered for a moment on the silky texture of her soft, warm skin. He pulled his hands out from under her shirt.

"Okay, now what?" Fascinated, David felt his eyes intent on every move she made.

She turned back around and, reaching inside her sleeve, pulled the bra strap down past her shoulder and elbow and then leveraged her arm through. She did the same with the other strap, before she reached inside the front of her shirt and pulled out the bra, tossing it into the back with her jacket. Her jutting breasts, now free, strained against the remaining buttons, but she left only enough buttons undone to allow an enticing view of cleavage.

"I think that'll work," she said, turning her collar up.

David swallowed hard—and more than once in those long seconds—feeling as though he'd witnessed a private striptease through her transformation from the everyday seductive Natalie who easily raised his blood pressure to a sexy temptress who caused it to boil.

Lifting her shirt's hem, she rolled down the waist of her skirt so that the length was shorter and the top rode just below her belly button.

"I guess I should keep on my garter, stockings, and underwear." She smiled as she turned to him. "You never know when they may come in handy inside."

"You're enjoying this, aren't you?" David's eyes had strained in the dim light to follow her hands to the top of the garters where she tightened them before he returned his gaze to her face, and saw that she was looking at him.

"Why are you looking like that?"

"Jeez, Natalie, what do you expect? I'm not dead and you're stripping in my car."

"Well, if you can't take it, then turn your head," she suggested. "I'm sorry to do this here, but I have no choice. Look." She pointed to a car not far from theirs. "The woman who just got out of her car—I'll bet she works here. I'm going to follow her in."

David sighed, and rubbed at his brow. "I'll stay in the car

and keep watch until you're inside. And for God's sake, please be careful."

"I'll be back before you know it."

"Look for me inside the club. I'll be waiting for you as close to the back entry as I can get without drawing suspicion. I'll give you ten minutes inside—"

"No, David. I need at least fifteen—"

"Okay, fifteen minutes, and that's it. If you don't join me in the club by then, I'm going to come looking for you—I don't care if I blow your cover."

While he had talked, Natalie had reapplied lipstick and fluffed her hair to put the finishing touches on her transformation. She now turned to him, and in the fluorescent colors that washed over them, she looked more delicate and ethereal than ever.

"Don't worry. I'll be okay." She opened her door and swung her legs from the car.

David swallowed the words he wanted to say, that she should be careful of men coming on to her, that she should call out if she needed him . . . he could go on and on; but this was Natalie, and she had this crazy sense of her own power. Never mind that she barely tipped the scale at a hundred pounds at five three.

"Promise me you won't do anything even more stupid than this."

"She's going in. I've got to go." Almost as an afterthought, Natalie paused and looked back at David, a gentleness softening her eyes. "Thanks for watching my back." She slammed the door shut and, adjusting her bag on her shoulder, moved toward the building.

David held himself from hauling her back in the car, and watched as she expertly maneuvered across the parking lot in the very high heels and very short skirt, the exaggerated sway becoming her own. He could easily watch a lot more than her back, he mused lustily.

She quickly merged with the woman, and the guard in turn

joined them. He opened a barely noticeable door set into the wall, and the women stepped through. Within a minute of leaving the car, Natalie was out of sight.

David released the breath he'd been holding, and got out of the car. And as he ambled his tall frame toward the front entrance, he thought to himself, what had he let Natalie talk him into?

The dancer that Natalie accompanied showed no interest in her, except that she was brand-new on the job. Natalie did gather from their short conversation that she wasn't Randi Synn, and followed her to the dressing room that was shared with the other dancers. Two were already in the room, and in various stages of dress—or undress, as the case might be.

Natalie wasn't frightened or even nervous over her charade; in fact, the playacting had become just another challenge she enjoyed. The dressing room was large and made even more airy by the multitude of mirrors. The row of makeup tables were attached together and set in a line on either side of the wall below the mirrors. She propped her bag at the empty table nearest the door when the woman she'd entered with called out.

"Hey, girls, we got somebody new joining us tonight. As usual, nobody told us a damn thing."

"I'm Jeri."

A blonde with golden skin and enormous breasts spilling from her wedding gown costume had looked up from her chair where she was rubbing body oil into her legs. Natalie would bet the farm that a quarter could bounce off those silicone breasts.

A pretty though sullen-looking black woman wearing a dressing robe applied makeup while she sat at another table. "I'm Carleshia," she announced without looking up.

"Hi," Natalie answered, and swiveled her head back to the mirror and played with touching up her lipstick.

"What name you dance under, honey?" Jeri asked.

"Ah . . ." Natalie looked down at her tube of lipstick for divine intervention. "Natasha Blue," she blurted out easily.

"Well, Natasha," Jeri said, looking her up and down, "you're a tiny little thing. I didn't think Tony was big on the short ones." She laughed. "Legs and boobs, that's all I've ever known him to look for."

"There's a freak out there for every shape and size," the dancer Natalie had come in with deadpanned as she left the room.

"So, what's your specialty?" Jeri asked.

"Well, ah, actually, I was waiting around to get some pointers from my friend Randi." She looked at the two women. "Randi Synn. You know her?"

The comment got a rise out of Carleshia. She stopped with her makeup and gave a hard squint to Natalie. "Randi's not gonna be here for a while. She doesn't go on till midnight," she said, frowning. "Why would she be giving you pointers, anyway?"

"Yeah," Jeri acknowledged. "I wouldn't consider her the most likely person to offer help."

Natalie turned back to her makeup, and tried to nonchalantly craft a believable tale that would snare information. "Well, we're not that close. I only met her recently through a mutual friend of ours—at that big company downtown. You know, Innervision. Anyway, this other friend told me to look Randi up. She could show me the ropes."

"Innervision. Yeah," Jeri said, recognition in her voice. "I heard of them." She turned around to Carleshia. "Isn't that where Randi's—" Jeri stopped. "So, where'd Carleshia go?"

Natalie looked around and she, too, realized the standoffish dancer had disappeared through the rear door. She crossed her arms and looked at Jeri. "What were you saying about Randi?"

"Only that the company you mentioned is where Randi's sugar daddy works." She let out a chuckle as she winked at Natalie. "It's no big secret since she lets it out every now and then for bragging rights."

"Oh—you know his name?" Natalie tried to keep her voice casual.

"Now, that she won't say. Course, Carleshia probably knows. They're pretty tight, which is why she wanted to know the dirt with you and Randi."

Natalie turned back to the mirror, and tried to contain the excitement in her eyes. Her hunch had been right. Although his name hadn't been mentioned, she was sure it meant that Blakely was involved in cooking the books at Innervision and paying his girlfriend from the company payroll. Sure that her fifteen-minute limit was up, she had to get out of here and find David.

"I'm going to make a bathroom run before I get dressed." She picked up her bag. "Which way?" she asked.

"Down the hall, on your right."

"Okay," Natalie said gaily. "I'll be right back."

She left the room and quickly headed down the hall, but two men in black, tuxedo-style dress stood at its end, talking. She could swear she heard one call the other Tony. From what the dancer had said, Tony would know she wasn't a new dancer.

Natalie immediately turned around to go to the opposite end of the hall.

When she reached the end, it was a toss-up on which direction would take her to the nearest exit, so she decided to go right and try to double-back around to avoid the men.

But the halls became a maze, and there were rooms busy with activities going on throughout. She doubled-back again, and tried to find her way to the dressing room, hopelessly confused by the layout.

"Hey, what are you doing back here?"

Natalie didn't like that official voice, and so she didn't stop, but continued on, using the sounds of party voices and muffled music as a guide to lead her into the club. But she could feel the security guard gaining on her.

"Hey, I'm talking to you."

This corridor did lead back into the club, and there was

David, straight ahead, with his head stuck through the doorway, looking for her. Natalie let out a deep sigh of relief, and slowed down to play her part.

David and security converged on Natalie almost simultaneously.

"Didn't you hear me calling you?" the security guard demanded. "What were you doing back there near the offices?"

"I'm a new dancer," she said, smiling and fiddling with her hair.

"What's with the pocketbook?"

"Oh, this." She looked at her purse. "I made a run to the bathroom before I planned to entertain my customer with a private dance, and I got so turned around that I couldn't even find the dressing room again to store this. So, I was just looking for my customer."

She turned to David as he came up. "Oh, there you are, big boy," she said with a wink as she faced him. "I didn't know where you'd gone."

"Ah, yeah, I was looking for you, too," David said as he watched her oddly. "Come on." He took her hand, and turned to retrace his steps.

"Hey, buddy, you know the rules. Hands off," the guard huffed. "And the private dance rooms are on the other corridor, not this one," he added as he regarded them with a bit of suspicion. "Come on, they're this way."

While the guard brought up the rear as they walked through another hallway, Natalie looked back and, reading David's displeasure, hoped he would continue to play along.

"Here you go." The guard whisked back a curtain at a doorway, and stood aside so David and Natalie could enter.

The room was little more than a ten-by-ten carpeted alcove that had music piped in and a coffee table with a couple of chairs, one a wide, curving lounge chair, ostensibly for the lap dance recipient's comfort.

"Thank you," Natalie said, thinking the guard would now leave, and they could make their escape. "You can go now."

He grinned. "You are new, huh? You know the rules, though.

I have to stick around to check and make sure your boy here doesn't do anything illegal."

"All right, big boy," she said, and turned to David. "Are we going to do this thing or what?"

David settled himself on the chair, and put his arms on the rests so he wouldn't touch her. Natalie sauntered over to the table and set her purse down before she followed him to the chair, awkwardly straddling his thighs as the black garters peeked out from her rising hem.

"I'm sorry." She mouthed the words only David could see as she noted his anger by his set face, his clamped mouth, and fixed eyes. He was mad, and rightly so. As she settled against him and could feel his control beneath her, she felt guilty for putting him through this, and in the presence of other people, to boot.

The nonchalant guard had already returned to the door, reaching over to turn up the music on his way out. Apparently satisfied that all was going well, he said "I'll be right outside the door." He gave David a hard final stare. "And remember, no touching."

"Got you," David said, his gaze never wavering from Natalie's.

The curtains were drawn with a crisp snap, and they were alone.

Natalie put her finger to her lips and turning her head, motioned to the door. "Play along," she whispered under the music. "Maybe he'll leave."

David's scowl returned to his face. "Do you see what your plan has led to? Are you happy?" he whispered, gripping the chair's arms.

Natalie was not proud now and she looked around to the door. When she saw the guard peek through the curtain for a moment, she leveraged her arms against the back of the lounger, and quickly began a bump and grind across David's lap.

"I found out that Randi Synn does work here and she's got a connection at Innervision," she whispered at David's ear. "It seems she has a benefactor over there. How much do you want to bet it's Blakely?"

"That's her picture on the wall."

Natalie craned her neck to follow his gaze, and saw the grouping of small, black-and-white composites of the dancers. Randi was tall, statuesque, and quite pretty. Natalie couldn't remember ever seeing her around Innervision; she didn't think she would have forgotten such a striking figure.

She turned back to David, and was met by the onslaught of his mouth. With her senses reeling, she realized his hands were already stroking the top of her exposed thighs.

"A man can only take so much," he said, and kissed her hard.

Her world tumbled from the twofold assault, and Natalie's body folded against David of its own accord. He opened his mouth on hers, and she accepted his tongue, darting and searching for the rhythm their bodies had now found.

Natalie's arms left the chair to clutch at David's neck, and stroked the soft hair at his nape, and she forgot everything except his touch. David broke from the kiss in his search for another sensual destination. Natalie raised her head and threw it back, as David's mouth dipped inside her shirt and licked the valley between her supple breasts, moving, unerringly, toward a ripe nipple.

As she tried catching her breath, Natalie turned her head and saw that the guard's shadow was no longer on the curtain. He had gone. David's hand had already begun to stroke the sensitive skin inside her thighs, and was steadily moving higher . . .

"David, he's gone," Natalie whispered huskily. "We can get out of here."

Lifting his head, he pulled his hands back and clutched the chair arms. Flushed from their foreplay, he took a deep breath.

Natalie lifted her leg over him and, standing, readjusted her clothes. David, too, now sprang up off the chair.

She grabbed up her purse and followed him through the door, where they promptly ran into the guard.

"You finished already?" he asked, a knowing grin on his face.

"Yeah," Natalie said, as they walked past him. "He got to the point pretty fast."

When they turned the corner, it was a simple matter of going back through the crowded main floor of the club and exiting through the front door. David had grabbed Natalie's hand as they made their exit, but a glance to the raised stage gave her a glimpse of Jeri's fantasy bride performance in progress.

As soon as they hit the front door, Natalie let out a whoop of relief, but David continued to drag her on to his car, and he didn't say anything until they were both safely ensconced in it once again.

"You want to explain to me what just happened in there?" he said. "And between us?"

Natalie let out a deep breath, and dropped her head back to the headrest. "I'm not quite sure myself. I guess we got caught up in the moment."

He inserted the key in the ignition. "And that's all you think went on? We got caught in a moment?" He straightened in the seat before he turned to her. "You think I wanted to kiss you and touch you the way I did in a strip joint's dance chair?"

"It didn't mean anything. We knew why we were there."

"It didn't mean anything," he mumbled, and shook his head in frustration. "You still don't get it."

"I'm sorry. I know it was unfair to put you through all this—"

"Do you think I was proud of you performing with a guard watching us there? It took every bit of self-control I could muster to stay there. But, I know you, and I know you were set to do this; so, damn it, I let you have your way." He looked at her. "I swallowed my pride for you tonight."

Natalie looked at him and saw that he was angry, but not at her. He was angry with himself.

"David, I . . ." A glance at the mirror showed a familiar figure nearing the car. "Look at that man. Isn't that Carter?"

David looked in his mirror, and sat up. "Yeah, you're right. It is him."

"He can't see me here. If he's involved in any of this, he may figure out what we know." She ducked in the car and buried her head against David's lap.

"He's almost past now," David said, his arm and hand blocking his own face from view. "He's not looking our way anymore."

After a few more seconds, David said, "He's going inside now."

At that moment, a rap sounded at the window. David moved his arm and looked up. Natalie stayed put. Just in case, she thought.

It was security.

David let the window down. "Yes?"

"Hey, you've got to move along. You know we can't be having any of that in the parking lot." His nod and gaze was to Natalie's head as it brushed the steering wheel.

"What?" Natalie quickly raised herself up to see the guard as he backed away from the car.

David turned the ignition key, and the car roared awake. "After all you've done tonight," he said, "you have no reason to be offended." He tightened his jaw, no sign of humor on his face, and drove the car from the parking lot, heading for her house.

Chapter 23

"I wonder what Carter was doing there," Natalie mused aloud. "It has to do with Randi, somehow. I want to go back and talk to her."

They had just arrived at Natalie's house and David, after closing the front door, was coming behind Natalie through the foyer. "Did I just hear you right?" he asked.

"Well, we know she works there," Natalie reasoned, leaning against the table at the base of the stairs and slipping from her shoes. "Why not build on that and learn what she knows about Blakely before our hand is tipped?"

David stopped in front of her, and even as his expression had worked into a frown at her comment, his eyes were drawn to her legs as she kicked the shoes away and then turned to go into the living room.

"How do you know that the man Randi is seeing at Innervision isn't your friend, Carter?" He followed behind her. "You already know enough pieces of suspicion to just turn them over to the proper authorities."

She tossed him a glance from over her shoulder. "That's just it. All I have are bits and pieces of the puzzle." She dropped onto the end of the sofa, and curled her feet beneath her. "Doesn't all this make you wonder where everybody fits in the big picture?"

"Right now," he said, shrugging from his jacket, "I'm more interested in where I fit in yours."

Natalie didn't know what to say, so rather than answer David, she watched him drop the jacket across a chair before he took up the other end of the sofa. When he extended his arm across the back and stretched out his long legs, the silk shirt clung to his muscular body.

She took him all in, down to the sleek pants that accentuated his brawny thighs; she knew he peered at her, too, and their earlier shared sensuality rose up between them like a physical force. Natalie swallowed at the memory and broke from the power of his invisible charm.

"Tonight ended up a little crazy, I admit that." She looked at him uneasily. Theirs had been a strained ride home after the performance they shared on the dance chair. With their intense awareness of each other, that dance had been like nothing Natalie could remember—like experiencing forbidden fruit, and getting away with it. The fruit had been their growing need for each other.

From the look in David's eyes, and like Natalie, he was still hungry.

"I didn't mean to pull you into it," she continued. "I didn't think it would end up—"

"Half of the time you don't think. You just jump in and worry about the consequences later."

It was as though something clicked in Natalie when she heard the criticism. Suddenly defensive and vulnerable, she leaned back and closed her eyes. "In that case, I'm figuring you aren't going with me when I return to talk to Randi." She could hear David straighten up from the sofa.

"I don't get it. What makes you do this crazy stuff? It's like you enjoy being the outrageous center of attention . . . the dance at the restaurant; this rogue investigation of your client; and now, cruising around a strip joint asking for information about a dancer who might know Carter or Blakely, or both. You've been getting notes left in your car, you could be in danger, and it all goes right over your head."

Natalie had heard enough. She uncrossed her legs and hastily rose from the sofa. "Why does it bother you so much that I make my own decisions and know what I want?"

"Do you?" he asked.

"You're damned right, I do. You want a life that's all planned in a nutshell with all the proper things done." She looked at him. "Well, I don't." She started to turn away.

David also jumped up, and he grabbed at her hand and twisted her back around to him. "You act like you're running at full speed, away from something, and if you slow up, it'll take you over. So, you just keep on running, no matter what happens along the way, to make sure you keep one step ahead of it."

Natalie's eyes flashed as she sank into memories better left behind. "I don't need to be analyzed."

"Well, then, grow up and stop making decisions like a child."

All Natalie could see was her father, belittling her cowering mother; and her hand, seemingly under its own volition, rose up.

"Don't talk to me that way." She struck David hard against his jaw; the resulting pain to her hand was deadening, and she let out a loud grunt from both the pain and surprise at what she'd done.

David turned her loose as he touched his jaw. Natalie expected to see anger, but she saw both confusion and surprise.

"I'm sorry," he said. "I let my frustration from tonight out on you." He stepped closer. "But I worry about you, Natalie. I've decided that what you need is for me to help temper that impulsive nature of yours."

As David's arrogance dawned on Natalie, he had already bent down and swept her into his arms. Caught off guard, she writhed in protest as he buried his mouth against hers, but it took only a moment before she melted against his deliciously hard chest. His mouth, his body, it was all good. But she had to stop this . . . this madness.

She pulled free of his embrace, dizzy with desire. But when she saw the self-satisfied smile on his face, she slapped him again before she stepped back. But, he kept coming toward her. The evening was getting out of her control.

"I want you to go," she demanded feebly.

"Not tonight," he said.

She backed up a step, matching his advance. "We're making a mistake, David."

"We'll worry about it tomorrow," he said.

"You would take a woman against her will?"

He had reached her and, with a tug to her arm, drew her to him again. This time, his lips were more persuasive than Natalie wanted to admit, and she wrapped her arms around him. With the drop of his hands, she was lost as they moved under her skirt to skim along her hips and thighs, and then pressed against her butt in a delicate caress, before she was raised to meet him intimately.

"Do I hear a no?" he teased as his lips moved to nibble her ear.

"Oh, shut up, and kiss me," she commanded.

With a throaty grunt, David complied with cruel mastery. Abruptly, he pulled away and, with his arms under her knees, picked her up and headed for the stairs and the soft bed waiting on the second floor.

"I got your phone message. So, what's going on?" Carter's glance around the club took in the late partygoers, primarily men, as he sat apart from the main floor at a small cocktail table near the back. He had waited an hour for Carleshia's break, at which point she'd slipped away to accompany him at the private table.

"When you said you'd pay me to keep an eye on anything

odd that happened with Randi, I figured you'd want to know that somebody else was asking about her tonight."

Carter now gave his full attention to the dancer. "All right, then. I came with cash, so you want to tell me what you know?"

She smiled, and prettily crossed her legs. "Another girl came in earlier tonight. She was in the dressing room, told us she was a new dancer; but later on, one of the other girls said she asked questions about Randi. She did say she goes by the professional name Natasha Blue."

"You didn't believe her?"

Carleshia let out an unladylike snort that contrasted greatly with her revealing sequined dress and wrap. "Well, first, she made like she was Randi's friend, and then she said, not really, but that they had a mutual friend . . . at Innervision." She flounced her hand. "That's when I left to call you. But guess what? I get back to the dressing room, and the chick was nowhere to be found."

She nodded her head in profound confusion. "Later on, one of the other girls told me she had been asking about Randi, and what Randi had going on with that dude over at your company." She fluttered her hand again in disdain. "Well, you know me. I walked right up to Tony and asked him about the new girl he hired, and you know what? He didn't know what I was talking about."

While she paused from the long story to sip from her drink, Carter said nothing, but continued to quietly study her as a few ideas of his own floated through his head.

"What did this woman look like?"

"Mmm . . ." She set the drink back down. "Let's see . . . pretty, but she's really short and what you call petite. That's not Tony's type for a dancer. Never was."

"Brown-skinned and shapely, too," Carter suggested, "with short, curly hair?"

"You know her?"

"I've got an idea of who it is." He tapped his long fingers against the table. "She used the name Natasha, huh?"

Carleshia nodded, her eyes searching out his hands. "So, you are still gonna pay me for the information, right? Even though you know who she is?"

Carter smiled and, reaching into his back pocket, took out his wallet and three bills. "Actually, you've been a lot more help than you know."

She looked at the bills, her eyes wide in appreciation. "Really? Well, thank you."

"Is Randi working tonight?"

"Yeah, she's back there getting ready. She thinks you're here reporting on her for the old boy you work for."

"Well, let's keep this information, especially a description of the woman, between us for now."

"You know me." She folded the bills, and after pressing them safely into a crevice in her bosom, stood up and patted down her dress.

Carter followed her back through the loud club, and with a nod, turned to head for the exit. Outside in the fresh air, he looked around before he headed for his car.

"Natalie, Natalie," he muttered in exhaustion. "What are you up to now?"

David had reached the end of the bed and lifted Natalie high, kissing her exposed stomach leisurely before he leaned forward and dropped her to the bed. As she lay there, sprawled in erotic abandon, his eyes didn't leave her. He peeled off his own shirt, and kicked off his shoes before he joined her on the bed.

"I want you so bad, I can taste it," he whispered, and raised himself up on his elbow to look down at her, already unbuttoning her blouse. "But, I'll be damned if I'm going to rush it. I'm going to savor every moment of making love to you."

Natalie held her breath as she pulled herself up on her knees so she could sit on the bed.

"So, you really want to make love, huh, as opposed to having sex?"

He smiled, and sitting up like her, unhooked the exposed garters attaching her hose, his hands lingering against the soft, warm flesh along her thighs.

"Wait until you find out how good love can be."

Natalie's emotions whirled with expectation as she reached over to unfasten his waistband. David pushed back her blouse; her breasts, like sweet succulent overripe fruit, sprang out under his gaze. The sight of her full breasts, unbound and eager for his touch, caused his erection to throb. He dipped his head and claimed one dusky nipple, and then the other.

Her low murmur was indicative of her pleasure at the tongue flicks that covered her breasts. Leaning in, Natalie gave David ample access while she unzipped his fly and then slipped her fingers into the waistband of his briefs, slowly working them down.

"You're a beautiful woman, Natalie," David said, raising his head. His eyes were darkly sensuous as he watched Natalie shrug from the blouse, exposing her beauty more fully.

He pushed her back onto the bed, and then followed her. His kiss was a hungry one, and his tongue sent shivers racing through Natalie as she gave herself freely to passion that left her mouth burning with fire. David's lips had begun to sear a path down her neck, and then her shoulders, and on to her breasts. His mouth, moist with passion, covered her sensitive, swollen nipples in turn.

Raising up, he quickly removed her skirt, followed by the garter and hose. He got up from the bed and dropped his pants and briefs before he stepped away from them, noting that Natalie had watched, with heightened curiosity, his already rising erection.

"You're a beautiful and . . . impressive man, David." Her eyes darted down. "Even more than I'd hoped for," she added with a smile.

"I try to please," he responded gruffly as he strode back to her and the bed. "I'm also aiming to respect you." He opened his hand and revealed two gold packets. Condoms.

Natalie took them from him, smiling. "You knew this would happen tonight?"

"A man can hope, can't he? I'm only sorry that I just brought a couple."

"Don't worry. I made sure I had fresh ones around, too." She raised her brows. "Just in case I gave in to one of your seductions one night."

Kneeling over her, he took both hands and pulled her lacy bikini underwear down her hips until he could see the nest of spry curls between her legs. He eased them along farther, past her thighs and knees, until she lifted her feet to free herself of them.

Now, as they were naked to each other's gaze, Natalie reveled in his open desire of her. Her own giddy sense of pleasure caused her blood to course through her veins like a surging river.

As he met her, Natalie curled into the curve of his body, her back arched in an open invitation of pleasure as his erection pressed her belly. They fell to the bed, on their sides, as Natalie rained kisses along David's neck and face. He, in turn, ran his hand along her sleek body, across her taut stomach, and back to the swell of her hips, where his fingers moved, unerringly, to the sweet juncture of her thighs. There, they dipped into her warm, silky flesh.

Even as Natalie arched against his hand's manipulations, her own sought out his erection, where she danced her bold fingers to an erotic tune along its length and breadth.

This began a lust-arousing exploration of each other's soft flesh, searching out pleasure points and marking them to memory. David had long left the sensuous area of Natalie's neck and shoulders and breasts with his kisses and moved to her belly, her hips, and farther downward to her inner thighs where his kisses ended with a bold invasion by his tongue.

Natalie's body reacted with volcanic force. She was on fire, but David held her hips to him and wouldn't let her escape his scorching mouth. She held on to his head, and as she found a rhythm for release, it left her quivering with waves of ecstasy and a need for total possession by David.

As she caught her breath, her eyes flew open and she saw David kneeling beside her, already spreading her knees apart.

"Enough foreplay," he said. "I don't want to wait."

"Neither do I." She reached for the condom under the pillow and tore it open. With hands trembling from exhaustion and anticipation, she kneeled in front of him and worked it onto his steel-hard, hovering erection. "There," she said, admiring the object of her handiwork.

"Just in time," David said, and arched his arms around her back and pulled her to him.

Natalie rested on his muscular thighs and could feel his erection brushing at her entrance. She wrapped her arms around his neck and covered his mouth with hers.

"I want you, David," she said, and tried to scoot closer to take him in. But David was surprisingly in control as he continued to brush against her core, though he wouldn't offer relief to either of them.

"I know," he murmured in her ear. "I've always known it. First, though, I want you to admit you want my love." He lowered his head to her hardening nipples.

The licking strokes sent pleasant jolts through her. In fact, his body had imprisoned Natalie in a web of growing arousal until she was at her breaking point. She pressed against his shaft, but he allowed only a tease of himself into her.

Her head lolled back in abandon. "I do, I do want it, David."

"Say it, then."

"Say what?" she whimpered.

"I love you."

She didn't know whether that had been his personal declaration or if he said it only for her to repeat. All she knew was the crashing waves that wreaked havoc inside her body were continuing.

Tears began to well in Natalie's eyes. It was true, any-way—it was something she'd known a year ago. The rhythm in David was building, and she could feel it in the shiver from his arms. She clung to him and, once again, begged him for release.

"Say it," he grunted with urgency.

"I love you, David," she cried out. "Oh, God, help me, I love you."

The words echoed throughout the room as David complied with his promise. "This is the way I always want you—warm and ready for me."

And with long and powerful strokes, he pounded home the relief she so desperately sought, and he wanted to give.

Wave after wave of orgasmic release rolled through them as they dropped back onto the bed. When her body arched to take him in fully, David felt her heated walls tighten around him; and in one final peak of exquisite delight, both let out explosive gasps amid volatile shudders of relief.

In the following minutes, as they crash-landed to earth again, the room became drowned in silence, contentment, and peace. Finally, they stirred. David, belatedly realizing he might suffocate her, raised himself from her chest.

Twisting around, he pulled her against him, spoon fash-ion, and let out a deep sigh. "How stupid are we, huh?" he teased.

She knew what he referred to and, reaching down, squeezed his hand firmly clasped around her belly. "We missed a lot of each other."

"Yeah, and I'm thinking that, since the night is still young, we have a lot of lost time to make up." Resting a possessive leg across Natalie's, he settled against her.

Natalie grinned at his reference that this was going to be a long night of sex—no, lovemaking, she corrected. She managed to curtail her squirm at the word. It was all new to her, granted, but she was looking forward to seeing where this might lead. David hadn't mentioned her confession, and she appreciated that. For now, though, she was happy in just enjoying the fruits of what it had produced.

She squeezed David's hand again. *I love you.*

Chapter 24

Natalie wasn't sure what it was that woke her up—maybe it was the cool air that licked at her body after the heat she'd experienced during the night with David. Turning on the bed, she stretched out her hand to an empty space. That's what was missing. David. Where was he?

She sat straight up, naked in the middle of the bed, only to have her eyes greet the headboard. Somehow, she must have gotten turned around at some point during last night. Natalie smiled with a particularly pleasant memory, and stretched like a satisfied cat as she perused her bedroom.

Only the pillows and the fitted sheet remained on the bed. The covers, along with the other sheets, were on the floor. It had been a wild evening, all right. She didn't see David's clothes anywhere, so she concluded he must have dressed . . . and left?

As her eyes circled back around the room, they hit upon the bedside table. There it was—a note propped against the Tiffany lamp. She scooted up to the head of the bed and opened it.

"Gone home for my suit," she read aloud. "Put some clothes on that lovely body of yours. . . ." Natalie smiled. "I'll be back to pick you up." As quickly as relief had flooded her that David had only left for a moment, she was filled again with anxiety.

It was Sunday morning. The christening was to begin after morning service. She looked at the clock settled over the door. *In an hour.*

At the same moment she pounced from the bed, the phone rang. She grabbed it up.

"Hello?"

"Good morning, beautiful."

Natalie's soul glowed in a smile. She dropped back onto the bed. "David. I almost forgot the time."

"You looked so comfortable this morning, I figured I'd let you get another hour of sleep."

"You could have thrown a cover over me."

"And spoil my view? Not on your life," he said, laughing.

"You are so bad," she said, smiling. "So, are you going to meet me at the church?"

"No way," he said. "I'm dressed, and I'm leaving now to pick you up."

"What about Davina? We were supposed to meet the family thirty minutes ago and go to the church together." Natalie groaned. "She's probably wondering right now what happened to us."

"No, she's not. I called her and told her we were coming together, and that we'd be there before the ceremony started."

Natalie let out a sigh of relief. "Oh, that's great, David."

"See? Didn't I tell you that you needed me? I'm going to keep you by my side for a while, or at least the next few days, so get dressed."

"Okay." She started to say the words she had said all night, but they hung in her throat, refusing to materialize in the light of day.

"Bye." He hung up.

Natalie held the phone in her hands a few moments before she was drawn from her reverie, shivering in her nakedness from the chill. She had to get dressed before David arrived.

* * *

With the advent of the christening, David and Natalie had no time to consider the impact of the big step they'd taken the night before.

Upon picking Natalie up, David only had time to enjoy a singular kiss from her, fly out to his car, and race to the church.

David pulled into a parking space in the church's crowded lot. Grabbing Natalie's hand, he helped her from the car just as he heard his name shouted from the building. Looking up, they saw Justin waiting at the church door, flagging his arm in their direction.

"Come on, you two," he called out.

David glanced to his watch. "I guess we're here in the nick of time."

And as Natalie double-stepped with him across the church-yard, she experienced what she considered one of life's perfect moments. David was next to her, and for this time, all doubts were erased; it was a beautiful day for a christening of life with the morning sun stretched peach-colored across the clear, bright horizon, and Natalie didn't have a worry. Not today. All was all right in this moment.

She smiled at David as he looked back at her. Yes, she would remember this moment forever.

They reached Justin, who greeted Natalie with a hug and a twinkle in his eye before he led them through a side entrance into the church's sanctuary and the family's filled pews.

Once they were settled in their seats saved by Alli, and Justin had returned to sit with Davina, Natalie felt a light nudge from David. When she looked at him, he nodded toward Davina in the front row. Davina had looked back over her shoulder with a wide grin. Natalie returned the smile, but gave a knowing one to David. There was no way their changed relationship would go unnoticed by the legions of friends who wished it so.

A glowing patina remained fastened to Natalie's psyche during the subsequent solemn christening ceremony, which went off without a hitch.

At the appropriate time, Natalie took her place in front of the church beside Davina and Justin, as little Jake wiggled about in his christening gown in Reverend King's arms. David followed to take his place next to her. They recited their prepared responses, without hesitation, to the litany of questions asked of them by the minister. The look of support offered her way by Reverend King was comforting, to say the least.

With their part done, David and Natalie stepped back to give little Jake his due and welcome into his church family and into the bosom of his family and friends.

Though short, the ceremony had been thought-provoking. At one moment, Natalie had indulged in a daydream wherein her and David's positions were reversed with Davina's and Justin's—they attended their own child's christening.

Natalie had shaken her head to dislodge the ridiculous thought before she realized she was wearing a broad smile during a serious moment in the ceremony. At David's secret squeeze of her hand, and nod, she landed back in reality. But, the idea had been interesting. Her, with children?

When the service was over, they all filed out into the early afternoon sun. The plan was to return to the Hardy estate for an afternoon and evening of fellowship to meet the baby.

"It's going to be a long day," Natalie whispered to David.

"Longer than you think," he said with a smile as he looked up to see his sister waiting for them outside.

Natalie stole a wary look inside the diaper before she breathed a sigh of relief. "Oh, thank God," she said, happy to see only a damp surface. "He only did a number one. I thought for a minute I was going to turn green."

David peeked over her shoulder, as he squeezed her waist,

and smiled down at the wide-eyed baby on the changing mat who was desperately trying to fit his entire fist into his mouth, without much success.

It was already late Sunday afternoon, and Natalie had offered to bring the baby upstairs when he needed changing. David had offered his help, expecting that they might grab some time together. They had been hard pressed to find any kind of a private moment with a houseful of people.

"Here . . ." David handed her a bottle of oil and powder from the shelf. "Aren't you supposed to use these, too?"

"Davina said these pull-up cleaning things would be fine," Natalie answered, pulling at one and then wiping the baby's smooth behind.

David chose a diaper from a stack in the corner, already pulling back a paper tab from curiosity and allowing it to stick to the diaper liner.

"Will you stop it?" Natalie scolded him playfully. "It's not going to stick worth anything if you undo the tab too soon."

"I see you've learned a lot in a week." He retrieved another diaper for her. "Do men really know how to do this sort of stuff? I've always heard that women have a special knack for knowing what to do, a natural instinct."

Natalie looked over at David and laughed. "Don't look to my family when you want to know what a good father does. I had a stay-at-home mother most of my life, and she did everything." She had tried to eliminate the anger from her voice, but she suspected it had seeped in, anyway.

"So, what's that about?" he asked. "Sounds like you didn't have a *Brady Bunch* childhood, either."

She slipped the clean diaper under Jake's bottom. "Your father was an alcoholic, turned into one after your mother's early death. Even with his addiction, though, your father still loved you and Davina."

"And yours didn't?" he asked. "What happened with your dad?"

Natalie thought a moment as she bit the inside of her lip.

"Do you really want to know that? Why spoil our nice day today with the Hardys?"

"I want to know about you." He tilted her chin up to him with his finger, and placed a light kiss against her mouth. "The more I learn, the more I understand you . . . and what makes you happy."

She gave her attention back to the baby, pulling down his gown over the changed diaper. Lifting him, she balanced him against her shoulder.

"My father was only around for the first half of my childhood and I spent most of it trying to get his attention because I was too young to realize that he was a louse. He didn't last during the second half, though. He didn't love my mama, and he made her life miserable.

"So one day, as a teenager, I had it out with him. Between me and my older sister, I always had the mouth, you know, and I told him if he didn't want us, why didn't he just leave?" Natalie looked at David, a sorrowful expression marring her beautiful face. "And he did. Just like that. He never came back, a fact that I think my mother believes I brought on."

"Wow, that's rough," David said. "But you know it's not your fault, right? He chose to leave because of his problems with your mother."

"Funny, but that's the same thing Reverend King told me," she said.

David looked at her, as though he had unearthed a wonderful discovery. "Hey, you're not thinking I'd do that?"

Would he? Natalie looked at David, and remembered that she had told him she loved him.

"Natalie—I would never walk out on my family."

"Everyone says that in the beginning of relationships."

"I'm not your father, and you're not your mother. Our differences are already obvious. We love each other, and we talk—"

"I know," Natalie said, stopping him. "I've been thinking about it a lot lately, ever since I talked with Reverend King."

"And last night?" He left it a question. "Morning regrets?"

She smiled and shook her head. "No, but let's not spoil our success so far, okay?" She hoisted little Jake up and, similar to what Davina had done to her, she placed the baby against David's shoulder. "He's all dry, so now there's no excuse for you not to hold him."

David looked at the small baby as he held him tightly against his body, his shoulders hunched as though that provided extra protection. "What am I supposed to do now?" he asked.

Natalie laughed. "Nothing. In fact, I think you look wonderful holding Jake. Just like a proud papa."

He grinned as he looked at her. "You think so?"

As the three of them crossed the room to return downstairs, Natalie caught a glimpse of their exit in the mirror. A vision of her future? Still not totally comfortable with the concept, she didn't hazard a second look.

The main floor of the Hardy estate had been tastefully decorated with whimsy for the many children that were present today, and elegance for the adults. All the Hardys—scores of cousins, aunts, and uncles—had shown up.

"Natalie . . ." It was Justin coming toward them as they reached the bottom of the stairs. "Davina said you were looking for me earlier." He chucked his son under the chin and prepared to take him from David's stiff arms.

"Yeah, I was," she replied. "But if David returns Jake to Davina, maybe we can talk for a moment."

"Sure," he said, retucking the baby against David. "Listen, if you want to find Davina fast, she's in the library," he said.

As David left them, Justin turned to Natalie. "Okay, what can I help you with?"

"I was curious about Connie. Did you introduce him and Carter?"

"No," Justin said as he stopped. "I believe I mentioned I had a PI friend at the restaurant, but I don't believe I even mentioned Connie's name. In fact, his name usually draws a whole conversation by itself." They resumed their stroll through the house. "Why do you think Carter and Connie know each other?"

"Because I saw them together. In the park a few days ago. And Connie was handing him something."

Justin laughed. "Don't be so suspicious about a businessman talking to Connie, and his meeting place is wherever his client wants it to be. His specialty is sought after in the city."

"Oh, what is his specialty, anyway?"

"People. Ninety-nine percent of his clientele want him to get information on people and their backgrounds. And, he's very good at his investigations."

"How can I forget?" she said, and cracked a smile at Justin. "Let's see now . . . when Davina found out you were investigating her, was that your second or third big blowout with her?"

"That's not fair. I didn't know her then, so it doesn't count."

"You know, Justin, when I think back to how you began with Davina, I wonder how you two keep it together. You're definitely not alike. In fact, you're the original oil-and-water couple."

"Sort of like you and David, right?" At Natalie's snort, he laughed, but continued. "Oh, we argue, but we've learned to let each other win just enough that we can't keep score."

Natalie grinned. "That's a good point. I'll have to remember that."

"David's a good man, you know. I don't think he was ever resolved over your breakup."

"Will he take off in a few days, and disappear out of my life again?"

Justin slowed his walk. "Tell him how you feel. If it's supposed to be, it'll happen," he said. "Look at me and Davina."

When he left Natalie to join another guest, she decided she'd seek out Alli.

David, meanwhile, had delivered little Jake to his sister, and they took the time to talk.

"You and Natalie sure are closemouthed about what happened to make you arrive at the church late."

"Yeah," David said. "But, give it time and I'm sure you'll finagle some information out of one of us, one way or the other." He couldn't help it as his whole face spread into a smile.

"So, you're back together?" Her eyes grew wide with excitement.

David knew that tone, and stopped to give her a nod. "We're getting there, but you know Natalie. She's pretty fragile about commitment and stuff. Please—don't get her all spooked with a lot of questions."

Davina put on a brilliant smile of her own. "I won't, I won't, I promise. But don't tell me not to be happy."

"Yeah, I'm happy, too," he said, grinning at his sister's enthusiasm. "What do you know about Natalie's family background?"

Davina looked at her brother. "What are you talking about?"

"Her parents are divorced, right? So, why does she blame herself for it?"

"She told you that?"

"I figured it out. She told her father to leave, and he did."

Davina looked around, seemingly torn as to whether she should say anything. "David, if you love her, please don't press her about this. She carries around this huge guilt."

"Didn't her mother explain it wasn't her fault?"

"You have to understand the whole story."

Frowning, David drew his sister to the sofa. "I've got time. Tell me."

"Well," Davina said, settling on the sofa, "Natalie watched her smart mother become this belittled woman with no ambition at the hands of her domineering father. Her mother didn't stand up for herself, so Natalie always did until finally her father left them. After that," Davina continued, "her mother was a basket case during our last years in high school."

"I'd already left for college by then," David said.

Davina nodded. "To make matters worse, at about the

time Natalie went off to school, her mother remarried, had another child, and it left Natalie feeling totally alone. She can't bring herself to connect with her mother, and she won't even try to get to know her little sister."

"And she swears she'll never become what her mother was," David said.

"You've got it," Davina said. "What are you going to do with her?"

"I don't know," he said and leaned back on the couch. "Tread lightly, I guess until she's ready to forgive herself."

David was ready to leave. He wanted to take Natalie home and finish what they'd started last night, and from the kiss she'd given him in the kitchen about an hour ago, so did she. He looked at his watch again. It was going on seven o'clock in the evening.

As he walked through the rooms, he caught sight of her sitting with a small group in the solarium. He walked up to them.

"Ah, can you excuse us for a moment?" he asked as he took her hand and then led her from the room.

"Where are we going?" she asked.

"Hopefully somewhere we can get ten minutes of privacy."

Natalie chuckled. "Ten whole minutes?"

They took the back hallway and when they reached the cloakroom, David stopped. He looked both ways, opened the door, and then pulled Natalie in behind him. Pushing the door closed, he leaned against it as he wrapped his arms around Natalie's midriff, and bent to kiss her. It was a deep, probing kiss that allowed Natalie to drink in its sweetness in leisure. His mouth moved to graze her earlobe.

"I've been wanting to do this all day," he said as his hands skimmed her soft curves molded in the sheath dress.

"We won't be missed for a while," she said, pressing against him.

David was pleased with her response. A delicate thread of understanding was beginning to form between them, and he intended to handle it with care. He gently squeezed her butt as he pulled her hard up against him, memories of last night fogging his brain. The need to make love to her overpowered him.

Abruptly, David set Natalie away from him.

"What's wrong?" she asked.

"We've got to leave," David said.

"We sure do make a fine pair of godparents, don't you think? Here we are, running out on little Jake."

"Jake is upstairs sleep. And believe me, no one will blame us, least of all his daddy; and just about everyone else thinks we've already left."

He took Natalie's hand into his own, bearing the knowing smiles of several guests who stood in the hall as they exited the room.

Chapter 25

"Mmm . . . I didn't realize I was this hungry," Natalie said as she sampled from another of the Chinese take-out boxes on the tray. She was sitting astride David; both of them were awake and refreshed in terry cloth robes, and sampled, as well as offered samples to each other, from the boxes.

"You're always hungry," David observed with a grin. He leaned forward and gave her a quick kiss. "Good for me."

Their evening, so far, had been very productive. They had made love, ordered in, showered, and now they relaxed at David's house in his bedroom. A lot had been crammed into the few hours since they'd left the Hardys'.

"In fact, you're good luck to me."

"I am? How so?"

"I went by BPR on Friday, and they were okay at extending my Atlanta time for another ten days."

"Oh?" Natalie watched David warily. BPR was the name the attorneys in his firm used for Bennett, Parker & Richardson.

"They're okay with loaning me an office for the time being, in case I need to be involved with any loose-end casework in D.C." He frowned. "Hey . . . I thought you'd be happy."

She didn't know how she was supposed to react to this—excited for the ten days, or angry that he considered ten days as enough time for them before he picked up his bags and headed out again.

"Are you happy?" she asked.

"I was. Come here. . . ." He set his carton on the tray, and then took hers and did the same before he pulled her forward onto him.

Natalie reclined against him, holding him close—loving the connection, yet fearing a disconnection even more.

"We're making some pretty big steps here. It's okay if you take a little one every now and then, so long as it's forward, though. No backsliding from either of us. Now, what's wrong?"

She sighed against his chest, not wanting the position disturbed. "Your temporary position in D.C. won't be over for a while. Why tease around with ten days? Maybe we should just let you go and get it over with."

David laughed. "Just like you—you don't believe in delaying the inevitable. Get it over with now." He set her back up. "Let's see what happens with the ten days, okay? Maybe things will work out for us, and I'll be returned to Atlanta. I'm a senior attorney, so there are some perks to that."

Natalie pushed back the opening of his robe and, exposing his chest, made soft, circular motions on it with her fingers. "I don't see myself on a red-eye every weekend, you know."

"If it comes to that, maybe we could split the trips," he teased, though concern wasn't completely shuttered in his eyes.

She rose up on her knees and, leaning forward, kissed David's chest, before she looked back up at him. "Or maybe we can try and find you some corporate clients right here in Atlanta."

David grinned at her comment, but it abruptly disappeared as a line of concentration deepened along his brows.

"What is it?" Natalie asked, tilting her head in concern.

"Funny you should mention corporate clients. Remember when I first came to town, I mentioned that the name Innervision sounded familiar, but couldn't remember where I'd heard it?"

"Yeah." Natalie sat back on her haunches, her full attention given.

"Well, when I was in the office, I learned that one of BPR's attorneys handles some things for Gilbert Blakely."

"Are you serious? Someone at your office does legal work for Blakely?"

David nodded. "I probably saw the names from a client list, or something like that, and forgot about it."

Natalie's brain was moving faster than a train. What was happening with all that money that wasn't showing up on the balance sheets? Someone had to be making a killing from the bad books. Blakely? That was obvious.

"We've got to go there."

"What?" And then he answered his own question as he looked into Natalie's eyes. "Oh, no, not on your life . . . not a second time am I going to be taken in by your—"

"David, listen. I need you to do this."

"Breaking and entering is illegal, and I'm an attorney, an officer of the court."

"Technically, you're not doing anything illegal. You're going to your office after hours, you're going to use your brand-new passkeys to get in, and you're going to look at your client list. If Blakely's on there, you're going to simply ask for the last billing statement, something like that—"

"You'd ask for the last work request from his attorney."

Natalie's eyes perked. "That's good. We'll be in and out, and it'll just be more information I can pass on."

When he exhaled deeply, Natalie knew he had come around. "Oh, thank you, honey." She leaned forward and planted a big kiss on his mouth, which he met fully and turned into a lusty exchange.

"We're not going anywhere just yet," he said as they parted and Natalie raised up again.

"I couldn't agree more," Natalie said and, drawing his

gaze, shrugged from the robe as she resettled herself astride David's lap, and then pushed him back against the bed. Unwrapping his robe, she pushed it wide.

David stared up at her naked body as she straddled him. When she leaned forward, and their hands met and clasped in the tangled sheets, Natalie's senses swirled as David's hungry mouth rose up to explore her hardening nipples floating above him.

"Now it's my turn to make you hungry," she teased, and started the erotic feast with nibbles and touches across his chest, and down his flat, flexed chest and belly, and even farther.

When she reached for his swollen member, and bent her head down, David's body began a sweet-paced rhythm, and his hands quivered against her neck and shoulders as the feast began.

Ring-Ring.

John Callaway heard his wife stir next to him in their bed. "No, I'll get it," he whispered at her, damning whoever was on the phone calling on a work night at this ungodly hour.

As his wife fell back into sleep, he reached for the phone. "Hello?" he answered.

"Did you know that the lawyer friend of the Goodman woman is a senior attorney at the firm I use?"

It was Blakely. John swallowed hard, his thoughts scattering. He tried to assemble the necessary facts to respond to a crazy man in the middle of the night.

"I knew, but I didn't think it was important." He glanced at his wife to assure himself that she was still asleep. "He doesn't even work for their Atlanta office anymore. He's in D.C. How did you learn about it?"

"Carter found out for me, no thanks to you. And I only got his information yesterday. Do you think the lawyer is helping her check things out somehow?"

"No . . . Natalie wouldn't compromise confidentiality. She'd come to me first before she'd go to anyone else. Give her some time. She'll come around."

"You've been wrong on everything else about her, so what makes you so sure on this?" He didn't wait for an answer. "I need to see you tomorrow."

"My schedule—I don't see how it'll be possi—"

"You're the partner who manages Innervision's account. Of course you can make it to my office. Now, I'll see you tomorrow. Call my secretary and get on my calendar." He summarily hung up the phone.

"Damn that man."

"What, dear?" John's wife spoke groggily from her side of the bed.

"Oh. Nothing." He replaced the dead phone, and dropped back onto his pillow. Had Natalie enlisted her boyfriend's help in her search for answers? If Blakely was running scared, then something must be going on at his attorney's office that might incriminate him.

John turned and faced the wall in the expansive bedroom. It would all be over soon, anyway. Deals with devils come to no good. All he wanted to do now was protect Natalie from the bad situation he'd put her in.

The offices throughout BPR were dimly lit at midnight, and the cubicle with the forlorn computer sitting on top of the empty desk, and two animated figures huddled over it, was equally dim.

As David pressed the keyboard, he motioned for Natalie to turn on the desk lamp. "I can barely read these account codes," he said.

Natalie scooted around the desk and pulled down the chain to the small banker's lamp. Bright rays spread out across the desktop.

"That's much better," David said, and pressed the enter key. He raised his eyes to the monitor just as Natalie worked her way back around the desk to view it, too.

"What is that?" Natalie asked. A file with an odd extension was slowly unloading on the screen.

"The Acrobat program is uploading a form Victor Barnes, his attorney, downloaded off the Internet. He apparently worked on it recently for Blakely."

"What else did the client info say?" Natalie asked.

"Your Blakely came on as a client a while back, but BPR has only done advisory-type services for him, and that only once. That is, until about two months ago. That's when Victor began getting requests to do some other work."

"There's the form, David." The screen blinked and the entire form appeared in a miniaturized version. "It's an application—"

"For an offshore account," David said. "This one is in the Turks in Caicos." He pressed the page-down button.

"Another one in Bermuda," Natalie said, reading the screen.

"He hasn't signed them yet. Vic's notes have the date entered as this Friday coming up."

Natalie turned to David. "Blakely's embezzling money from Innervision, and he's getting ready to hide it in an offshore account, safe from everybody."

David sat back from the computer and rubbed his face. "It's today's white-collar crime. You don't pay U.S. taxes on the money, choose a country with no tax treaty with the U.S., and the country doesn't care—they know you're avoiding taxes."

"Yeah, I've been hearing a lot about it lately. These accounts also can issue the holder credit cards—with no names, just numbers—and they're used for just about anything here. Only, like you said, the money was never taxed."

David had already shut down the computer, and then replaced his keys in his pockets. "Let's get out of here." He put his arm around Natalie's shoulder as they left the cubicle. "Tomorrow you've got a big decision ahead of you."

"Huh?"

"You're going to turn what you know over to some authority. This has gotten way out of hand, and with the two notes you've received, I'm even more worried about your safety."

Natalie grasped David's hand at her shoulder as they walked back through the office. He was right. She had a lot to think about. And though he was worried about her safety, she was worried about John. How would she bring up all this when she saw him tomorrow?

Carter unwrapped his hash brown at the local eatery and took a bite from it. It was early Monday morning, the beginning of a watershed week, and he still didn't know all the players in the game. Hopefully, Connie Preston was about to shed some more light on the situation.

He looked across the small, cramped booth at Connie just as the big man passed him a plain, oversized envelope.

"What does it say about George Webster?"

"You don't want to read it yourself for all of the details?"

"I can read it in good time later. So you tell me the high points. Where is George Webster now?"

Connie sighed. "I'm sorry, but he's dead, going on six months now."

Carter stopped chewing for a moment and digested the fact. "Okay, back up a bit. Pick up from when he left Innervision."

"You already knew Innervision let him go due to poor performance over a year ago?"

Carter nodded and bit into the hash brown. "Start there."

"He left the city, seemingly blackballed for a job around here, for a lucrative offer in another state."

"Bad employee does good?"

"Not quite. He couldn't get a job recommendation here; but interestingly enough, Innervision relented for some reason and gave him a glowing record for any position he'd take out of the state."

"Do you know which Innervision officials gave the recommendation?"

Connie flipped through the small notepad. "If I'm not mistaken, it was a gentleman named Ford, and the other was Gilbert Blakely." At Carter's nod, he continued. "George Webster picked a New Jersey offer with a large accounting firm, and he was doing quite well, flourishing within their ranks, in fact."

"And what happened?"

"About six months ago, he was a victim of a hit-and-run in Atlantic City."

Carter sat up. "Any suspects?"

"Not a one. Still on the books as an unsolved accident."

Carter's brows braided in deep thought as he looked across at Connie. "You've been a great help." He extended his hand across the table. "It's hard to believe you were able to get this much information in a matter of days."

Connie shook the offered hand, and prepared to get up. "It's what I do best," he said with a grin. "If I can be of any further service, you let me know."

When Connie had disappeared from the eatery, Carter opened the envelope, and the first thing that fell out was a grainy photo of an unsmiling man with dull eyes behind black-rimmed glasses. George Webster, victim. Carter had always known Blakely could be dangerous. It appeared that no one knew how dangerous that could be.

He pulled out his cell phone and dialed a number. It was answered quickly, with loud music blasting in the background.

"Hello, Sean?" Carter asked.

"Hey . . . I'm on the way in now. You need me to do something?"

"I'd like to see you this morning, in my office. I'm on my way in, as well. Say, in an hour?"

"Fine with me," Sean said. "See you then."

Carter clicked off the phone and eyeing the envelope, decided to read the package now.

* * *

When Carter reached his office at Innervision within the hour, Sean Miller was already hanging over the receptionist's desk in the security division, trying to be cool with lame one-liners. Carter shook his head. He was like a kid who wanted to be streetwise, and so he learned all he could from music videos and movies.

Carter opened his door, and Sean followed him, closing it behind him.

"What was so important this morning?"

"Sit down. I want to ask you a few questions."

"Sure." He sat in one of the chairs in front of Carter's desk.

"You know I'm aware of your history as a key man."

Sean was an urban experiment. It seemed that after acquiring juvenile records for years, and petty larceny charges, he moved up to the big time and tried his first car theft. He was a key man for a local chop shop—he could start any machine. However, the social workers got him into Innervision's Inner City Youth program. It didn't matter that Sean wasn't from the inner city. But he was a kid who needed intensive guidance to avoid a life of crime. After years of attending feel-good boys' camps and technical schools, he was finally employable. He had been put under Blakely's tender tutelage, going on two years now.

"Yeah, and your point is . . ." he answered smartly.

"You've admitted you've been in Natalie's office, uninvited. So, it doesn't take a rocket scientist to figure you've stolen her keys and made a set. Maybe for Blakely." Carter came around his desk and sat on it, crossing his arms. "You had them copied, right?"

The young man smiled. "Yeah, I got plates for her car, house, everything. Hell, some of 'em I don't even know what they go to." He chuckled. "I turned it all over to Blakely, though."

Carter kept his temper in check. "Are you sure you didn't keep a set?"

"Hey, you think I'd cross our boss, Blakely? Hell, no." He

held his hands up. "I didn't keep any." He looked at Carter. "What's this all about, anyway?"

"I don't like it when you and Blakely plan these little things and I'm not involved. I am security, remember? I'm supposed to know everything so I can plan necessary follow-up. Remember the almost screwed up burglary because your pair of nincompoop friends got greedy?"

"Okay, so I won't ever suggest them again. You fixed it, though. Blakely likes that you fix things up."

"If I'm so good, why didn't you tell me your part in the plans for George Webster?"

Sean's head shot up like a rocket. "Who?"

"George Webster? You know him."

"Never heard of him," he said, his eyes avoiding Carter's. "You need to take that up with Blakely. I mean, I don't know nothing about that."

"Is there any link between you not knowing George Webster and Blakely wanting Miss Goodman to be at the gala?"

"He wants Natalie at that party?" A look of surprise suffused the young man's face.

"Yeah, he specifically requested that I get into her good graces so she'd come. Let's face it, he hates the woman, and makes no bones about it. Understandably, she wants to blow his well-established operation."

"She's really smart, and she talks to me. I kind of like her."

"In that case, if you hear anything, you'll let me know? Just between us?"

"Yeah, sure." Sean got up and with a nod at Carter, left.

Alone again, Carter rubbed his forehead in deep thought. What else was going on with Blakely and Innervision?

Nora Watts, Justin's able executive assistant at Hardy Enterprises, waved Connie through to her boss's inner office conference room.

"Thank you, Nora," Connie said, and walked up to where Justin met him at the door. The men shook hands.

"I heard the christening went off without a hitch," Connie said.

Justin nodded. "I'm sorry you were out of town and couldn't make it."

"Yeah, I had to physically chase some information down for a case that I just closed out this morning."

"Good, maybe that means you can do something for me in a hurry. Go on, have a seat." He pulled out one of the chairs from the table for himself.

Connie sat down and immediately got down to business. "So, what is it?"

"I'd like you to learn what you can about a man named Carter Johnson."

Crossing his leg, Connie chuckled. "Is this some kind of joke?"

Justin shook his head. "Dead serious. I had dinner with him. . . ." He held his hand up. "There were others present; it's a long story, so don't ask. Anyway, I mentioned your profession at dinner and how good you were, but I never mentioned you by name. He apparently made it his business to find you because Natalie saw you talking with him in the park the other day."

He shifted on his chair. "Justin, you know about confidentiality."

"I'm not asking you to tell me what you were investigating, but I am asking you to find out if this man can be trusted."

"I can tell you he's an employee, a high-level security guy, over at that high-tech manufacturer, Innervision. Why would you be concerned?"

"He works with Natalie, and she's concerned."

"Our little Natalie?"

Justin finally smiled. "Yes."

"Well . . ." Connie studied the toe of his shoe for a moment. "Technically, Mr. Johnson is no longer a client." He looked up. "I closed his case out this morning."

"Good. There's no conflict of interest, nothing you have to disclose. But look deeper than the surface." He stood up.

"I talked with David. He doesn't think the guy smells right, either, and I think—well, he's got a lot of secrets."

Connie nodded as he stood, too. "I'll see what comes up."

It was after four when Natalie picked up the phone from her desk at Innervision. It was Carter.

"Carter, I was going to call you before I left today," she said, apologizing for not giving him an answer sooner.

"I figured you would, but I've been in and out of my office all day, and didn't know if you had tried." There was a pause. "Are you going to attend the gala with me tomorrow night?"

Natalie cupped her face in one last-ditch effort to figure out what to do, knowing that her answer would upset David. He didn't trust the man, and rightly so. But, Natalie had an innate sense that Carter wouldn't harm her; however, the anxious belief that he was involved in Innervision's illegal goings-on continued to plague her.

"Yes, I'll go. In fact, I'll meet you there, since I have some things to do."

"Good. Look for me at the door or, better still, I'll give you your own ticket tomorrow."

"That'll work for me," she said, and bidding him goodbye, hung up.

"Are you crazy?" Natalie chastised herself relentlessly. How was she going to tell this to David without him blowing up? It was her own fault. She could have told him when Carter first asked her. At least then it wouldn't have been such a shock to learn about it.

And when was she going to turn over all she knew? David had suggested today. She wanted to get one more crack at Myra, though, and maybe work on the figures one more night at home. Tomorrow, before the stockholders' big Wednesday afternoon meeting, she would make it known that she'd uncovered a horrendous stack of overstated, misrepresented figures.

She slammed the book closed that she'd been thumbing through before Carter called. She was going home, she'd take a nice hot bath to ease her neck muscles, and she was going to tell David about the gala when he came over.

With her bags packed, she left the office and took the elevator to her car in the parking garage. It was still light out and at this normal hour others were leaving as well, so she felt quite comfortable, in light of the recent notes.

Natalie unlocked her car, and her eyes immediately scanned the recently cleaned out space for a note. Not a thing. Except for the familiar bump that was her spare tire, nothing else occupied the trunk. She hadn't realized she had held her breath the entire time. Smiling at her self-induced drama, she untied the bungee cords to her briefcases and set them into the trunk.

With everything secure, she closed the trunk and hurried around to the driver's side to get in.

She wrenched open the door, and as she made to launch herself into her seat, she saw it. It was folded, but she could see the bold words bleeding out from the other side. Natalie looked around. No one was coming in her direction, and everyone else seemed quite normal.

Picking up the note, she slowly opened it.

PLAY ALONG WITH THE GAME.

Chapter 26

Natalie had arrived at Lang & Myers's offices in record time. Unnerved by the third brazen message, she had left David a frantic call, but he had not returned it. Her only alternative left was to see John. No matter, enough was enough, and David was right. She was no detective, and all of this secretive stuff and so forth was out of her league.

As she waited for the elevator to take her to her floor, she thought about the notes. They were definitely written by the same person, and they were definitely warnings. For what? To go along with Blakely's game? Who would want her to do that? Who would want her to be careful, and watch her back for enemies?

The elevator door opened, and Natalie jumped, startled as she came out of her reverie and saw people stepping in. It was her floor.

"Excuse me," she said, and quickly stepped out before the doors closed.

Carter. It had to be him. He was, no doubt, vested somehow in Blakely's game, but he didn't want her to get hurt. That had to be it. She opened the doors to L & M's suites, and headed to the executive wing, greeting Belinda as she passed her desk.

"Hi, dear," Belinda responded. "What are you doing here so late in the evening? I'm getting ready to leave myself."

"Looking for John." She slowed to a stop. "Is he in his office?"

"Ah, no, I don't think so." She craned around. "I saw his secretary a while ago, but she was running around like a chicken with its head cut off."

"I'll find him," she said, and continued through the executive suites.

When Natalie reached John's office, his secretary, Carol, wasn't present, but his door was ajar. In fact, now that she noticed it, the entire wing seemed pretty empty for five o'clock, but it was obvious, with things about the desks, that everyone had not gone for the day.

Natalie peered into the room, calling his name as she did. His conference and work area, where they usually discussed problems, was empty. She walked over to the table and saw that he'd been working with a white board set up on an easel. Circling around it with nervous energy, she touched her purse where the note was safely contained. She had yet to figure out how she would tell all this to John. He was going to think she was nuts—but not if her thoughts were better organized.

Without hesitation, she picked up one of the fat tube markers from the table and made the easel useful. She began to list the events that had caused her worry from the beginning, hoping this would better arrange her jumbled thoughts.

"The notes, three of them," she said aloud, and frowned at her downhill words. "Overt accounting errors—invalid transfers and renamed accounts," she said, and wrote that down, too. Something struck her as wrong, but she didn't know what, and continued. "Bogus vendors?" She began to write the words, but the clumsy marker began to streak, and she turned it to a better position.

Natalie dropped the marker, and gulped a breath as it dawned on her what was wrong. The words on the easel . . . they had the same split markings as the notes. She picked up the marker and looked at it. It was old, and probably needed to be replaced. She looked at the others that lay innocently on the table. They were all old, and that was her John. He believed in using a supply item to its end. Mild panic began to trickle through Natalie, and she capped the marker, stuffing it into her purse. She had to get out of here.

"Oh, Natalie, you're here." The cry came from the door. Natalie walked back through John's office, her discovery temporarily put aside for an obviously upset Carol. Tears were flowing down her cheek.

"Carol, what's wrong?"

"You haven't heard, have you?"

"No." The hackles at her neck began to rise. "What is it?"

"It's Mr. Callaway," she said, dabbing her eyes. "He's announced his resignation, and it's effective tomorrow."

Natalie felt a shock course through her several times before she trusted herself to speak. "What? Where is he?"

"He's been meeting with the partners for maybe the last hour. I knew something big was going on, and then they called me in there and told me officially." Her tears choked her. "He's still in there with them."

Natalie drew the taller woman close in a hug. "It'll be all right, Carol." Would it? They both cared about John, and this was a shock to the system.

Carol pulled back. "Do you think he has some kind of cancer and only has six months to live, or something like that?" she said, smothering a sob.

Natalie didn't think so. She thought it had something to do with the notes, Blakely, and Innervision's crooked books. It had to be. She felt her eyes becoming damp.

She drew away from the secretary. "Carol, I've got to go." She remembered the board and, walking back to the easel, tore off the sheet.

"You don't want to wait to see him?" Carol asked, watching Natalie move through the room.

"No, I . . . I'll talk with him later." Natalie quickly left and headed for the doors, folding the sheet from the easel as she left. She had to get out of here.

Carter was in his car when his phone rang. He immediately picked it up. "Yeah," he said.

"I hear you've been busy."

"Sort of. I'm getting some unexpected help from a few friends, though."

"I didn't think you had any of those."

Carter smiled in the dark car. "Neither did I, but you'd be surprised."

"So, what's up?"

"I believe the proverbial shit is about to hit the fan, and on gala night. I want you to be ready for it."

"I'll pass it on. Anything else?"

"One small thing. Call New Jersey, and check out a hit-and-run DOA, name of George Webster."

"Gotcha. Is that it?"

"For now."

"All right. Later."

Carter clicked off the phone, and darting a glance to the clock, headed for his emergency meeting.

When the doorbell rang, Natalie ran to it, throwing it open. "Oh, I'm so glad you're here."

David caught her as she sailed into his arms. "What happened?" he asked, and pushed the door closed behind them. "You sounded desperate in your message." Holding her away from him, he looked at her intently, his concern full blown. "Did someone try to hurt you?"

"I got another note."

"What? Where is it? What did it say?"

"It's in the study," she said, and turned to go there, with David on her heels. "That's not all, though, David. I went to

John's office because I just knew right then that it had to be Carter leaving the notes; I had to tell John not only about the notes, but about the stripper and even my suspicions on Blakely's embezzling." They had reached the study, and she stayed at the door. "There they are."

David strode over to the desk where Natalie had lined the three notes together. "Play along with the game?" he asked. He looked back at Natalie before he looked at the notes again. "Someone thinks you ought to go along with the program."

"Yeah." Natalie's voice was curiously flat from exhaustion. "I'm being warned to be careful, to watch for enemies, and to sign off on that review, regardless of my suspicions."

David walked back to her, holding the latest note, his face a constant frown as he studied it closely. "And you feel pretty confident it's Carter, huh?"

"No, it's not Carter," she said, and crossed her arms over her chest. "It's . . ." She swallowed hard. "It's my boss, John."

David's head snapped back to her. "John? But, I thought you said—"

"I did until I went to John's office and couldn't find him. So, I waited in there for him, and I found these old fat markers that John loves to use." She reached into her pocket and pulled out the marker she'd taken.

"I played around with writing like the notes, David, and it's the same. The same streaks, the same split at the top of the letters, everything."

"And you told him what you suspect?"

"By the time I realized he did it, the news was out in the office that he'd suddenly resigned, effective immediately."

David took in a deep breath before he let it out. "Whoa . . . he resigned?"

"Yeah, that was my reaction, too," Natalie said.

"Did he say why the sudden decision?"

"I haven't talked with him, but I can guess."

"Yeah, so can I."

"The office called me a while ago and it was so strange.

They want to assign me a temporary partner that I can report to."

"Are you going to turn all the evidence you have over to him?"

She nodded. "We're meeting Wednesday, since our official statement to Innervision has to be filed one week from today about why I haven't signed off on the review. After that, I'll have to make a presentation to their board."

"You still have all the disks with your downloaded evidence?" he asked.

"Yes, and my notes, too. I've been trying to organize it all, and it's a lot." She looked at David. "I just don't want to think I'm jumping the gun on this. There are lives at stake out there."

"It'll soon be in their hands, and they'll see the same things you have." David walked back to the desk and picked up the sample pages of writing Natalie had made with the marker. After flipping through them, he left them all on the desk and came back to her at the door.

"Come on," he said and, hugging her to him, walked back into the living room.

They curled up together on the sofa, with Natalie in David's lap and arms, and his legs stretched down the length of the couch.

"I think I'm exhausted," she said. For the first time in a while, though, she managed to make a smile. "Between you and my investigating, I haven't been getting much sleep."

"You've gone through a whole lot the past few hours: fear, relief, shock, even distress over John's resignation." David kissed her forehead. "You know this has gotten way too big for you to handle? So, I'm going to call Justin and see if I can have him loan us the expertise of one of his attorneys tomorrow night. And, between the two of us, maybe we can offer you some sound advice before you meet with the partner."

Tuesday night was the gala. Natalie nodded, knowing she had to tell David about the invitation.

"Since Carter didn't send the notes, I only wish I knew more about how he fits into this."

David stroked her hair, pressing it back from her face. "He's playing around with snakes; therefore, he's one, too."

Natalie leaned back and looked up at David, enjoying the attention he gave her. This must be what it was like every day for Davina. No wonder she loved Justin. But how long would this last?

"The Innervision gala is tomorrow night. I think it would be perfect timing if I attended and picked up more evidence to turn over to the firm."

"Oh, no, don't even think about it. Look at you, you're already exhausted as it is."

Natalie pulled herself up and turned around so she could look at him. "I think I should go, David."

"What makes you think Blakely will invite you to his corporate bash, anyway? He hates you."

She took a deep breath. "Carter got me an invite."

"Carter?" David's expression was a mixture of anger and disappointment, and he stiffened with the emotion. "This is a man you don't entirely trust. He works for a snake whose dislike for you is well known, and John's resignation even tells you something fishy is going on. Yet, you're still not convinced that the man is dangerous?"

"Not entirely."

"You've already made up your mind; so what's the point in telling me?"

"Even if you don't agree with me, I figure you'd want to know."

"You think I'm going to feel better knowing you're out there with him?"

Natalie moved from his lap and folded her arms. "It's my decision."

"Yeah, right." He pulled himself up from the sofa. "Maybe you're infatuated with him and can't help yourself."

"That's not true, and totally unfair of you to say."

"Isn't that what your pleasure principle is about? Whatever comes along, find a way to enjoy it?"

What could she say? A dull ache of foreboding began to build in Natalie, and she was speechless as she watched her relationship with David prepare to combust.

He stuffed his hands into his pocket. "I've been back, what, almost two weeks, and we've been intimate about three days?" He looked at Natalie, the hurt vivid in his eyes. "I guess that's about your attention span for commitment."

"I thought you said you would stick around and help guide my impulsive nature." She gazed at him in despair. "You're backing out so quickly?"

"I thought it was what you wanted, but maybe I was wrong. In either case, maybe we both need to sleep on it . . . apart."

He turned toward the foyer and strode toward the front door; and although Natalie wanted to stop him—the advice from all of her friends crowded into her head to do it—she couldn't. Years of denying herself the possibility of a long-term relationship had stifled the ability.

David opened the door and looked back at her. "Keep yourself safe tonight, okay?"

His was a sad smile that didn't reach his beautiful gray eyes, and all Natalie could do was nod in silence.

"I'll check with Justin about an attorney. Davina can call you tomorrow and give you the details." Stepping outside, he didn't look back.

"Good night," he said.

When the door closed, Natalie also closed her eyes, feeling utterly miserable; and with her heart aching with the pain she had always feared she'd suffer if she dared admit she loved David, she cried.

Chapter 27

As Natalie walked briskly through the halls at Innervision on Tuesday morning, she reflected on the horrible night she had survived; it was almost a welcome relief to return to the office and its rut of numbers. She had hoped David would call last night; in fact, she had worked into the wee hours of the morning on the accounting issues, hoping that he would. He never did.

Today was important: it could very well be the beginning of the end for so many innocent people at this company. At last count last night, Natalie had totaled close to two hundred million dollars in questionable entries and practices, and that was just in one quarter. That made their financial statement a sham.

First, though, and to make sure there was no legal explanation for the inaccuracies, Natalie planned to conduct informal confrontations with the main players who held authority to enter figures into the corporate books. That would be Merlin Ford, accounting director, and Myra Grayson and Bill Daniels, senior accountants who reported to him. Of course, all of these people were under the authority of the chief financial officer, Gil Blakely, and Natalie didn't need another confrontation with him to know his reaction to her questions. But the others' comments had to be a necessary part of her record for both her firm and ultimately, Innervision's board.

Even with all the information she had amassed, Natalie was still unsure how far up misrepresentation of the company would go. The CEO, Mr. Monroe, had requested there be an openness in this review of the books, because it was what the stockholders wanted in view of a sign of declining profits. Natalie had her suspicions that it had all begun and ended with Gil Blakely. He had an uncanny power over a lot of people in this company, and she didn't know why.

Now, armed with her file notes, she knocked on Myra Grayson's door.

"Come in."

The timid offer filtered through the door to Natalie, and she opened it. To her benefit, Bill Daniels was also in the office, seated across from Myra at her desk.

"Ah, Miss Goodman," Myra exclaimed, standing. "I didn't know you'd be coming by here today." She gestured to Bill, who had also stood, and who looked like he wanted to be sick. "We were just deciding on whether we were coming to the gala tonight."

"Please, call me Natalie, and I thought senior managers were required to attend for the benefit of the shareholders?"

"Well, I can't think what I might be able to add to their celebration," Myra said, her voice cracking as she tried to keep it light. "So, what can I do for you?"

"I'm glad that you're here, too, Mr. Daniels." Natalie looked at him, and noticed that his color had begun to drain under her gaze. She returned her attention to Myra.

"I believe by now both of you are aware of my extensive review into Innervision's accounts. Even though Mr. Blakely has not given me express permission to question any employees, I am coming to you, informally, to ask about serious misrepresentations that have been uncovered by my team over the past months, and specific issues during the last weeks."

Natalie took a deep breath as Myra dropped back down into her chair. Bill, with his mouth slightly agape, remained standing, his stare aimed at Natalie.

"Myra Grayson, is it true that you made entries into the capital accounts, made transfers between accounts, and used your authority to rename certain operating expense accounts, placing them in capital accounts, as well?"

"Oh, my goodness," Bill said, his hand cupping over his mouth. He sat back down and now looked over at Myra.

Myra, on the other hand, seemed as stoic as a put-upon farmer's wife, as if she had expected this. She now nodded.

"Yes, I made entries in those accounts. Not all of them, but I did make some."

Natalie turned to Bill. "And you, Bill Daniels? Did you make likewise entries into these accounts?"

He darted his eyes to Myra. "Y-yes, I did," he stuttered.

"Can either of you provide the documentation to support the entries you've just attested that you made?"

"Ah, Mr. Ford told us to make the entries," Bill blurted from his chair. "In fact, he said that if anyone asked, to say that he told us to do it."

"Mr. Ford, the head of accounting, said that?" She looked between the two people. "Did anyone else direct you to make entries that had no documentation to support them?" Both Myra and Bill remained quiet.

"Well, I guess that's it for now," Natalie said. "Thank you for your time."

"Ah, Miss Goodman," Myra started. "What are you going to do now?"

"I'm going to speak with Mr. Ford next. Where I go from there depends on what he tells me."

"I see," she said quietly.

"Oh," Natalie added. "I'll be preparing a memo today with the gist of what we just discussed, and I will make it available to both of you."

She surveyed the two people who had become paler versions of their former selves right before her eyes. "I'll be in my office today if you want to further clarify anything you've already said."

Natalie almost felt sorry for them. They weren't wealthy, not like Blakely, but she was sure they did what they did at his and Ford's behest, never considering the consequences that would wreak havoc on their lives and careers in the process.

"Thank you for your time," Natalie said.

She left them there, scared by the trouble that would seek them out, and backtracked to the elevators where she headed to Mr. Ford's domain.

When she arrived at his suite, his secretary said he might be busy. Natalie explained it wouldn't take long, continuing to his office before the woman could stop her. Knocking on his door, she received a tepid invitation.

Natalie stepped through the office and saw that it was large, though only half the size of Blakely's space.

"We've met before. Mr. Ford, I'm Natalie Goodman."

"I know who you are. My two managers already called me, told me you were on your way up here." He sort of shifted his brows in a helpless manner, his round shape seemingly forced to sit still in the executive chair.

"So," he said. "What is it that you want from me?"

Natalie repeated the litany of questions regarding the accounts, as she'd done with the senior managers. He answered almost exactly as they did, though he didn't pass blame.

"In some cases, I figured it was a stretch, the principles we applied. Who knows? Maybe we can go back and reconstruct the support for the entries." He paused. "But, that's not gonna happen." He looked down at his hands, and took a deep breath before he looked back up.

"Would you like to explain any accounting principles that might support the way the entries were made?"

Natalie noticed that a light bead of sweat had begun to form along the robust man's brow.

"No." He cleared his throat. "And, uh, in retrospect, I suspect the entries shouldn't have been made at all."

Natalie closed the tablet she'd been making notes in and looked at the man. "Sir, can I ask you something?" At his nod, Natalie said, "What did you plan on telling your internal auditors, your own board, even the SEC about your flagrant lack of substantiation?"

He shook his head as though the answer eluded him as well. "I guess I never thought it would catch up with us. No one asked much until you came along. Anyway, it was to be a short-term fix until the next acquisition and merger came along." He looked up. "Unfortunately, it's taking too long for that next one to get here."

Natalie could sense his disgust with himself. She bade him good-bye, and then she left.

So they were finally realizing their backs were against the wall. Still, Natalie thought the principals of this fraud might at least argue for reconstruction. But, how do you reconstruct a half-billion dollars in false entries? In the end, the short-term answer for their problems had ballooned into their downfall, possibly even for Innervision.

Back in her office, Natalie typed away at the report, preparing interview notes for each person. And in each statement, the words that jarred her very being every time were the same.

They have no support.

As Natalie said the words out loud, it seemed to give them life, and she stopped a moment to put her head in her hands as she sat at her desk.

She would brief her firm tomorrow, and she would be required to go before Innervision's board shortly after that. The board, as well as her firm, would then have to take this to the SEC. Natalie would wait for the consequences that followed, and hope that she was not forever damaged as well.

Suddenly, both her personal and business lives were in tatters.

* * *

Blakely sat back in his chair and enjoyed the classical overture. Bach was very civilized, and Blakely sometimes needed these things to keep his feet to the earth. He wondered if he'd miss any of this once he was gone.

It didn't matter. He would be out of the country by the end of the week. It would take at least that long for the board to decide on the issues the Goodman woman had amassed. And so much for his own staff's honor to him. All they had to do was keep their mouths shut, not admit to anything— not even if there was a camera catching them in the act. But all of them had, in turn, openly stated that they had committed fraud.

So, where did things go wrong? He had acted too late with the Goodman woman, the dangerously weak link between Innervision and Lang & Myers. Blakely had wanted to bribe her and then dispose of her—just as he'd done when Webster, one of Innervision's own internal auditors, had started to snoop where he shouldn't. But, at John's insistence, he had let the woman poke around through any- and everything, and in her own time.

John had held a dangerous soft spot for the woman, and look where it had gotten him.

He shifted in the chair, and wondered if Carter would develop a soft spot, too. Carter was a good man. He did as he was told, and wouldn't let emotion get in the way. In any event, he would find out tonight when Ms. Goodman appeared for the party. And, tonight was as good a time as any for her to disappear.

The phone rang. It was his private line. There had been many calls coming in this morning, but he only chose to answer his private line.

"Hello."

"It's done." The loud music in the background almost drowned out the voice.

"Good. You got everything there?"

"A pretty good haul of stuff."

"I'll see you tonight, then, and take possession." He hung up the phone and allowed a rare smile this day to appear.

Everything was proceeding along as Blakely had planned. Well, mostly. He was ready to transfer money from six different accounts. It would all be done in a matter of days. Friday, to be exact. He wondered, again, if he'd miss this life. Of course, island life had its benefits as well. Especially if you had millions at your disposal for the rest of your life.

Tilting his head, he allowed the music to lull him into a more peaceful place.

The statements from the managers had been prepared, and Natalie was printing them from her computer when her office phone rang. When she picked it up and identified herself, she discovered it was David. Her heart somersaulted in her chest.

"Are you okay today?" he asked

"Yes, I am," she said, keeping her voice steady and calm. "After what happened yesterday, you can imagine I've got lots going on to keep me busy around here."

"I talked with Justin, and he's arranging for an attorney. I didn't offer any details, and he didn't ask, either. Let him know when you can talk, and he'll set up a meeting."

"Thank you. That does help my peace of mind." There was an awkward pause between them, as though the unspoken screamed. Natalie, having never been good at playing coy, broke the silence with words from her heart.

"I missed you last night."

"So did I." They both sighed, as though with relief. "I started to come back three different times."

Natalie's heart began to sing. "You did? Oh, why didn't you? I was up, trying to work, and hoping you would."

"I don't know. I guess I wanted to be a comfort to you yesterday, and give you my advice and you . . . well, you didn't need me."

"But I did. I was so relieved when you showed up. But, in the end, you felt like I stepped on your ego?"

He chuckled. "All over it. You're right, Natalie. I don't have a corner on the best judgment, and in the end you have to go with your gut. If you feel there's something there that needs to be exposed, I can't argue against you."

She leaned back in the chair. "Oh, David, you don't know how much I wanted to hear you say that. I know I sometimes don't think ahead, but I honestly thought this gala thing through. I was just worried about how you'd take it, which is why it took me so long to tell you."

"We have to stop this, you know."

"I know. But I've decided I don't need to go tonight. Innervision and probably Securities and Exchange will take care of Blakely and Carter and all the rest of them. I don't have to do it."

He chuckled again. "I was thinking—if you really wanted to go, I could take you."

"Oh, how thoughtful," Natalie said, smiling. "But, I'm not going. That's final."

"In that case, you want to come over to Davina's tonight? I'll tell Justin to have the lawyer meet you there."

"That sounds fine," she said.

"Great." There was a slight pause. "Hey," he said.

"Yeah?" Natalie answered.

"I love you."

Natalie grinned from ear to ear. "I love you, too."

Arriving home later that evening, Natalie felt a lightness—as though a burden had been lifted. She would speak with the lawyer tonight, and she would give her report her best shot with the partners at L & M tomorrow. Beyond that, to hell with everybody else involved in this sticky mess.

She climbed the stairs to her bedroom.

One thing did continue to haunt her. She had still not spoken to John. No one answered at his home, and Carol from the office had told Natalie that his office had been locked—and sealed. Did that mean he had admitted something to the partners? In view of the fact that she had not been called in for questioning, it could only mean he had not, in some mean-spirited move, implicated her in any wrongdoing.

Thankfully, she had covered herself from the beginning with documentation. Some had been downloaded from Innervision's computer system. Other files had been copied, and notes had been carefully compiled, an accountant's back door, she thought.

Natalie looked at her watch. She was to meet Justin and the lawyer at seven-thirty, and it was already six-thirty. She had called Carter and left her regrets for tonight on his voice mail. He had not been around all day that she knew of. She walked over to the closet.

When she opened its wide door, Natalie immediately knew something was wrong. Shoes had been pushed back, as though with a swing of the hand, and the clothes hung irregularly along the rack. It didn't look the same as she'd left it that morning.

Looking behind her, she gave her bedroom a closer look. She turned slowly, and saw her lamp, the clock—her eyes moved on. No pictures were off-kilter. Her eyes swung back to the lamp. The scarf that draped it was missing. She walked over and saw that it had fallen behind the dresser. It had been there, as it was every day, that morning when she left.

With a sharp draw of breath, Natalie rushed downstairs to the study. Her desk was cleared. Tablets, the notes, files, data CDs—they all had been stacked together on the floor and table near her computer. And they were all missing now. Blakely had done this, and it made her more angry than scared.

Natalie raced back upstairs and, plying through her closet, looked for a suitable evening dress for the gala. She was going to Innervision's party and face off with Mr. Blakely.

Chapter 28

Natalie stood outside the atrium in a resplendent strapless gown of spun gold with a tulle shawl—just something she'd grabbed from her closet in her anger over having her personal space violated by the likes of Blakely.

Who had broken into her home without sounding the alarm? The idea that it may have been Carter angered her even more since she'd done a good job of defending him to herself ever since she'd met him. What of Sean, who always hung around him and Blakely—

"Natalie, is that you?"

A wolf-whistle sang through the air and many of the white-haired attendees walking by raised their brows in disdain.

"What are you doing standing out here by yourself?" Sean asked.

Natalie gave him a smile, though her caution around him was high. "I need to get in. I don't see Carter anywhere, and . . ." She didn't explain that she had canceled and he didn't expect her out here.

Sean, dressed to the nines in tuxedo tails, held his crooked arm out for her support. "He told me he had invited you. I'll have to get on the old fella not to leave a beautiful lady waiting," he said.

Natalie let out a pretty sigh of relief for him. "Thank you. I owe—" She stopped herself. That old trite comment had already gotten her into trouble. "Thank you."

"No problem," he said.

Once they entered the building, Natalie tried to forge together a plan that would get her upstairs, past the guards she noticed at the elevator entrance.

Every so often, the guards would move aside and allow someone through. The person must be wearing some sort of identity badge or else the guard must know the person. The room was moderately filled, though it was only now eight-thirty. The string quartet had already set up and begun to play on the stage.

"Natalie?"

She turned back to Sean and realized he was talking to her.

"I'm sorry. What were you saying?"

"I was going to get us something to drink and then check out the buffet." He grinned. "I'll also look around and see if I can find Carter."

"Okay," she said. "I'll be waiting right here."

The minute he was out of sight, Natalie hiked up the long skirt of her dress and hightailed it across the room to the elevator bay, where she stood just beyond the curiosity of the guards and watched who got through.

Two men nodded as they walked past the guard and into the bay. When they turned around, Natalie peered at their coats. The only thing they had in common was a pin on their lapel. It was the Innervision logo, shaped into a pin. It was probably expensive. The men got onto the elevator.

Natalie decided she'd have to lift a pin off someone. She looked over the group, staring at more lapels than she wanted to.

"Oh, excuse me," she said to a small woman she bumped into.

"Why, that's all right, young lady. No damage done," she said, smiling.

"Oh, but there is. Here, let me straighten your collar." Natalie reached up to straighten the fluffs in her chiffon collar, and expertly pulled the icon pin from its holding place, palming it as she removed her hand. "There," Natalie said, her face beaming. "Good as new."

"Thank you." The older woman gave her a gracious smile. "And what a beautiful gown you're wearing. I'll bet it's an Ungaro? I can tell by the lines, you know."

Natalie nodded with a twinkle in her eyes. "You're so smart. Have a great time." She pranced off, heading directly for the elevator bays. By the time she reached them, she had fastened the pilfered pin, which boasted a single diamond on the front, on her gown. No wonder they were hard to come by. They were probably a keepsake for only the most worthy investors. She wondered if her gown really was an Ungaro. When she picked it out at the consignment shop, the designer's name had been missing.

She offered the guard a smile, but did not suffer his permission to pass, so she didn't slow down. The rich seemed to know they had access to anywhere they wanted to go. The poor didn't comprehend that concept.

The guard's trained eyes swiftly perused her chest, and then returned to their active duty straight ahead, just as he'd been taught. Natalie took a deep breath only when the elevator opened and she was safely ensconced within its walls.

She pressed the button to her floor, fifteen, intending to learn if her office had been ransacked, too. When the elevator stopped there, she stepped into a deafening silence. Instead of cutting through the accounting division, she took the back route, skirting the internal offices. As she rounded the last corner for her hallway, she heard sounds—low voices, with gentle laughter following.

A man and woman, with their backs to Natalie, had stopped in the middle of the hallway. More giggling was accompanied by a masculine voice.

Pulling up her step, Natalie backed into the shadowy corner, and then peeked out at them. Shocked by what she saw, she stepped back and stood stock-still against the wall.

Having only gotten a side view, the woman was, without any doubt, the tall and unmistakable beauty, Randi Synn. The gentleman with her was distinguished by the fact that he had a full head of dark hair, and was shorter than Randi by a good six inches. The oddest thing of all was that both had stopped in front of Natalie's office door.

She risked yet another look, and saw Randi turn the key and enter the room; the man followed, and then closed the door behind them.

Swallowing hard, all Natalie could think was, what was going on?

The first thing that made David anxious was that Natalie's car was not in the Hardys' drive and it was after nine o'clock. The second thing was that Justin was standing in the turnaround, as though he waited for him. Aw, hell, he thought as he jumped from his car, slamming the door. What had happened?

"Where's Natalie?" he asked Justin.

Justin's hands were pushed deep into his pockets as he came down to meet David. "She's not here, and she's not answering her house phone or her cell. Davina's been trying for the last hour."

"Damn. I know exactly where she is."

"You do?"

"She told me this afternoon that she wasn't going to that big Innervision bash they're having for investors and company brass tonight." David's brows knitted with anger as he crossed his arms and explained. "She got an invite, courtesy of our friend, Carter; but I believed her this afternoon." He chuckled nastily. "I really did believe her when she said she didn't want to go after all that was going down at the office, and we agreed that she'd meet me here."

"I think you ought to go over to Innervision and find her," Justin said. "She may need you."

David dropped his arms and turned to his friend. "What are you talking about?"

"The other night at the christening party, Natalie told me that you two saw Carter talking with Connie in the park."

He nodded. "We did. It looked like they were meeting for business or something."

"I talked with Connie yesterday and asked him to find out what he could on Carter. Where did he come from, last job, that sort of stuff, because of the bad vibe Natalie was giving off about him."

"Really? And . . . ?"

"I just talked with Connie. There is no history on our Carter Johnson before eighteen months ago. It's as though his name and history materialized from nowhere."

David turned and walked back to his car. Justin followed him.

"I'm waiting for another call from Connie. He's using some other searches, including photography."

"I've got my phone," David said, opening the car door. "If you find out anything else, call me."

"Hey, do you need me to go with you?"

"No." David saluted his brother-in-law from the car. "You've done more than your share already. Just stay close to my sister and Jake."

"Will do," Justin said, smiling, and stepped back at the roar from the car's powerful engine.

Natalie stepped from the elevator bay and walked past the guard into the main dancing area, still shocked by what she'd witnessed upstairs. She wondered if Carter could shed light on it. She wasn't stupid, and she knew Randi wasn't some principal investor in the company. So, the only reason she'd be going into a locked room with a man who wasn't her husband would be for illicit purposes. Was Blakely arranging sexual favors for his executives or was it something even more difficult to fathom?

As she waded through the people, she felt her elbow being tugged, and then pulled hard enough to stop her motion forward.

She whirled around, ready to become indignant, only to face Carter's stern frown.

"Natalie—damn it, Sean told me you were here, and I didn't want to believe it."

"He let me in on his ticket."

"I thought your message said you wouldn't be able to attend anymore."

She drew a deep breath. "I changed my mind." She didn't intend to tell him that her house had been burglarized and she wanted to see if her things were in Blakely's office. "But, that's not important. I was just on fifteen and I saw a woman going into my office upstairs. With a man."

"How did you even get upstairs?" He sighed. "Never mind."

"Carter, are you going to tell me what's going on or do I have to go up there again, knock on my damn door, and ask?"

He looked around, as though for someone. "I've got to go, but I'll explain later. What I need you to do is go home, and please don't fight me on this."

"Now that I'm here, I'm not going anywhere until you tell me something about that woman on fifteen. You're security, so I know you know."

"Later, Natalie, and stay out of it." His curt voice lashed out at her. "Now, go home." With a sharp stare at her face, he sauntered off and disappeared into the crowd.

"Well, he sure as hell doesn't know me." She smirked. "I'll go home when I'm damn ready," she said aloud. She'd worry about Randi later and get back to figuring a way to get into Blakely's office, one way or the other. Turnaround, she figured, was fair play since someone was in hers.

As she walked through the group to head back to the elevators, she ran into Myra.

The small woman wore a beige tailored sheath dress that only seemed to accentuate her lack of curves.

"Hi there, you're looking lovely this evening," Natalie said graciously.

"Oh, thank you. And you . . ." She shook her head. "You dazzle the eye, Ms. Goodman."

"Please call me Natalie." She looked around. "Did the other manager, Bill Daniels, I believe, attend?"

"No. It's why I had to come. For both of us not to come would have been a slap in Mr. Ford's face. Since I don't have a family, I told him I'd show up."

"I hope my visit to you and Mr. Daniels this afternoon didn't set too hard with you," Natalie said. "I'm only doing my job and protecting my company's integrity," she said.

"Which I didn't." With those words, tears began to spill down Myra's cheek.

"Come on," Natalie said, and drew her through the crowd. "Let's get some privacy, away from these people."

By the time they reached the ladies' lounge, Myra had controlled the tears, but she had seriously damaged her eye makeup.

"I don't know what gets into me sometimes," she said. "I think I've given up everything for this job. I'm not married, I have no children, and I have no prospects for either. But here I am, almost forty, and I could be going to prison."

Natalie understood the woman's reality. "Have you consulted a lawyer?"

"After you left, Bill and I decided to pool our money and get one. We have a meeting set up for tomorrow. I'm here tonight because we don't want to tip our hands too much." She looked up. "Bill and I are going to try and become whistle-blowers before wind of the scandal hits the authorities."

"Oh, Myra, I hope it's not too late."

"Being here tonight, I almost want to get on the microphone, stand in front of the crowd, and just announce that the report they're getting is filled with lies, errors, and misrepresentation. I can't live with the lies anymore. I thought about it a lot the other day when we met in the cafeteria."

"You seem like a good person. Why did you go along with Mr. Ford's requests? And you don't have to say it, but I know his orders came directly from Blakely." She watched as Myra tried to repair her eyes. "You're going to have to admit that fact to the authorities down the line so that Blakely will get his due."

Myra turned to Natalie. "Everybody's scared of him. Except you." She turned back to the mirror. "You should hear some of the rumors riding around about him. He's like the bogeyman your mama told you about when you were bad."

Natalie shivered from the woman's words. "What kind of rumors?"

"That he blackmails people, but nobody knows how he does it." She sighed as she wiped her hands. "And people who question his authority don't last long in the company. You wouldn't believe the turnover in accounting over the past couple of years. There's even rumors of mysterious disappearances."

"Good grief," Natalie said, and rose up to leave. "I'd be willing to bet whatever will incriminate him is probably in that fourteen-carat office of his."

"Probably," Myra said as she stood up, too.

"I wish I had a key to get me up there on his floor."

"My executive key will get you into conference rooms and bathrooms all over. I don't know if it'll work in his private office. Maybe you can get into his office from a conference room."

Natalie's eyes widened with excitement. "Where's the key?"

While Myra fished it from her evening purse, Natalie pulled her cell phone out. "Do you have a cell phone with you?"

"I, ah, I don't use those things."

Natalie sighed and grinned at the simple woman. "You're

giving accountants a bad name, girl. Here—keep mine with you. I've got it turned to vibrate so it keeps quiet." She showed her how it operates. "I'm going upstairs to Blakely's office. When I get in, I'll call you. Think you can do it?"

She nodded as she looked over the small phone. "Sure, I can do it."

"All right. Wish me luck. With your key, maybe I'll find something that'll bust Mr. Blakely for more than just cooking his corporate books."

Natalie had successfully used Myra's universal passkey to enter Blakely's conference room. She now had begun frantically to wiggle at the office's door knob. But it wouldn't budge. Her featherweight didn't even make a noise. At her wits' end, she finally fiddled with the top lock and voila, the door opened. It hadn't even been locked.

Feeling like a total klutz, she peeked around the door and into the room. Slipping through, she quietly closed it behind her.

Now, where would I hide something? she asked herself as she looked around the dimly lit room. The window blinds were up and the corner office's northwest view was spectacular.

Natalie peered into a china cabinet, opened drawers, and looked under the sofa, including the cushions. There was nothing to be found. The cherry-wood cabinet near the door had no secrets to give up when she opened its double doors, and she pushed them back. But one wouldn't close correctly.

She looked to the floor, and saw that there were five drawers in the bottom, and one had slid out when the doors had been opened.

Natalie pulled the drawers out, one at a time, and found nothing. The final drawer was a different story. The others were filled with memorabilia and such. This one was empty. She reached in, and the floor of the drawer wobbled. A false bottom. She got down on her knees and, as quietly as she could, removed the false bottom. Below the piece of wood was a flat surface that required a key.

"Damn." Natalie muttered the expletive and looked around, running her hands along the smooth edges of wood. There was no key. She gave up, going over to the desk.

It was a magnificent piece of furniture, Natalie thought, and probably cost a fortune, seeing as it was the size of a small bed. She went around to the other side and yanked at the long top drawer, expecting it to be locked up; but it wasn't, and Natalie barely landed on the chair from the force of her pull.

Scrabbling about in the drawer didn't bring up a key. She checked the left-side drawers and hit the jackpot. She rushed back over to the cabinet, almost tripping over her gown, and kneeling behind the sofa in front of the cabinet, tried the keys, one at a time, in the lock. The third key looked like a court jester's hat, with five flanges sticking out in all directions. She tried it, and it was a perfect fit. She turned it and the cover lifted up.

What met her eyes were neatly stacked rows of black plastic casings of videotapes. There were also CDRs and CDRWs, the kinds of media that record video with a computer.

"What in the world . . . ?" Natalie muttered to herself. None of the tapes had names written on them, just dates, some as recent as two days before.

Natalie's brain cruised along with questions. Why would Blakely keep tapes locked away, and in such a complicated fashion? Unless they contained something he didn't want to come to light. Natalie needed to learn their contents. Maybe he had a VCR. Grabbing up the keys, she returned to the desk.

This time, she yanked open the right side of the desk. When she was faced with another wooden panel, she grinned. "I'm thinking you've got a wood fetish, Mr. Blakely."

Natalie pushed the panel aside and revealed three small,

attached television screens. She let out an unexpected expletive at this surprise discovery.

"Mr. Blakely, you've got all kinds of secrets, don't you?"

Manual controls stretched out below the screens, but with no instructions. Natalie began to push buttons and, suddenly, hit pay dirt. All three screens flashed on. And there, playing out before her eyes, was an X-rated film.

"Huh," Natalie said, squinting at the small picture. "Why, that little pervert, watching porno videos at work."

At first, Natalie thought she was viewing three different movies. But then, as she looked harder, she recognized the short man, with the dark hair straddling the woman—he had been in the hall not too long ago. And now, he was on the video. She looked carefully again. The woman . . . it was Randi Synn.

Natalie put her hand over her mouth to stifle her scream of surprise and shock at what she'd uncovered. This was her office on camera, and somehow Blakely received a video feed. In some region of her mind, the puzzle pieces were rapidly forming a picture.

Furniture bolted to the floor to stay stationary . . . for cameras. This could explain Blakely's almost Machiavellian influence on his superiors, employees, board members. He used blackmail. And he used Randi Synn. Her name in Innervision's books meant payoffs to her, ostensibly for helping Blakely blackmail his business partners.

This was major, and she had to tell someone quickly.

She reached for Blakely's phone and dialed her cell number that she'd left with Myra.

"Hello."

"Myra? It's me."

"Where've you been? I was getting worried."

"Listen, I don't have much time. I need you to call a phone number for me. Jot this down in your hand." She gave Myra David's cell number. "His name is David. Tell him I need him to come to the gala ASAP. He'll give me flack, but he won't if you call him."

"Okay, I got it. So, did you find anything up there in Mr. Blakely's office?"

"Oh, Myra, you'll never believe what I came across," she said. "A whole cache of videos and film, and even live—"

Natalie was unceremoniously yanked away from the phone by the back of her shawl. She turned and saw it was Sean.

"Sean," she demanded, as he now dragged her bodily from behind the desk. "What are you doing?"

"Aww, damn, Natalie. Carter said he sent you back home. So why didn't you go?" he asked, as he dumped her onto the sofa.

"How did you know I was up here?" she asked as she regained her footing.

"We didn't. But when you picked up Mr. Blakely's private line, it lit up in the other room." He nodded to the far side of the office that boasted a fully paneled wall. "We were in there." He looked over at the wall as a panel of the wood opened, becoming a door that revealed Carter stepping through.

Natalie put her hands on her hips and sighed. "I should have known."

Carter was a glowering mask of rage. "Tie that mouth of hers up right now, Sean. Do it first."

David realized he was severely underdressed—in a light summer suit and no tie—for a formal dance. But it was the least of his worries. The biggest worry was Natalie. Where was she?

His cell phone on the seat rang out. "Hello," he answered.

"Ah, David. This is Myra." David looked at the caller ID. It showed Natalie's name.

"Myra?" Apprehension swept through David. "Where's Natalie?"

"Well, she told me to call you and tell you she found some crazy stuff up in Mr. Blakely's office. She wants you to meet her over here at the gala."

"I'm already on my way there now," he said, trying to keep the cold knot of fear down.

"I'll have to meet you outside, or otherwise you can't get in."

"Where is Natalie now, Myra?"

"I'm not sure. When she called me from upstairs, we were interrupted."

David staved off his growing panic. "Wait for me outside the building, Myra. I should be there in less than fifteen minutes."

"How will I know what you look like?" she asked.

"You'll know me. I'll be mad as hell and inappropriately dressed."

David clicked off the phone, and sped down the expressway toward downtown.

Carter looked down at Sean's handiwork. Natalie had been tied to a chair, and her own shawl had been used to gag her mouth. But the daggers she threw from her eyes were unmistakable, and never missed their target.

"She was talking to Myra," Sean said. "I told security to be on the lookout for her. She can't be that hard to find."

"When they find her, I'll take care of it. Blakely will be here soon. I want you to keep Natalie healthy, is that clear? Nothing goes off unless I say so."

Myra jumped up and down on the entrance patio when she saw the stern-faced David appear from the parking area, his light jacket flapping against the light breeze.

"Thank God, you made it. I'm Myra," she said, extending her hand.

"I'm David." He looked around before he quickly escorted her back to the doors. "Have you seen Natalie or heard from her again?"

"No, but I'm really worried," Myra said, doing double steps to keep up.

"Where was she the last time you talked? What floor?"

"In Mr. Blakely's office." She gave him the suite's location on the twenty-fifth floor. "She hasn't tried to call back at all."

David's heart floundered. "How can I get up there? What's the security like?"

"Natalie . . . You know, she's so resourceful. Well, anyway, she slipped one of those tiny little VIP pins off of some lady. And, security let her right through to the elevators without any questions."

They had entered the main floor, and David began to receive more than his share of stares at his state of dress.

"It's gonna be pretty hard for me to slip up on someone unsuspecting and snatch a pin. But, I'm going to have to try," he said, looking around.

"Not to worry," Myra said, and grinned. "Natalie said I should believe in myself." She produced one of the pins. "I knew you'd need one, so I began to check out the room before you got here."

David hugged the woman. "Bless you." He slipped it onto his lapel. "Keep Natalie's phone handy. If I'm not back down here within an hour, I want you to call the police and tell them everything you told me—that Natalie was upstairs, she found something incriminating, and she was abruptly cut off from the phone."

Myra nodded at the instructions. "Okay. Now, you go on, see if you can find her. She's so nice, you know."

"I do know," he said with a smile, and then sauntered off toward the elevator bays and the vigilant guards.

Chapter 29

David's bold stride into the elevator bay was almost a dare to the security guard. But wisely, the young guard did not challenge an already nerve-racked David. He pressed the numbers for the executive suites, holding his patience during the long ride.

When the elevator doors opened, David cautiously stepped out and surveyed the area, unsure of what might be waiting. He remembered the number of the suite Myra had given him and headed in that direction.

Farther down the hall, a receptionist area loomed. He walked through and came to large, double doors that led into an office. He tried the lever, but the door was locked. To his left was another door labeled CONFERENCE ROOM.

Silence penetrated the air as David laid his head against the door to detect a sound. Nothing.

He slowly pushed down on the latch and eased the door open, and then, wider still. Sitting in the middle of the room, tied down in a straight-backed chair, was Natalie. The lower half of her face was fully covered with the shawl. Only her eyes attested to the fright she must feel.

David's rage was immeasurable, and he made the mistake of not reading her eyes, wide and darting.

"Jeez . . . what have they done to you?" he asked, and rushed up to her.

"The same thing that's going to happen to you, I'm afraid." Sean pushed the flat-nosed gun into David's back. "Hands up, please."

David slowly rose from Natalie's side, and tried to see who held the gun. "You've got me now. Let her go," David offered.

"Unfortunately, that's not my call, because I do like the lady. But I'm afraid a lot of people think she's more trouble than she's worth." He pressed the gun at David's back. "And since Carter's not around to help, I sure can't tie you up and hold the gun at the same time, so . . ."

A sharp pain drove into David's right temple before he crumpled to the carpeted floor.

Natalie had prayed, she was sure, a hundred prayers since David had rushed in. Each one had asked God to make sure he was all right, and she had watched with cautious optimism, as he had quickly roused himself from the floor, but he was incapacitated enough that Sean was able to tie his legs and hands without David's brawn overpowering him. Natalie blamed herself for their predicament. If only she'd adhered to her promise; if only she'd let David come with her; if only . . .

David raised his head and gave her a wink above the gag Sean had tied.

Natalie's relief was so great that she wanted to cry. He still had his sense of humor. She looked about the room. Sean seemed to be constantly on the phone with someone, in and out, between the conference room and Blakely's office. He was also obviously impatient for Carter's return. He'd barely spoken a word to her or David. And where had Carter gone, anyway? After reminding Sean to keep her safe, he'd left, not to return. And the big question: what did they plan to do with her and David?

Natalie felt more than heard David next to her. He was edging closer to her. It seemed each time Sean left them, or turned his back to them, David would powerlift his entire chair and move a fraction closer to Natalie.

With a flourish of his arm, Sean turned from the window. "Mr. Blakely is going to make a little visit before he leaves," he said. "He's coming up right now."

Natalie and David shared a glance before Sean said, "What?" He crossed over to them. "I bet you don't have a clue about what you've screwed up, do you, Natalie?"

He didn't have time to explain because at that moment Blakely walked in through his office. Dressed in formal attire, he took on an almost patrician air as he paraded across the room, studying them at length down his long nose. Sean brought him a chair and he sat on it as he regarded them with a malicious smile.

"You say you'll show up, and then you don't, and then you show up again." He shook his head. "You're something else, Ms. Goodman. You sure kept me on my toes these last weeks." He smiled again. "It's almost a shame to end your life." He turned around to Sean. "Where's Carter?"

"Security located Myra. She was in cahoots with Natalie down on the floor; Carter wanted to handle it himself, so he told me to watch her until you came up. He should be back soon, sir," Sean said.

"That Carter is more hands-on than I am, damn it. Get him on the phone. Tell him our double package here has been ready for delivery for a while."

"I've been trying, sir, but I'll try again." He stepped back to the window and began dialing.

Blakely looked at David. "You, Mr. Spenser, were not supposed to be involved in any of this; so I'm afraid you'll have to join Ms. Goodman in her long sleep. Both of you will be found in your vehicle together, where you, unfortunately, took the curve too quickly on a steep road near a lake, or a river—it doesn't matter."

He now gave his attention to Natalie. "I can hear that analytical brain of yours working overtime. And whether anyone believes it was an accident or not won't matter too much, because by the time they decide it was connected with a company being investigated for irregular bookkeeping, I'll be out of the country, and I won't give a damn at that point."

A faraway buzz could be heard, like a bee flitting through the air. Blakely stood up, and turned toward the window where Sean was still dialing the phone.

"What is that noise?" he asked, his ear cocked toward the window.

Natalie believed another one of her prayers had been answered.

Sean let out an expletive. "Sounds like sirens." He looked at his boss. "Lots of them."

"I'll go downstairs and see what's going on." He turned to Natalie and David. "Keep them for Carter to pick up. But, if they give you problems, or if they try to get away, shoot them."

When he left through the conference room door, Sean peered down the twenty-five floors, seemingly impressed by the lights. "Man, there's a flood of cars down there. I gotta find Carter."

The minute Sean left the room, David looked over at Natalie and motioned for her to try and meet him with her chair. Together, they covered the distance in a short time, positioning their chairs back to back. Reaching through the rails, David clutched at Natalie's bindings and worked at them. After what seemed an eternity, the knots were sufficiently loosened that her small hands could squeeze through the slack spaces.

The sirens outside had not abated, and each screech gave Natalie hope. She quickly reached up and unbound the shawl from her mouth.

Touching her bruised mouth, she took no time to savor freedom, and bent over to untie her legs.

"David." She looked around at him. "I'm glad you came for me, but I'm so sorry I did this to you."

He grunted his understanding, but urged her to keep moving, winking in the process.

"I know," she said. "They'll be back before we know it."

Finally free of her leg bindings, Natalie hopped up from the chair and moved over to David. Her nimble fingers made quick work of his mouth gag, and the moment it was removed, she landed a kiss on his parched lips. "I feel so much better with you here," she said. "Listen to those sirens. Maybe the police will come up here."

"Can you untie my hands?" he asked. "We've got to hurry."

She moved around the back and worked on the knot, but it was especially tight, and she couldn't get it to unravel. Aware that she was losing precious time, she stooped to his leg bindings, which were not as tight; in fact, they fell away quickly. As Natalie returned to try his hands, Sean's curses could be heard coming from Blakely's office.

"Stoop down, stay behind me, Natalie," David whispered. "Pretend I'm still tied."

Sean walked back in, and at the sight of Natalie's empty chair, he whirled toward them with the gun. "What are you doing?" he asked, dumbfounded. "Get over here, now," he said to Natalie.

"No," she said. "You're going to kill us, anyway."

"That's right, stay right behind me, Natalie," David commanded. "You like her, Sean, and she's never been anything but nice to you. Let her go."

"I . . . I can't, man. You don't know Blakely. If he says she's gotta go, she's gotta go."

An outer door could be heard opening, and they all turned toward it.

Sean realized the visitor was coming in through Blakely's office. He quickly took a position behind the door and out of view, pointing the gun at David in the process.

"If either of you say the wrong thing, or if she runs, the other gets a bullet." He cocked the gun, and the deadly click sounded through the room. "I swear."

Outside, sirens continued to scream their presence to the city.

Carter walked into the room, and Natalie let out a loud gasp when she saw him brandishing a gun this time.

"You were able to get loose," he observed, and walked toward David and Natalie. "Well, the cavalry is here now." His face then broke out in a grin as he faced Natalie, with Sean coming up from behind the door. "Finally," Carter added.

"What the hell?" A shocked Sean raised his gun, but turned the muzzle from David to Carter.

Carter looked over his shoulder and, belatedly, saw Sean coming up behind him, with his gun raised, ready to fire.

"You liar," Sean shouted, his face screwed up in anger as he pulled the trigger; but David had already hoisted his legs up and a hard kick sent Carter sprawling across the carpet and out of the way of the bullet.

Natalie screamed as Sean prepared to shoot again, and this one aimed at her and David. Carter, however, with a quick roll on the carpet, came up, took aim, and shot first.

"Owww . . ." Sean doubled over and howled in pain, the gun dropping from his injured arm.

Carter quickly jumped up and kicked the gun out of reach before he pulled Sean up by his shirt and dragged him near the window.

"Carter, what is going on here?" David asked.

"I thought you were . . . Well, I don't really know what I thought," Natalie said, as she worked to free David's hands.

"You bastard," Carter said to Sean, before he holstered his gun.

"Aw, man, I can't believe this. I'm bleeding," Sean cried.

"Believe it," Carter said, and walked over to help Natalie untie David. "The police will be up here to get you in a minute."

"You've got a lot of explaining to do," David said, as he stood and flexed his hands and wrists.

Carter gave a wide grin as he turned to face them fully. "I couldn't—"

David had already reared his right shoulder back, and brought it forward with a hard jab to Carter's corner jaw, and a stumbling Carter crashed into the wall.

"David," Natalie exclaimed, running to him.

Carter pulled himself off the wall, working his jaw into position even as he gingerly fingered it. "What the hell was that for?"

David was already back in Carter's face, as though he was ready to throw another punch. But Natalie stood in front of him.

"With that jab, though," Carter said, "the Bureau could use you in the field."

Natalie looked from David to Carter. "What's he talking about?" she asked.

David shook out his hand and walked away from Carter. "He's FBI, Natalie, and he let you come too close to being killed tonight. That's why he got the punch."

Natalie turned to Carter. "You're what?"

It was only now that Natalie took the time to take in the differences about Carter. For one, he wore a dark windbreaker over his tuxedo, and when he turned to pick up the kicked-away gun, she saw, boldly displayed across the back, the letters FBI.

"You really are FBI?"

"Actually," he clarified, "I'm with the Securities and Exchange Commission. This is our joint effort with the FBI, IRS, GBI, and even a few ATF agents tagged along, too. I borrowed a jacket since I couldn't get to my own."

"This?" David questioned, drawing Natalie in front of him.

"The undercover operation at Innervision."

"What?" Natalie exclaimed, and looked up at David.

"Come on over here; I'll tell you about it." They joined him at the conference table as he explained. "The probe has been going on now officially for about seven months." He smiled as he crossed his arms. "We thought their books looked too good when their counterparts were going through hell. We got lots of tips, but no evidence. So, we planted one of our own. Me.

"Of course, you even uncovered some things we didn't know about initially, like Blakely paying off his partners out of Innervision's funds, and his applications for offshore accounts."

"How did you know that? I just found out about it on Sunday."

"When I learned Blakely had Sean make a set of your keys—"

"Is that how everybody got into my property?"

Carter nodded. "I told Sean to deliver the stolen files to me. I had a chance to read some of your notes. That's when I saw copies of the offshore account apps you made. It's all safely marked as evidence."

At that moment, a commotion was heard in the halls, and a burst of armed men, some in flak jackets, some in suits, maybe ten in all, came into the room. They took over the gun Carter had confiscated, others pulled a crying and injured Sean to his feet and escorted him out, and still others moved into Blakely's office.

"I'm sure you want to get out of here; unfortunately, you and David can't leave until you give a statement."

"When will that be?" David asked.

"It shouldn't be too long."

Natalie looked over at Blakely's office. "Are you aware that he has a video system in there that records my office downstairs?"

"He has what?" David asked.

Carter nodded. "The man has a wide range of vices, which is why I became concerned about you, Natalie. I tried to position myself to know what was going on in your life; that's why I kept asking for those dates."

"Even though I kept saying no," she said with a smile. She looked up. "It all makes sense now."

He looked at David. "You have to know that it was my job to get into Blakely's inner circle, and gain his trust. But I always tried to keep Natalie's best interests in hand."

"Well, a lot of things are beginning to make better sense," David admitted.

"Do you know anything about my boss, John? I haven't heard from him since he resigned yesterday, and I'm afraid he's way deep in this, too."

"I had a meeting with him last night. You know he wrote those notes?" At Natalie's nod, Carter continued. "He was convinced that Blakely was ready to harm you, and when he confessed to his partners, he had to resign; but the authorities wouldn't let them tip you off—not when we had this big bust planned for tonight."

"What's going to happen to him?"

"I suspect he'll turn into a witness and testify against Blakely."

David turned to Carter. "Where's Myra? She was really helpful tonight."

"She's safely sitting in a police car outside, and out of Blakely's harm."

A woman stuck her head in the door. "Carter, we're ready for their statements," she said, and then left.

"That brings us back to Blakely," David said.

"Yeah," Natalie chimed in. "Where is he?"

"Mr. Blakely was waylaid as he tried to leave the building. He's being questioned, as well; however, he's a flight risk, so he'll probably be booked immediately, and his passport confiscated."

"Good," David said. "That makes me feel better."

"Yeah, that'll make a lot of people feel better." Carter stood up. "So, are you ready to give your statements?"

"One more thing," David said. "What is your real name?"

"What?" Natalie asked.

"It's Carter Randall," he said, grinning. "Now are you ready?"

David nodded, and with a smile, he rose, too. "All right. After tonight, I think I'm ready for anything."

"Well, I'm just feeling good about being alive." Natalie grinned and squeezed David in a hug. "I can't wait until we tell little Jake about this adventure."

It was after midnight, and Innervision Industries was still lit up with official law enforcement vehicles like the proverbial Christmas tree.

David held the doors open for Natalie, and they walked out of the building together, she in the drop-dead beautiful gold formal dress with a slightly wrinkled shawl, and he in the linen sports jacket and slacks, also slightly wrinkled. They were a sight to see walking along the downtown sidewalks at this time of morning, but they were just happy to be together. And for a while, they simply walked, hand in hand, with no particular destination.

"Thank you, David," Natalie finally said.

"For what?"

"Believing in me, and letting me make God knows how many mistakes, and best of all, letting me find my way out of them." She darted a glance at him. "I have made a few, haven't I?"

"Well, if you're counting, then we both have some under our belts." He glanced at her. "Maybe it's our imperfections that make us right for each other. We know them better than anybody else."

"I never thought of it that way." They walked awhile longer. "Until tonight, I was afraid of leaning on you, of leaning on anyone."

"I understand. That way, you're never disappointed."

"Right. Tonight, though, it was bad all around, but you didn't care. You were there for me; even with your own life at stake, you wanted to protect me."

David laughed as he drew her hand in his and crossed over Peachtree Street. "Why are you surprised?" He stopped when they reached the other side of the sidewalk, and tilted her head up. "I love you, Natalie." He kissed her eyes.

"I know." Tears began to trail down her face. "And because I know that, it makes all the difference in the world. I need you to know that I love you, too."

"I've known it for some time." He kissed her eyes again. "It's why I didn't give up on you, even when I was in D.C."

He drew her arm through his and continued walking. "Which brings me to some other news I had planned to share with you tonight."

"Oh?" she asked. "And what news is that?"

"I'm back in Atlanta."

She stopped and turned to him, grinning from ear to ear. "Are you serious? For good?"

"Forever, if I want."

She threw her arms around his neck. "So you don't have to go back in a few days after all?"

He squeezed her to him. "Not right now. I will have to go back to pack and move my things here."

When they pulled apart, they realized they had stopped in front of the wide verandah that was the Westin Hotel.

"I have an idea," Natalie said, looking up at the hotel as a devilish smile overtook her face. "Why don't we check into a hotel, shower, stay naked, and order room service?"

"Already thought of it. I made the call here about an hour ago," David said, laughing. "See? You're rubbing off on me already." He picked her up and swung her around. "I've got a feeling, Natalie, that life with you will be anything but boring."

Natalie giggled out loud into the night sky. God, she loved this man.

Epilogue

Two Weeks Later

"You made the green bean casserole we're having for dinner today?" Carolyn asked. "What in heck brought that on?" She was comfortably snuggled against Michael on the sofa.

"It was a friendly bet, and Justin won," Davina said, squeezing Justin's arm from where he crowded next to her on the other sofa.

"Oh, goodness," Natalie exclaimed with a laugh as she perched on David's lap. "Not another one of *those* bets."

It was almost time for Sunday dinner at the Hardys', and the young friends had gathered to lounge in the salon while they waited for the tardy arrivals. In the meantime, a variety of subjects got tossed around during these laid-back talk sessions on Sunday afternoons.

"Well, I have to admit," David said, "I'm in love with a woman whose talents definitely lie outside of the kitchen."

A host of hoots and laughs followed his comment.

"No," he said, laughing, too. "Not like that." When Natalie turned her face up to his, he kissed her. "Well, okay, maybe like that," he joked.

Another round of laughter rose up between the friends.

"Natalie, when is that *60 Minutes* interview you did on corporate greed airing?" Justin asked.

"Not until next month, I believe."

Carolyn sat up. "Can you believe how many people Gil Blakely was blackmailing with those tapes? And then, he uses that stripper to seduce his partners? I mean, he had tapes of everybody, from the CEO on down."

"That's how he got his way and became so powerful," Michael offered. "I don't see how he can defend himself in court."

"Yeah, he and the other manager, Ford, are going down from what I hear of the evidence," Justin said. "Everybody else is testifying against them."

"Aren't you going home for a week next month?" Davina asked Natalie.

Natalie looked back at David. "Yes, and David wanted to go, too." She then exchanged a private smile with Davina before she explained the occasion to the others.

"It's my little sister's birthday, and my mom's planning a big party. And, I mean big. In fact, I think she's turning it into a family reunion."

"Don't forget, Mom wants to know when they come to Atlanta for a visit," Justin reminded them.

"So, did you decide to stay with Lang & Myers now that John Callaway has gone?" Carolyn asked.

"Would you believe, after all the publicity I've been getting for helping to crack this case, they now want to train me as the staff forensic accountant?"

"I've heard of that. It's a brand-new field," Michael said.

"Yeah, for a brand-new kind of twenty-first-century criminal," David added.

"I just might do it," she said, turning her gaze on David. "Or"—she reached for his hand—"I might join David in a private practice."

"Hey, that sounds like a plan," Justin said.

"I'm just waiting for her to give me the word," David said. "No pressure."

"I'm hungry," Davina announced. "Is everybody here?"

"Anyone see Alli around?" Carolyn asked.

"Hey . . . we just got here." Alli's voice floated out from the doorway. She entered with a towering Carter close behind her.

"Carter, glad you could make it," David called out, with the others chiming in a similar greeting.

"Okay, it looks like the gang's all here," Davina announced. "So, let's eat."

Later that night, Natalie sat cross-legged on the bench at the foot of her bed, her robe tied loosely around her. David had knelt in front of her.

"Are we officially a couple again?" he asked.

Natalie scowled as she brushed back his hair. "I don't like how that sounds . . . too nineties."

David grinned. "All right . . . what about going steady?"

She laughed. "You aren't serious, are you? That's too juvenile."

"Something grown-up, maybe, like lovers?" he suggested.

"In that case, why don't we just tell everyone we're sleeping together and they can draw their own conclusion?"

"So, we agree, then? We don't need a label?"

Natalie leaned forward and kissed him. "Only the classic ones, like we're in love, or—"

"We're engaged?" David's hand reached over Natalie's and he left a tiny silver box there.

"Oh, my God, David." Natalie gasped in surprise even as her eyes widened with pleasure.

"Go ahead," he urged, enjoying her shock. "Open it."

She popped the box open and a sparkling diamond sitting atop an exquisite platinum band bedazzled her. She gasped again before she began to cry. "Oh, David. It's beautiful."

"Here," he said, stealing a glance at her eyes. "Let me slip it on for you." He did, and she held her hand out to admire it.

"I don't know what to say," was all she was finally able to get out.

"Well, how about, yes, you'll marry me and make me the happiest man in the world?"

She nodded as she laughed with her tears. "Okay, yes, I want to marry you, David Spenser, and make us the happiest couple in the world."

Natalie threw her arms around his neck, and allowed his demanding mouth full access to hers. "Oh, God," she said against his mouth. "You're so good to me, you're so good *for* me."

David grinned and, pulling her close with one hand, he was already peeling away her wispy underwear with his other.

"So, you want to kiss me some more and seal the deal?" she teased.

He loosened his embrace and pushed Natalie so that she fell gently back to the bed.

"You're insatiable," he teased. "And I love it." He followed her to the bed.

ABOUT THE AUTHOR

Shirley Harrison has enjoyed writing all her life and is employed in the tax accounting field. She lives in the metro Atlanta area with her husband and two sons, where she is an accomplished artist, gardener and avid reader. You can write to her at P.O. Box 373411, Decatur, Georgia 30037-3411, or email her at sdh108@aol.com

More Sizzling Romance From
Gwynne Forster